Set in a sun-kissed Caribbean paradise, this third book in the Shad detective series explores a love triangle gone wrong—and how class divisions create a perfect storm of tr

Sarah, a talente , arrives at the perfect llage of Largo Bay, Jama ation of a Jamaican artist but falls in love with Danny, an American businessman visiting Largo Bay. Soon, Sarah runs afoul of her host as well as Danny's local lover, and her fate, along with Danny's plans, becomes endangered.

Meanwhile, Shad Myers—"bartender by trade, investigator by vocation, and unofficial sheriff of Largo Bay" (*Publishers Weekly*)—has another set of problems to solve, alongside his friend Eric, an American who owns the bar. The two friends court Danny, the investor who can help them rebuild Eric's hotel, left in ruins by a hurricane. Eric wants to make Shad a partner in the business, not just a worker. But the two must first overcome the social and political forces that make it difficult for local partners in the business to accept Shad's new, more important role.

The Sea Grape Tree is a delicious blend of suspense and soul. Gillian Royes once again delivers a vivid, thought-provoking novel with passion and punch.

Also by Gillian Royes

The Goat Woman of Largo Bay

The Man Who Turned Both Cheeks

Business Is Good

Sexcess: The New Gender Rules at Work

THE
SEA GRAPE
TREE

A Novel

GILLIAN ROYES

ATRIA PAPERBACK

NEW YORK   LONDON   TORONTO   SYDNEY   NEW DELHI

ATRIA PAPERBACK

A Division of Simon & Schuster, Inc.
1230 Avenue of the Americas
New York, NY 10020

First Atria Paperback edition July 2014

ATRIA PAPERBACK and colophon are trademarks of Simon & Schuster, Inc.

For information about special discounts for bulk purchases, please contact Simon & Schuster Special Sales at 1-866-506-1949 or business@simonandschuster.com.

The Simon & Schuster Speakers Bureau can bring authors to your live event. For more information or to book an event, contact the Simon & Schuster Speakers Bureau at 1-866-248-3049 or visit our website at www.simonspeakers.com.

Cover design by Laywan Kwan
Cover art: Background, easels, and border images from Shutterstock; images of sea grape leaves © Cuboimages SRL/Almay and © Stockfolio®/Almay

Manufactured in the United States of America

10 9 8 7 6 5 4 3 2 1

Library of Congress Cataloging-in-Publication Data is available.

ISBN 978-1-4767-6238-8
ISBN 978-1-4767-6239-5 (ebook)

For my daughter, Lauren, whose ever-blossoming creativity inspires me every day

Art is the stored honey of the human soul,
gathered on wings of misery and travail.

—THEODORE DREISER

U ncle Obediah's cigarette-hardened voice came back to Shad as he removed the fairy lights from their box.

"Don't fall over, you hear," Uncle would rumble from the stern as they rowed out for another night's fishing, the light from the kerosene lamp glinting off the water, "because the onliest thing between you and a shark is a miracle." There was no sinking boat tonight, no fishing net entangling arms and legs, but Shad felt as if he were back in the old canoe—his eye on the circling shark of failure—and he sent up a brief request for a miracle.

The main reason for the bartender's prayer was his conscience. Raised by a God-fearing grandmother who still nagged at him from somewhere off his left shoulder, Shad was trying to suppress his guilt. He hadn't been this sneaky, this dishonest, since he was nineteen and had started stealing ladies' purses after he'd lost his bus conductor work. The resulting year in the Kingston penitentiary had cured him, until now.

Here he was, seventeen years later, taking the boss's money from the cash register when he wasn't looking, and spending it on something Eric Keller would not have condoned. It was a rash decision but, being a man who followed

1

his heart, Shad had decided that the risk was worth it. Because Danny Caines was worth it.

"He's never been to Jamaica before," the boss had explained about Caines a few weeks earlier. "He wants to get to know the island real well before he decides if he wants to go into business with us or build a hotel in Largo." Eric had lit his pipe, his dry, ashy elbows squarely on the table as he sucked in and puffed out. Then he'd leaned back and exhaled, twiddling his black eyebrows. "And *we* need to know him before we go into business with him."

The project was at a delicate stage. It was like a newborn baby, eyes shut tight and fists curled, needing nourishment to stay alive. If Caines didn't like what he saw, there'd be no hotel. Of course—Shad sighed at the thought—the investor himself might turn out to be a *samfie-man,* a big-talking con man who'd carry the village down even further. Unwinding the last of the lights, Shad sent up a second appeal, this time that the newcomer might not turn out to be the shark.

Samfie or savior, Caines was to be the guest of honor at a welcome party Shad had planned down to the last detail, from the Spam in the sandwiches to the white rum in the punch. One way or the other, the party was on and half the village about to arrive. Shad had decided that this celebration was going to be a real party this time, not the boss's idea of a party, where the guests had to buy their own drinks. This time the invitees had been promised one free drink and one sandwich each. But they would have come anyway, would have bathed and put on the deodorant and clothes they saved for church, just to feast their eyes on the main attraction—the American man who could change their withering lives.

No one had more to gain or lose from this encounter than Shad. Squatting down in front of the bar with the fairy lights, the bartender remembered his grandmother's prediction.

"You going to be a *busha* one day, watch me," Granny would say, always squeezing her lips together at the end like a punctuation mark. It was a prophecy that the other old ladies agreed with, because the color of the boy's skin was as black as the night sky between the stars, and his forehead round and high, sure signs that he would be a big shot one day, big as the white overseers in sugar days.

The image of being a *busha,* complete with a large concrete house and a Mitsubishi in front, had begun to form in Shad's mind six months before, shortly after a real estate man had said that a client of his was interested in partnering with Eric in a hotel venture. Right away, the boss had declared to the Realtor—in front of Shad, no less—that his bartender would have to be a partner. Shad knew the reason. Eric had built one hotel already and he had no intention of exhausting himself again to build another hotel from scratch, not at the age of sixty-five. Nonetheless, making a poor bartender a partner was a bold suggestion in Jamaica, one only an American who'd never understood the island's class barriers would make.

The possibility of being a partner in a hotel had been keeping Shad awake at night, Beth snoring softly beside him, because it offered a thread of hope in a place where a man on the bottom had little or nothing to pull himself up with. And being a practical man, the bartender would remind himself, almost as soon as he started imagining the new house and car, that he was happy doing what he did and being who he was.

3

Shad hung the fairy lights over the last tack under the counter. Despite his guilt about taking Eric's money, he was looking forward to the party. He and every man-jack in the village needed cheering up, because they were tired of grieving the lack of work, the youth lost to Kingston and crime.

Granny would have understood. After she got the news that Obediah had drowned, and after she'd thanked God that Shad had stayed home with a fever and missed the storm that killed her son, she'd dried her eyes.

"Nothing that a little curry goat and white rum can't cure," she'd said with a sniff and a wipe of her kerchief. Then she'd asked her neighbor to tell everyone to come and mark her son's passing.

Shad plugged the lights into the wall outlet and stood back. They were blinking just the way the man in the shop said they would. On sale for half price, the Christmas lights had been hard to pass up, even if it was late January. Maybe they'd distract Caines from the drab truth of the bar, its open sides, rough concrete floor, and thatch roof held up by telephone poles. Maybe he wouldn't notice right away that Eric—his prospective partner—didn't have two shillings to rub together.

Laughter leaped over the kitchen partition behind Shad. "More work and less frolicking, please," he called, "and remember to put the fruit in one of the nice glass plate."

"Yes, *sir*," women's voices called back amid titters.

He brought out the mixers from their plastic cases under the sink and set them beside the row of glasses. The white and brown rums he placed within easy reach, and the vodka, gin, and whiskey farther away. His movements were swift and sure, those of a man who thought of liquor as a business, not a beverage.

The clatter of the kitchen's bead curtain announced Beth at his elbow, one hand smoothing her hair. "You want us to make a fruit salad or just slice the fruit?" She had on her light-blue dress, the one that showed she still had half a waist after birthing their four children.

"You mean your mango or my banana?" Shad replied with a grin, wiggling his hairless eyebrows like an underage scamp.

Beth sucked her teeth, pulling the air in between her teeth quickly, a flirting little suck, not the long drag of air she made when she was disgusted. She ran her hand over the back of his shirt, ironed earlier that afternoon while yelling at the older children to finish their homework. "You think you still a playboy and I still a young girl? After we done with the party, you know we going be too tired for anything else."

Shad walked her to the side of the bar facing the ocean, his arm around the familiar rolls of her waist. "Come watch the sunset with me, then." He looked at her sideways. "We can pretend we having sex."

Their laughter died away into the late-afternoon softness, into the postcard scenery that Largo Bay's residents usually ignored. In front of them, a short grassy lawn ended abruptly at a cliff, the waves crashing fifteen feet below. To their right, a beige beach extended in a graceful, one-mile curve, and under its arc of coconut trees lay the fishing canoes, the lifeline of the village.

A quarter mile in front of the bar, in choppy, turquoise water, sat a tiny island. Eric, its owner, had officially named it after the woman who'd lived on it the summer before, the woman named Simone. Uninhabited now, the island housed only two roofless buildings that remained as testament to Eric's old hotel, the Largo Bay Inn, which Shad had helped build fifteen years before and where he'd first worked as a bartender.

Small by North Coast standards, with only fifteen rooms, the inn had been known for its spectacular location on a peninsula at the end of the bay, the narrow driveway perfumed by frangipani trees. It had become a beacon of light in the village, employing workers and makers of shell necklaces and tie-dyed shirts. The boss had been the proud innkeeper for seven years, waving aside advice about the need for a retaining wall for the driveway. Better to spend the money on magazine ads, he'd countered, to entice guests to come to this eastern end of the island, far from Negril and Montego Bay.

Eric's day of reckoning had come, however. A monster hurricane called Albert had wiped out the thin strip of land that had been the hotel's driveway, leaving the battered buildings stranded on an island. With the demise of the inn, the village had lapsed into its former rusty state, one of the few signs of life being the roadside bar that the boss had built with the meager insurance money.

"You still don't answer the question," Beth said, bumping him with the side of her hip. "Sliced fruit or fruit salad? Maisie waiting in the kitchen."

"Fruit salad," Shad said, kissing her on the cheek, "with cherries on top."

She returned to the kitchen and he to the slicing of limes, oranges, and mint sprigs for the garnishes. Spry and trim, he looked more like a teenager than a man in his midthirties planning the future of sixty families. Being short and without prominent features, Shad was not a man who was noticed at a distance. You had to get up close to see the shine in his eye, the glow from his pores, the glow of a man who still laughed with his family. The bartender's other distinguishing feature was his smile, an ear-to-ear grin that displayed all his teeth, especially the two front teeth with the space between, the smile that had, in his boy days, saved him from licks from his grandmother and earned him money running errands.

Darkness was now blanketing the bay, and preparations for the party were complete, the radio tuned to an old Peter Tosh reggae. One naked bulb hung over the bar and two over the restaurant tables, the blinking fairy lights like giddy children below. At any moment Eric would be bringing Caines from the Montego Bay airport and pulling up at the boardinghouse next door.

"Don't worry, I won't tell them nothing," Miss Mac, the boardinghouse owner, had promised. "I just tell them to follow me."

If it were up to the boss, there'd be no welcome party, and probably no new hotel. The bar had almost not come into existence. Embittered by the destruction of his inn, Eric had only grudgingly constructed the Largo Bay Restaurant and Bar at Shad's suggestion, and it was the younger man's belief that anything built in anger could never make a profit, forcing the bartender to stay on constant watch, reining in expenses, robbing Peter to pay Paul.

Eric, on the other hand, didn't seem to care about the status of his bank account, and if it wasn't for Miss Ferguson's calls from the bank, he wouldn't even inquire. When Shad reminded him about payments to suppliers, he'd shrug his shoulders and say they'd have to wait. It didn't matter to him that after seven years of fitful existence, the little roadside bar was sliding deeper into debt.

"Like his spirit dying every day," Shad had explained to Beth the afternoon before. "We have a man ready to put up money to build another hotel—and the boss hanging back."

"He kind of old to start again," Beth had reminded him over the pigeon peas she was picking.

Shad had nodded. "And like he don't even understand that this hotel must-must happen. He don't understand how the sea getting fished out and is a good night when a fisherman come back with one, two dozen fish nowadays. All it going to take is one bad hurricane and the village going to dead, you know." Shad had spread his hands, urging Beth, as if she needed convincing. "Things tough now, but better can come again." Beth had nodded and picked two more pea pods.

"The only hope," Shad had concluded, "is this investor man, Danny Caines. I think we should give him a party, kind of warm him up from the beginning, you know, use a little *psychology* on him."

The guests were arriving, starting with one of the regulars, a gaunt man in his sixties who approached the bar rubbing his hands. His name was Triumphant Arch, a man who enjoyed a good argument.

Shad placed a glass of rum on the counter and Tri slid his fingers around the glass. His teeth clinked against its rim as he took his first blessed gulp.

"Big bashment tonight," he said when he set the glass down.

Shad ran his hand over the bald scalp his children loved to rub for good luck. "Mas Tri, do me a favor, nuh? No talk about political corruption, please. We want to make sure the man know that Largo is a *decent* place and that the hotel belong here, you get me?"

"No problem, man," Tri agreed, and took another gulp.

"And stop drinking out Mistah Eric's free liquor!" a grumpy voice called over the partition. The kitchen's bead curtain parted and a towering, somber man emerged. Solomon, the bar's part-time cook, descended from his status as chef of the old hotel and deprived tonight of his usual shot of white rum, threw a glare at his drinking buddy as he plodded past holding a tray of sandwiches. He was wearing white as usual, the tall chef's hat, double-buttoned jacket, and immaculate pants at odds with the gigantic, crusty feet, the toes of which hung over the front of his flip-flops. Depositing the tray on a table in the middle of the restaurant, Solomon returned to the kitchen without another word.

Fifteen minutes later, the place was full of Largoites, most holding glasses of rum punch, everyone looking *tidy,* as Granny used to say. The older women wore dresses with careful necklines, the young girls short, bright outfits, all with dustings of talcum powder to the chest to keep them fresh. Faded shirts were tucked neatly into the older men's pants, while T-shirts slouched outside the young men's jeans. Neighborly comments were passed in low murmurs, everyone leaning on one leg and then the other, tamping down their excitement.

The murmurs stopped when Eric appeared in the parking lot, Miss Mac and a strange man in tow.

"They come!" Shad called, turning down the radio. Beth

and Maisie rushed out of the kitchen with plates of fruit as the bar's owner waded into the crowd.

Taller than any villager, out of place among the well-dressed folk, Eric looked like he should have been on a dock somewhere in his old shorts and sandals, his flowing white hair, reddish face, and small paunch those of the captain of a vessel. The newcomer behind him—the man Shad had told everyone must be *treated with respect*—was looking around and smiling. Mahogany-colored, his big scalp bald as a baby's, Caines appeared to be in his early forties. He was muscular for a tall man, almost as tall as the boss, and he stood with his chest high in its banana-patterned shirt, as if he had a world, or an island, to conquer.

"What's going on?" Eric called to Shad, and raised his arms, the flabby skin underneath shaking with indignation, questioning the cost already. The bartender lifted his own skinny arms and grinned, and everyone laughed. An elderly man with a shock of fluffy gray hair patted Eric on the back.

"A little surprise business, suh," said Old Man Job, village elder and contractor on the old Largo Bay Inn, a man who made up for his lack of teeth with his common sense. "We know you want to welcome the gentleman to Largo, give him a nice party. Not true?" Eric shot a look at the bartender under his thick eyebrows and lowered his arms, and Shad exhaled, knowing he'd have to endure only a couple days of grumbling before all would be forgiven.

"A party for me?" the visitor said. His voice warmed the room, and when he laughed the sound came straight from his big chest. "I love it!"

Shad circled the bar and grasped the man's hand. "Mistah Caines, welcome! My name is Shad, and I run things for Mistah Eric." The newcomer had a firm, friendly hand-shake, making you want to shake it again. "We *privilege* that you come down to see us. You going to love Largo, I know it."

Shad swung around to the crowd and held Caines's arm high like a boxer's. "Give the man a Largo Bay shout-out, people!" he yelled. The crowd clapped and whistled, and a few even stomped their feet.

"Thank you, thank you," Caines said, loud enough for everyone to hear. "Nobody's ever thrown me a party before!" He spoke with a nice American twang, but his proud, al-most arrogant stance said something different.

"What about a beer, a nice, cold Red Stripe?" Shad asked, a man who liked to guess his customers' drinks.

"Perfect."

"I'd better change," Eric grunted before he escaped to his apartment at the end of the building.

Shad got busy with the drinks. When he looked up, Caines was chatting with his new landlady, and Shad won-dered if they were talking about the old woman's house and land next to the bar, the property that he and Eric thought would be just right for a hotel. Miss Mac wanted to sell it—so she said, anyway, but if old ladies didn't like you, they wouldn't sell to you, no matter how much money you had.

The bartender placed the visitor's drink on a tray and added a Coke. "One beer," he said, approaching the two, "and one Coke for the lady."

Caines removed his glass with its perfect head of foam and Miss Mac took her glass. "And I didn't even order noth-ing." She laughed, the gold fillings flashing at the back of her mouth.

Shad was about to answer when he felt a stiffness in the air, heard the falling away of chatter. A woman had stepped onto the floor of the bar. It was Janet, the village seamstress who visited the bar almost every night, on the prowl for the American man she'd predicted would marry her and take her away. Fishermen could only buy her rum, she'd declared, and she was a *champagne girl* (a girl still at forty).

Short and well-padded, Janet walked carefully on her high heels, the plunging neckline of her tight white dress putting the church dresses to shame. A vision of village sophistication, she wore a new wig that framed her rounded features and curled around her ears. Looking left and right as if she'd never been in the bar before, stopping with one leg bent like a beauty queen, she looked at Danny and smiled.

"You ever see such a thing?" Beth hissed when Shad got back to the bar.

"He don't stand a chance." Shad nodded, watching as Caines, a red-blooded man with no ring on his finger, turned toward the woman.

"Queen of diamonds," Beth muttered.

Shad shook his head, remembering the dressmaker beating some regulars at twenty-one in the bar with a pack of cards she'd brought. Janet had slapped down the winning card and said, "That's me you see there, in America, the queen of diamonds."

The bartender closed his eyes and pressed his fingers into the lids. *Jeezum peace,* he groaned, *plenty shark in the water tonight.*

CHAPTER TWO

Stepping high to avoid the prickly nettles, Eric plodded through the grass, still damp with morning dew. His flip-flops were already slippery and he was annoyed he'd forgotten to wear sneakers.

"Watch out for rocks," he said, looking over his shoulder. "The place hasn't been cleared for a long time."

In Reeboks and neat white socks, Daniel Caines was walking with hardly a sound, staring at the ocean through the coconut trees. It had been his idea to walk Miss Mac's land the day after his arrival, and it had turned out to be the perfect morning to show it. The sky was clear, the sea wasn't too rough, and a light breeze was blowing through the palms.

"The property is nine and a quarter acres," Eric said. "The beach is coral sand, a really good-quality sand, and it runs to the end of the bay over there, about a quarter mile long. The village is on the other side of the point and that's where the fishermen keep their canoes, so we wouldn't be interfering with them."

He stopped walking and waved toward the water, strands of white hair blowing across his face. "There's no reef, which is why it's a bit rough, but there's a—a kind of natural wildness to it, don't you think, that makes it different from the usual tourist spot." He hoped Caines wouldn't ask about sharks and currents, because he'd have to tell him that, yes, there'd been a couple sightings over the eighteen years he'd lived there, and, yes, a woman had drowned in the old hotel days, which was why they'd written in a lifeguard for the new hotel.

"By the way," Eric added, feeling a blush spread up his face, "I never thanked you properly for the gift, the new laptop. I was a little thrown off last night with the party and all."

"I mailed it ahead to Miss Mac's so I could surprise you," Caines said with a chuckle. "Little did I know you guys had a surprise for *me,* eh?"

Eric gathered up his hair and pulled it back. "Yeah, right. It's going to be—I haven't used a computer in—sheesh, I don't know how long."

"You said you didn't have one," Caines replied, brushing away the sweat already collecting on his bald scalp, "and if we're going to do business—"

"I know, I know." Eric turned away from the man to sigh as quietly as he could (still chafing at the cost of the party and Shad's deception, annoyed at Caines's assumption that he couldn't afford a computer, irritated most of all that he had to learn to operate the damn thing).

When they reached a cliff on the far end of the property, the bar owner stopped under a tamarind tree. Two nightingales quarreled at the intruders from a branch, the noise almost drowned out by the crashing of the surf in front of them.

With large, square hands, Eric mapped out the acreage. "The land slopes uphill from the beach to the road. It's long and rectangular. Closest to my bar on the eastern end, it's about eighty feet wide, then it broadens out coming west, to four hundred feet across, perfect for a hotel site. That area over there is where we think the main building should go—like you saw in the drawings we sent you—twenty guest rooms, swimming pool and Jacuzzi like you want, restaurant and bar area facing the ocean. Over here, we'd have a separate housekeeping and maintenance building."

Caines pointed to the bungalow partly visible through the thick foliage. "Would we have to knock down Miss Mac's house to put up the main building?"

"That's right."

"Has she given any conditions, caveats?"

"I—we never—well, it would be our land. I guess we could do anything with it, couldn't we?"

"She might want some graves or—something, trees maybe, preserved."

"I guess, out of respect, we can ask—"

But Caines had already started loping down to the beach. Eric followed, stepping gingerly over the weeds and vines that snaked along the ground. By the time he reached the sand, the visitor was standing with legs apart and arms crossed, his gaze fixed on the sapphire water in the distance.

"Nothing like the smell of the sea, eh?" Caines said, taking a slow, deep breath like he was sucking in the morning.

"Are you from the Caribbean?" Eric ventured. "Most Americans wouldn't ask about graves. Where are your people from?"

Caines glanced at him and back out to sea. "St. Croix."

"Oh, yeah, the US Virgins. I've been there. I used to travel around the Caribbean looking for a place to live when

I retired, using all my vacations to go to different islands. I went to St. Thomas and St. Croix on one of those trips. It took me years, but I finally found the spot. . . ."

When Caines didn't answer, Eric walked to a driftwood tree trunk and sat down. A small crab scurried around his sandals and disappeared into a hole. Over the water, a pelican dove and snatched at a breakfast tidbit. This was the bar owner's favorite time of day in Largo, just after the sun had risen and before the village had sprung to life. Within a few minutes he felt his shoulders relaxing, felt more tolerant of Caines, who was ignoring him, his strong legs in their khaki shorts still planted in the sand. On the trip from Montego Bay, he'd said he was forty-five, a good age, the bar owner thought, for a man to go into a venture like a hotel. If it failed, there'd be time to recoup. He wouldn't be throwing his retirement savings down the drain.

A passing car blew its horn, the sharp rat-a-tat-tat startling Caines. He walked over to the log.

"Beautiful spot, man," he said, sitting down and brushing sand off his shoes. "Seems like a waste, all this undeveloped land."

"Probably didn't occur to them. It was originally a larger parcel of about fifty acres owned by Miss Mac's father, and when he died it was divided among the heirs. I think they must have done a little farming on it at one time."

"Don't people use the beach?"

"Not much. They prefer the beaches near Port Antonio."

"We'd have to be real careful about guests swimming in the ocean," Caines said, and bit his lip. "We'd need a lifeguard, for sure. We don't want no law suits from families back in the States."

"I know. That's why—if we build the place—we should put in a swimming pool, like you suggested. We'd also have our registration form include a waiver in the event of a drowning, that's what the lawyer said. We can't be too careful."

The morning passed with a number of *we'd have to*s and *what-if*s tossed back and forth between the men, trying on for size how it would feel to be partners. Questioned about his hotel experience, Eric told of his successes and failures. The inn had always been full in the tourist season, from mid-December to mid-April, and they'd depended on repeat business and referrals. But he'd made a mistake with the size: fifteen rooms had been barely enough to cover operating costs. Caines confessed that, although he was good at managing small businesses, he had no experience in the tourist industry and would need help.

"I made my money with beauty salons and a few strip malls," he said.

"Then why go into a hotel?"

"I guess I'm tired of fights between stores that want to sell the same products, salons going belly-up halfway through their lease. I really want to get out of those businesses altogether, but it's not the time to sell, you know, so I thought I'd make some other investments, like this."

"Why here? It's beautiful, true, but it's—there's more than meets the eye to doing business in Jamaica. There's a ton of government paperwork to begin with, and we have a problem with crime. You know that, I'm sure."

"Heck, the whole Caribbean has crime, the Virgin Islands, probably the whole Third World, even the US. I mean, look at Detroit, New York—"

"But we have some serious stuff here."

"I know it's risky," the visitor said, shaking his head. "But I like to take calculated risks, that's just me. And for some reason, I love the idea of owning a hotel here. Maybe it's the idea of owning a piece of Jamaica. When I was coming up, we spoke of Jamaicans with respect, you know. To us in the Virgin Islands, Jamaicans stood up for their rights. When they got their independence—"

"In '62."

"I heard about it from my people—they felt that that was what we should have been doing, that we should have fought the Danes, not just sat back and allowed them to sell us to the US in 1917. A lot of Crucians were ticked off that they had no say in the deal. Then when Jamaica and Trinidad got their independence, my grandfather used to say that we should have been getting ours, too. He used to talk about Jamaica like he was talking about the Holy Land. He and my great-grandfather were Marcus Garvey men from way back, when they used to get Garvey's papers from Jamaica on the docks in Frederiksted. It's like I'm honoring the old men with this business, you know. And I want to see what it's like operatin' in a black-run country that's independent of Big Brother. You mightn't understand it, but—"

"It's different from doing business in the US, just know it."

"Cameron warned me already." The man was not to be deterred, it seemed, and Eric, who'd been wondering if Caines had the stamina to endure, realized that the man's resolve to build a hotel probably outstripped his own, because Caines had a motive greater than money.

"You've done business with Cameron before, right?" Eric asked, tipping one shoulder down to his companion.

"Yeah, nice guy. Know him long?"

"His sister was living on the island out there last year." Eric's throat tightened. "Then Cameron came down to find her and we became friends." Caines didn't need to know that Eric and Simone had been lovers, that he and Cameron hadn't talked for a while because Eric wouldn't let him take Simone off the island against her will, or that he still thought about her at night while he sat on his verandah listening to boleros on Radio Santiago de Cuba.

"Cameron and me go back about nine, ten years," Caines said. "He's sold me most of my malls in Queens and in the Bronx. I never had no reason to doubt him." He rubbed the fist of one hand into the palm of the other. "Good man, Cameron, good man."

Eric looked sideways at Caines. He seemed solid, sure of himself. One had more reason to trust a man who wasn't handsome, whose nose was more square than round, whose lips were unusually thin for a black man. And there was something about his eyes, eyes that looked straight at you and burned with intensity at times.

"What's *your* story?" Caines asked with one brow lifted.

"Oh, I had enough of New York. I went there from Shaker Heights, Ohio, right out of high school, worked with a paper company my whole career. But I always wanted to live in a warm climate." Eric blew out of the side of his mouth. "Hell, I couldn't wait to get out of New York when I retired. Like I said, I'd started scouting for a place to live before I moved down. Then I found Largo and decided I wanted to run a hotel here."

"And a hurricane wiped it out, Cameron told me."

"Yeah, sank the land connecting it to the main road. I swam to shore in the middle of it, from there to there, close to where my bar is now." They both gazed at the bar. Even from this distance it was embarrassing, the thatched roof Simone's rent money had paid for already looking shabby.

Caines clapped his hands. "At least you didn't fold up your tent and run back to the States."

"You mean, with my tail between my legs."

"The bar was a good idea."

"Shad's idea," Eric said, nodding. He'd always liked to give people their due; it took the responsibility off you, anyway.

"I like Shad," Cameron said. "He's a straight-up kind of guy. I'm glad you're thinking of making him a partner. We'll need someone from the community, someone who know the lay of the land." A twist of St. Croix had slipped into the man's language, like he was feeling more at ease.

"Since we're both foreigners, we'll need a local partner, anyway."

"The island," Caines said, turning to it. "The report said it might be leased to a Horace—I can't remember his name—for a campsite."

"Horace MacKenzie, Miss Mac's son, our lawyer. He wants the right to lease it from us in exchange for doing all our legal work, free of charge. He jumped on the campsite idea."

"Not a bad idea, passive income for us."

Eric looked down at his old, sandy toes. He saw Joseph's handsome profile outlined by the dim light coming from the bar. "My son and I were sitting on my verandah one night and he brought it up." Joseph had asked if Simone had lived in a tent on the island. It had made him think of camping, he'd said, and of using the island as a campsite.

Caines stood slowly, easing his shorts away from his thighs. "When can we go and see the contractor?"

"Lambert Delgado? He's away for a couple days, but he gets back at the end of the week."

"And I'll talk to Miss Mac about the property."

"I think she'll sell," Eric said. "Ready to head back?"

"I'm going to stay here awhile."

"If there's anything else . . ."

The visitor's face remained blank and Eric started back toward the bar. When he got to the brow of a hill, he looked back at Caines, now standing shoeless and sockless on the sand. He was stripping off his T-shirt, followed by his shorts and his briefs. With hardly an ounce of fat on him, he stood still for a few seconds, an Afro-Greek sculpture. Then he waded into the foam, the waves crashing around his legs and thighs, dove into an oncoming wave, and disappeared.

Just when Eric began to worry, he popped up farther out and swung around to face the shore, his upturned face gleaming with joy, a man returning to his roots—the hotel an excuse to do it.

CHAPTER THREE

An icy winter evening and darkness had descended earlier than usual, forcing the city's residents into the warmth of pubs and homes. Sarah rushed up the stairs to the flat without turning on the passageway light, feeling her way to the keyhole.

"Hello, lovely," she called when she got the door open.

"Hello, not working tonight?" her flatmate shouted from the lounge. A television woman was announcing casualties in an earthquake.

"No, I have to finish packing."

In her bedroom, Sarah changed into pajamas, drew on a dressing gown, and looked around the room, deciding what to tackle first. She stepped over a pack of new paintbrushes to examine the overflowing suitcase on the bed. It was definitely overweight, according to the airline's website.

"Repacking time," she muttered. Some of the clothes would have to go. The art supplies couldn't be eliminated.

"Bring everything you need," Roper had declared on the phone, "because my place is in the bush, and it's a long, rough road to town."

She dumped the contents of the suitcase on the bed. No need for a fancy wardrobe if the place was as remote as he said. The lavender outfit she'd bought that afternoon, after hours searching for summer garments, would be enough for special evenings, if any. The rest would be more practical gear, old painting pants, shorts, underwear. She repacked, rolling every item of clothing to save space, and added a wide-brimmed straw hat, purchased at the last minute when she had an image of her face turning as red as her hair.

She glanced at the bureau mirror, daring to look again at the woman who stared back, this person she didn't yet know. The mousy brown hair she'd had all her life had been replaced by bright red locks, the fringe hanging like fiery exclamation marks above her eyes. The rather ordinary blunt-cut bob that had been a convenience now looked edgy and aggressive.

Three days before, when she'd emerged from the bathroom after the dye job, Penny had been standing in the hallway talking on her mobile. She'd stopped abruptly to shriek.

"Oh, my God, Sassy's gone and dyed her hair *red*!" she'd said to someone on the phone.

Sarah had given her hair another rub with the towel. "What d'you think—I mean, honestly?"

"It's fabulous, totally not you!"

Penny was right, of course, because standing out had never been on Sarah's radar. Ironically, it had been the very desire to melt into the background that had driven her to the opposite of her intention. She'd been sure—having experienced the vibrancy of Notting Hill Carnival more than once—that if anything would stand out in Jamaica, it would be her pallid and very temperate appearance. And the last thing she wanted was to look like a pale tourist, a target for beggars and con artists.

To blend into a tropical country, she'd decided, she'd need to be a bit more colorful than usual, and she'd start with her hair. A likable sales assistant had talked her out of Topaz Glow and into Poinciana Passion, a more fashionable color, the girl had assured her, and, conjuring up images of exotic flowers, Sarah had taken the plunge.

The instant she'd looked in the mirror after emerging from the shower, Sarah's heart had sunk. Her first thought was that it looked like a fire had broken out on top of a five-feet-ten-inch pole. Her entire face looked different in contrast to the blindingly red hair. The pale skin had become paler, the lean face leaner, and the cheekbones more prominent and dramatic. Her long neck, which her mother had compared to that of a swan (and she to an ostrich), looked longer than ever. She'd stand out like a bloody sore thumb, she'd thought glumly. The hair would be the first thing everyone would notice, because Jamaicans didn't have red hair—at least none that she'd ever seen. She would be the only person on the island with Poinciana hair.

Retrieved from the dustbin, the dye box condemned her to a flaming future. *Do not apply fresh color before four to six weeks,* the instructions had read.

Bad enough that she was going to live with total strangers in Largo, but now she'd be living with a face and hair that looked disturbingly unfamiliar for at least another month, maybe longer. The whole experience was beginning to feel bizarre, but it was too late to turn back. The agreement had been made and the ticket had been bought.

Swallowing hard, Sarah returned to the last of her packing, adding several large sheets of paper in a plastic bag, which she fitted into the lid of the suitcase. On top of the clothes she added two pads, one for sketching and one for watercolor painting. (Jamaica, she'd known instinctively, would call for the hues and subtlety of water rather than acrylics.) A separate bag she started packing with her paints and new paintbrushes.

"Aren't you taking a swimming costume?" It was Penny, leaning on the door frame, her very existence filling the small room.

Sarah tucked a lock behind her ear. "I don't actually have one, come to think of it. The sun and my skin—"

"Nonsense, I'll lend you mine."

"I probably won't wear it," Sarah muttered, following Penny to her room. "I'm not a great swimmer, didn't even get my twenty-five-meter badge. I'll just sit in the shade."

"You can't sit around in the shade the whole time you're in Jamaica, you know. You'll miss the point of going." After digging in the bottom drawer of her dresser, Penny handed her a bathing suit. "Here, it'll match your eyes."

"Not much to it, is there?" Sarah said, holding aloft what looked like three strings of vivid green, imagining her ample breasts spilling out of the top.

"What do you expect? I bought it in the South of France last year to fit in."

It was a flippant remark, because Penny knew she always fit in and wouldn't need a dye job to do it. Everyone wanted to be around her, attracted to the pleasurable ease with which she moved through life. Sarah had come to the conclusion that marketing people were successful because they had personalities like Penny's that others wanted to buy.

"I'll put the kettle on," Penny said, sashaying down the

corridor. "When you're finished, come for a cup of Rosie Lea." Their name for tea, courtesy of Gladys, their sometime cleaning lady.

The kitchen was the brightest place in the Camden flat, its mustard-yellow walls and potted plants making it a cozy gathering spot for whoever was around. It felt best to Sarah, though, when the two of them were alone together, sipping Earl Grey or cocoa, tattling about the latest man, always Penny's, or the royals. That was the time when Sarah laughed the most, when the messy bathroom didn't matter.

When she'd moved in, the artist had hoped that some of her flatmate's joie de vivre would rub off on her, but it hadn't and she'd reconciled herself to being who she was—reserved, unwitty, a bit of a bore. And she'd become comfortable with that and allowed her art to speak for her.

Departing her tiny flat in Maidstone and moving to London two years before had been a new phase of life for Sarah, who'd spent all of her thirty-two years in quiet Kent, south of London. At first she'd had minor panic attacks thinking about her survival (*Suppose Penny gets married and sells the flat? Suppose nobody buys my paintings?*), which had soon lessened. Thus far Penny had not found the right man to marry and didn't even seem inclined, and a few of Sarah's paintings had actually been sold by Eccentricity Gallery, enough, along with waitressing, to pay her rent.

The fame and fortune that Penny had said awaited her had not appeared, but it was enough to be in London. There were galleries and museums to browse, hundreds of parks and public spaces to sketch in, endless churches to photograph, and people to watch. When she sat on the Tube, she'd count the number of races on the bench facing hers, examine the national costumes, eavesdrop on the languages. Her favorite coffee shop (with coffees from thirty-six nations) became her window on the behaviors of lovers and parents and students. It was an ever-changing scene, this city. She was at the center of things in London, she'd told her mother; one never knew what to expect.

The move had been Penny's idea. "You can't stay here the rest of your life," she'd said, licking lager from her top lip. It was early afternoon, and Maidstone's oldest and largest pub was already occupied by the regulars.

"There's nothing wrong with it," Sarah had replied, still in awe at Penny's news that she'd bought her own flat. "I'm perfectly happy—"

"But you haven't gone out with anyone since John moved out, what, two, three years ago? I mean, *really*, Sarah."

"He wanted children, Penny, for God's sake, and you know where I stand on that. We're still good friends. I wish him the best, honestly, but it was a relief when he left." Sarah took a sip of her beer. "I'm not in the mood to go out with anyone, to tell the truth. They talk about their jobs and their sports, and I start yawning. I must have dried up or something, it's just not happening."

"They're probably dull men, that's all." Penny played with one dangling earring. "Maybe your friends can introduce you. How many friends do you have here, anyway?"

"I don't really need friends. I just joined the—"

"Don't be ridiculous. Everyone needs friends. It's not good to keep things bottled up inside, and you know you tend to do that."

"Leave me alone, Pen, I'm fine. All I need is my painting and a bit of cash, and I have that all here. Maidstone suits me."

"Nothing happens here," her friend said, lowering her voice and looking around. "I mean, this place hasn't changed in thirty-five years. It still smells the same!" Sarah couldn't help but laugh, remembering them peering into the pub as children, sniffing the stale beer.

"Look at you," Penny said and clucked her tongue. "You're a fan*tas*tic artist, and what do you do? You only paint in your free time! I would die for your talent, I'm telling you. But you're like a *hollow* person here, killing time in Maidstone, marching towards death." Her friend's eyes had widened at the thought of a life unlived.

"I'm not—"

"You won all the art awards in Maidstone Grammar, again in MidKent College, and what are you doing with them? Nothing! You've got to move up to London. I mean, what's holding you back, your mother? You said yourself you only see her once a month. You can do that from London, just hop on the train and come down. It costs a few quid, but you'll be making more money up there, you know. Seriously, Sassy, you need to come up and get into the art scene on the King's Road or something. They'll love your stuff, wait and see. And you definitely can*not* keep working in that awful restaurant."

The cubbyhole in the restaurant where she stuffed her coat and handbag came to Sarah's mind. "It's not too bad—"

"With a maître d' you call Percy Pervert?"

"They're a nice lot, really, and I get good tips. Besides, there's a new gallery opening up and I have an appointment to meet with them. I've painted one or two new things. You never can tell, maybe they'll appreciate something other than wildflowers."

Penny had clunked her glass down on the bar's counter. "Listen, I have a friend who owns a small gallery in Kensington. It's really posh, high ceilings and classy clientele, you know the type. Let's show her your work, shall we? Come and visit me for a few days and bring those pieces you've painted."

In the end, it was Penny's comment that she was a *hollow* person—the kind of statement soon forgotten by the speaker but embedded in the listener's mind—that had pushed Sarah to change the trajectory of her life. Events had followed swiftly: a short visit to Kensington and a contract with Eccentricity, the upscale gallery owned by Naomi Whittingham; the sale of three of her pieces; then the invitation to move into Penny's flat after her boyfriend had left in a rant (according to Penny), breaking the teapot he'd given her. She'd talked Sarah into moving in and buying a new teapot.

"I'm going to miss you, you know," Penny said over the rim of her cup. "Are you taking your mobile?"

"They said it wouldn't work there. I'll email you, anyway. Roper said he was on the Internet, although I can't imagine the Internet in the middle of the jungle, can you?"

"It's not the *jungle,* Sarah. You said yourself it was a fishing village in the northeastern corner of the island. I looked it up. Gorgeous scenery, the article said." Penny snapped a biscotto in two. "It's quite romantic, you know, running off to Jamaica with some man you've only met once."

"I'm not running off. Naomi said he has a perfectly nice girlfriend and I have nothing to worry about."

"Whatever it is, I think it's a super idea. You've needed a great adventure for a long time, and it's not like you're going to disappear into the mountains or anything."

"Hard to disappear with this hair in Jamaica, I imagine," Sarah said with a sigh.

"What's his name again—the man you're staying with?"

"Roper—that's how he signs his paintings. Everybody calls him that. Naomi's visited him and says his home is quite comfortable, maids and whatnot. She thought it was a good idea that I go. She said something about wanting to see me *explore new vistas*." In fact, Naomi had been so enthusiastic about the trip to Jamaica that Sarah had known instantly that the gallery owner did indeed hate the new acrylic series she was planning.

"*Eggs in dirt!*" Naomi had shrieked the month before when she heard the name of the series.

The art diva's reaction hadn't lessened Sarah's desire to create five paintings of five white eggs. The larger ends of the eggs were to be buried in dark brown earth, shiny lumps cradling the shells. Her goal was to paint the first one as soon as she got finished with her Mermaid in the Cathedral series, the last of the twelve disciple-mermaids near completion.

Before Naomi's outburst, Sarah had been mulling what the new eggs-in-dirt series should be called. It had to be a name signifying fertility and the unity of all life—the idea of baby chicks taking the place of grass. Both eggs and dirt would have to be safe and contained, of course. Otherwise the viewer would think about the crushing of eggs and the resulting slimy yolks. And like all her other paintings, each piece would be small, exactly four inches by four inches.

Sarah painted nothing but miniature canvases. They had become part of her personal style and no one had questioned her choice in the last eight years, not since her father had died.

"Why not try it even once?" he'd suggested while he was driving her to her job one day. "Try sketching, just take a big sheet of paper and let things flow, as they say nowadays."

The very thought of a large piece of paper always resulted in a knot in Sarah's stomach, the way it had when she was forced to do it in art school, and she'd ignored her father's advice. The unfettering of self that came with painting large, the unveiling to others, left her far too vulnerable. Her paintings remained small, the ornate frames more than double the size.

The subject of an eggs-in-dirt series hadn't been raised with her mother, who'd never been particularly interested in her work.

"Hello, my dear," she'd always say, pressing her cheek to her daughter's, when Sarah paid her monthly visit. Arthritis-bowed spine pushing through the back of the sweater set, her mother usually launched into descriptions of her latest ailments as soon as they sat down. The subject of her only child's art never took longer than two minutes of the one-hour visit and, over the years, the artist had gotten used to nursing her work within the privacy of her own breast.

There was even some pride, admittedly, in knowing that few people understood the minuscule, surrealistic paintings. Only a buyer with an unusual eye would appreciate mermaids lying before church altars or the safety offered to an egg by warm, brown earth. But the egg series was to be put on hold, thanks to Roper's invitation, and a Jamaican series was to take its place.

"A free vacation." Penny snorted. "I'm totally green, you know, thinking of you being in the Caribbean in the middle of winter."

"And the sea's right there, at the end of a path."

"How'd you get this invitation, anyway? I know you mentioned it, but—"

"I don't know why I tell you anything, Penny Clutterbuck." Sarah took a slow sip of tea, relishing the suspense she had few opportunities to create.

"Get on with it."

"Naomi represents Roper in the UK, and he was in the gallery one day and we started chatting. Actually, he was chatting and I was listening. He kept looking at my paintings and asking me if I didn't want to paint something larger than four-by-fours, like a bloody teacher or something, and I finally got upset because he kept pressing me, and as I was walking away he called out something about paying my ticket to Jamaica and putting me up if I painted one large painting. *You can't paint Jamaica small,* he said. Had a rather arrogant tone, too." Sarah shrugged. "I said no, thank you, of course, but Naomi was standing right there. She started going on about how wonderful a Jamaican series would be." Sarah drained her cup and filled it again from the teapot. "No way out, really."

"Lucky bugger, you are. Don't even know the man's full name and he's paying for your ticket, *plus* board and lodging."

"Yes, but it's sort of like holding me hostage, isn't it? No return ticket until he approves of one of my paintings."

"Suppose he doesn't approve of anything and you're *stuck*?"

Sarah ran a finger around the lip of her teacup. "He's rather a character, I think, but he strikes me as a fair sort. When I've had my holiday and painted what I want to paint, I'll just give him the painting *he* wants and get done with it. In the meanwhile, my expenses will be taken care of in Jamaica, and your cousin will be renting my room here until I come back. No harm done." She hunched her shoulders forward and hugged her arms. "The great adventure, right?"

CHAPTER FOUR

S ay that again!" Shad said. He pushed himself up on one elbow, Beth's arm still on his hip. The unexpected evening of romance had descended into a web of manipulation.

"So that is why you left the sandwich on the dinette table—"

"With the crust cut off, the way you like it."

"—and the nightgown and perfume, because *you want to work in Port Antonio?*"

"What wrong with that?" Beth asked, almost innocently.

"Just because Jamaica get a woman prime minister, all you women think you can—"

"Why you going on so?"

"You have four children to look after, a baby to nurse, Ashanti with her problems, a garden in the back to tend, market on Saturday to sell your vegetables—and you want to get a job? You don't have enough work to do here?"

He dropped back on the pillow, his head on his arm. Above him, the ceiling was streaked by the neighbor's porch light sneaking in above the curtains. "Who going to take care of the children? I working mornings at Mistah

34

Eric's bar and evening shift until all hours, so I can't take care of no children, if that what you thinking. You going to spend almost one hour each way to Port Antonio in the route taxi every day. It don't make no sense."

Beth rolled onto her back. "Joella have to finish high school in Port Antonio, like how she want to start dental assistant school next year, right? She going to take taxi there every day, starting September. Like how she don't know the place, and I come from Port Antonio and know it good, and we nervous about her traveling with all the boys on the bus, I can travel with her. You know what can happen if we let her go on her own? You said it yourself. Next thing she end up pregnant and the studying gone through the window."

Shad rolled his eyes in the dark, hearing what Beth was not saying, that her own downfall had started on a Port Antonio bus when she'd smiled coyly at him, the new bus conductor, and five months later had agreed to go back to his room behind the butcher shop and lie down on his old iron bed.

"What about Joshua?" Shad argued, changing direction. "He still breast-feeding—who going to take care of him?"

"He gone one and a half years now, time to stop the feeding. Miss Livingston say she will look after him in the daytime and I will pick him up when I come home."

"But who going to look after Ashanti, like how she so difficult with the autism? Nobody going to want to take care of her."

"They have a school in Port Antonio for children like her, and that is another reason I want to work there. I call the number on the pamphlet the doctor gave us, remember the one? They say that they have a day school for children like her, children with *disabilities,* that's what they call it. They say that since she going on five, she should start school now, and when Joella start school in September, she can help me with her in the taxi coming and going."

"And Rickia? She can't stay by herself when she come home from school. And I can't be here to make sure she do homework and everything."

"She going over to Miss Livingston after school and help with the baby. She always good about her homework, anyway, so she can do it there."

"Miss Livingston agree to this?"

"I tell her I will pay her little money and she say yes. She need the money and she like the company." A lot of thinking had gone into Beth's new plan, Shad realized. Without a word to him, she'd done her research and made calls and arrangements with other people, and he, a man who was known as a *sniffer and snuffer* (according to Miss Mac), a man who knew everything about everybody in Largo, had been clueless about his own woman's goings-on.

As hurtful as the news was to Shad, it was even more painful because he hadn't been consulted. Although he was unable to read and write beyond a fifth-grade level, Shad had established himself as Largo Bay's problem solver. The role had started from childhood when, as the self-appointed village messenger, he'd earned access to the villagers' lives. He'd seen who was sitting in the obeah man's waiting room when he paid a bill for Miss Hilda. He'd known who was coming from England when he delivered invitations to Mas Josiah's party, and overheard the pastor cursing his wife once when he went to collect his dollar.

With knowledge of their secrets, the little barefoot boy had morphed into the village's go-to man as an adult. Yet Shad was keenly aware that he was looked down on by many who were higher up the food chain—even while he was looked up to by his peers. He understood the social context in which he operated, understood the complexities of his people and how they thought. He was a man who observed, who analyzed, who hung back until it was time, and acted when it was. He was a man of street smarts, an Anansi—the African spider of folk tales that had traveled to the Caribbean with the enslaved thousands—a man who, in another time and place, would have been a financial genius.

"Stop right here," Shad said as he turned on the bedside lamp. "What you planning to do with this money you going to make? I know you, and you always have a purpose for everything."

Beth closed her eyes. "We can always use little extra, not true? Like how Joella going to high school—"

"I can manage that now, so what else?"

"What you mean?"

"Don't act so innocent. You want to buy a car? Another house? Talk to me."

She took her time, followed by the crick-crack of her rollers as she turned to look at him. "You said we going to marry, right? But you say the—the wedding have to wait until we have the money. I was just thinking I could find little work, you know, cleaning house to pay for the wedding, and we wouldn't have to wait."

Shad sat up, propping his elbows on his knees. "Everything going along nice-nice, and we about to build the new hotel. I going to have to work harder, supervising the hotel going up *and* running the bar. Everything already going to be in confusion, and you want to cause more confusion by traveling to Port Antonio, twenty miles each way, every day—just for a wedding? It going to mean that you coming home late, that dinner going to be cooked late, that nobody here when I come home for my lunch—"

"Shad," Beth said, sitting up beside him, "I tired of being your woman. All these years we together, seventeen, going on eighteen years now, and I just your common-law wife. We have four children—not one, not two, not even three—*four* children." She held up her fingers one by one.

"When you lost the conductor work and you start to rob people purses, it was *me* who tell you to stop the foolishness, and when they catch you and put you in the Pen for the year, it was *me* traveling to Kingston every week and taking food for you, with my belly getting bigger with Joella. And after you get out, is *me* make you come to Largo to live with your grandmother, and when she was sick, is *me* taking care of her and the baby while you building the hotel. Then you start the bartending at the hotel, and is *me* start planting garden so we could have little extra money and eat fresh food." Shad slid down to rest on the headboard, allowing her to get the memorized list off her chest, the way a woman had to.

"I have Rickia just before your granny dead," she continued, "and I sew the dress for Granny to bury in with the baby nursing at my breast. You lose the work when the hotel mash up in the hurricane, and we live off the garden and your fishing, barely making it. Then the bar build back and you bringing in steady money, and I have Ashanti and Joshua." She exhaled hard and short, a train letting out steam. "I done now with the baby making, you hear me, and is my time now, my time to bring in steady money—like you."

Shad stroked her arm. "We have enough money, even added on a second bedroom for the children last year. I don't know what you talking about, Beth. We making it, we making it."

"But you need little help, and the wedding—you told me last year to set a date, and I set it for July this year. Then you tell me to hold off because we don't have the money for no wedding."

"Like how you was sewing wedding dress and soaking fruit and talking about invitations, you sound like some English princess. You make me afraid of the whole thing. That kind of wedding cost plenty money."

"I just saying we should have a good-good wedding—after all this time. We need to set a example. We need to show the children that we respectable and married."

"You mean we not respectable now? We don't need no wedding to show that."

"Talk the truth, Shadrack Myers." Her voice had gone cool, chilling him already. "You don't want to marry me."

"I want to married to you, sweetness, but we don't have to rush it."

"Four children and eighteen years, and we—"

"I love you until sun don't shine, you know that."

The mother of his children lay down again, straightening her nightgown under the sheet, her face to the wall.

"Beth," he reasoned with her back, "how many people you see married in Largo Bay, apart from the Delgados and pastor? Miss Alice and Mistah Jethro is the onliest ones, and they only marry right before Jethro died, because pastor tell him he going straight to hell when he dead." Above the sheet he could see the baby hairs on the back of her neck and resisted the urge to stroke them.

"*Boonoonoonoos,*" he said, calling her by the name Granny called him when she was in a good mood. "People in Jamaica don't get married, you know that. It feel like bondage, from way back, from slavery days. Is only when these ministers start to come and say that we living in sin that it shame us, but you and I not living in sin. We don't sleep with nobody else but us, you know that. The Bible say we shouldn't commit adultery, but show me where it say we must marry in long dress and suit with a minister and plenty people in a church, and that we must feed all of them afterward."

Her voice was muffled. "Corinthians say every man should have his wife and every woman should have her husband."

An old argument that was beginning to get stale, one that even he was getting tired of, the wedding question had intensified over the past year. It had all started with the last minister, a self-righteous man who had departed over a matter related to sexual preference, but now the new minister had taken up the slack. Like all the other villagers, Beth at first had ignored the threats of hellfire for the unmarried, even though her own parents had been married. But she'd finally concluded that she and Shad were doomed and she'd been planning a wedding since late the year before. A contributing factor, Shad suspected, was that she saw that the island's well-to-do families were headed by married parents and, since middle-class people were respected, and since she was an ambitious woman, Beth had decided to claim her place among them by becoming a married woman.

Whenever he raised the topic of marriage, Shad had received advice to the contrary from several local residents, including his own boss.

"Stay away from it as long as you can," Eric had remarked once. "If it doesn't drive you to divorce, it will drive you to drink. A wedding ring makes a woman go crazy, I'm telling you. She suddenly thinks she can run your life." Eric had been reading a newspaper when he said it and Shad still remembered the black eyebrows above the paper.

Shad touched Beth on the shoulder. "Name me one thing that marriage is good for," he said.

"Com-mitment." She pronounced the word carefully, as if she'd heard it on one of the soap operas she watched while cooking dinner.

"We not committed now?"

"No. You can go off any time and leave me with the children and—"

"I come home every night to you for sixteen years now. I don't love another woman for more than eighteen years. What you call that, not commitment? I bring home all my money, all my tips. I don't spend a penny on another woman, on nothing outside the house, not even on liquor. I buy you a television, a refrigerator, and me and Frank put on the back room last year. You don't call that love?"

Beth turned over. "I know you love me, and I know you will think about it *because* you love me. If you can't afford to pay for a nice wedding, like you say, you will understand that I need to have a job so we can have a nice wedding.

Now get your rest, because Miss Livingston's cock going to crow soon." He felt for the lamp switch without looking, turned it off, and reached for her.

"One more thing," she said, rolling away from him. "No sex before marriage, so Pastor say."

CHAPTER FIVE

Roper's home was nothing as Sarah had imagined. Instead of a rustic cottage surrounded by palms, she'd found a very modern, wood-and-glass structure clinging to a mountain. The view too was a surprise, particularly the colors. The greens of the bamboo around the house and the blues of the ocean visible from its deck were more brilliant than any colors she'd ever seen in nature. She had the sensation of almost being pummeled by the stimuli coming at her.

The Caribbean Sea—with at least six different blues she'd identified—filled everything with its presence. The smell of salt had assailed her from the minute she stepped out of Immigration, the trade winds wrinkling her hair into a frizzy mess within minutes. Most constant in subsequent days was the drumbeat of the waves, which seemed to pursue her all day.

There was noise everywhere. The villagers spoke and laughed loudly. Passing taxis played their radios at top volume and blew their horns as they tore down the road. Even the night air was pierced by the bellowing of frogs—mercifully segueing into the cooing of doves in the early morning. She'd lain awake the first couple of nights convinced that she'd never sleep with the racket of waves, wind, and frogs, but on her third morning Sarah awakened to find that she'd slept deeply, deeper than she had in months, maybe in years.

She'd started setting up her traveling easel—not as portable as she'd hoped—on the beach across from Roper's house. There was a clearing under the coconut trees that gave her a view of the ocean while providing shade. She was relieved to find that this eastern end of the beach was almost deserted, the fishing activity being concentrated on the opposite end, and there'd been few interruptions since she'd started working. On one occasion a gaggle of children had come and stared at her from ten feet away before running off, jabbering in patois.

It had taken her a few jet-lagged days to settle into her new routine after being met at the airport by Sonja, Roper's girlfriend. The woman had held up a handmade sign that said *Sarah Davenport* and smiled broadly when the new arrival nodded. She'd apologized for Roper's absence (he was opening a show in Toronto, apparently) and for being sleepy, the result of working late the night before.

"I'm a writer," Sonja had mumbled as they started off toward the parking lot, "and my best time to work is when everyone else is sleeping." Roper had apparently woken her that morning to remind her to meet the London flight.

"Totally forgot, of course." The writer's hair stood in a spiky Afro, and Sarah wasn't sure if she'd styled it that way or forgotten to brush it. "Anyway, if I fall asleep, just shake me and take over the wheel!"

The driver had proven to be more awake than her guest. Having had only snatches of sleep on the flight, Sarah had fallen asleep for most of the four-hour drive back to Largo. When the SUV ascended the steep driveway to the house, she'd jerked awake. Together the women had lugged the bags and easel into the house and deposited them on the rug inside the door. The maid—called *helpers* on the island, Sonja had whispered—had met them at the door.

"My name Carthena," she'd informed Sarah. She looked to be in her mid- to late-twenties and wore capri pants and a T-shirt with a gold design on the front. A shower of pink and white beads decorated the braids that cascaded to her shoulders.

"How long you planning to stay, miss?" the woman asked on the way to Sarah's room.

"As long—as it—takes, I suppose," Sarah had answered, struggling with her suitcase down the stairs. She was already regretting refusing Carthena's help with the bag because of her guilt about being served by anyone.

"A real English lady," the helper remarked. "I never meet one before."

The guest room on the lower level contained a sitting area and a bedroom with twin beds, a desk, and a ceiling made of bamboo woven in a herringbone pattern. Left alone, Sarah slid open the glass doors leading from the bedroom to the terrace, absorbing the reality of her surroundings. Somehow, she was in Jamaica—and without spending a penny, thanks to a kind and wonky artist. She'd collapsed onto one of the beds, smiling broadly and giving herself two full days before starting her painting routine.

On this, her fourth morning, the light on the ocean was breaking into a mosaic of glitter and Sarah pulled out her sketch pad to capture it. She drew a square in the center, a rough four-by-four. Her goal was to spend a week or two painting the unfamiliar in the familiar way, sticking to her miniatures, followed by a gradual expansion to a thirty-six-by-twenty-four-inch sheet—Roper's required size for a return ticket. The five large sheets she'd placed out of sight on a high shelf so they wouldn't annoy her.

A noise overhead made her look up, holding on to the crown of her straw hat. She was being inspected by a large black bird with a bald head and a red ring around its neck, a vulture of some kind, sitting on the stem of a coconut leaf.

"Hello? I'm not dead yet," Sarah shouted, and the bird flew off to soar on an air current.

Settling again on the kitchen stool loaned by Carthena, Sarah got back to her drawing of the waves. Water was not her strength, especially tossing, rolling, foaming water like that of Largo Bay. She'd done some work on the beaches of Kent, but that was a different ocean—heavy, dark, and certainly cold. The water of the Caribbean seemed lighter and friskier to her by comparison. Although she hadn't stepped into the surf yet, she knew it must be warm, hot even, in line with everything she'd encountered so far.

You'd never think Jamaica was once British, she'd written Penny in an arrived-safely email. *It has a character all its own. It's loud, crude, beautiful, and utterly unpredictable.*

The night before, Sonja had asked what she thought about the island. "It's terribly alive, isn't it?" Sarah had answered, frowning into her wineglass. "Everything is in motion."

"You either love it or hate it. There's no in-between about Jamaica." Sonja leaned forward for a handful of almonds. "Most poor countries, the ones I've been to, anyway, never seem passive. Nothing is easy, nothing has soft corners. I guess that contributes to our strong instinct for survival."

"I had no idea, none whatsoever, that being here would make me feel so—different, might be the word. I'm a total bloody foreigner here. I can't understand one word of the dialect, probably never will. And everything feels new, the night noises, the smells—from dead dogs to flowers, even the touch of the sea breeze. I never know what to expect next."

"It takes a while." Sonja nodded. "I was living in the States for fourteen years, and when I first came back I remember being in culture shock—in my own country. Took me a few weeks to settle in and start writing again."

"What kind of writing do you do?"

"Business books, would you believe? I used to work in strategic planning with an insurance company, then I worked in training. After I got tired of the nine-to-five, I left and started writing training manuals for the insurance industry, then human-resource-type stuff."

"How do you write from so far away?"

"Everything I need is on the Internet, from the *Wall Street Journal* to the latest books and research data. I can write from anywhere, even Largo."

Several inches shorter than Sarah and some ten years older, Sonja had a kindness to her rounded features, despite the spiky hair. Before dinner that first night, she'd taken Sarah on a tour of the house. There were three floors: the lower level, where Sarah was lodged; a middle floor with a living and dining room, Sonja's office, the kitchen, and a deck; and a top floor, where three bedrooms and bathrooms opened off a sitting area.

Roper's office and studio were in a separate building be-hind the house and up a path of flat stones. The smell of oil paint and turpentine greeted them when Sonja opened the door to the high-ceilinged room. Canvases of all sizes, most between three and six feet tall, were stacked against the walls in various stages of completion. One painting had the artist's bold one-name signature scrawled on the bottom (the *R* in *Roper* dominating the other letters). On two easels were half-finished paintings, one of a nude woman with a basket of flowers on her hip, the other of a group of market women, the artist's style a blend of realism and impres-sionism. The women's features were symmetrical and their expressions peaceful, their skin painted with hues of browns and blues and greens.

"Now that I look at his paintings," Sarah commented, "I see Jamaica in them. I didn't really understand them in Lon-don. They seemed overwhelming, full of passion and color."

"Like the man himself, wouldn't you say?"

"I don't really know him—"

"You will," Sonja said with an impish grin. "He's larger-than-life."

"And all his subjects are women."

"Women are the creators, and he's reaching for the eter-nal through them." Her hostess winked at her. "So he says, anyway. I have to respect that."

"Don't you get jealous? He must have models."

"I used to. When you live with an artist, though, you have to accept the whole package, and that includes his subject matter. So far," she said, knocking on the table she was leaning on, "his philandering has been limited to canvas—as far as I know, anyway."

It turned out that Sarah was not to be the only guest. "We're expecting a couple from New York," Sonja had explained over dinner. "He's a trumpeter, an old friend of Roper's. I have to check, but I think they're coming in a day or two after Roper comes back." Sarah had gone to sleep that night certain that the couple, along with Roper and Sonja, would turn into a foursome, herself the odd one out, as usual.

A wave broke in front of her and pushed up the hilly slope of sand. Turning the sketch pad to a fresh page, Sarah drew another four-by-four square. The constant motion of the water was starting to frustrate her, her attempts to capture it unsuccessful. Her rapid pencil strokes quickly became irrelevant as the foam pulled back and prepared for another onslaught.

There was only one way to capture a close-up of a wave's movement, she decided, and pulled her digital camera out of her bag. After turning it on, she rested her elbows on her knees and steadied the camera. Focusing on the slope of the beach in front of her, she zoomed the lens in and waited. As soon as she heard the pause of another wave curling over, preparing to crash to the sand, she clicked—and photographed a large brown foot planted in the middle of the foam.

"Shit!" Sarah muttered, and looked up. The owner of the foot had already passed and was streaking toward the end of the beach. Wearing only a pair of red trunks, the invader was a strapping local man, by the looks of it, his shoulders thick with muscle, his bald and shining head held high.

Discombobulated, as her father would have said, her heart beating fast, she pushed the camera into the bag. If she hurried, she could get away before he returned.

Carthena greeted her when she returned the stool to the kitchen. "You come back early."

"The heat," Sarah said, fanning herself with the hat. "I still have to get used to it."

"Jamaica plenty hot," the young woman said, and threw the scallion she'd been chopping into a bowl. The beads rattled when she looked up. "You must be careful you don't burn, you hear?"

CHAPTER SIX

The words and numbers swam before Eric's eyes. He groaned and patted the top of the refrigerator, his hand finding nothing but gritty dust.

"Shad, do you know where my glasses are?" he called to the bartender wiping a table at the rear of the restaurant.

"On the middle shelf, boss. You put them down after you fix the blender last night."

Glasses found, Eric returned to his usual chair at his usual table and scrutinized the document.

"I think we have a problem," he said, reaching for the pipe in his pocket.

"A problem?"

"The budget doesn't include the cost of putting electricity and water on the island. We can't have the people in the campsite without water and lights."

While Eric lit his lignum vitae pipe, Shad peered over his shoulder at the report. "Can't we run a water pipe out there?"

Eric blew out a column of smoke. "A quarter mile offshore? Cost a fortune."

"What about rain barrels?"

"They're going to need water to bathe in, to drink, to wash dishes, you name it—too much for barrels."

"And they going to need electricity to cook with. They can't use charcoal, like Simone used to use."

"Next thing, they burn down the tents."

Shad wiped a corner of the table absently, his eyes on the report. "We going to have to tell Mistah Caines, nuh?"

The problem hadn't come to Eric while examining the business proposal, which he had never fully read since it was completed in December. He'd thought about it for the first time during his drive from Port Antonio earlier that day. His mouth still aching from the dentist's injection, he'd been ambling from one self-pitying thought to another, most of them revolving around Simone.

Talking about her with Danny had made him miss her again, almost as much as when she first left Largo six months earlier. He remembered watching her brother's rental car disappear down the main road—Simone's thin, brown arm waving out the passenger window—and how he'd walked back to his apartment and sat on the side of the bed facing the island.

Before her arrival, the rocky little island had been loaded with bittersweet memories from years past. Seated on his verandah every night, staring into the blackness, he'd reminisce about the seven years he'd been the head honcho of the small inn, lingering over incidents like when a guest had had a heart attack and he'd taken him to the hospital in his Jeep and the man had lived. And the two guests who'd met at the hotel and married in one week—and he'd wonder if the marriage had lasted.

Everything had changed when he and Shad had discovered Simone living on the island. His nightly verandah vigils had become consumed by things she'd said, by her safety, by her needs. After they became lovers, he'd arrive on the island with treats, imported cheese and olives and wine, which they'd enjoy on her bed before making love. When she left Largo, they'd agreed there'd be no phone calls. Long-distance relationships didn't work, he'd said. But he'd broken his own vow and called her a couple of times since, once to ask her permission to name the island after her, once to tell her that the island was now officially Simone Island. She'd met his calls in a cool yet friendly way and even called back once.

He'd been looking for another excuse to call her and had now found one. If the island were to be a campsite, he was going to say, they'd need her advice about outfitting it properly. It had then dawned on him that, although a canoe had been enough to transport her supplies, it would be way different for a slew of people. Fifty guests plus staff living and working on the island would need a lot more water than a few bottles a week. They'd need *running* water, and lights and power.

By the time Caines appeared later that evening in another tourist shirt, Shad and Eric were a grim duo. They watched him bouncing in, greeting the few customers as if he were already an owner, introducing himself, charisma flowing out of his pores.

"Had a good day?" Eric inquired, motioning for him to sit down.

"Great!" Caines said, and pulled out a chair.

"Anything to eat?" Shad asked with a strained smile. "We have some nice stew peas and rice tonight."

"Miss Mac took care of me, thanks. But I'll have a rum and ginger."

Eric asked about his day and Caines mentioned he'd started running on the beach, the first time he'd run in a couple of years.

"I'm feeling like a new man," he added. He looked boyish, wiggling his shoulders, excited by his discovery. "You feel like a youth when you running, you know. It takes years off your life. Ever tried it?"

"No, I'm not a runner."

"It's a great run, that beach. How long is it?"

"About a mile."

"Two miles altogether. I'm going to do it every day. All the stress just goes away, man. Being on the beach does something—takes me back, you know?"

"Watch out for the jellyfish. Sometimes they wash up and sting you when you least expect it."

"I'll be careful, don't worry." Caines dropped the smile. Small lines appeared around his mouth, making him look older. "I've decided to rent a car, because I need to know the area, Port Antonio and the other towns, you know. I'm going to start driving around every day."

"Don't forget that we have to see Delgado, the contractor, tomorrow."

"I won't forget, and I want to meet Horace Mac."

"MacKenzie, Horace MacKenzie," Eric said, glancing at Shad, who was twisting off the ginger ale cap, his forehead in a rare frown.

"I'm liking the idea of a campsite more and more. Leasing the island could be cash money at the start, don't you think? Setting the hotel up, running it, advertising, all the expenses in the first couple years is going to mean more money going out than coming in until we get our guest numbers up. And we'll have to hire a marketing agent—"

"I used an agency in Miami for the old inn. I don't know if they're still in business—"

"And with all the initial outlay, we're going to need the cash from that campsite," Caines said, rubbing his palms together. "We need to talk details and terms, and start getting something down in writing with Horace Mac."

There was nothing of the ingenue in the investor that Eric had expected. He'd assumed before meeting him that an African American with a few small properties in Queens and the Bronx would be green around the ears. Danny was anything but green. Amiable and easygoing, he deceived at first, but there was a hard core to him when it came to business.

"Shad," Eric called. "When you're coming, bring some of those mints in the green wrappers, will you?" The ones that settled his stomach. He turned to Caines. "Do you want peanuts or anything?"

Eric's discomfort with the idea of a new hotel only increased listening to Caines, now sounding more like an entrepreneur than an island man returning home. His business acumen clearly went deeper than that of a human resource manager of a paper company. Although running the inn had taught Eric one or two things (he'd called his bumps in the road *the school of hard rocks*), he was just getting the hang of it when the hurricane had come along and school was out.

After Caines took his first sip of rum, Eric put his hand on the business proposal. "Speaking of Horace—we need to talk to him about how the campsite is going to get water and electricity. We thought we might negotiate—"

"There's no water on the island?" Caines said, leaning forward, eyebrows high.

"There's nothing but—walls. The hurricane destroyed the pipes running out there."

"It has to have water." The investor's voice dropped an octave. "Does Horace know?" He frowned at the island, dimly outlined by the three-quarter moon rising over the water.

"We never discussed it."

"If I were him, I'd want some kind of infrastructure. Who's going to pay for that?"

Eric cleared his throat. "About the electricity, I thought we could—"

"We can use solar power," Caines interrupted. "All the sunshine here, it shouldn't be a problem. Expensive as hell to install, though."

"I was thinking solar, too."

"We'd have to add that on to the budget, though," Danny snorted, twisting his upper lip.

Ten minutes later, the bar owner departed for his apartment, mulling his partnership with Caines. Several things were becoming clear. First, the man would argue for every penny he had to borrow or spend. Second, there was nothing about building this hotel that was going to be a cakewalk. And third, Caines was sounding more and more like a man who wouldn't think twice about dragging someone into court. Eric sighed and tuned the radio to his favorite Havana station.

CHAPTER SEVEN

The big man slid onto the bar stool opposite, scowling brows low over his eyes.

"Another rum, Mistah Caines?" Shad asked.

"Yeah—and call me Danny."

Shad turned the radio dial, cutting off the strident soca with a woman singer describing the grinding of cocoa beans for her man's breakfast (complete with panting between grinds), and found a soft country and western with a woman crying over a heartless man.

"Why you turn off the good-good music?" Tri called from the far end of the bar counter where he'd been arguing with Eli about Kingston politicians.

"Pshaw, man," Shad said, grabbing the bottle of Appleton rum. "Too much grinding make a person stupid." And only served to remind him of his own lack of grinding, Beth's body being off-limits, at least for the time being.

"I saw you running on the beach this morning," he said to Danny as he placed the drink in front of him. "Look like you enjoying Largo."

"It's beautiful." Danny sipped and licked his lips. "But I don't like surprises."

"You get a surprise?" Shad said, keeping the smile bright to fight off the sinking feeling in his stomach.

"Yeah, I need to put more money into the budget for water and solar panels on the island."

After he'd gotten a round of drinks for a distant table, Shad settled down on his bartender's stool. "Why Horace can't help with the cost of the solar panels?" he asked.

"It's not his property."

"Maybe he can put up some money, and we can take it off the rent, slow like—you know, not all at once. That way he have to rent the island a long time to get back his money."

"Possible, possible," Danny said, and looked up at Shad. "So how come you all didn't think of this before?"

"We was waiting for you to come down. We know you would ask some good questions, get us thinking. That's what partners supposed to do, right?"

"Yeah, but not surprise you with a new bottom line, man."

Even though Shad didn't understand what *bottom line* meant and he wasn't going to ask, he knew that Danny had eased up in his anger, because the grooves on his forehead weren't as deep and his accent was starting to sound more Caribbean.

Shad leaned in. "I know you have an answer for the water, though. What you think is the best way to get it out there?"

"Cisterns," Danny answered with a firm mouth.

"Cisterns?"

"Almost every house in the Virgin Islands have them, because we don't have rivers like you guys." Danny rested his elbows on the bar and put his broad fingertips together in a peak. "See, you have a house with a pitched roof and gutters. The gutters lead the rainwater down a pipe that drains into a big underground tank—that's the cistern—and every time it rains, the cistern fills up—"

"And we can collect the rainwater."

"Exactly." The investor nodded.

"We just have to build a tank under the ground."

"And we have to put in pipes and a pump to bring it up to the surface. But it'll be even more expensive to put roofs on the buildings for the rain to collect on."

Shad ran his fingers across his scalp. "We could use zinc, right? Zinc is cheap; all our houses have zinc roofs. I could get the men in the village to help put them up over the ruins. We could give them a little goat-head soup and make it into a party. We could put that up in one day, put up some beams and nail the zinc to them."

"And we could run the gutters around the zinc when that's finished."

So it was, on that night at the end of January, that Shad and Danny solved a problem and became friends, one man respecting the other's ideas. And just when Shad was beginning to feel comfortable enough with his new friend to talk about Beth and the wedding problem, the arrival of a third party shifted everything, the way it always did.

"Good night," Janet purred, depositing a large handbag on the counter. She flashed a smile at Danny that showed the gold tooth on her incisor to full advantage.

The dressmaker took Danny's outstretched hand and clambered onto the stool beside him, wriggling her hips around until she was comfortable. She was wearing a red dress with a neckline that framed her breasts and made her skin look more coppery than usual. Her arms were gleaming like she'd rubbed them with some kind of oil and she was smelling musky sweet—a scheming woman on a hot night.

"I want whatever he's having," she said with a simper that would have made Beth roll up her eyes. Shad turned to the fridge and sighed.

"I remember you," Danny said behind him. "You came to my welcome party, right?"

"That's right."

"You had on a white—"

"We talked for a few minutes, but you was so popular . . ."

"I'm sorry, I don't remember your name. There were a lot of people—"

"Janet."

When Shad placed the drink in front of the woman, she raised her eyes over the rim of the glass and gave the bartender a look that told him to back off. She turned again to Danny, the hoop earrings swinging as she eyed him up and down.

"So, what you think of Largo, Mistah America?"

"It's great," Danny said. "I want to see the rest of the area, though."

"It sound like you need somebody to show you around," she replied, batting her eyelashes. Shad tried not to suck his teeth.

"I do, yes," Danny said. He kept rubbing the glass with his thumbs, sliding them up and down.

Shad folded his arms. "I can show you around during my lunchtime," he said, "from two o'clock to five."

"If you're free tomorrow," Danny said, looking at Shad but leaning toward Janet.

"I can't go tomorrow," Shad said. "I have to go to the clinic with Beth and Ashanti. The nurse come on Friday."

"I can go," Janet piped up.

"You can?" Danny said, turning to grin at her. "That's cool. Where should we go first?"

"Blue Hole," Shad said, trying to ignore Tri's beckoning finger. "You should take a trip to Blue Hole in Port Antonio, man, beautiful lagoon with deep, deep water in the middle. We can go Monday. Is my day off."

"What about tomorrow?" Janet asked.

"Tomorrow is good," Danny said. "I have to take a taxi to Port Antonio to rent a car, but then I'm free."

"My cousin Marvin can take us to Port Antonio," Janet said. "He always charge me half fare."

Shad strolled to the other end of the counter and refilled Tri's glass. The aging fisherman slurped a bit off the top. "Look like Janet have the hotel man under heavy manners already," he said.

"If she get her claws into him is worse than a crab," Eli whispered. "She never let him go."

"I just hope he don't catch crabs." Tri snickered, slapping Eli on the arm, and the two men doubled over.

"Shush your mouth," Shad muttered. "Next thing, the man hear you."

"Is not true?" Tri said, his thin frame still trembling. "You don't see how she working it?"

"She a seamstress, you don't know?" Eli hissed. "She sewing up the business."

"You mean, she going to pump his treadle?" Tri laughed

so hard he almost fell off his bar stool, and his friend had to steady him.

Waving their foolishness away, Shad moved back to his stool in front of Danny. He might as well not have been there, the man was so engrossed in Janet's description of the sights she was going to show him. She was waving her hands around, telling him which beach was best, and then talking about a night club in Ocho Rios she wanted to show him, and how she would teach him to dance the reggae like a real Jamaican. And Shad could see that there was no going back now, just by the way Danny was smiling, his fingers tapping the counter halfway between him and the woman, a few beads of sweat on his forehead above the delighted smile, the increased budget forgotten. When he laughed, he gave a throaty laugh, full of desire and of feeling desired, and if the two of them didn't sleep together tonight, Shad knew, they would do it tomorrow night.

After they'd left—Danny insisting that he had to walk Janet home—Shad washed up the dirty glasses at the bar sink, worrying, sometimes bringing God into it, that the dressmaker would mess up the hotel deal and his dream of a prosperous Largo. Maybe he should warn Danny that Janet was only looking for a husband to give her a green card. But if he warned him, Danny might think that Largo people just wanted to use him and his money, and he wouldn't see that they were good people who talked the truth most of the time.

He tried to see how it would end if Danny fell for the *leggo gal,* the hussy, and it made his stomach go from a churn to a knot. No scenario had a happy ending. He saw them lying side by side on a beach, drinking and dancing in a club, ripping off each other's clothes, and tumbling into a bed. He visualized (too clearly, he chastised himself) Janet straddling Danny, her sumptuous breasts swinging as she worked him and worked him, felt the sweaty exhaustion as they lay together in a heap afterward.

This was followed by the even more troublesome thought that, a few months down the road, Janet might dump Danny because his penis was too small or he was too cheap or he was already married, and Shad was sure that, having found fault with Danny, she'd put his business in the street the way she always did. Then (*oh, God!*) he envisioned the opposite: Danny dumping Janet and going back to America without her. She'd be enraged and tell everyone what a *bumba claat* no-good he was, because she was not an easy woman. And, either way, Danny wouldn't come back to Largo. Every possibility Shad imagined concluded with the investor pulling out of the deal and the death of the new inn.

The next morning over breakfast, Shad told Beth about Janet's offer to be Danny's tour guide.

"I telling you," he said, and slurped his ginger tea, "the woman just outsmart me. I was offering to take him around, but she just bounce me out of the picture."

"We know she only after one thing."

"And you know what I realize yesterday? Is not only a conniving woman that can mash up the hotel plan. An innocent woman can do it, too." While Beth unbuttoned her blouse and settled Joshua at her breast to feed, Shad told her, scene by scene, the way he always did, something disturbing he'd seen the previous afternoon, a wake-up call about the future of tourism in Largo.

It was close to five o'clock, and he'd been making his usual trek back to the bar for his evening shift when he'd glanced across the road. Between two houses, he'd had a straight view of the beach, where three people were in conversation under a coconut tree. He'd strained for a better view of the three, because one was a white woman he'd never seen before. She was so tall and lanky, her hair so red-red, that he would have remembered her if he had. And her legs and arms were so pale, pale as the sand she was standing on, that he knew she'd just arrived.

Standing on either side of her had been two local layabouts, one thin and the other stocky, both a head shorter than her. The youths were doing all the talking, it looked like, and the woman was looking uncomfortable but smiling politely. The bartender had waited until a pickup passed, crossed the road, and walked between the cottages to the beach.

"What up?" he'd called out as he approached the group. The boy who was talking had broken off and all three had turned around. The woman had started edging away.

"You just come to Largo?" Shad had said to the redhead, speaking slowly so she'd understand. She nodded, and the flaming hair nodded with her. She'd been a nice-looking woman even if she was thin—*mauger,* Beth would call her— the kind of woman who was too well mannered to say no. Trouble waiting to happen.

"Zebediah," Shad had asked the skinny youth, "you not bothering the lady or anything, right?"

"Why I want to do that?" the boy had said, and glanced at the other. "We making friends with her, seen, like how she just come to Largo."

"Well, I come to take her to the restaurant," Shad said, waving the two away. "So both of you can go about your business now."

"We not doing nothing—"

"Go on," Shad insisted, and the two teenagers had sauntered away, sucking their teeth.

"You mustn't do any business with them, you hear, miss," Shad had explained. "They want to take your money from you. Don't have nothing to do with them." The woman's face had relaxed and she'd thanked him for helping her.

"They wanted to sell me some marijuana, I think," she'd said in a nice English accent. "I couldn't understand them, but they said something about *ganja* and I know what that is."

"We don't have a lot of visitors, you know, and they see a chance to make little money. The boy Zeb, his grandmother can't handle him, you know. He sell weed now and again, and he getting his friend into it, too. Bedward was bright-bright in school, but he stop going to school and start making mischief with Zeb."

Guiding the woman back to the main road, Shad had told her he worked at the bar. "You want to come and have a nice drink, a coconut water or something?"

"I better be getting back," she said. "I was taking a walk on the beach—"

"Better you walk with somebody else," Shad had advised, smiling so she wouldn't be too afraid, "or walk on the road. Not that anybody going to hurt you, but some people might see you as a stranger and want to take advantage of you. They think you have a lot of money."

The woman had thanked him again and they'd gone in

opposite directions. Shad had walked back to the bar in a trance, realizing for the first time that Largo might not be ready for the inflow of tourists that would come with a hotel because, in the eight years since the boss's hotel had closed, the young people had gotten more desperate, their options fewer by the year. A new hotel would attract every lazy, good-for-nothing youth for miles around, every one of them looking to make easy money off the guests. If they didn't get work, they'd be all over the tourists with offers of weed and sex and hair-braiding.

Shad looked at Beth, shaking his head. "Next thing, people in America hear that they going to be harassed in Largo—"

"And the tourists stop coming."

"Innocent or guilty, a woman can mash up everything the same way, yes." Shad stood up, stretching his arms overhead. "Nothing simple, eh?"

CHAPTER EIGHT

The wide silver bangle on Sonja's wrist reflected the candlelight, making the flame appear fatter, brighter. Everything about the writer sparkled with her delight at Roper's return, her full lips and cheeks glowing.

"Where've you been playing lately, Ford?" she asked. All heads turned to the end of the dining table where the newest guest was sitting.

"New York, right?" Roper said. He wore a scarlet mandarin shirt that matched the wine he was sipping.

Fordham Monroe looked up from his roast beef. He was tall enough to have to bend over the dinner plate, his slim fingers extending almost the lengths of the knife and fork in his hands. The furrow between his eyes seemed to be debating his answer.

"Didn't you tell me on the phone you were taking a gig in the Village?" Roper prompted, stroking the deep grooves beside his mouth that brought carved furniture to mind.

Ford dropped his hands to his lap. "I've been giving the trumpet a rest since London, man."

"A rest?" Roper asked. "What do you mean?" Probing ever deeper was always his pattern, it seemed, and Sarah winced inwardly in sympathy, remembering how it felt to be the subject of Roper's scrutiny only two days before on his return to Largo. Strolling around the studio, he'd pointed out that the dimensions of his life-size canvases allowed the onlooker to *connect* with his subjects, and he'd lectured her about her own work as if she were a wayward student.

"What I love about your work," he'd said in an agonized voice, "is the perfection of it. Your symbolism is strong, your intricate composition is wonderful, your strokes clean and precise. But, *why,* in God's name, do you have to contract life to a few *inches?* It's as if you create these masterpieces and don't want anyone to see them."

"I believe," Sarah had said after only a second's hesitation, "that my work is a microcosm of life. Whatever my subject matter is, I like to scale it down to force the viewers to look inside my frame in a totally focused way."

"You want to frustrate them, you mean." Roper ran his hand through his wiry gray hair while he said it. She hadn't made up her mind if she liked him or hated him. The experience of living in the home—a beautiful home, to boot—of an affluent black man was still sinking in with her. It was the first time she remembered being the only white person in a group, certainly in a home, and she still didn't know how she felt about it. True, Sonja had been sweet and nonthreatening, Carthena had been civil, but Roper's arrival had given her the clear understanding that she was the guest of a black man, eating his food, living under his roof, having to please him with her art. And Roper was no ordinary man. He was eloquent, arrogant, stylish to a fault, and fully confident of the rightness of his opinions.

"Tell me the truth, how many do you sell a year?" Roper had raised one eyebrow like a mandarin in judgment. "Maybe you don't have to live off your work like the rest of us, but the question is, do you paint for yourself or for others? It's all well and good for people to appreciate your work, but you want them to take it home and put money in your bank account."

Her mother's favorite expression had come back to her. *Don't make a fuss, dear,* she'd say, always accompanied by a patting of Sarah's hand.

"The kind of buyer I'm looking for, Roper, is someone who sees the layers in my work, who understands the intimacy of my connection with them." She didn't mean to imply (even though she'd thought it) that a man in his midfifties who enjoyed being the center of attention, who painted large nudes of women because he knew they'd sell, wouldn't understand true intimacy.

Roper was not a man to be contradicted, however generous he was to his household guests, and few had the stomach to oppose him for long. Sarah had already concluded that her host relished the presence of his guests and whatever muse they brought to his home for one reason—he enjoyed controlling them. Confident and paternalistic, he'd throw out his opinions, emphasizing every word, sometimes spacing them so that each lingered in the air with authority.

"It's time to let your audience *live* the work, to put *themselves* in the scene," he'd said, a smile playing around his large, square lips. "They can't do that if they have to shrink like Alice to see them."

Halfway through the afternoon, Sarah realized she was no match for the man, especially since she was his guest, and she lied that she was already sketching larger works. "Do you have anything to show me yet?" he wanted to know.

"I'll tell you when I'm ready," she'd answered, and made an excuse to go back to her room.

Ford looked down at his roast beef and resumed cutting it. "It's not just that Jewel couldn't come, man. She had a miscarriage. It hit her hard, it hit us both hard." He was talking so softly in his Southern accent that Sarah strained forward to catch his words. "We've had a rough time of it and she's moved out. It's over."

"Oh, God," Sonja said, her carrot-laden fork in midair. "We had no idea, Ford. I'm so sorry."

"How awful," Sarah mumbled. She liked Ford and his gentle, studied manner. He seemed like someone who would appreciate small paintings.

"That's life, right?" Ford's voice got matter-of-fact as he refilled his glass with burgundy. "Thought it might be best if I got out of the city for a few weeks. There are worse places than Jamaica to chill out. Sorry I didn't give you a heads-up before I came, but I—"

"We're glad you came," Sonja said. "It'll give you both some time to get over it. Maybe things will change by the time you get back." Roper was looking at Sonja, allowing her to speak for him, but the writer had run out of words, and the sound of silverware chafing against plates took the place of conversation.

The swing door to the kitchen opened. "Finished?" Carthena asked, her puff sleeves and aproned skirt reminding Sarah of a chocolate Swiss maid ready to burst into song.

"I'm done," Ford said. He laid his fork down and looked up at the young woman with a dutiful widening of lips.

"But you haven't finished," the helper protested, shaking her beads.

"I've had enough for tonight."

"You didn't like it?"

"It was delicious. I don't have much of an appetite."

"I going to cook some nice food for you. We need to fatten you up." Carthena's smile remained fixed while she collected the dinner plates, and Sarah wondered if she'd heard some of their earlier talk.

"Carthena cooks a mean escoveitch fish," Roper said. "Can we have that for breakfast tomorrow?"

"Nobody make it better than me," the woman said, beaming. "I'll buy some fresh snapper in the morning."

By the time they moved to the deck with a pot of coffee and a tray of cups and saucers, some sense of normalcy had returned, although the hostess made sure to serve Ford his coffee first. Around them, fireflies—*peeny wallies,* Roper called them—buzzed in and out of the darkened bushes.

Settling back into a lounge chair with her coffee cup, Sarah pointed to the lights on the far end of the bay. "I went walking over there a couple days ago. There's a bar there, right?"

"A bar and a house on the hill—there on the left. It's a beautiful house where a family called the Delgados live," Sonja explained. "That other light—lower down, see—is the bar. It's on a cliff overlooking the water."

"Sounds lovely," Sarah said. "I met the bartender when I was taking a walk." She decided to say nothing about the man's warning, which, remembered on a soft tropical evening, now seemed like an overreaction.

"We'll take you there," Sonja said. "It's a cute bar, very—rustic."

"It's right across from an island," Roper added. "We'll go before sunset so you can see it."

Ford leaned forward, showing some energy for the first time. "Do they have music in the bar?"

"Not much live music," Sonja answered, shrugging. "An American man owns it."

Roper entertained them with the bar owner's saga, and they all tsk-tsked about the hurricane that had wiped the roofs off the villagers' houses and resulted in the death of the hotel and the birth of an island.

"You think your problems are bigger than everyone else's," Ford said, "but there's always someone with a tougher story."

"I hear an investor's come down to talk to Eric about building another hotel," Roper interjected. "Maybe there's hope for him after all."

After the hosts had excused themselves, Ford and Sarah continued sitting on the deck. They listened for a while to a CD that Roper had put on before he went to bed, and the trumpeter explained that he and his band had recorded it live last year at Ravinia, an open-air theater near Chicago. All around them, the squeaks and honks of crickets and frogs accompanied the music. Sipping a second cup of coffee, Ford commented on the many bright stars overhead, and they compared notes on the difficulty of stargazing in urban centers, a mutual pet peeve, it turned out.

"When I was little," Sarah said, "my father took me to this village where my uncle had a church—he was an Anglican minister—just south of Scotland. We went walking on a country road one night, and I remember being all bundled up and my father pointing out the stars. They were so bright, just amazing."

"That's a great memory."

"Funnily enough, I don't have a lot of memories from childhood." She laughed. "There are these great blocks of time that are blank, for some reason. Maybe that comes from living a pretty monotonous life."

Ford had lots of memories. He talked of watching the night sky in the summer. He would sit on his aunt's dock in South Carolina in the evening with his cousins, and they would see how many stars they could count. "When we gave up, we'd count the shooting stars."

Listening to Ford, seeing one half of his face dimly lit by the living room lights, Sarah guessed that he was anywhere between thirty-five and forty-five. There were no wrinkles on his face, despite the late nights he kept, so he might have been younger rather than older. There was something likable about his mouth with its raised outer edges, something refined about his nose. And while he spoke nostalgically, she began to suspect they'd been left alone on purpose by Sonja and Roper.

Her companion now talked about playing the trumpet in the South, and how much he enjoyed jamming with musicians from New Orleans since Hurricane Katrina, and she noticed for the first time a diamond on one side of his long nose that glimmered when he turned toward her. And while he spoke, she wondered how it would feel to run her hand over his close-cropped head, if it would feel coarse or smooth, although there was no chance of them becoming lovers even if she wanted to—which she didn't. His wounds were too fresh.

It was only later, while she was changing into her pajamas, that she knew that the real reason she wouldn't sleep with Ford, or even flirt with him, was more about the fact that she'd never found a black man appealing. She'd had a few high school and art school classmates who were first-generation West Indians or Africans, but no close friends who were anything other than white. Penny, of course, had all kinds of friends, including Zoey, a Barbadian TV producer who dropped in at least once a month, and her roommate's circle often included a black boyfriend.

"I was telling my mother," Penny had commented after starting an affair with a Nigerian engineer, "that it's a different time and place. People are just people, for God's sake."

Sarah had nodded but hadn't been sure how she felt about it herself. She had nothing against black men per se, but they didn't start the adrenaline rushing for her. At the bottom of it, she thought, was the awkwardness of cultural differences, even if it was a new day. It was enough of a nuisance meshing with any boyfriend, much less one who ate strange food and had a mother you couldn't understand.

Somewhere between pounding her pillow and laying her head on it, Sarah decided that part of the reason she'd accepted Roper's invitation was that Naomi had confirmed that he had a lovely home and a live-in girlfriend. He was middle class and she was safe. No, she was not having a relationship with anyone in Jamaica. It was definitely not in the cards.

CHAPTER NINE

I t was no secret that Daniel Caines had become a tourist, had gone to see the lagoon at Blue Hole, had shopped in the Ocho Rios craft market and gone into the underground caves in St. Ann, according to his reports to Eric. It was also no secret that he was having a nightly romp with Janet. By way of announcing it, the seamstress was now hanging on to his arm wherever he went, and Eric had more than once imagined the woman's rounded buttocks pounding up and down on Caines.

When the investor and his girlfriend had come into the bar one night, the man almost luminescent, like he'd just had a monstrous orgasm followed by a hot shower, Eric had decided that he better move things along at a faster clip, since Caines clearly had too much free time. The next morning he'd called Horace MacKenzie to set up their meeting.

The meeting with Lambert Delgado the week before had gone well. Eric and Caines had walked up the Delgados' driveway to that meeting, between the mango and grapefruit trees, with Eric again describing his swim across when the eye of the hurricane was passing over and dragging himself up onto Lambert's verandah, "naked as a baby," and pounding on the door. Caines had only murmured, "Hmm," his eyes roaming over the modern, plantation-style house before them.

They'd finally arrived, with a fair amount of panting on Eric's part, at two minutes after eleven, the appointed time. Lambert, large and beige, had come through the elegant living room with arms extended to his visitors, welcoming them. He apologized for not making it to the party. He'd been in Kingston buying lumber, he said.

The middle-aged contractor was Eric's best friend. Apart from sheltering the homeless hotel owner during the hurricane, Lambert had given him a room to live in for a year after, before the bar and apartment were built. He'd let Eric's son, Joseph, use an office in the house when he came to write the business proposal. And now he was giving his services as contractor for the new hotel at a major discount—as a gift to Largo, he said.

After the introductions, Eric, Lambert, and Danny had moved to the long verandah and its white rocking chairs and were served Red Stripe beers by Miss Bertha, the chunky housekeeper whose hips just fit into her plaid uniform.

"You don't come up here for a long time," she'd teased Eric. "Now that your son is gone, you scarce as good gold."

"Don't worry, Miss Bertha, you going to have plenty chance to see me," Eric had answered in his American patois. "When we start building, you see me every day."

An easy icebreaker came up at the start of the meeting: the city of New York. All three men had lived there at some point. And although Lambert and Danny had lived there in different decades, they acted like they shared something that Eric didn't, and he knew it was that they had both been Caribbean men struggling through college in a big white city. Eric had joined in the discussion about living in Manhattan in the seventies and eighties, referring to the Village as if he'd gone there often, careful not to mention that he'd never attended university and had lived a very different life from theirs.

Having warmed up to the matter at hand, Lambert had run his fingers across his handlebar mustache. "How long are you planning to be here?" he'd said, nodding to Caines.

"It's kind of a working holiday, so I'd say another couple weeks. I want to get to know Jamaica better if I'm going to make an investment here, you know. I've been visiting places, reading up about stuff—about the economy, the recent election."

"And you know we have political confusion, right?" Lambert joked, winking at Eric. "But I bet you never read about the time it takes to get government approvals—"

"I heard about that."

"Then you'd better plan to stay another month, my friend, because we need to get permits from the Parish Council here, and we have to attend several meetings to justify the construction. I really think you should be here for that. The Council will want to ask you about your businesses overseas."

"I don't know—it's been difficult connecting with my business, what with poor cell phone coverage here and Miss Mac not being on the Internet. My mother is handling everything back home, but I like to stay in touch. I may have to come and go."

"I'm telling you," Lambert had assured him, "it takes the patience of Job to do business here, just bear that in mind." By the time the meeting ended, Caines and Lambert were calling each other *my man,* had made a date to go out on the golf course, and were sounding more and more like black Americans.

In contrast to the visit with Lambert, the meeting with Horace went poorly from the beginning. Eric had forgotten to warn Caines that Horace had never been on time since he'd known him and, one hour after they'd arrived at Horace's office above a Port Antonio bread shop, they were still waiting. Caines kept looking at his watch and recrossing his legs. The stale *Lawyers Today* magazines displayed on the side table remained untouched. On several occasions, Danny paced to the open window and looked down at the lane outside.

"What time was our appointment?" he asked the elderly receptionist on one of his trips. She assured him that Mr. MacKenzie knew he was to meet with them but had to go to court. She was expecting him *momentarily,* she said, frowning at his American petulance.

When the slender lawyer appeared two hours after the scheduled time, his black robe thrown over his arm, Caines appeared to be in no mood to be civil, but he held his tongue, his thin lips thinner than usual. Eric got the conversation rolling with a question about the campsite. In answer and without asking for their approval, Horace lit a cigarette with his graceful mocha fingers and exhaled a cone of smoke that was quickly dispersed by the overhead fan.

"I've spoken to some guys, friends of mine, and we're ready to lease the island once you get the hotel construction started."

"Everything is going well so far," Eric said. "Your mother has agreed to sell the land—Danny spoke with her—so that's okay. We've started the construction discussions with Lambert Delgado, no problem there. And we're on board about leasing you the island. But there's one thing, the electricity and water—"

"We had a thought," Caines interjected. "Since there aren't any working utilities on the island, of course, since the hurricane, we were wondering if your group would want to install solar panels and cisterns for electricity and water. Make the place self-sustaining, you know, cheaper than paying utility bills. You could design and build just the way you want, in the locations you want. And it would be the kind of eco-friendly stuff your tourists would go for."

Horace scrutinized them, his cigarette at a right angle with his fingers, and his bony chin jutting toward them. "Are you telling me that you're expecting us to put in the infrastructure for you, to pay for it ourselves, is that what you're saying?"

Caines stretched his neck to one side. "We thought you might be open to working with us—"

"You're joking, right? That was never mentioned before."

"If you construct, we can deduct it from the lease, month by month, you know."

Horace sat back, shrugging the shoulders of his cream linen jacket. "We already have to install tents and a kitchen and bathrooms. Now we're talking basic infrastructure." His eyes narrowed. "How much more is that going to cost?"

"Not much, probably twenty, twenty-five thousand US, mostly for the purchase of solar panels and the construction of an underground cistern and plumbing. The installation of the roofs should be fairly cheap if you use zinc sheets and gutters." Horace glowered, Caines wouldn't budge, and things seemed to have reached an impasse until Eric asked about the necessary documents to form a company.

An hour later in the afternoon-empty bar, the bar owner poured himself a scotch, a rare indulgence, and sat down at his table with the newspaper.

"Didn't go well," he complained to Shad, who was leaving for his lunch break.

"What happen?"

"We had to tell Horace there were no utilities and—"

"Danny didn't tell him that if he did it, we would deduct the cost from the rent?"

"How'd you know?" Eric said. He finished the scotch in one swig and grimaced. "Horace didn't like the idea one bit. I can't imagine where Caines got it from."

"I give it to him," Shad said, to which Eric stared at him—his trusted employee, whom he'd insisted should be a minority partner in the new hotel, giving advice to his business partner behind his back. The bartender disappeared with an apologetic shrugging of shoulders, while his boss poured himself another shot and opened the *Gleaner*.

Unaccustomed to drinking hard liquor, Eric soon had trouble making sense of the words in front of him. He put down the paper and looked across at Simone Island, baking in the two o'clock sunlight. Six months earlier, he would have rowed out to see her, would have told her about the meeting with Horace, and she would have said something he needed to hear. He poured a third shot and swallowed it quickly, rebuking himself at the same time. A tingling started in his groin, the scotch going to places he'd almost forgotten, places that made him think of her, and of Caines

and his after-sex glow. He stood up with inebriated determination, went searching in the drawer where he kept his
ledger book and odd notes, and found a pink Post-it note
with an Atlanta phone number. She answered right away.

"How you doing, Simone?" He was trying not to slur,
holding his tongue and teeth apart.

"Great! How is the hotel coming along?"

"Danny Caines is here, your brother's client."

"How is that going?" She sounded like she was eating
something.

"So far, so good, you know, long way to go. Do you know
him, Caines, I mean?"

"No, but Cameron seems to like him a lot."

"I think he's on board, but you know how it is here.
He's finding some things hard to accept, and then other
things"—thinking of the man's shining face—"he seems
to like a lot."

"Like what?"

Eric cleared his throat. "He loves the ocean, kind of like
you. He runs every morning on the beach, swims, that kind
of thing."

"Like a Jamerican." She laughed. It was a term she'd
used to describe herself once. They'd been eating June
plums, he remembered, the juice dripping down her chin.

"He's from St. Croix."

"Cameron hadn't mentioned that."

"So," he said, and looked up at a car pulling into the
parking lot, "what have you been doing? Still not working?"

She paused, either to chew or think. "I'm working on
Celeste's room, deciding what to keep and what to store.

I'm still working that through, you know. I've joined a group for parents who've—it helps a lot—knowing that other people have . . ." Her voice faded away, then got stronger when she started speaking again. "And I've been applying for jobs with nonprofits, working with troubled youth, that kind of thing. I'm not going back to corporate, like I told you. My head just isn't into the whole advertising thing anymore."

"I mish you." It had come out wrong, his lips and teeth getting lazy. The customer, a man in jeans, was locking his car door, would soon want a drink.

"What was that?"

Eric licked his lips. "I miss you."

"You miss me? That's very sweet, Eric."

"I was thinking about you all of a sudden, looking at the island. Shumtimes—"

"Are you okay, Eric?" She almost sounded like Claire, his ex, her concern laced with criticism.

"I had a drink. Hard day today, you know."

"Maybe you should call back another time and we can talk about it. I was just going out, anyway. What about tomorrow?"

"Okay, I'll call you."

Eric replaced the phone and nodded to the man approaching the counter.

"A beer? Coming right up, shir."

CHAPTER TEN

Leaning into the full-length mirror, Sarah layered on a coat of bright red lipstick. Her lips were not too bad, the bottom one almost pouty.

"Blessed from birth," Penny had pronounced while making Sarah up for an exhibition. "The celebs would pay a fortune for them."

After dabbing on face powder (*geisha white,* Penny called it) and some blush, Sarah swished mascara on her lashes. Her skimpy eyebrows she left natural, hating penciled brows like her mother's, and pulled a few strands of hair over the eyebrows. The smile on her lips ended with a shake of the head. The image reflected back to her was undoubtedly the tallest, palest woman on the island, swan neck and all. To make matters worse, the lavender dress looked like a dowdy country cousin to her wild urban hair, which had frizzed into a red dandelion. By tomorrow she'd be the laughing-stock of the village.

The Friday-night expedition had been announced at dinner by Roper the evening before. They were to go to the Largo Bay Bar for a drink before sunset.

"They have an excellent cook," he'd added, "so maybe we'll stay for a bite."

After moussing her hair one last time, Sarah ascended the stairs to the living room, and she and Ford waited for the others on the deck. To Ford's delight, a hummingbird was poking its beak into the hibiscus flowers in a large pot. Her fellow guest, she'd discovered, was a member of the Audubon Society, a wildlife organization in the States.

"I'm usually the only black guy on the trips," he'd said once with a sad smile. "It takes the other birders a while to get used to it."

Over the five days since he'd arrived, she had become friends with the quiet trumpeter. They'd walked on two afternoons along the main road, she under her floppy hat and he in a Panama hat he'd bought in Ecuador. While he scouted the trees for birds, pointing out a woodpecker to her once, they talked about her life in London—tame compared to his in New York—and described Harlem and Camden to each other. On a few occasions, he'd referred to Jewel by automatically saying "we," but he never brought up the miscarriage or the breakup, which was fine with Sarah.

Roper joined them on the deck, followed in a few minutes by Sonja in a long cotton dress, her hair held back by a scarf with an African print. Carthena came out of the kitchen as they were preparing to leave.

"Miss, since you going out, can I leave early tonight?"

"No problem," Sonja said. "Enjoy yourself." The young woman wished them good night and returned to the kitchen.

When they arrived at the bar, there were already a few people scattered around.

"Shad!" Roper called to the bartender as soon as they seated themselves at a table.

"Coming right up!" the petite man called from behind

the bar, the same man who had shooed away the teenagers. Within a few minutes, he rushed to the table and Roper introduced him to the visitors as "Shadrack, the power behind the throne of the Largo Bay Bar."

"I know this lady already," he said, tipping his chin at Sarah. "She was walking on the beach." She smiled to thank him again and he answered with a broad grin, complete with the gap between his teeth, and the thought crossed her mind that, had she been a portrait painter, she would have asked him to be her model.

"Who you painting now?" Shad asked Roper.

"A young girl from Port Antonio," the artist reported. "How Miss Beth doing?" The easy, affectionate way the men talked about their personal lives showed Roper as very much a part of Largo—a surprise to Sarah, who'd assumed he was an outsider.

"Boss man," an emaciated man said as he shook Roper's hand. "Miss Olive want you to paint her before she die. She say if I see you I was to tell you. She say she want a painting more than a photograph, because a photograph going to fade, but a painting last long after you dead."

"Tri," Roper said with a big smile, "tell Miss Olive I stop by her house next week." The artist switched from Standard English to Jamaican dialect without batting an eye, something that made Sarah now appreciate why Sonja (whom she'd been pitying) might want to be with him.

Ford inquired about the island a few hundred yards out, its ruins bathed in the orange-gold light of sunset.

"That's where the old Largo Bay Inn was," Sonja answered. "A woman was living out there by herself last summer. It caused quite a commotion."

"Why was she there?" Sarah asked.

"She wanted to be alone, I guess. I never met her, but—but I always admired her. It takes a lot of guts for a woman to do that in Jamaica."

A tall, middle-aged man with a shock of platinum hair approached the table and Roper introduced him as Eric, the owner of both the old hotel and the bar. For a bar owner, Sarah thought, he seemed odd, even shy, perhaps an introvert like herself. Blushing, pulling back his hair, the American asked if they were staying for dinner and Roper said yes. Shad took their order and the four were left to wait, commenting on the streaks of color filling the sky. The bar's lights were turned on, including a string of blinking white bulbs under the bar's counter, and the crowd grew by a few more tables.

Ford turned to Sarah. "Not exactly a London pub, is it?"

She liked that he knew a lot about England from his frequent trips, and she'd already promised to attend his next performance in London. Penny would encourage her to sleep with him, no doubt, but it was enough for Sarah that Ford was her friend, an admired musician and her first black friend, and she was looking forward to introducing him to Penny as exactly that.

Dinner came with Roper sucking on goat bones, Ford and Sonja on chicken bones, and Sarah using a knife and fork to separate the bones from her snapper. When the dishes had been cleared away, Eric approached again.

"Mind if I join you?" he asked with a hangdog expression, like he needed the company.

"Have a seat," Sonja said. The bar owner sat down heavily between Sarah and Ford.

"How is the new hotel coming?" Roper said. "Lambert told me the investor guy was down."

"He just came in," Eric replied. "I'll introduce you." He waved Shad over and said something to him.

Shortly after, four people approached the table with drinks in their hands. In the lead was a couple: a man Eric introduced as the investor, Danny Caines, and a plump woman named Janet wearing a bright floral dress. Two men, who looked to be in their forties, trailed behind them. They were friends he'd made in Ocho Rios, Caines said, and they were visiting Largo for the evening. One of them, Alphonsus, a man with an imposing belly, wore a large gold necklace with a cross, and the other, Emile, was a slim, intense man in a busy gray shirt. The two men stood a step behind the couple and soon moved back to the bar.

By far the most imposing member of the group, Danny Caines carried himself like a man who was proud of who he was. He wasn't handsome, but he had strong features, and his bald head made Sarah think of gangster films with villains who were really good guys. And there was something about his complexion that stayed with her, a deep brown with a hint of auburn, like old blood.

The woman with him, Janet, smiled broadly at everyone and sat down, keeping her knees tightly together. Caines shook hands with everyone at the table and, for a long time after, Sarah could feel the warmth of his large hand wrapped around hers, see the eyes, soft gray like a dove's breast, eyes that beamed straight into hers before they blinked. She'd never known that a black man could have gray eyes and, embarrassed, she looked away even before he moved on to shake Ford's hand.

Two additional chairs were added to the table, and no sooner had the couple taken their seats than Roper started drilling Danny about the hotel and, after fielding the questions about his intentions and the progress thus far, Danny asked a few of his own. He wanted to know how long Roper had lived in Largo, why he'd chosen the village to live in, and what the prospects were for future development in the area.

While they talked, Sarah observed how the investor controlled the conversation, had controlled it from the beginning. He didn't do it by talking louder or faster or more than anyone else. He did it with the power of his personality, which pulsed across the table, encircled them, held them captive. Without even seeking the spotlight, he owned it.

It wasn't long before Danny Caines inquired about everyone else at the table. He was pleased to hear that Ford was a musician in New York and wanted to know where he could go to hear him play. They spent a few minutes talking about the trumpet and about Danny's lack of musical talent.

"I play business instruments, man," he admitted with a rich laugh, "not musical ones, but I love to hear people who can play." When it came to Sarah, he asked only where she was from.

"England—London, actually," she said, adding quickly, "I'm an artist."

Danny looked down at his drink and back up at her. "I dabble a bit myself. We should talk." He turned to Roper, switching gears easily. "Tell me something, how often do you have hurricanes here?"

"About every five to eight years," Roper told him. "We're expecting one anytime soon, but then, it could be another ten years. You never know with hurricanes."

"Do you think the bay back there, Miss Mac's land, would be protected enough?" Caines asked.

Eric jumped in for the first time. "If we strap the roofs down, like the new building codes say, Lambert says we should be fine."

"What about tsunamis? How high do the waves rise in a storm?" Caines continued his research, making the locals squirm. Then he suddenly changed the subject to the last election, and Roper started in on the politicians.

For the rest of the evening, Sarah was more conscious of Danny Caines than of anyone else at the table. She wanted to ask him about his interest in art, which was ridiculous, since he only dabbled in it, but she spent the time listening, wondering if Caines and Janet were sleeping together, wishing she'd had something brighter to wear. Every now and again she held a sidebar conversation with Ford and Sonja, once with Eric, but Caines ignored the parallel chatter and never addressed her again.

When Roper insisted on paying for the evening's expenses, Ford leaned over to Sarah and whispered, "I guess that means I'll be paying next time."

"Better start saving," she muttered, "because I can't, penniless as I am." They laughed quietly, her eyes following Danny as he rejoined his two friends at the bar. Close beside him was Janet, who had thus far smiled wordlessly.

The bill paid, Sarah's party started back to their car, walking in front of a table at the rear of the restaurant where Carthena sat drinking a beer. She was wearing a pink striped dress that matched the beads in her hair. Her companions were two older women, perhaps in their forties. One, a slim woman with bulging eyes and a straight nose, fingered her cigarette as they passed, her hair piled high in a fancy braided hairdo. The other woman was dressed in a glamorous purple one-shoulder blouse, but she'd had too much to drink already, her lips set in a crooked smile and her eyelids having trouble staying open.

Carthena smiled at Roper and Sonja, smiled wider for Ford. When it came to Sarah, the last in the line, the housekeeper looked away almost guiltily, as if she'd just been talking about her. Settling into the car and buckling up, Sarah thought about the woman's averted eyes. Carthena was probably moody, she decided, or she had expected to be tipped, and she reminded herself to ask Sonja about the protocol for handling helpers.

The thought lasted only a few seconds. By the time Roper swung the car onto the main road, it had been erased by the memory of dove-gray eyes, eyes that had stared at her and blinked.

CHAPTER ELEVEN

W atch your toes!" Shad called while the young man
handed Beth from the riverbank into the seat of his
bamboo raft.

He watched her sit down carefully, avoiding the spaces
between the logs and adjusting the straps of the bathing
suit borrowed from Joella. Under the seat she placed a
tightly folded plastic bag (*we don't want it to get wet,* she'd
told him) with their clothes and money.

Still on the riverbank, Shad handed a covered basket to
the raftsman. "Put the food somewhere safe," he instructed,
and the man passed the basket to Beth.

"You okay?" Shad yelled at her, but his words were
drowned out by the roar of the river filling the valley. Only
thirty feet across in its upper reaches, the Rio Grande galloped down the mountain under overhanging trees, lashing
at the rocks and coarse gray sand lining the banks.

"Your turn," the raftsman said, and held out his hand to
Shad, who insisted on jumping onto the raft without help.
The long, narrow craft lurched and the youth—Carlton was
his name, he'd said—sucked his teeth.

"You ever see my *raas claat* trial?" the teenager exclaimed
as he pushed his pole deep to balance the raft.

A few yards away, Danny and Janet waited on another raft—the American's red trunks filling most of the narrow seat. Janet's hips, threatening to erupt out of a gold bikini, were crammed into the space that was left. At the front of their raft, the raftsman held his long bamboo pole in the water, poised for takeoff.

"Let's go!" called Carlton, and both boys pushed off with their poles, maneuvering into the center of the river, heading for the ocean.

"I never thought I would ever ride a raft on the Rio Grande," Beth shouted into Shad's ear.

"I hear you," Shad shouted. He arched his back, tried to get comfortable on the bamboo seat, tried to unkink his lower spine, a daily ritual that came with a sagging mattress.

The invitation from Danny the Saturday evening before had come as a surprise and even caused Shad some confusion. Rafting on the Rio Grande was reserved for people with US dollars to burn, not people like him. But he'd loved the idea and looked forward to telling Beth that night when he got home. It was a good way to end their weekend, which had started badly with Beth's announcement that she was going into Port Antonio on Monday to look for work.

"Like how my sister still living there," she'd said while he was eating breakfast, "she can help me inquire around." She'd sat down opposite, putting the baby on her lap and a bowl of mashed banana in front of him. Shad had kept buttering his johnnycake, the fried roll he loved.

Beth put a spoonful of mashed banana into Joshua's mouth. "Valerie tell me she hear of something with a lady in a big house, cleaning and washing. She tell the woman her sister looking for a job."

Plastering guava jelly on the johnnycake, Shad pictured Rickia seated at the bar counter doing homework while he poured a drink for a customer, Joshua on his hip. "Sound like more than *inquiring around* to me," he said. "You talking about interviewing for a job. You talking about leaving me in charge of Rickia and Joshua while you working."

"I tell you I make the arrangements already," she insisted. "You don't have nothing to do."

Gulping the bread down, Shad held up a warning finger. "You and me know that when one thing go wrong, when Rickia have no school because of a teacher meeting, that is *me* have to do the mothering. You can't take care of them all the way in Port Antonio when something happen to Miss Livingston. Who going to look after them, not me?"

"You mean to say, Shadrack Myers, that five thousand dollars a week more not going to help us?" Beth had countered, waving a spoon with mashed banana in front of Joshua's open mouth.

"You realize that five thousand Jamaican dollars sound like a lot, but that is not even sixty US dollars? If you not careful, you going to spend the whole thing on taxis from Largo to Port Antonio."

The argument had gone round and round, circling Beth's now-firm decision. When no agreement was reached, his partner had switched to another reason why she had to work miles away.

"And I going to find out how much it cost to put Ashanti in the autism school. If I working, we might can afford to send her. She not learning nothing sitting down here. The teacher don't spend no time with her."

Shad had shaken his head and left for his morning shift

feeling unsettled. At lunchtime, he decided not to go to Saturday market, where Beth was selling vegetables from their garden. Instead, he trotted next door to eat with Miss Mac. Feared as a schoolteacher (her reputation enhanced by the tight gray bun and steel-rimmed glasses), the elder had softened in retirement and become Shad's mentor, the person he sought out when something was troubling him.

"Beth just hard of hearing," he complained over his bowl of red pea soup. "She won't listen to no reason."

"You sure you're listening to *her*?" Miss Mac said, clasping her hands in front of the twin mounds on the table. Even in school days, the woman had rested her breasts on the desk whenever she sat down, much to the children's delight.

"She do all the talking," Shad protested. "I doing the listening."

"Did you ask her exactly why she want to work in Port Antonio, why she not looking for work here?"

"She have all kind of reason. We going to have more money coming in, she can drive on the bus with Joella, she can pay for wedding, she can put Ashanti in school—every kind of reason."

Miss Mac put her head on her fist, the moles on her face standing out more than he remembered. "Maybe she just want some freedom."

"Beth have plenty freedom, man. She don't have no work to go to."

"What you mean? She working all the time, taking care of you and the children, growing vegetables, selling them in the market, sewing clothes, cooking, cleaning. She don't have no time for herself. A woman need a little freedom sometimes."

Shad had frowned. "Next thing—"

"Didn't you say she want to get married in a church? If she want to marry you, she not looking to run off. If you keep putting her off, though, and don't marry her like she want, she going to be miserable, and is you going to pay."

The Saturday-afternoon lunch had ended with Shad admitting that Miss Mac had a point, although it still puzzled him that a woman would want her freedom and a wedding at the same time. And since it was obvious that Beth wasn't going to back down, he decided that simply allowing her to do what she was going to do anyway was probably the only solution, since he'd already lost the battle.

When he got home that night, Beth was in bed with her face turned to the wall and her head full of rollers for church. She was awake, he could tell, no snores coming from her.

"I know you vex because I didn't come to market today," he said, offering a truce to the rollers. "I had lunch with Miss Mac." She turned over and sighed, her eyes closed, and he knew she was listening, angry but listening. "But I have something nice to tell you."

She opened her eyes and squinted at him in the lamplight. "First, you must say you sorry for not coming to market. I have to mind all four children, and Rickia have a quarrel with Joella, and Joella go off and leave me with the three of them. You know I need you to come help me Saturday, 'cause I can't handle all of them and sell vegetables at the same time."

"Sorry."

"Promise me you not going to do it again."

"Promise."

"What you have to tell me?"

"Danny invite us to go rafting on the Rio Grande with

him and Janet." He knew what it was about but didn't say. The investor wanted to see them close up so he could decide if he wanted to be in partnership with a bartender.

"We can't afford no rafting—" Beth started.

"He going to pay."

The announcement had been met with slow, almost reluctant pleasure, if not the lovemaking he'd hoped for. Instead, she'd let him snuggle up to her while she planned her preparations, that she'd get up early to cook fried chicken, and that Joella would take the younger children to church and keep them after. Before they drifted off to sleep, he'd lifted his head and worked his lips between the rollers to kiss her on the ear.

"And you can go work in Port Antonio, even though I don't like it," he'd muttered, to which she only harrumphed.

The Rio Grande took a deep curve to the right and Carlton used his pole to push them off the bank. Around the corner, the river widened and calmed and Shad leaned back in his seat. The ride between the rapids had been frightening for Beth, who, holding tightly to the basket on her lap with one hand, had squeezed his hand bloodless with the other and given yelps whenever they bounced against a rock. To make matters worse, another raftsman toting a tourist couple had competed with Carlton to shoot some of the rapids, both bellowing war cries like Indians as they shot through.

"You want to stop?" the youth asked when they approached a wide stretch of sand.

Shad looked back at Danny's raft. "Ask the man behind us."

Danny agreed and they heard Janet call, "Yes, stop, driver, *stop*!"

The two rafts were beached and tied up together. After balancing his way off the raft, Shad took the lunch basket and helped Beth jump onto the gravelly sand.

"Thank Gawd!" Janet said when her raftsman helped her off. "I feeling sick. The thing just rocking and rolling. My belly feeling funny." Plopping down on the old blanket Beth had spread, she rubbed her abdomen, large enough to make Shad grateful for his partner's one-piece suit.

"Here, have little tea to settle your stomach," Beth coaxed Janet, feeling guilty, Shad knew, that she'd called her *a little opportunist* before they got into Danny's rental car.

Janet took a sip of ginger tea. "This taste good," she said. "I still feel kind of—I wonder if I—I hope I not—"

"Not what?" Danny said, and sat down cross-legged on the blanket. "You mean—oh, *no,* don't even go there!" He was laughing but shaking his head with such force that it left no doubt that making babies with Janet was not part of his plan.

After lunch and while the raftsmen ate the leftovers Beth had given them, the two couples waded knee-deep into the river. Another raft passed with waving passengers and they waved back. As soon as the raft passed, Danny waded out deeper, rolled over, and swam backward away from them. Janet stood watching him, her hands on her hips.

"I can't get my hair wet," she called to Danny.

"Well, don't come in," he shouted back.

Looking pretty in a pink shower cap, Beth waded in up to her waist. "I want to float," she told Shad. He obliged, holding her while she looked up into the overhanging tree, and he dug his toes into the sand against the current.

"This feel sweet," she murmured. "I could do it forever."

"You can't do it forever," Shad chided her. "You have to go to Port Antonio to find a work tomorrow, remember? My time to stay home now." He tickled her side and she, giggling and protesting, tried to keep her legs up. He'd just gotten her relaxed and floating again when Janet waded out beside them.

"Pshaw, man," she said, pouting. "Watch him, he just swim off and leave me."

"He soon come back," Shad said.

"What he doing over there?" Janet said, and sucked her teeth.

Shad scanned the gushing river, unable to spot Danny. After a minute, he saw the investor standing in the midst of a shady grove on the opposite bank. He was standing under a massive cedar tree, his hands flat against the bark and his eyes fixed on the branches above, almost like he was listening to the tree.

CHAPTER TWELVE

M istah Eric, the phone want you, suh!" Solomon called, his tone indicating that answering the phone wasn't part of subbing for Shad on his day off.

"Take the message and tell them I'll call back," Eric yelled. He was sweating like a pig, the round stain made by his paunch now connecting with the stain on his back. With only ten more conch shells to fit in place along the new path to the road, he didn't want to stop. The plan to create the path had waited long enough—months, in fact—while the salmon-colored conch shells turned paler and paler in a heap behind the building. On the other side of the bar, Carmichael, his sometime gardener, was bent low, swiping at the grass on the cliff with a machete.

Solomon slouched over to Eric with the phone. "Is a lady."

"Okay, give it to me." Eric sat down on the edge of the concrete floor. The bank manager again.

"Yes?" he said, pulling the bandanna off his forehead and wiping his face with it.

"Eric?"

"Simone?"

"I'm sorry I rushed you off the phone last week. When

you called I was going out and—you didn't sound like yourself."

"I've been meaning to call you back, but it's been kind of crazy."

"I understand." She paused long enough for him to realize this was a big step for her, calling him after his drunken call, trying to get back to normal. "I've been worried about you."

"About me?"

"You sounded—you told me you'd been drinking when you called last time. I've never seen you drink more than a glass of wine."

He could feel a blush creep across his cheeks. "I'm sorry—I shouldn't have called—you know, in that condition."

"It was kind of early in the day."

"I was—stressed out, I guess, about the whole hotel business."

"Is the investor still there?"

"Yes, but I'm not sure for how long. Everything has gone sort of weird. He and Horace—the lawyer—they're like oil and water, you know. Our first meeting didn't go well, and the second was even worse."

He told her about the problem with the utilities on the island. "And when we went back to see him yesterday to discuss the partnership arrangement—he's drawing up the papers—Horace suddenly says we shouldn't make Shad a partner, and he and Danny argued about it. It got pretty heated. I didn't want to get into it, because things were chaotic enough as it was."

"Why doesn't he want Shad to be a partner?"

"He says Shad doesn't have enough education and that having Shad in the mix could cause a lot of problems, misunderstandings, you know. Another thing he didn't like was the share split, with Shad having ten percent, Danny sixty, and me thirty. He said Danny would always have the power, and that I was on the ground here running things, and if I'm going to throw in the land, the island, and the bar, I need more shares. Danny fought him, I'm telling you, and I had to back him, because I don't want all the responsibility again. Heck, it's the man's money putting up this hotel, not mine. But Horace kept saying we need to change the share split and we need a local person who's educated—I don't know if he was talking about himself. Danny just got up and walked out of the meeting."

Simone sucked in her breath through her teeth. "Oh dear, doesn't sound good."

Fanning his face with the bandanna, Eric sighed. "Horace even said we need *a better class of person*. I couldn't believe my ears. You'd never think he was from Largo."

"What about Miss Mac?" Her voice softened with the name of the landlady who'd nursed her back to health after she left the island. "Horace is her son. She should be able to handle him, especially if she wants to sell her house and land. Plus, she knows Shad is a good guy."

Eric ran the toe of one lime-green Croc across the pebbles. "I don't know—I wouldn't want to bring her into it."

It was easier to talk to Simone about the hotel than about the things that really nagged at him. The ugly words *erectile dysfunction,* for example, had been mocking him recently from magazine ads, labeling him as over-the-hill. But his deeper, darker secret was that he was now the owner of a sleek, new laptop that was sitting in his apartment, barely touched. Simone wouldn't understand that a man two decades older than her—who'd left American civilization before the digital age had taken hold—might never have used a computer. She wouldn't understand how humiliating it was to have Shad's eleven-year-old daughter giving him lessons, starting with how to turn on the thing.

Standing over him, the child had clicked a couple keys and a blank page had opened up on the screen.

"How did you learn this stuff?" Eric had asked, looking at his dwarf teacher.

"We have two computers at school," Rickia had said, straightening her glasses. "See, you can type a letter now."

"Why would I need to write a letter," Eric had countered, "if I can just write it with paper and pen?"

"This way you don't go to the post office. You just send it in an email."

"But I don't have the Internet."

"You only need a phone, teacher says, and they will give you the Internet. You have a phone, right?"

Already behind on his telephone payments, Eric had promised her he would type letters to practice. She'd gone off to the kitchen and he'd heard her boasting to her father that she'd taught Mistah Eric how to use the computer.

"The good thing," Simone was saying in an unusually maternal voice, "is that if the hotel falls through, you still have your bar."

"Yes, but just barely."

"What do you mean?"

"I've been running the bar on my overdraft."

"It's got to work, then."

"From your lips to God's ears." After hanging up, Eric scraped the area beside the path clear, pulling up the weeds and flattening the spot with his trowel. He placed the next conch shell close to the pebbles.

Simone knew he'd been drunk last time, heard him slurring like an idiot, and she'd still called because she was worried about him. And he'd confided in her, told her about his financial problems. It might turn her off, his being broke, but she needed to know. If she had any sense, she wouldn't be in a relationship with him, anyway. She certainly didn't need him as a lover. Gorgeous, with those almond-shaped eyes and caramel skin, she was every man's dream.

For a minute he allowed himself to feel older and poorer and sorrier than ever, until he remembered that she'd been worried about him and called. It almost made up for Danny not inviting him to go rafting.

CHAPTER THIRTEEN

The time of day, the location of sun and shade, the amount of exposure to passersby, the placement of the kitchen stool away from ant nests had all become part of Sarah's decisions about where to paint. In the previous week, she'd sat deep in the shade of the coconut trees and out of the sun, and out of sight of anyone walking on the beach. With the easel set up so she was looking straight out at the ocean, she'd been sketching the waves as they rolled toward her.

On Valentine's Day, a Tuesday, she made a decision, a small one, that changed her life forever. It was prompted by the still-fresh memory of Penny calling her hollow. She'd had time in the two years since to mull the fact that she did in fact *feel* hollow inside, that she'd felt it as long as she could remember. The word had come back to her the day after meeting Danny Caines, the man she'd seen running on the beach, the man she'd feared, the successful businessman that everyone spoke so highly of, and she'd upbraided herself for being a spineless coward because of her negative assumptions.

It wasn't that her family was racist, but the parties given by their neighbors, a friendly Indian engineer and his wife who celebrated Diwali and every birthday, or news of a crime committed by a West Indian youth, had usually resulted in the wordless raising of her father's eyebrows and a tsk-tsk from her mother. And despite the multitude of races in London, despite her awareness that times had changed, Sarah had never thought of countering the parental message. Until meeting Sonja and Roper and Ford, that is. Her new friends had opened an unfamiliar world, and she, a captive audience, was finding herself outside her comfort zone. Yet something was telling her to push into this unknown area—if she was to release the dark, empty space inside herself.

In light of that, she'd decided to throw caution to the winds and get to know Danny Caines as she had Ford. She felt differently about Danny, nothing romantic, of course, since he had a girlfriend already. If anything, she was curious. She wanted to see what color his eyes were in daylight, what he painted and if it was any good. Was he a collector, she wondered, a man who'd appreciate a miniature series of eggs in dirt?

Being open to friendships, especially male friendships, was unusual for Sarah. She routinely shut out male customers in the restaurant even before they gave her a compliment. She didn't know when it started, but she'd always experienced some level of anxiety around men. Roper made her tense, even raised her hackles. Ford, on the other hand, left her with only slight unease, their talk about birds and music making friendship possible. When it came to Danny Caines, she felt both cautious and intrigued, but, satisfied now that he offered no threat, she was ready for the challenge.

Even before she got out of bed that morning, another Valentine's Day with no card or flowers, she'd known she was going to place her easel a little closer to the water's edge, in full view of passersby. Her decision had come after seeing Danny jogging on the beach the morning before. She'd been too deep in the shadows for him to see her and she'd watched his muscular arms and legs pumping like a machine—and been a little disappointed that he hadn't seen her.

The morning sun was streaking long shadows from the eastern hills when Sarah set up her easel, the coconut leaves making their shushing sound above. While taping her paper to the board, she saw Danny flashing by on his way to the eastern end of the beach. She continued her preparations to paint, telling herself that if he wanted to stop, he would. On his return trip, he saw her, the sun catching the frame of his sunglasses. He waved but didn't smile. In response, she waved and smiled with her lips clamped shut.

That evening, while the discussion around the dinner table raged—Roper declaring that Barack Obama didn't communicate well and Ford and Sonja defending him—she asked herself why she was interested in Caines or his eyes or what he painted. During dessert she decided that it was the life force he exuded, a force that nothing could hold back. He gave one the feeling of unlimited growth and expansiveness. She was fascinated by people like that, people like Penny and Naomi with the power to motivate others. Only this time it happened to be a black man.

The next day, a Wednesday, she placed her easel in the same exposed position but faced it east, allowing someone running from the west to see that she was painting. She was still settling the easel into the sand when Danny ran by too fast for her to wave. She taped her paper to the easel board and sat down, opening her watercolors and jar of water, deciding to give a bigger smile when he passed. But on his return he stopped running and walked across the dried seaweed on the sand between them. He was still wearing sunglasses, with a T-shirt this time.

"You're the artist, the one from England." He stopped a few yards away and wiped his forehead with two fingers.

"We met on Friday night," she said, taking off her hat.

"I'll never forget that hair." He had a wavy smile on his lips. "Sorry, I have a terrible memory for names."

"Sarah."

"And I'm Danny." He glanced behind him at the ocean. "Great place to paint, eh?"

"I hope I can do it justice."

"I was wondering—would you mind—can I join you tomorrow—painting, I mean? Ever since I saw you out here, I've been thinking about it."

"Yes, of course."

"Tomorrow then." He dipped his sweaty scalp and ran on.

On Thursday, Sarah slathered more sunblock on her now-pink legs and put on shorts, the green ones without holes, because her legs weren't too bad when she was sitting down. She placed an extra jar of water, a few more paint-brushes, and some snacks in her backpack.

"You leaving early these days," Carthena commented after she'd supplied her with bottled water.

"It's cooler in the morning," Sarah replied.

On the beach she prepared her spot, closer to the trees

where there was more shade and privacy. Just when she was settled and already glancing down the beach, there was a tap on her shoulder. She jumped and looked around. The big man was standing behind her.

"I didn't mean to frighten you," Danny said. He was carrying a small case and a folding chair.

"You came from the road?"

"I drove, too much stuff to carry." There was an island lilt to the way he said it.

After placing the chair a few feet away from her, he sat down and took off his sunglasses. He opened a bag with his paints and paper, everything still in their original packages, all brand-new.

"You have everything, do you?" she said.

"I think I forgot water."

"Don't worry, I've got some."

They started painting, not talking much, leaving space for the noise of the waves and the calling of gulls. She became aware of his breathing, going from heavy to light to silent, then of his smell: the crispness of soap and a man's deodorant. Sometimes he moved his feet around in their leather sandals, and beneath his shorts the muscles on his thighs shifted. Once she glanced at the side of his face while she rinsed out her brush, saw his lips working as he concentrated. Every now and again she would look over at the pad on his lap, watching his painting of the sand and the sea progressing from a pencil sketch to a swirling watercolor in blues and yellows, filling the letter-size page. Although his work was raw and untrained, he had some talent with color.

"When do you find time to paint?" she asked, dabbing lemon yellow on her clouds.

"This is the first time I've painted in—in at least five years."

"You're quite good."

"It help me to relax," he said, and she pictured him in a Manhattan apartment painting the skyline. He left after a couple hours, after they'd taken a break eating peanuts, throwing the shells on the ground.

The next day dawned cloudy but not rainy, and she wondered if he was a fair-weather painter, but he came back like he'd said and they continued painting, changing their positions to face west and the island in the distance. He asked a few questions about her use of colors, but most of the time they talked as if they were in art class at neighboring easels, sticking to banal topics.

Throughout a quiet Saturday and a Sunday drive to Ocho Rios with her housemates, Sarah waited, the hours creeping by, recalling how he'd wiped his scalp with a handkerchief, how his sentences went up at the end, how he chuckled when something he said tickled him. Her chest tightened when she thought of him, and she tried not to think of him.

On Monday morning, she asked him why he'd started painting. "I was married to this woman," he said. "Lots of drama, every evening more drama. You know the kind, eh?" His gray eyes with their thin spokes of black laughed with her. "I had to find a reason to stay out of the house and I always loved to draw and paint, from when I was a child, so I decided that instead of killing her I'd go to an art class after work, and—that's it—that's how I started. The marriage didn't last long, but it got me painting. I can thank her for that."

He had left St. Croix (explaining where it was, because

she'd never heard of it), when he was fourteen. His mother had been offered a job as a maid by a man who'd been visiting the island on vacation, a widower with three small children. She'd moved to San Francisco to take the live-in job.

"I stayed with my grandparents for a year after she left, until she sent for me and I flew over—my first airplane trip. I thought San Francisco would be wonderful, you know, Golden Gate Bridge, cable cars and everything. But I arrived in July, and the place was so damn—so freezing cold that I had to wear a winter coat!" He laughed at the memory. "We lived in the man's house in the Presidio. You ever hear of it? It's an old military base near the Golden Gate Bridge, and the fog just comes sweeping up the hill off the water. But you couldn't swim or nothing, it was so cold." He looked over the long stretch of beach he was painting. "I really missed the islands, man."

During a water break, he talked of his mother and how she'd studied to be a hairstylist in San Francisco, going to classes on Saturdays. She was an ambitious woman, he said, and he admired her for that. Two years after he arrived in California, she'd graduated as a hairdresser and announced they were moving to New York.

"I was glad, because the kids in the school in Frisco were kind of snobbish. They didn't mean to be, but there was no other black kids in the place, you know, and they treated me like I was a mascot. They kept saying my accent was cute. The girls wouldn't go out with me or nothing, but they liked how I spoke."

He didn't speak perfect English, his language and accent a mixture of St. Croix and America, but they were full of life and harmonized with the landscape. He seemed to make the setting more complete and she was glad he'd come back.

On Tuesday he asked her about her family, and she told him about growing up as an only child in Maidstone, having a father, now deceased, who was a physician and a mother who was still alive and still in Kent. She never mentioned that she'd loved her father, even if he'd lectured her, but she didn't know how she felt about her mother. She kept short her descriptions of their comfortable, sedate family life in three separate bedrooms, not wanting to sound like she'd had advantages that he hadn't.

When she finished, Danny stood up and pulled off his sandals. "You ever swim in the Caribbean Sea?"

"Not yet."

"But if you're going to paint it, you must know how it feels." He peeled off his T-shirt. "I'm sweating like crazy, aren't you . . . ? Let's go for a swim."

"I don't have a suit."

"We swim in—whatever." He laughed and took off his shorts. He ran toward the water in his briefs, a boy again. Biting her bottom lip, she slid off her shorts, pulling down her T-shirt to cover her panties, and hurried across the hot sand. Danny had already plunged in and was underwater by the time she stood with the water crashing around her hips. He came to the surface farther out.

"You have to pass the waves," he called, wiping his eyes. "It's calmer out here."

"I don't swim very well."

He swam and then waded up to her. She kept her eyes on his to avoid looking at his underwear.

"I walk you out," he said. Holding her hand, he pulled her one step at a time past the breakers—while she shut her eyes and turned her head against the slapping waves—into calmer water where her toes barely touched the sandy bottom.

"Don't leave me," she said, holding on tight to his shoulder.

"I'm not leaving you." They bobbed around, her feet lifting off the bottom sometimes. He told her to duck her head under the water and she quickly followed his instructions.

"Keep paddling," he said, and she paddled with one hand, knowing she looked like a wet, red rat.

"I told you you'd love it." He was totally at home in the water, showing her how to ride the waves, his eyelashes covered with droplets, telling her about swimming as a boy. Every few minutes, he'd dip his head under a wave, and when he pulled up the water would stream off his scalp like it was rolling off a rock.

Seawater was about healing, he told her, that's what his grandfather always said. And she believed him, because he looked healed and whole, happier than ever. She closed her eyes and turned her face up to the sun, felt its heat penetrating her pores, felt her heart swelling in the midst of its fear—even while she held on to his shoulder and made sure she never got completely out of her depth.

CHAPTER FOURTEEN

S unlight falling through the mango tree speckled the children's arms as they gathered around the kitten. Skinny legs folded under her, Ashanti sat on the floor to one side, in her own world as usual.

"Can I hold him, Dadda?" Rickia said, and picked up the black-and-white ball of fluff before Shad could answer.

"Where you get him?" Joella inquired. She had Joshua in one arm, fanning the other hand to let her nail polish dry.

"I found him under the bar counter this morning," her father answered. "He drank a whole bowl of milk."

Baby Joshua held his hand out to the kitten and Rickia pulled the wide-eyed animal away. "Can we keep him, please, please?" she begged.

"If your mother says yes," her father said. "No spoiling him, though, no sleeping in the bed."

Joella frowned. "Is he going to wee-wee in the house?"

Shad stroked Ashanti's hair and the child pushed his hand away. "I don't think so. Where your mother?"

"She gone to Port Antonio," Rickia announced.

"I in charge," Joella said, patting the baby's bottom like any big woman.

"Everybody do homework?"

"No homework today," said his eldest. "Teacher meeting this afternoon."

"I reading," said Rickia, and held up a book.

"You don't buy no book, right?" Shad asked. "We can't afford to—"

"Mama borrow it from the library for me."

"Good," Shad said. "I going to take my nap. Keep it down."

"A sandwich on the table for you," Joella announced behind him, sounding so much like Beth he could have confused them.

After Shad woke from his nap, he walked out to the kitchen, where Beth was washing rice in a strainer in the sink. She was still wearing her good green dress with the belt, and in her ears were small earrings he hadn't seen before. Their eyes met for a second and she lowered hers and turned off the tap.

"I get a job," she said, sighing as if she was sorry, although she wasn't. When he didn't answer—not trusting his feelings or the words to express them—she continued. "Is not the first job I was telling you about, is another job."

"Doing what?"

"Cleaning, Port Antonio library." She half filled a pot with water and put it on the fire.

Shad leaned his hip against the counter and crossed his arms. "You going to clean toilets for a hundred people, people with all kind of sickness? I hope they paying you good."

"The hours suit me, from eight to four, better than the housework with the woman. I was going to the school for autistics yesterday, and I see the library next door. I went in and ask about work, and they tell me to come back today."

She looked out the window. "I always like books. The manager take me on. You want little soup before you go?"

"No, I had a sandwich already and I going straight back to work. The boss say he want to talk to me about something."

"What kind of something?"

"He don't say. Must be about the hotel." He kissed her on the cheek. "I tell you tonight."

"Mistah Shad," she called behind him, "I see you bring a puss in the house, another mouth to feed."

He laughed over his shoulder. "We can afford it now, man, like how you have a big job."

When Shad arrived at the bar, Eric rose from his table. "We're going over to Miss Mac's for a minute. I left Maisie in charge."

They walked the hundred yards around the fence to Miss Mac's front door. The boardinghouse owner was standing on her verandah with Danny Caines. Closing the wire gate behind him, Shad felt his throat go dry. Jumbled thoughts came to mind, none pleasant: it had to be either bad news or something he wouldn't understand.

"Miss Mac," Shad and Eric said at the same time as they walked up the verandah steps.

"Danny," Shad greeted Caines, and the two exchanged fist bumps. The men followed the old woman into her front room, where glasses and a tall jug of juice were waiting on a tray.

"I feel like I coming to a wake," Shad said, and everyone laughed, maybe a little too much.

When they were all seated and drinks handed around, there was an awkward silence until Danny spoke up. "You know that Eric and I talked about having you as a partner. You not only work hard, but you helped to build the first hotel and the bar. Eric says he couldn't have done it without you, and I believe him." The investor put down his glass and leaned back in the heavy mahogany chair.

"Miss Mac says you was a good student in the old days," he continued, and the bartender bit down on his lips. "And I also hear you spent some—some time in prison—had a little run-in with the law." Shad looked from Eric to Miss Mac, neither looking at him, their eyes fixed on Danny. "But since then you prove that you're a good, solid man, churchgoing and everything. You work hard and you take care of your wife and family. I seen that with my own eyes."

He threw a hand toward Shad. "What I'm saying, man, because I don't want you to worry, is that we all know you deserve a break. You paid your dues."

It was coming, Shad thought, the news was about to come. He took a sip of June plum juice, but its acid stung his throat and he coughed, almost choked. Danny stopped talking while Shad wiped his mouth with a napkin.

There was no reason why he should hope to be a partner in a hotel. He couldn't read well, couldn't write well. He liked words, big words, and tried to use them sometimes so his children would learn them. But it didn't matter that he traced the shorter newspaper articles with his finger and read them out loud to Beth, or that she helped him sometimes with words he couldn't recognize. He wouldn't be able to keep up with these men who had gone to high school and college. No way he could understand all the hotel papers. Even the young employees would be more educated than him. Nobody would respect him if he had to hire them or fire them. It didn't make sense that a little man like him should be a partner with a rich man like Danny or a white man like Eric.

"Shad," Miss Mac followed up. "It's going to be different with the new hotel. When you a partner, you have different things, management things, you have to do. You must stay informed about all the comings and goings of money and government documents and everything."

"I thought Beth could . . ." Shad started but stopped, thinking of how little time she would have to help him now.

"You're going to need more than that, my friend," Eric said, shaking his head.

"Well—well, I just want you to know," Shad said, "that I not going to hold up anything to do with the hotel." He rubbed his scalp with one hand and closed his eyes. "I don't have to be a partner. The hotel more important than me. I just want a job—"

Miss Mac's forehead was folded into a deep crease when he opened his eyes. "Wait, Shad, they not forcing you out. They just saying that if you want to be a partner, you have work to do, some catching up. Like how you left school at nine to start fishing, you miss out on a lot of learning."

"What kind of learning?"

"I think," the boss said, "we should be straight with you. Danny and I are foreigners here, and we need a local partner. We want you to be that person. But there has been—there are people who think you might not be in a—a position to be a partner. I think you can do it, because I know you, and I've stood up for you, and Danny here has stood up for you. We think you can handle it. But the truth is that there's going to be a lot you might not understand about running a business."

"I can learn."

Eric leaned back and crossed his feet in the old flip-flops. "That's the point. You *can* learn. I remember when we were building the hotel, Old Man Job taught us how to build with block and steel, and you learned faster than me. And when that finished, you got yourself to Port Antonio and learned bartending from your cousin in two weeks flat. I remember that. But this is more complicated."

"You just tell me what to sign, boss, and I will sign."

Miss Mac rested her elbows on her wide-spread knees. "Is not for Mr. Keller to tell you what to sign. You have to make up your own mind about everything. If you're willing to take up the reading and writing lessons again, I will teach you, because you going to have to read legal contracts and sign your name to things you understand. I can read you the documents, we can discuss them, and then you can decide what you going to do." She looked at him above the metal rims of her glasses. "Are you willing to do that work, though? Do you really want to be a partner? *That* is the question."

Shad stared at Miss Mac, the elder who'd held him, a grown man, like a baby when his grandmother died. He was more than aware, the bile starting to crawl in his stomach, that she was forcing him to make a choice that would change everything for him and his family. He could either remain a bartender for the rest of his life or venture into the land of the *bushas*. The downside, he knew, was that— ignorant, untraveled, burdened with a criminal record—he could also make a fool of himself and fall flat on his face.

He held her gaze and swallowed hard. "Miss Mac, how I going to learn if you do all the reading?"

"You will learn as you go along, I will teach you. And what I don't understand, we ask Mr. Eric to explain."

Looking first at the men to see if they had any doubt, Shad turned to his old teacher. "If you have the patience, Miss Mac, so do I."

"It going to be hard work, you know," the woman said, shaking her head.

"I never afraid of hard work yet."

"When you can start? They have a document right now for you to sign."

"Tomorrow?" Danny said.

"I just have to tell Beth I not coming home for lunch."

"You can have lunch here every day, you know," Miss Mac said.

"No problem." Soon there'd be no lunch at home for him, anyway.

After shooing Maisie home from the bar later, Shad climbed up on the counter and replaced the burned-out lightbulb overhead, still thinking about the meeting. The three other participants had clearly been discussing the difficulties of having him as a partner. Miss Mac, who'd always been disappointed that he'd dropped out of school, had probably been the one to suggest that she teach him to read big words so he could understand all the legal business, and the men had gone along with it. If he wanted to, he could have made something of it, this talking about him behind his back—but he wouldn't, because they'd made decisions for his good, ones that gave him a chance to be a partner in the hotel.

Later that night he slid into bed, cuddling into Beth's back, and she rolled over sleepily in his arms. "Something bothering you, I know."

He described the meeting in its entirety, including the part about someone suggesting to Eric and Danny that he shouldn't be a partner.

"Why they would do that?" she asked.

"They think I don't have enough education. I not the right class, must be." His heart started racing as he said it, his chest burning. "The person think I not good enough to own a hotel."

"Who you think the person is?"

"Only two people possible. One is Lambert Delgado, but it not him. He don't have it in him to be a small man."

"The other one?"

Shad rolled onto his back and folded his arms under his head. "Mistah big-shot lawyer, Horace Mac. It have to be him. He always know everything, always have to have the last word and like how he was the teacher's child, he used to get away with murder in school. Then, after he go to university in Kingston and become a lawyer, he think he somebody. I went with the boss to see him once, about the woman living on the island, remember, and he act like he don't even know me, and I pretend like I don't know him neither."

Beth snorted and, although he couldn't see her expression in the dark, he knew her upper right lip was curling. "Horace Mac?" she said.

"He too *bad-mind*."

"You don't remember he went to Titchfield High with me?" she said. "I never tell you, but he used to want to talk to

me. I couldn't stand him. He was so skinny and stupid looking. Even though he was bright, I just . . ." She shuddered.

Before he went to sleep, Shad had a word with God. First,
a short thank-you for good friends like the boss and Danny
and Miss Mac, people who would look out for him the way
they had. Then a request that he be restrained from killing
Horace–*bumba claat*–MacKenzie the next time he saw him,
because he didn't want to leave his children fatherless.

CHAPTER FIFTEEN

F ore!" Lambert shouted. A tourist couple in matching shorts looked up just as the golf ball landed in a patch of weeds beside them.

"Damn!" Lambert spat, and stalked a few paces to one side.

Next up, Danny placed his ball on the tee and spread his legs, rocking until he was comfortable. After shielding his eyes to peer at the distant flag, the man wrapped his fingers around the handle of his rented club. He rocked again from one leg to the other, settled, and drew the club back—his left arm straight as a board. When he hit the ball, it soared high and landed neatly in the middle of the fairway.

"*Damn!*" Lambert murmured, glancing at Eric.

The three men walked back to the golf cart and Eric climbed in behind the wheel, relieved he didn't have to swing a club. When Lambert had invited him to join them at the course where he was a member, the bar owner had been tempted to say no. Instead, he'd volunteered to drive them from one hole to the other, because his back was acting up, he said. He didn't want to miss the outing, but he hated golf. The few times he'd played in New Rochelle with

Arnie, his office mate at the paper company, he'd embarrassed himself so badly he'd avoided the game thereafter. His rationalization was that only people with money had the stamina to learn golf. The rest, with the exception of Arnie, got depressed.

At the next hole, the tenth, Lambert declared that it was too hot today and that they'd started out too late. By the fourteenth hole, Danny had become the clear leader, having parred three holes and even birdied one. While the two men chatted, analyzing their strokes, Eric stood to the side trying to remember what a par and a birdie were, eventually having his memory jogged by the men's talk. At the sixteenth hole and limp with sweat, Eric stayed in the cart and wished his companions every par and birdie to get them through quicker, reminding them that there were other golfers behind.

In the clubhouse bar at last, Lambert ordered a round of Red Stripes before they made their way to the patio overlooking the course.

"The third hole," Danny started as soon as they'd sat down, "the way you had to drive from the tee across that huge pond—that was crazy!"

Lambert gave his big guffaw. "That's the first thing every visitor mentions." He turned to Eric. "You're kind of flushed there, boy. You okay?"

"The damn heat," his friend answered, pulling sticky hair away from his neck. "I don't know how you guys do it."

"It's the melanin." Danny laughed and left for the restroom.

"How's the project going?" Lambert asked as soon as the man had disappeared.

"Shad is taken care of," Eric said, and outlined the meeting two days before. "He's going back to school with Miss Mac."

"I'm glad to hear it," his friend agreed. "He's a good boots-on-the-ground man."

"Like I'm not?"

"You know what I mean. He's loyal, and you need somebody who can negotiate with the Parish Council guys in patois."

"And make sure that you keep construction within cost, right?" Eric said, swatting his friend on the arm.

Lambert pulled the corners of his mouth back. "Would I cheat you? How long have you known me, man?"

"Just kidding," Eric said, only half kidding. "So what do you think?"

"About what?"

"About Danny."

"Plays a decent round of golf."

"As a business partner, man. He's kind of a perfectionist, don't you think? I don't want to be in business with somebody looking over my shoulder all the time. I thought he was going to be a silent partner, so Cameron had said, anyway, but he seems very hands-on, you know. He has an opinion about damn near everything."

"I think he's a good businessman."

"How so?"

"You can tell a lot by how a man plays golf. Didn't you notice how he wrote down every stroke he made? He kept notes on each hole, comparing the hole before with the hole he just played. He even wrote down my strokes."

"So he's going to be a pain in the ass."

124

"He's going to make sure you both make money, that's what I mean. I think he's a—" He broke off while the waiter served the frosty beers and Danny took his place at the table.

"Great game!" Danny said, and clinked his glass with the other two men. "I'd love to do it again sometime."

"Definitely," Lambert replied, holding his mustache away from his drink with two fingers while he took a sip. Below the clubhouse, the greens were in shadow and the sea beyond them navy blue. The disappearing sun was glinting off the ribbon of foam along the reef.

"How's Jennifer?" Eric asked Lambert.

"She's in Florida at her sister's. Her mother is going down fast. She's been in and out of hospital with this spinal cancer thing. It's not going to be long now, the doctors are saying."

"Jeez, Lam—"

"And I'm in the doghouse." The contractor grimaced. "Seems I forgot Valentine's Day, first time since we've been together."

"Valentine's?" Eric said.

"That's right, last week Tuesday," Danny weighed in. "Janet invited me to a friend's party in Port Maria. It was crazy, man. They'd blocked off a street and the whole thing was in the middle of the road." His fingers were dancing up and down on the wooden table. "There must have been a hundred people there, all kinds of people, and there was this deejay guy who kept yelling into the mike." He shook his head. "The music was loud enough to kill every dog in the neighborhood. I know the neighbors couldn't sleep."

"That's a Jamaican party, for sure," Eric murmured, his

head still filled with Valentine's, and that he'd forgotten it. Maybe Valentine's wasn't important to Simone and she wouldn't be expecting anything, anyway.

The first man to finish his beer was Danny. "What's the next step with the job, guys?"

"Permits," Lambert said. "Now that you've formed the corporation and set up a bank account, we can submit the applications for permits. Then you folks have to appear before the Parish Council committees. They're going to have a lot of questions."

"What committees?" Danny asked.

"The Planning Authority's committees, they have to approve the drawings—fire, health, and roads committees," Eric said. "Then the whole thing has to be approved by the Authority at the end."

"Before we do that, I want to meet with the architect," Danny said. To Eric he raised his eyebrows. "You've met with him, right?"

"I saw the drawings and they looked fine. Lambert said he was a good—"

"*She,*" Lambert chimed in. "I can set up a meeting with her right away. She called me yesterday and asked if there was anything we needed to change."

"Let's do it," Danny said. "I have a couple questions for her, anyway."

"Like what?" Eric said, chewing the inside of his cheek, back on the golf course and out of the game. "You never said anything about the drawings before."

"Like the size of the guest rooms. They seem too big to me."

"That's the standard size for small hotels," Lambert said.

"I did the research. But we can talk to her about it. Anything else?"

"I was thinking we could use some of that empty land between the main road and the buildings to plant vegetables, you know. We could supply the kitchen with tomatoes, carrots, lettuce, herbs, that kind of thing—and save some money, have a kind of farm-to-table restaurant. And if we do that, we going to need a couple more workers and a shed for the garden tools."

Eric uncrossed his feet under the table and planted them on the ground. "I thought we could have a nice garden with flowers there, some frangipani trees, a lawn, maybe a fishpond. Guests like that kind of thing. I had Joseph put that in the budget."

"I saw it, but I was thinking—"

"We can have both," Lambert interrupted. "Flower gardens in the front where the guests can see them, and a vegetable garden behind. You have nine acres to play with—shouldn't be a problem." His companions sat back, the quashed argument still in the air. Discreet patio lights appeared around them.

After a minute, Danny looked at Lambert. "I wanted to ask you—I'm driving into the Blue Mountains tomorrow and I've been looking at some maps, but I'm still not sure. What's the best way in, you think?"

While the discussion between the two continued about roads into the hills, Eric looked out at the dark sea, still pissed about the loss of his garden with its fishpond and benches. True, it made sense to grow their own produce— he hated to admit it—but it was one more sign that Danny wanted to be in charge. If he needed Eric's experience, as

Cameron had assured him, he wasn't acting like it. He had a mind of his own about everything, even if he was twenty years younger and knew nothing about running hotels.

A clap from Lambert made Eric start. "One more round, gents?" his friend was asking.

"I guess I'll have to," Eric said, tugging at the neck of his T-shirt so he could breathe better.

CHAPTER SIXTEEN

S he tried and failed to focus on the many blues of the clouds and the mountain peak, her paintbrush hovering over the paper, her thoughts hovering over the man at her side. Danny seemed to have gone into some deep place while he painted.

That morning, while she pulled up her skirt, wishing again that she'd brought more presentable clothes, she'd tried to think of everything they might need for the painting trip in the Blue Mountains. Would he remember mosquito spray? Probably not. Should she take bottles of water? Yes. Gym shoes, yes. A book, why not? When she'd finished stowing them in an extra bag, she collected the sandwiches Carthena had made for her and, laboring under her bags and boxes, had bumped into Ford at the front door. On his way to the Port Antonio post office in Sonja's car, he'd dropped her at the bottom of the hill.

"Remember to stay on the left," she'd called while he was driving away.

Minutes later, Danny had appeared in his rented car. At first, they had driven along the coast road, unable to find the road into the Blue Mountains. They'd stopped four times to ask pedestrians—including a woman carrying a live chicken—if they were on the right road. They'd eventually found it and wound upward, a cliff always on one side, only the occasional car barreling toward them blowing its horn.

Soon they were getting valley views between the trees, the mountains browner here than around Largo Bay. Every few hundred yards there were fruit stands and above them, clinging to the side of the hill, were wooden houses with flights of concrete steps leading up to their doors.

"Not very sturdy, is it?" she'd said, pointing to one. "Looks like it'd blow away in a good storm."

"Or wash down the mountain."

"I can't imagine a whole family living there."

At a wide part of the road, Danny had parked the Toyota to allow them space to paint safely between the car and the cliff. He'd selected a spot under a large mango tree, so she wouldn't need to wear her hat or sunglasses to paint, he'd pointed out. When they'd climbed out of the car, he'd exclaimed that he'd never known a road with so many curves. He was dressed today in brown khaki shorts and matching T-shirt, looking like a model in a fashion show for big men, and she was glad she'd worn a skirt, her legs now bright pink. They'd stood together on the edge of the cliff and admired the view for a minute before off-loading the easel and chairs.

Today, she'd announced, she was going to paint straight onto the paper with no pencil. In answer, he'd laughed and picked up a pencil. Within an hour, she had finished one painting and started another, and he was still fitting color within the lines he'd drawn.

"I love how you paint," he said, swishing his brush in the water jar they were sharing.

"Thank you." She'd been wondering when or if he'd comment on her work.

"It's small," he added, "but it has a lot of detail."

"Probably how my mind works." A car roared up the hill past them and they could hear the engine climbing and fading away while they continued working and she thought about Danny liking her work, noticing the detail.

It was early afternoon, a warm one and getting warmer, and soon sweat was forming under her breasts. Her companion's scalp was glistening, one artery pulsing as he bent over his paper.

"I want to ask you something," he said.

"What?"

"How do you get your watercolors to bleed into each other like they do, without making a mess?"

She had him squeeze out a color, water it down, and load the brush. Standing over him, her breast grazing his shoulder, she held his hand and showed him how to approach the edge of one color and nudge it with the brush. While her fingers were wrapped around his thick hand demonstrating the delicate stroke, she felt an exchange of electricity between their hands, almost like being shocked. He looked up at her—his gray eyes with their spokes and yellow rings inches from hers—and she knew he'd felt it, too.

"I've got sandwiches," she said, straightening. "Would you like one?"

"Sure, what do you have?"

"Only cheese, I'm afraid. I thought it would be safe for a long trip."

They sat munching the half-melted sandwiches, he finding it funny that the crusts had been sliced off the bread.

Ladies' sandwiches, he called them, but he seemed to enjoy them well enough.

"I was going to buy us something to drink—" he said.

"I have water, but they're probably warm by now. A cold Britney would be nice, though."

"A what?"

"A Britney? A Britney Spears?"

"The singer?"

"No, a beer. A Britney is a beer, that's cockney rhyming." A little thing, but it started them off with banter that ended the painting for the afternoon.

"Stairs are called *apples and pears*?" he said, shaking his head. "Now I know you're kidding me."

"I'm telling you," she protested. "Cockney rhyming is a real language. Londoners created it. There's books written about it."

"But why? They already speak English."

"It was a kind of secret code, probably to avoid the police or something." She handed him a bottle of water.

"You're making this up, I know it. Nobody would say *apples and pears* instead of *stairs*."

"Nobody in America, maybe. Everything has to be bloody convenient for you—roads, spelling, shopping."

"Have you ever been to America?"

"Not yet."

"Well, you'll see. We get things done, and we like to do it fast."

"But, like painting, sometimes the difference is in the detail, and that takes time."

He picked up another sandwich. "Tell me more about this rhyming thing. Tell me another word."

"Let's see. There's *cream crackered*. That means knackered."

"I don't even know what *knackered* means."

"Knackered? It means tired."

"Where did you learn this stuff?"

"We have a cleaning lady from the East End of London, a big, chatty woman. She comes and gives the flat a good spit-and-polish when we can afford her, and she started telling us about things in the kitchen. She calls milk *satin and silk,* and tea *Rosie Lea*. She uses it all the time, so we got to know what she was talking about. We're starting to get good at it."

"You English are scary, that's all I can say," he said, laughing and slapping his knee.

"Have you ever been there?"

"No, but I want to go to Europe, travel all over, maybe rent a car and drive, you know, to France and Spain." He took a long swig of water. "My mother went, though. She wanted a trip with her girlfriend for her sixtieth birthday, so I gave it to her. They had a blast, took some bus tour around. I think they met some guys on the tour and had too much fun. They're still talking about it."

"So your mum isn't married?"

"No, never was." Looking at the now-glary hills, he told her how his mother had gotten pregnant in her late teens, just after leaving school. He spoke without bitterness, his openness making her uncomfortable.

"Do you have any brothers or sisters?"

"One sister, two years younger than me. She's married in St. Croix and has a couple kids. She never left the island. I think my grandmother wanted her to stay because they were close. She found me kind of difficult to handle." He made a face. "Teenage boy, you know. I used to give her a hard time—stay out late, that kind of thing. My mother knew how to handle me. She knew what tough love was, I'm telling you."

A piercing, almost ringing sound coming up the valley made her lift her head. "What's that, a car alarm?"

He gave a big smile, showing his American teeth, all straight and white. "That's a donkey braying. You never heard that before?"

"We don't have donkeys walking the streets of London, thank you."

"Come on," he said, standing. "Let's get you a Britney. Maybe we'll hear a few more donkeys braying or even see one."

"But you haven't finished your painting."

"I'll do that tomorrow. Lambert told me about this place farther up where they serve tea and scones or something, very English. You going to like it."

"What's it called?"

"Strawberry Hill, I think."

When they'd loaded everything back in the car and were well on their way up the winding road, Sarah heard Penny's voice as if it were coming from the backseat.

It's not like you're going to disappear into the mountains or anything.

CHAPTER SEVENTEEN

Y ou seen Danny?" Janet said, and threw a big handbag on the counter, the gold chains on the front clinking.

"No," Shad said. "I just know he play golf yesterday—"

"I can't find him nowhere," the woman said, looking behind her as if she was expecting to find him hiding under a table. "Miss Mac say he gone from early morning, and he didn't say nothing to me about leaving town."

"Maybe he have some work to do in Port Antonio."

"On a Friday night?"

Shad grunted. There was no way he'd mention that he'd seen Danny speeding down the road early that morning, heading toward the east end of the bay. Shad had waved, but the big man hadn't noticed, which had been fine with the bartender, because he was going in the opposite direction, anyway, and he'd needed more time to think about his last conversation with Beth.

"They want me to wear a uniform," she'd announced as soon as he stirred that morning. He'd groaned and she repeated it to make sure he'd heard.

"That good," he said, his head half hidden by the pillow. He hoped she would get up the way she usually did, get the

135

children ready for school, and leave him to sleep some more. The bar had been full the evening before with folks who'd abstained over the Ash Wednesday holiday, and they hadn't left until the first cock was crowing.

"If it was a nice uniform, yes," she said, "but this uniform look terrible. The color terrible, the style of it terrible."

"It going to save you money," he said, opening one eye. Between them, the rump of a sleeping Joshua was high in the air, his thumb in his mouth.

"I prefer to sew it myself, though. I can make it look nice."

"Ask them, nuh?" There would be no getting up, he remembered. The children had just started Easter break.

"I going to ask them on Monday. First thing after they show me what to do, I going to ask them."

His best line of defense was not to answer, he'd decided, and rolled over to go back to sleep.

"If they say yes, you have to fix the sewing machine leg for me," she said, undaunted. "I need you to fix it, anyway, like how I have to finish the wedding dress."

He turned over and squinted at her. "What the date, again?"

Beth turned toward the curtain, where the sun was already peeping through a gap. "Look how many times I tell you. You tell me last year I was to find a day, not a holiday weekend, not Father's Day or Mother's Day, and I tell you Saturday, July twenty-eight. Like you not listening to me."

"Why we can't just live together in peace, the way we living now?" he asked, beating the dead horse one last time.

Beth sat up violently, making the mattress shake. Joshua raised his head. "How many women and children now with no man, where the man just go off to Kingston or America or go live with another woman? Plenty, right?"

"I tell you, I not—"

"That's what you say now, but you can still leave. If you don't want to married, maybe I should be the one to leave, like how I have a job now. Is not only man can leave, you know. You ever think of that?" She picked up the whining Joshua and stalked out of the room, her swinging rump in the blue T-shirt chastising Shad in her wake.

Sleep had been impossible afterward, and he'd eventually taken a cold shower and gone to work early, spotting Danny along the way. He'd blundered through mopping the floor of the bar, kicked over the bucket of dirty water when he finished, and had to mop all over again. After dusting the shelves and bottles, he'd sat down in the kitchen and listened to Maisie complain about Solomon and his drinking. Lunchtime was spent with Miss Mac going over an application for a permit, but her words about the Parish Council's requirements kept getting mixed up with Beth's threat to leave. While Miss Mac read, her glasses sliding down her nose, he pictured himself walking around the empty house, tossing and turning in an empty bed.

Miss Mac's stew peas did nothing to ease his mood. When he returned to the bar that afternoon, he served drinks to the customers without cracking jokes and took food orders without making recommendations. Even Triumphant Arch and two other locals at the end of the counter hadn't been able to engage him in their wrangling.

"You listening to me or what?" Janet said. "I want a Coke, and put little rum in it for me, nuh?" She climbed onto a bar stool, her mouth sour. "I don't know what get into Danny the last few days. Like he always busy, have to do this and do that."

"He working on the hotel."

"Something different, I saying."

"He getting down to business, man." He placed a rum and Coke in front of Janet and started wiping down the counter.

"I don't know about getting down to business." The woman bent toward him, her chin brushing the rim of her glass. "The only thing he getting down to is painting."

"He *painting*?"

"I telling you. Every day he painting—beach and coconut tree, even the bar." She crowed, a sharp hoot of a sound, and shook her head. "You should see them. They look like a child paint them! He ask me if I want to learn and I say, *No, sir*. I tell him that big people don't play with paint like pickney. I tell him I busy, I have to sew people's clothes." She cupped her chin with her hands. "If you ask me, is pure *foolishness*." The word came out with such venom that Shad didn't tell her how he'd watched Jennifer painting the fish mural at the old hotel and thought it would be a joy to paint on a wall and get paid for it.

By the time Shad got back from serving whiskey to three foreigners at a table, Janet's drink was nearly finished and she was feeling better.

"I have a plan, though," she said with a smirk.

"What kind of plan?"

"I going to the obeah doctor."

"What you talking?" Shad breathed, eyes wide, thinking of the obeah man, an intelligent man, who'd worn a white suit to his daughter's wedding in the bar.

138

"You going to work *obeah* on Danny? You joking, right?"

"I telling you, I going to get some Oil-of-Never-Stray."

Shad leaned across the counter with a fierce frown. "You don't know is devil business that? Danny is a modern man. You can't work no obeah on him!"

Janet emptied her glass and sucked a cube of ice into her mouth. "I just going to sprinkle little bit on him," she said, like she was gargling.

"If he ever find out, you know what would happen?" No hotel, no partnership.

She crunched down on the ice and chewed it. "If he find out, I will know who tell him." She pushed away from the counter. "Mistah Daniel Caines not going to get away just so. He a big fish, but I a bigger fisherman."

"You mean you want you married to him." The public secret from the minute she stepped into the welcome party in the tight, white dress, the bridal omen.

"What you think?" she said with a smile that set the gold tooth leering. "He a good-looking man and he have money. He tell me he own all kind of business, hairdressing parlor and mall. And," she added with a wink, "he like a tiger in bed. He know where to put it and love a *pum-pum*. Watch me, he not going to get away. Miss Janet going to put some oil on Mistah Danny, and he going to put a ring on her finger."

At the end of the bar, Tri called for another shot of white rum and two Red Stripes. The bartender nodded to Janet. "Don't go nowhere."

When he returned, the seamstress had disappeared. Her glass sat empty, all the ice cubes eaten.

CHAPTER EIGHTEEN

'm being lazy tonight," Sonja declared as the party of four pulled out chairs. "Our helper is off and I don't feel like cooking."

"Glad to have you," Eric said, smiling at the two attractive women, pleased that he'd slicked his hair back in a neat ponytail and had on a new cotton shirt. He raised his arm to signal Shad, but the barman was already on his way to the table.

Roper gave his drink order in a monotone, unusual for him, and complained of his tiring drive from Kingston that day. Their guest, the Englishwoman, looked pretty tonight in a blue dress with straps, her face and arms pinker than Eric remembered. On the group's last visit to the bar, she'd been silent and sad looking, despite the fiery hair, her eyes constantly circling, observing. Beside her sat the tall African-American man, the trumpeter, who'd been with them the last time. A couple, maybe?

"What's on the menu tonight?" Sonja asked.

"I think jerk chicken," Eric said. "Shad will tell you." He slapped at a mosquito on his arm and walked back to the refrigerator. Shad returned to the bar after taking the order and tuned the radio to a soca song, something with a fast beat and a man shouting, *Jump, jump*.

"Do you have to play that?" Eric complained, pulling the top off a ginger ale bottle.

"It make the crowd happy."

"You don't look too happy."

The younger man stroked his chin. "Boss, I have something to ask you."

Eric took a sip of his ginger ale. "Go on." And while Shad poured Merlot into a wineglass and three Red Stripes into beer glasses, he told him about Beth's threat to leave.

"I wouldn't take her seriously," Eric said, and rounded the counter. "Women have a way of saying things to. . . . Bet it blows over in a couple days."

"No, Beth don't blow over. She want to get married, and she going to move mountain and river to do it. Her father was a preacher and her parents married, you know. You would think that, like how they dead now, she would forget about it. But no, we living in sin, and the older she get, the worse she get. All she thinking about is marriage."

"Marriage!" Eric blew out of the side of his mouth. "You know my opinion on that subject. So what d'you want to ask me?"

Shad placed the drinks on a round wooden tray and folded four napkins. "I asking you, boss, about your mother and father. You say they was married a long time. You think they had a good marriage?"

Eric sat down on a bar stool. "And you want to know this because . . ."

"I was just thinking—hold on, I coming back." Shad rushed off with the drinks to Roper's table, but he was back in five minutes, after handing in their food orders to the kitchen. "As I was saying—maybe, if your parents was miserable, that is why you so against marriage. Maybe if they had a good marriage, you would more favor it, you know. I notice that people from families with happy parents, those people want to get married, like Beth. I was wondering if it go the other way—when the parents miserable, the children don't like marriage."

It was an awkward moment for Eric, who knew that, as a white foreigner, he occupied a rare status in Largo. Although he was gossiped about and sometimes laughed at (even to his face), he was also considered a man of the world with an American passport, on par with the preacher and the obeah man. Advice from him was taken seriously and he was careful about giving it.

Eric shifted his buttocks on the stool, trying to get comfortable. "Well, no marriage is a hundred percent happy."

"I hear you, boss, but were your parents *irie,* you know, cool? They like one another?"

"Why you asking me this now?"

"Miss Mac was saying that sometimes a person have an opinion that form from when they was growing up, and it influence everything they do when they big. She said her mother used to tell her all the time that a woman is better off living alone, and that make her live without a man. So I was thinking, maybe the reason you don't like marriage was because of your parents' marriage, you know." He looked over his shoulder toward the partition. "Stick a pin."

While Shad was in the kitchen checking on his orders, Eric looked out at the black vastness beyond the cliff. It was a moonless night, the waves beneath breaking the darkness. The memory of the brown belt—once his immigrant grandfather's—was so etched in his mind he could even remember the dent on the silver buckle, remember his father's hand reaching under his brother's bed to haul him out, remember every lash the old man had given him. And if he closed his eyes, he could hear the man slamming through the house in the middle of the night, drunk as a skunk, calling for his dinner, and hear his mother's complaining footsteps as she rolled down the corridor to the kitchen, hear it like it happened yesterday.

When Shad returned, Eric put his elbows on the counter. "My mother only stayed because she'd been a housewife all her life and didn't have a choice. I never knew how she stuck it out, though. They quarreled all the time, about everything. Why you think I left home so early and moved to New York?"

After draining his glass, Eric walked to Roper's table. "Enjoying the stew?"

"Delicious," the Englishwoman said with a nod.

"Have a seat," Roper said, and the bar owner sat down, enjoying the delighted moans from the table about Solomon's dishes.

"I'm glad you joined us," the trumpeter said, his voice like Brooklyn and the South mixed up.

Sonja put down her fork. "Ford wants to ask you something."

"Shoot," Eric said. A night of questions, it seemed.

"Would you like some music in the place?" Ford asked. "I notice you have a radio, but I was wondering if you'd be interested in some live music."

"I couldn't pay anybody," Eric said quickly.

Ford's nostrils flared, the diamond sparkling in his nose. "I wouldn't charge you anything, man. I just thought if you wanted to have a party or something, I could blow my horn, you know."

"You're serious?"

"That I am."

Roper leaned toward Eric. "He's terrific, I'm telling you. You can hardly get into his gigs in Manhattan."

"Why do you want to play here?" Eric asked. His bar was a dive; no decent musician would want to play in a place with a thatch roof and concrete floor. And chances were that Largoites might not appreciate a foreign musician playing foreign music. All they wanted was reggae and calypso. It could be a quiet night like tonight, no breeze, just mosquitoes buzzing around and only a few customers. It could be embarrassing.

"I'm getting anxious to play again, I guess, but I'm not ready to go back home," Ford replied. "It would be my way of giving something back."

"You can't pass this up, Eric," Sonja urged. "It would cost you thousands if you were in the States."

"Just a minute," Eric said, holding up his hand, signaling toward the bar. When Shad approached the table, he recounted the offer.

"What you going to need?" Shad queried Ford.

"I'm going to need somebody to play drums."

"And guitar? My cousin play guitar in Ocho Rios. He'll know a drummer." And before the dinner was digested, it had been arranged that Ford and a pickup band would perform in Eric's humble venue, date and time to be decided.

While they were all beaming with the new plan (Eric already calculating money out, money in), two customers entered the bar. The large man looked serious and calm, his date jubilant and wearing a dress with a waist so tight she looked ready to explode out of both ends.

"Danny!" Roper called.

The couple turned toward them. Danny's face clouded over for a second before he smiled. He seemed uncertain about whether to join them until the woman tugged at his arm. There was no doubt in Eric's mind about the reason for the man's hesitation. He was still unhappy about the trip to Simone Island that afternoon.

From his arrival, Danny had been curious about the island. He wasn't the only one. Almost every visitor who passed through the village wondered what the moldy buildings had been, wondered who would have taken a boat a quarter mile out to sea to occupy those buildings. Many asked at the bar while sipping a beer and Shad or Eric would recount the tale of the broken peninsula and marooned hotel.

When Danny's curiosity had reached its peak, he'd told Eric he wanted to examine the future campsite and, rowing an old canoe rented from Minion, a retired fisherman, Eric had taken Danny over before lunch, his first visit since Simone had left. That midday, the water had been as choppy as usual and the trip unremarkable. When they got to the island's small beach, Danny had leaped over the side of the canoe and hauled the boat onto the beach. Then he'd looked up at the fifteen-foot cliff in front of them.

"Is that how you usually get up, by climbing that steep path?"

Eric had nodded; Danny had frowned. He said nothing more until they'd ascended the path, their bare feet slipping back every few steps. At the top, they walked between the lemongrass to the almond tree in the center of the island. There they had stood examining the two long, roofless buildings. The southern one, Eric pointed out, had housed the registration area, the bar, and the guest rooms, and the northern one—at a right angle to the other—had served as dining room, housekeeping, and maintenance offices.

"We had a great view of the open sea from the dining room," Eric added. "Everyone loved it." The remnants of Jennifer's ravaged mural mocked his words.

"The lobby was great, too, high ceiling, and it had a giant mobile of fish swirling around. I had some guy in the village make it. Took him forever, then we had to get a crane to hoist the darn thing up and get it balanced right."

"And everything came apart in a few hours during the hurricane?"

"That's right." Eric recounted how he'd crouched on top of the registration desk while the waves washed through the lobby, remembered halfway through the story that he'd already told it to the investor, and rushed through the rest.

While Eric was memorializing the old hotel, his companion had been looking around. "About the campsite," he said after Eric had paused, "we need to bring Horace over to discuss what they're going to need, from day-to-day needs to emergency hurricane evacuation."

"I thought we'd just rent it to him," Eric said, scratching the side of his nose, "as is."

"We have to make an agreement with them, and we need it in writing. We don't want to be liable for any accidents. And there's a lot of stuff missing *as is*: no landing dock for boats, no steps leading up from the beach, no cooking facilities, no toilets. We might not even be allowed to rent it to them in this—" Danny broke off, the thought clearly alarming him. "If I were Horace, I'd want at least those things."

"We could just put up some wooden stairs—"

"Shit, Eric," Danny had said, turning with suddenly hard eyes, "you don't understand. If anything happens, we could lose our shirts, man."

The ride back in the canoe had been quiet other than the slapping and dripping of the oars. Overhead, seagulls circled around the boat looking for a fisherman's catch and, disappointed, drifted off.

"Let's get Horace out there," was all Danny had said before leaving, and a miffed Eric had sat on his verandah for a full hour to recover.

"Come and join us," Roper was saying now, waving Danny and Janet toward the table. Eric moved his chair over a few inches and looked at Sarah beside him to see if she would do the same, but the woman seemed frozen. She was staring at the two people approaching, her face paler than usual.

CHAPTER NINETEEN

Sarah's chest tightened as soon as she saw them walk in. Danny's stance remained proud when he noticed her, but his eyes flickered around, uncertain about where to land, the cause of which she knew. He'd said he had to rush down from the mountains that morning for an appointment with Eric, nothing about being with Janet. She'd half expected him to be there since the bar was the only place to go in Largo, but she'd thought that this time he'd come alone.

"Let's join two tables," Shad said, and he and Danny moved a nearby table to accommodate the expanded party. The new arrivals settled down, their faces turned to Roper, who was offering wine.

"I'm going to pass," Danny said and, over his shoulder to Shad, "Two rum and Cokes, please."

Sarah looked down at a tie-dyed circle on her dress. Sonja had encouraged her to buy it with the matching earrings in Ocho Rios that afternoon.

"Try this on," her hostess had called across the tourist shop. "It'll look great on you, like how you're long and slim." Sarah had tried on the dress with its splotches of bright blue and purple, colors she never wore, and she'd bought it, aware that a dress with spaghetti straps would get little wear in chilly London, aware that she was using up half her remaining funds to buy it. But the lavender outfit wasn't turning any heads, and she'd wanted to turn Danny's head, especially after their last outing.

The drive to Strawberry Hill the day before was over an hour from their mountainside painting spot, the time passing quickly as they veered around one sharp bend and then another, the air getting cooler as they climbed.

"This is more like England," Sarah had commented, feeling light-headed. The vegetation had changed to lily-like plants and mossy banks beside the road. More substantial wooden houses with gingerbread trim—vacation homes, they both agreed—began to appear, followed by a park with pine trees. They got out of the car to look at the view, both of them surprised by the large city on the southern side of the mountain that filled the entire plain below and ended at a harbor.

"Hey," she'd said with a mock pummel to his arm, "you never told me you were taking me to Kingston!"

"We're just going with the flow." Danny had chuckled. "Let's see where it take us." He seemed unperturbed that Largo was far behind.

Looking down at the sprawling city, Sarah wondered how she'd gotten here with a man she didn't know from Adam, who was driving her to a place where no one could find her. There seemed to have been some shift within her. They painted together and they'd become friends, but it was more than that. Just being with him made her feel more alive than she had in years, and she liked how it felt. And she'd decided, standing there looking at the tiny houses and streets below, hearing the distant hum of the city at rush hour, that she wasn't going to shut down this time. She would open to her fate—against her better judgment, perhaps—and see where it led her. To go with Danny's flow.

Sarah had gotten back in the car and exchanged a tight smile with her companion. They kept driving, searching for Strawberry Hill. Rewarded with a sign, they entered a winding road up to the main building. It turned out to be not only a restaurant but an elegant guesthouse, and they spent the first fifteen minutes exploring the old plantation and its very modern infinity pool. Danny got into a conversation with a gardener, who showed them a century-old palm tree, a coffee bush, and a variegated hibiscus flower.

In the restaurant they ordered cucumber sandwiches, with Sarah explaining that they were the queen's favorite, and two glasses of sherry. When the sandwiches came, Danny declared Jamaica a British colony after all, based on the crustless sandwiches, to which she'd slapped him on the arm again. By the time they finished, the sun had disappeared behind the western mountain range.

"You know it's too dark to drive back," she'd said.

"Come on, where's your sense of adventure?" he'd chided her.

"I saw you swerve into the right lane when we came out of the park. My confidence in your ability to drive down the mountain in the dark has drastically diminished."

He'd eased smoothly into talking about spending the night and she began to have a sinking feeling. "No, we have to go back," she'd urged. "I don't have the money for a place like this, not even one night—"

"Separate rooms, my treat," he'd said, grasping her fluttering hand. "Call Roper and tell him you're not coming home tonight. Tell him exactly where you are, if it will make you feel better."

He wouldn't listen to her protests. "You given me free art classes and I want to thank you. The least I can do is repay you with one night in a nice hotel, right?"

She'd eventually called Sonja to say she'd be home in the morning while Danny booked them into two rooms a building apart. They stopped at her room first and admired its white hammock on the balcony overlooking what was now a black valley. Danny called room service when they got to his room, and while he was speaking softly and firmly, asking for menus, Sarah began to see him as a man who might not speak perfect English but who knew his way around the world, expecting a positive response to everything he wanted. They'd sat at the table on his verandah to have dinner and, when it came to the wine, he admitted his ignorance to the waiter and left it to him to decide. When the waiter left, he'd breathed a deep sigh and stretched his legs out in front of him.

"I needed to leave Largo and get away from—from everything, to tell you the truth. I been thinking about the new hotel too much and I need to clear my head."

"Probably a good thing, then."

"This is the biggest project that I've gotten into and it's more of a headache than I thought. It could end up costing me everything if it pulls down my other businesses. I'll either go ahead with it or get out early. I don't like to waste my time."

Dinner was a well-done steak for him and crispy duck for her, washed down with a wine they agreed was miraculous. He'd walked her back to her room along the path connecting the buildings, aromatic bushes lining the walkway, the trip made shorter by the wine and the brushing of elbows.

"Is this what you thought Jamaica would be like?" he'd asked her.

"I thought it would be just sand and sea, really."

"I thought it would be edgy," Danny had said. "In-your-face, kind of, the way Jamaicans talk, you know? I didn't expect it to be—I don't know—*civilized* like this."

"You said it yourself, they *were* a British colony." He'd ruffled her hair, and she'd laughed with him and had a sudden desire to kiss him.

When they got to her room, she'd opened the door with the old-fashioned key and stood with her hand on the knob. She wasn't going to ask him to come in. Half turned to leave, suddenly quiet, he'd stood still while she floundered through a thank-you. He started to walk away—and returned, like he'd made a decision, and, when she started to say something, he'd placed one finger on her lips to silence her and she'd looked up at him, unable to see his eyes in the dark. He'd moved his finger from her lips down to her chin, raised it a few inches, and lowered his face until his lips brushed hers. Then he'd wrapped his arms around her, surprising her, and kissed her, his tongue playing with hers, and she hadn't resisted, asking herself why. And just when she'd started relaxing into the kiss and the embrace, he'd pulled away, and there was a startled silence before he left.

Afterward, she'd sat contemplating the fact that Danny had kissed her, a kiss that hadn't been unwelcome. She'd felt strangely protected being close to him, his large, brown presence enfolding her. After she'd climbed into the four-poster bed in her underwear, the mosquito net pulled tight around the posters, she'd fallen asleep feeling his finger beneath her chin.

They'd arranged to leave early the next morning so he could keep an appointment with Eric. Danny had knocked on her door soon after the sun was up and they'd greeted each other as if nothing unusual had happened. Munching on leftovers from the day before, they'd driven over the mountain and arrived back to Largo in time for his meeting. Everything seemed normal on the surface, except that Sarah had been left off at Roper's door feeling abandoned, wanting more. No word had been said about getting together again, and she hadn't been in the least mood to paint. When Sonja offered to take her into *Ochy,* she'd immediately agreed.

"You don't need to tell me about last night," Sonja had said when they got on the road, but the way the writer had opened her eyes, wide with mischief, had encouraged Sarah to describe the overnight trip.

"And nothing happened?" the writer had exclaimed when she finished.

"A perfect gentleman."

"Sweet," her friend had declared.

A bright blue dress and a few hours later, Sonja was again opening her eyes wide, this time at Janet. "And what have you two been up to?" she asked.

"We just out on the town," the woman replied. She seemed pleased to be included in the conversation this time, her voice and the makeup on her eyelids sparkling.

"I know you need it," Roper said to Danny. "Starting a business in Jamaica is hard work."

"You can say that again," Danny agreed, showing only

his profile to those at the other end. "There are so many details—"

"But he have time to paint," Janet interjected with a little laugh.

"You're *painting?*" Roper said.

Danny turned to Sarah, his body turning before his eyes. "I've been getting some tips."

"You're painting with Sarah?" Roper responded. He was playing the innocent as much as Sonja, Danny's painting on the beach having been the topic of discussion a couple evenings before.

"We had a few sessions together. She's a good teacher." Sarah bobbed her head to acknowledge the praise.

Janet took her drink from Shad and sucked her teeth. "I don't know how you have time to paint and is business you come to do."

"It take my mind off business, I told you," Danny answered.

The dressmaker took a sip of her rum. "You can't make no money doing no painting."

"Some artists actually make money, madam," Roper said in a British accent that delivered the sting of reproach.

"Yes, but you painting long time," the woman countered with a wave of her chubby hand. "He don't know how to paint, just wasting his time."

"Art," Sarah said in a low voice, "is not about making money. It's an act of creation that comes from the soul. If one makes money from it, so be it."

Sonja lifted her glass. "Well said, even if the form of art is a book on sexual harassment." Everyone laughed, except for Janet, who looked confused, and there was a sudden drop in temperature around the table.

Smoothing back his ponytail, Eric turned to Danny. "Guess what? Ford is going to be playing here one night." An enthusiastic discussion started and Sarah got up and walked to the bar.

"The lavatory?" Shad responded to her question.

"The ladies'," Sarah said with only a slight quiver in her voice.

He pointed to a door beyond the kitchen. "We only have one bathroom. I tell the boss we should have two, one for men and one for women, but we only have one."

"No problem, it'll do," she said, and opened the flimsy door. The restroom was lit by a bulb above the sink, revealing the uncovered toilet tank and its innards. After latching the door, Sarah leaned into the low mirror over the sink, which cut her off above the nose, showing only her high cheekbones and the blue shell earrings like a magazine advertisement.

She needed to put space between herself and Danny, needed to slow her heart down. Last night's kiss, she reasoned with the earrings, had been the result of good wine and being on holiday. She was the guest of two people who'd befriended her and whom she liked, Roper having shown himself as a pompous but likable character after all, and she'd developed a friendship with Ford, a gentle man in pain, and become his confidante. She was expanding here, although not to the point of having Danny as her lover.

She was attracted to him, without a doubt. When he was with her, the unevenness of her breathing sometimes disturbed her painting. When he wasn't, he dominated her thoughts. But not every infatuation had to be acted on. She'd experienced that already with a waiter in Kent, a married man named Richard. The vibe between them had been almost unbearable, his jokes making her blush, until she asked about his wife one day and the feelings had fizzled. She should do that with Danny, talk about Janet and let the beastly thing fizzle out.

She used the toilet since she was there, felt the vibration from the waves below traveling up through the toilet seat to her legs. After washing and drying her hands, she bent to check her hair in the mirror, noting that the red dye was growing out. She opened the door—only to take a step back.

Janet was standing a few inches in front of the door, one hand on her hip and the metallic eye shadow glowering.

"I coming to join you," she said. She pushed Sarah back into the bathroom and closed the door. The toilet was still noisily refilling, going about its business. "Keep me company, nuh?"

"I'm sorry—I was just leaving."

The dressmaker squeezed past Sarah to the toilet. She placed her purse on the ledge of the closed window. "You don't come from a family where plenty people use one bathroom, eh?"

She pulled her dress up and sat on the toilet, the high heels splaying out on either side. "Too much rum make you want to pee." She giggled as she started urinating.

"Do you mind—"

"Like how you new to Jamaica," Janet said, her face suddenly going cold, "I just figure you and me should understand each other."

Sarah nodded, hoping someone would knock on the door, anybody.

"You and Danny is friends, right?" Janet finished her business and stood up while Sarah looked away. "I know you

spending plenty time painting with him, helping his *soul* to
paint, even though his paintings look like baby finger paint
them. But he a nice man, you don't think so?"

"Yes, he's—" Sarah said carefully.

"I hear you go somewhere with him last night and spend
the night. A little bird tell me. They see you coming back
with him this morning." She nudged Sarah away from the
sink and began washing her hands. "Is lie they telling me,
or is true?"

The artist's heart started pounding. "We—we went up
into the hills—"

"So is true?"

"Yes—but—"

"You don't have no answer for me, right?" Janet wiped
her hands on a paper towel. "I going to give you some advice, Miss Englishwoman. If I was you, I wouldn't fuck
with other people's man, you hear me?"

"I'm not—I know you and Danny—"

"Let me tell you something." The woman leered up at
her, the gold tooth reflecting the bathroom light. "Danny
and me tight. You don't want to make no trouble for us,
right? Next thing, people say, because you white, you think
you can take a black man away from his woman. You don't
want people to say that, right?"

"Of course not."

"You don't want them to say you have no *respect* for black
women, right?" She looked up, smiling suddenly as if they
were now friends, fake friends forever. "No, I know you
don't want that, you too polite. You look like a nice, well-
brought-up woman, the kind of woman who wouldn't want
them to say you don't respect people."

"Of—of course, I respect you."

Janet's voice slowed and deepened. "So, if you respect me, how come you *fuck* my man last night?"

Sarah backed up to the door. "Nothing happened, I'm telling you."

"You think I born yesterday? Let me tell you something, Jamaican woman is the *baddest* woman in the world. Somebody should have tell you that before you come down here, because Jamaican woman is pure trouble, you hear me?"

"I can explain—"

"I don't need no *raas claat* explaining."

Janet opened her purse and pulled out a lipstick in a silver case. "A word to the wise, that what they say on TV." She pulled off the lipstick cover and turned the tube of lipstick, holding it upright like she was loading a handgun. "Stop fucking Danny Caines and stop fucking with me." She leaned into the mirror and applied the lipstick with care, back and forth, back and forth. "Danny and I making plans and you not going to interfere with that, you hear me, English?"

Sarah felt behind her for the door latch. "I hear you."

"One more thing," Janet said, closing the lipstick and dropping it into her purse. "Don't tell *nobody* that we have a chat, you hear? Largo is a small place and I going to hear about it and next time . . ." She looked Sarah up and down with eyes as hard as boiled eggs, pushed her out of the way, and left.

Sarah latched the door and held on to the sink until she could breathe again. When she emerged, the little bartender was standing near the counter wrapping and unwrapping a dish towel around one fist.

"I saw Janet go in there with you, miss. She trouble you?"

She tried a smile. "She's a strong one, isn't she?"

"You must let me know if she do anything to you, you hear?"

"It's fine, honestly, just a little misunderstanding. Thanks for asking."

She patted the bartender on the arm—more to steady herself than to reassure him—and started toward her table, the two empty chairs mocking her with every step.

CHAPTER TWENTY

It was almost dinnertime and a barrage of smells of scallion and thyme and fried fish were pouring into the lane from the wooden houses, making his mouth water. Remembering that his own kitchen was cold, Shad left the verandah to start dinner. He chopped an onion and carrots, browned the onion with the cubes of stew meat Beth had left thawing in the fridge, and threw them into a pot with the carrots.

It was his first day off since Beth had started working, and he'd been alone all day. In his old undershirt and shorts, he'd weeded the vegetable garden, watched a shopping channel on the small television in the living room, and practiced the reading exercise Miss Mac had given him, practiced until his eyes were tired. At half past three, his daughters' noise had filled the house again. He'd picked up Joshua from Miss Livingston at five, as instructed, and turned him over to Joella.

While dinner was cooking, he resumed sitting on the verandah, waiting and checking his watch. It was close to six thirty by the time Beth came down the lane. The new uniform she'd sewn was wrinkled and she looked weary, almost stooped, carrying a heavy bag and Ashanti.

Shad ran down the steps and opened the garden gate. "Let me take her," he said, reaching for the child.

"Thank you," she moaned, handing over the girl. "Where the other children?"

"Doing homework, but I don't know how much they doing. They playing in the room with Josh and the kitten." They went into the house and into their bedroom.

While he was rolling Ashanti onto the yellow bedspread, Beth sat down heavily on the side of the bed with a groan.

"What you cooking?" she asked, pulling off her shoes.

"Stew beef and rice," Shad replied, leaning on the door frame with his arms crossed, "like you told me."

"You remember to put in garlic?"

"I put in onion."

She loosened her belt and her eyes darted up at him. "Your clothes dirty."

"I was weeding."

Joella and Rickia came into the room, Joella carrying the baby. Rickia touched her mother's shoulder and smoothed her hair, commenting on how she looked like *a working lady*. After she chased them back to do homework, Beth stretched out on the bed beside Ashanti, who had curled up in the plaid dress her mother had sewn for her.

"How was it?" he asked. "The job, I mean."

"It kind of boring. The lady who was to show me everything didn't come in until lunchtime. Her son was sick. So I didn't do much at the beginning, I just walk around and introduce myself. The librarian ladies kind of funny, though, don't talk to me at all, like they think they too high to talk to me. Then I had my lunch and the woman come and show me around. I clean the floors like she told me, but

161

they dirty, dirty, and I clean the bathrooms, six toilets, three male and three female, and start to dust the books. Then it was time to go and everybody pick up their bag, so I pick up mine and leave, too."

"What about the school, the autism school?"

"The head lady talk nice, a white lady from New Jersey, and she have plenty experience with autism."

"Ashanti give them any trouble, like how she have tantrums and thing?"

"They say she don't pay them no mind. She not *responsive,* the woman said. I tell them that normal, she don't do nothing we tell her to do. But they say she going to be responsive after she get used to them." He sat at the foot of the bed and put her feet in his lap. While he pulled at her toes, she told him that the teacher at the school said they were going to teach Ashanti how to dress herself and how to go to the bathroom on her own.

"That good," he declared. "Even if they don't teach her nothing else."

"Now we need to register Joella at Titchfield High, too, for September."

Looking at his woman collapsed on the bed from first-day exhaustion, it occurred to Shad that the mother of his children had the same stubborn streak that Granny had, a woman who had taken on raising her baby grandson in her sixties and never complained. Beth would travel twenty miles on bad roads to clean dirty toilets for the sake of the family.

"I know what you doing not easy," he said, pushing his thumbs into the middle of her soles the way she liked. She closed her eyes, her eyebrows raised, and he continued, finishing the thoughts that had been forming over the course of the afternoon. "And like how you making extra money for us—I was thinking—"

"I listening."

"I was thinking, since you start making the wedding dress and you set date and everything—we should just go ahead . . ."

She sat up on her elbows. "We talking about the same thing, right?" He nodded and she narrowed her eyes at him. "What change your mind? I know you, and you is not a person to change your mind without a fight. What happen to you now?"

"I see how hard you working for the family, so I know you not leaving me. And I know a wedding will make you feel good, make us official like. You know me, I feel good, anyway, but I know you want a wedding." Shad looked down at his woman's tired toes. The reason for his change of heart lay unspoken like most truths. That afternoon, Rickia had asked him in the kitchen, asked him so casually that it had stunned him, why he didn't want to marry her mother, and he'd blundered through an answer. Afterward, he'd sat on the verandah thinking of his own distaste for marriage, and about the boss's parents and their unhappiness (still wondering how people living in America could be anything but happy), and it had occurred to Shad—the bolt of recognition making him stand up just thinking about it—that he, like Eric, had come from parents who hadn't had a loving partnership.

Beth, on the other hand, had come from a family with two parents who loved each other, even though her preacher father had ordered Beth out of the house when she got pregnant and she'd had to live with her sister in a rented room. Through everything, her father had loved her mother and she'd loved him back and their children had seen that.

Unlike his partner, Shad knew nothing about the man whose blood he carried in his veins. He didn't know if he was a thief or an idiot or a lady's man or anything else. All Granny had said was that he didn't have a father; she'd never explained. Asking his mother had been out of the question because he barely knew her. When she came from Kingston to visit every few months, always bearing a few sweeties for him and maybe a new shirt, she seemed more interested in gossiping with her mother than paying him attention. Before she left, she'd always plunk money down on the kitchen counter, and by the time he was fourteen he'd concluded that his mother was paying his grandmother to save herself the trouble of raising him.

He'd paced the narrow verandah that afternoon with the new understanding that the bad feeling he'd always had about marriage had come because he'd had no role models to show him anything good about it. He'd been angry with his mother and especially his father, who'd disappeared as if the baby he'd spawned was worthless. And because of that, Shad's highest goals had been to be a good father and to raise his children to be decent people. Being connected to their mother had never been important, and being tied to her in front of witnesses had been out of the question. Now he understood that everything would have to change. Not only was he moving from bartender to businessman, but his family goals would have to change as well.

Beth flopped back on the bed, raising her eyes to heaven. "Married, Jesus be praised! I never think I see the day."

"One thing though," her future husband warned. "Is just a small wedding we talking. We can't invite the whole village."

"Like how much, you mean?"

"Around twenty-five people."

"Twenty-five?" she said with derision.

"What wrong with that?"

"By the time we invite my sister and her family and your aunts and their children and our four children and Mistah Eric, we done reach twenty-five. We can't even invite Solomon and Maisie, not even Miss Mac."

"But we can't afford—"

"I tell you what," she said, covering her eyes with one arm, "let we decide how much money we have to spend, and I will see we don't spend more than that." Shad stood up to check on the rice, shaking his head, knowing she'd won again.

CHAPTER TWENTY-ONE

S imone was laughing so hard she was almost braying into the phone. "I've never heard that before, Happy *Un*-Valentine's Day! You're one of a kind, Eric Keller."

"I just thought that since February is Valentine's Month, with all the hoopla around Valentine's Day and everything, then the twenty-ninth—when it comes—should be Un-Valentine's Day. You get to forget the whole nonsense. What do you think? Every four years you buck the trend."

"Is that the day when you take back your roses or something?"

"They'd be dead by then," he said, walking with the phone toward the kitchen and away from the ears of the customers. "Just thought I'd make you laugh, and it worked, apparently."

"Are you feeling guilty for not calling on Valentine's Day?"

"Of course not," he protested. Ever since Lambert's and Danny's reminders about Valentine's, he'd been thinking about it. Had she expected him to call? Would he now have to remember—in his case, with Post-it notes—upcoming birthdays and rituals? He'd reassured himself that, in this day and age, *she* could have called him or sent him a card, but she hadn't.

"What have you been up to?" he inquired.

"Working on getting the foundation started. It's a long legal and accounting process. I've been filling out forms."

"What are you going to call it?"

"Either the Celeste Foundation for Young Adults or the Celeste Hall Youth Foundation. What do you think?"

"I like the second one, with her full name. Makes it sound more, I don't know, action oriented, maybe. What's the foundation going to do?"

"We're going to be working with college students who are floundering emotionally, and with parents of those kids—because it's about the parents as much as the young people. That's what I've come to realize with the therapy I've been having. The parents are as damaged as the children. I'm as much to blame as—"

"I didn't know you were going to therapy." He pictured her lying on a couch talking to a man with a beard, pictured the therapist trying to avoid looking at her perky little nipples, although she was probably wearing bras in Atlanta now.

"It's group therapy where we meditate and then write in a journal and, afterward, we share what we've written. A nun runs it. It's been really helpful. Maybe you should try it sometime."

"Too late for me, I'm afraid."

He heard three beeps, perhaps from a microwave, followed by a clunk, before she spoke. "Is the investor still there?"

"Yes, he's still here. He has to be, there are a hundred things to do. We formed a company with Shad, the three of us, and opened a bank account, lots of paperwork. Oh, God,

I'm sick of it already. Anyway, next up is to appear before a Parish Council committee, some environmental impact assessment thing."

"Everything going smoothly, then?" She was stirring a drink, the spoon clinking against the cup. Eric sat down in the kitchen chair, hoping the customers didn't want another drink or would last out until Shad came for his evening shift.

"We went to see the architect a couple days ago." She was a short, butch woman, he wanted to say, but decided to be politically correct and say nothing. "Danny has these ideas for things he wants to add on, a farm and a gardening warehouse—he calls it a shed, but it's really a warehouse—and five or six other things. I kept trying to tell him it's going to cost more than he wanted to put in, but he said they would pay off in the long run. So now the woman has to go back to the drawing board, and I know the financing is going to be out of whack—what with putting in some infrastructure on the island. I think he's going to be in shock when he sees the sticker price for everything."

"I guess your son will have to redo the budget." She took a sip of something close to the phone. "What's his name again? Joseph? Maybe he can come down and—"

"That's not going to happen."

"Why not?"

The thousand miles between their phones filled with silence, not even a slurp. Struggling with how to tell her, or if he should tell her, Eric walked to the kitchen window and creaked it open. He'd hardly known his own son before he came down to Jamaica to write the business proposal that Caines wanted, and what had happened to Joseph after he arrived he'd never mentioned again. It had been hard enough dealing with it himself.

"You know how Jamaica is," he said. "Some of the villagers thought he was gay—it was all—just speculation, you know—but one day, something happened—thank God, he escaped . . ." It wasn't true that he'd escaped. Someone had ended the madness, but saying he'd escaped gave Joseph his manhood back.

Her voice slowed. "Oh no. You should have told me about it."

"There was nothing you could have—"

"I would have listened. That's what friends do. If you want me in your life, Eric, and it seems like you do, then we have to be there for each other. I know you don't want to go there," she said, undaunted in her Simone way. "I don't know what happened to you in the past with women, and I'm not sure I even want to know, but you're going to have to trust me if I'm going to be your friend. And whether we go forward as nothing more than friends or continue being lovers, we're going to have to keep working at a friendship. It all starts there."

"Why'd you want a friendship with an old geezer like me, anyway?"

"You're a good lover, what can I say?" He heard a sigh. "You're honest, down-to-earth, kind, and you don't make demands. Plus, you live in a nice place. And while you're thinking about that," she said without a pause, "The woman is supposed to propose today, by the way, since it's February twenty-ninth. But don't worry, I won't. I couldn't handle it right now."

"Thank you," he answered, and they laughed quickly and loudly, pulling back from dangerous ground.

CHAPTER TWENTY-TWO

The brochure that Danny had placed in Sarah's hand said that Bucket Falls was *one of the island's most stunning waterfalls with a large, clear pool suitable for swimming,* and Shad had endorsed it, apparently. What neither the brochure nor the bartender had said was that the falls were reached by a long, uneven path from the parking lot, a path unsuitable for carrying easels, chairs, and bags of supplies.

After they reached the falls and dumped their load, Danny and Sarah stood beside the pool, sweaty but satisfied that the brochure had been accurate—the falls were exquisite. About twenty feet in height and thirty across, they cascaded noisily into a circular pool beneath. Trees towered up from the steep valley walls, sentinels keeping out the heat. The clarity of the pool was questionable, however, since the water had been muddied by groups of swimmers, tourists and locals, some climbing the mossy rocks beside the falls. One brave girl balanced her way out to the middle of the falls and dove into the pool to cheers from her friends.

"Here all right?" Danny asked, gesturing with his chin to a spot facing the falls, and Sarah agreed, despite an urge to wade in and swim away from him. He set up their chairs, his a few yards behind hers.

Once she started working she almost forgot him, almost forgot Janet's caustic words. She loved the translucence of the water sheeting off the overhang and tried to capture it on one of her panes, as Danny had started calling her four-by-four images. *Windowpanes into her soul,* he'd said, laughingly referring to her definition of art. When he said it she'd wanted to reach out and touch his lips, lips that had described something she'd always felt about her own work and never put into words. But she'd turned away instead, and repeated the phrase in her head.

Bucket Falls continued falling, morning turned into afternoon, sandwiches were eaten, and swimmers came and went. Sarah finished a second and a third painting, one of bubbles touching the dark, pebbly sand at her feet, and she decided that she'd had enough.

"I'm going in," she called to Danny behind her.

"Don't swim out too far."

She put her last painting on the stool to dry and washed out her brushes at the edge of the water. Removing her sandals, feeling Danny's eyes on her, she took off her shorts and T-shirt.

She stood in the shallows getting used to the chilly water, aware that he was probably examining her breasts, too big for the bikini, and her bottom, too flat for any bathing suit.

Don't forget, you're a swan, she reminded herself, resting a hand on her neck. *You are graceful and elegant.*

She waded into the cold water with gritted teeth, avoiding two children who were splashing each other. When she looked back, Danny was bending over his painting, his face expressionless. After dog-paddling in a circle to get used to the cold, she turned over on her back and tried to relax. It had been a stressful week. She hadn't slept well to begin with. When she did fall asleep she'd had dreams of women shaking her by the shoulders. One woman battled her with a toilet tank ball.

Danny had shown up on the beach Monday morning, somewhat subdued but ready to paint. She'd struggled with telling him to leave, but he was so intent on setting up his chair just like hers, facing the road going west around a bend, and she was so happy to see him, that she hadn't protested.

Two hours had passed in sweaty tension, in the midst of which she'd decided that there would be nothing more between them. Not only was there Janet, but she was sure that any feelings she might have had for him were imagined. He'd been gracious in paying for her room at Strawberry Hill and gotten carried away when he'd kissed her good night. If there was any feeling between them it was platonic. There was no obligation on either side, and her attraction to him only offered a lesson in not stereotyping.

Before he'd shown up, she'd been sure he wouldn't come, reasoning that Janet would have warned him off or he'd be too embarrassed to come. There was even a part of her that wanted him to stay away, for her sake and his, the part that kept seeing Janet looking up at her with steely eye shadow. But he'd come that Monday, and shortly before noon he'd gotten up, saying he had to leave. He'd folded his chair and started walking away, then put down the chair.

"It's difficult," he began, and chewed on his bottom lip. "I'd like to—I'm just—oh, shit." He'd leaned against the trunk of a coconut tree and rubbed his jaw with one hand.

"Listen, I don't think you should come back," she'd said, putting down her brush. "This is not a good idea, you know, painting together. There are people—people won't understand."

"I'm coming back," he'd said, spreading his hand flat to make the point. "Nobody is going to stop me doing what I want to do. If I want to paint, I'm going to paint."

"You—"

"And I like painting with you."

She'd picked up her paintbrush again. "You have a girlfriend, Danny, in case you forgot."

"She's not my—it's tricky."

"You don't have to say anything." She'd put down her brush, wanting to hear more.

"I have to say something, because that's how I am. I don't want to be one of those guys who—who lead women on, you know, and don't give no kind of explanation. I just need some time. That's what I'm saying, just give me a little time." He'd left without explaining.

To her surprise, he'd come running down the beach the next day, like the first time she'd seen him, barefoot and bare-chested, making her heart thump. He'd waved at her coming and going and she'd waved back, but he'd kept on running and left her wondering in his wake. The day after that, he'd been waiting for her when she got to the beach. He'd helped her set up the easel and asked if she would like to go on a painting expedition to a waterfall Shad had recommended.

"I'll pick you up tomorrow."

"I don't think so."

"Trust me," he'd said, holding on to her arm. "I have

this under control, I'm telling you." He wore her down, showing her the brochure, telling her not to worry.

"Okay," she'd said, and looked down at his hand on her arm. "But I don't play games."

Before he picked her up that morning, she'd allowed his statement that he had things under control to rise to the top and hold down her doubts. She had to stop worrying and be a big girl. Let life take its course, not anticipate anything, and keep her mouth shut.

Thus far, she hadn't confided in Sonja about her feelings for Danny, and she hadn't written Penny one word on the subject. Her rare emails had stayed on the topic of the village and her painting, and talked only in generalities about the place and people she'd met. She was having a good time, doing lots of painting, she'd written. To her mother she'd sent two postcards with even less information.

Floating, she looked up at the sunlight twinkling between the leaves of the trees overhead. A water gnat hovered over her and she swatted it away. Settling back, she decided that this was as good a time as any to practice being in the present, like that philosopher had written, Eckhart something or the other. She was going to stay in the present, be literally and figuratively present wherever she was, observe what went on around her, and detach from the outcome. She turned her attention to the sound of the falls echoing through the water and into her submerged ears, to the coolness of the river against her skin.

A spray of water in her face made her jerk to her feet. The boys playing nearby were throwing a ball back and forth. She swam away from the children and toward the falls. A Rastafarian man with long gray dreadlocks was standing up to his knees in the water.

"Go into the cave, man." He gestured with both arms, urging her on. "Swim around and go behind the falls. It nice, go on."

Feeling she had no choice, a little scared but determined to prove some point to herself, she swam in front of the falls, the noise deafening. After swimming through the opening in the water, she climbed onto a shelf of cream-colored rock behind the falls, the splashing making her scoot deeper along the shelf. She wiped the water out of her eyes and pulled her hair away from her face. She was sitting in a magical place, a damp cave where the water blocked her view of almost everything outside, enclosing her in noisy intimacy.

Danny appeared through the gap in the falls. "Are you trying to hide?" he shouted above the din of the water. He clambered onto the rock shelf, his red bathing trunks looking garish in the tranquillity of the cave.

"What am I hiding from?" she yelled back.

"Me." He sat down a foot away from her. She shook her head, smiling, evading. They sat in silence for a few minutes staring at the falls in front of them. She started feeling dizzy, perhaps from the noise, and she signaled that she was ready to leave. He held on to her hand and brought it slowly to his lips, his bald head glistening over her arm. She pulled back her arm, but he held it fast, no hesitancy about him now.

She mouthed the words *no games* when he looked up at her and he mouthed them back at her, and leaned over and kissed her arm higher up, her shoulder, her neck, and then her lips. *It was not my imagination,* she thought, grasping one of his powerful shoulders. When he slid his arms around her and pushed her gently back against the rock wall, it felt for a second as if they'd done this before, primordial people making love in a cave.

His hand moved down to her right breast, caressing it, pushing the bikini top aside. She held on to the strap and pulled away. "No, we can't—"

"We can," he said in her ear, licking it with his tongue between words. "I've—taken care of—everything." Repeating his words to herself, she allowed him to release her breast and lick it, his chocolate scalp over her raspberry nipple, licking and sucking.

The drive back to Largo went slowly, Sarah tingling in her wet bathing suit and shorts like she hadn't for a while, still agonizing about her decision to invite him back to her room, wondering if Roper and Sonja would be okay with it, thinking of Janet, wanting him and yet afraid. At the wheel, Danny started talking about her work, his voice calm like they weren't midway between foreplay and intercourse.

"I notice you're still painting little panes." He looked at her sideways, a smile playing around his lips.

"I'll get up to six inches next week," she said, and he burst out laughing. "I mean—"

"It's okay," he said, and reached for her hand, kissing her open palm, still tickled by her joke. He pulled up to a shop with a sign above the door that said *Doctor's Pharmacy,* and she was puzzled when he got out and left her with no explanation. Returning to the car, he held up a small brown bag and grinned.

There was no one around when they got to the house, although noises were coming from the kitchen. She softened her tread going down the stairs to her room. Danny walked behind, the floorboards creaking under his weight. When they reached the small lounge outside her bedroom, he dropped the easel and bag onto an armchair. She went into the bathroom, returning to find him still outside, doing something over the easel box, his back to her.

She wondered if he was going to enter after all, the moment lost, perhaps for the best. The twin beds had been neatly remade by Carthena. Should she push them together? Maybe they wouldn't need them. Then he was behind her, sliding his arms around her waist, the length of his bulky body against her narrow one. She turned and wrapped her arms around his neck. He walked her backward to the bed and, when she felt the bedspread against the back of her knees, she knew that the bed and its size were irrelevant.

"Close the door," she managed to whisper, and he obeyed. He returned to her, his eyes boring into her as he removed his shorts while she did the same, avoiding looking at him, her fingers trembling.

They kept their shirts on—something, she thought later, she'd done as protection. His kisses were vigorous this time, one hand playing with her hair and the other stroking her, all of her, the innards of her, until she moaned for him to stop. He opened the brown bag and deftly put on a condom, his penis browner and larger than any she'd seen. Her mouth got dry as he slid inside her and her heart started beating fast, faster.

He lay on top and carefully entered her, and it started again: the urge to end it, revulsion churning her belly. She wanted him to stop, but it was too late, so she held on to the low wooden headboard, wishing it over, the way she always did, his organic smell like the very earth coming at her through his pores, the bamboo in the ceiling above him making him look like a tropical Pan, half-human, half-animal, with horns coming out of his head, the voice inside her saying, *No, no, no.* She didn't climax, as usual, but he didn't, either.

He got up slowly, his body gleaming and his penis still at attention in the pale brown sheath. She lay on the bed, still wanting him but relieved it was over, watching his muscular buttocks and legs as he walked to the bathroom. She heard the toilet flush and he returned and pulled on his shorts.

"I'm glad you're still painting small," he said, his tone matter-of-fact. He leaned over her half-naked body and kissed her. "You'll be here longer."

"You're barmy," she said to his back.

Later, still moving around in a dazed state, she discovered something he'd placed on top of her bag and easel. It was the single painting he'd been working on all afternoon, not of the falls but of her. He'd portrayed her leaning into her easel, brush poised in the air and hair aflame above it.

getting married, boss."

"Say that again. I couldn't have heard you right."

"I not joking, Beth and me getting married."

Eric pushed away from the table and the stacks of dollar bills in front of him. "You proposed?"

"Nobody propose in Jamaica. The woman just harass the man, and he either leave or give in."

They'd just finished doing the weekly accounts, an afternoon routine performed at the square wooden table in Eric's apartment, the door ajar so they could see arriving customers. It had been another sad week moneywise, the bar's cash flow meandering downhill despite the bump over Christmas, and Shad had decided it would be a good time to change the subject.

"Did you set a date?" The boss's eyebrows made a rooftop over his eyes, the look he wore when he knew he'd lost his case.

"I think she set the day in July, July twenty-something. I can't remember."

"This year?" Shad nodded, and Eric gave a deep sigh.

"It keep peace in the house."

"Where's the reception?"

"We was hoping we could have it here, in the bar." Eric

blinked, like he was weighing the cost and the effort. "We going to take care of the drinks, food, everything," Shad rushed on, spreading his hands comfortingly. "You don't have to worry about nothing."

"You can afford that?"

"Beth get a work in Port Antonio, say she want to help with the wedding."

"That's a good woman."

"She give me four children, bring them up right. She deserve the best." Shad stood up, straightening his jeans that she'd starched and ironed just like he wanted. "Only thing, though. I want to give her a ring, a diamond ring, you know, a proper ring to go with the wedding band."

"That's going to cost you, man."

"God will provide, yes."

The rings had come to him the night before when he'd climbed into bed. He'd thought of the diamond ring he'd seen on TV that afternoon and he'd realized that, if he was to do the marriage properly, like a man, he'd have to buy Beth an engagement ring. She probably wouldn't fuss if she didn't get one, but all the married women he knew had two rings: a plain band and an engagement ring, even if it only had a small-small diamond.

He'd just served his regulars—Tri, Eli, and Solomon— and just tuned the radio to an uplifting Garnett Silk song, when Danny Caines walked in with a glum face, like somebody had died. The bartender popped a Red Stripe open and placed it in front of the man. He was wearing a black shirt this afternoon, too hot for Largo at five o'clock, and small beads of perspiration were already forming on his forehead.

"I signed the last paper you give me," Shad said. "The one for the next application. It seem like this application business just going on and on. We have plenty more to sign?"

"A few more. After we meet with Horace next—what the—?" A screeching noise was coming from the thatch roof.

"Is just an old croaking lizard." Shad waved. "He live up there."

"A lizard?" Danny said, his eyes fixed on the roof.

"He a regular customer," the bartender said, flashing the grin that gained forgiveness for the bar's inadequacies. "He been living there for years, like he can't dead."

"If he's that old, maybe he's getting ready to—to croak."

"Or drop some doo-doo on you," Shad said, letting out a gleeful yelp.

"Don't even say that, man. A lizard dropping its stuff on me? That's bad luck!" The big man was smiling like he'd forgotten whatever was bothering him when he walked in. After the croaking stopped, the talk about lizards went on with Danny recalling how he used to catch them when he was a boy.

"I like to see them sitting in the sun," Shad said. "I used to creep up on them and just watch them."

"They're beautiful," Danny agreed. "Come to think of it, maybe I should paint one."

"You still painting with the Englishwoman?"

"I love it out there on the beach, just the wind in your ears. We don't talk much, you know. It feels good."

"She look like a nice woman."

"Very nice, no drama. She's kind of low-key, quiet and

deep. She has a beautiful, steady spirit about her. I really like her, but . . ."

"But what?"

The investor pulled back and looked at his hand, flexed the thick brown fingers. "I don't know, man. I've dated a few white women, but to tell you the truth, I never been comfortable with it. America is a real prejudiced place, and I been burned a few times—shit, a lot of times, from high school on. If you're a black man trying to do business in America, you have to keep figuring out how to survive around white people, so when I'm kicking back I don't really want to be around whites that much. I was married to a Dominican woman last time, and I always think that if I marry again, it would be to another black woman, I just haven't had any luck with one yet. But Sarah's good people, good people, and I like her a lot. She's good for me, I can feel it, but I still don't know, man."

Shad pulled up his jeans and settled on his stool. "Pshaw, man, you talking about America. In Jamaica, we don't notice things like that. If you get along with her, then that important, not what color her eyes or her hair or her skin is. When you talking about relationships, it's about what's *inside* the person, not what's outside. You can't make a little thing like the color of a woman's skin stop you from loving her. God create us all, right? He create her and he create you."

Danny shrugged. "I'm not used to thinking like that."

"Maybe is time to think about it like that, then."

Shad rubbed a cloth over the counter, rubbed his way to the end of the counter and back. "You know," he began, examining the cotton rag as he hung it over a nail, "not every

woman nice like—Sarah she name, right?—like Sarah.
Some women just plain wicked, let me tell you."

"What you talking about?"

"Who you think I talking about? I talking about Janet.
You think she going to let go of you so easy?"

"It's none of her business—"

"Trust me, star, to a woman like Janet, your business is
her business."

"I told her already, I want to slow down. She knows it."

"When you told her?"

"Three nights ago. We had a talk and I told her I wanted
to take it easy. I told her the truth, man."

"What kind of truth?"

Danny glanced up at the thatch. "That I wasn't here to
start anything, you know, didn't want to get committed."

"How she take it?"

"She was cool."

"You heard from her since?"

"Not till this morning. She left a message to meet her
here, said she wanted to show me something."

"I don't like how that sound," Shad said, and put both
elbows on the counter, looking Caines in the eye. "If there
is one thing I know something about is women. My grandmother teach me. Two things she believe in: God and me.
Even though she call me a *worthless no-good* when I went to
the Pen, she make sure to get me a work with Job when I
come back to Largo the next year. She never give up on me.
That is how it stay with women. Once they set their eyes on
something, nothing going to stand in their way. They like
a dog with a bone, and you is the bone."

Danny pulled at his shirt collar, chuckling. "I can take

care of myself, man, don't worry. I'm twice her size, remember?"

At the back of the restaurant, high heels clipped on the concrete floor. Janet was wearing the bright smile she'd been wearing for the last few weeks, but it now looked pasted in place.

"*Yes,* man," Shad said, pushing away from the counter. "We used to catch lizards and put them in a glass jar, and Granny used to make us throw them back outside."

Danny didn't turn around, and his shoulder muscles had bunched up a little higher. The men continued their conversation, chuckling about how the reptiles' tails would fall off when you caught them wrong.

"You talking about lizards?" Janet said, climbing onto the stool next to Danny and plopping her bag on another stool. "I hate them. I don't know how you can even touch them." She shivered and squeezed her breasts together.

"There's one right above you," Danny said with a toss of his head.

"Oh, God," Janet squealed, and looked up in horror.

"We was just saying that he sound like he getting ready to do something," Shad commented, and the woman made a face.

"You finished your drink?" she said to Danny.

"Just about." The investor took a last sip and looked at Shad as he set down the bottle.

"Marvin waiting in his taxi for us at Miss Mac's."

"I can drive, I still have the car," Danny said, straightening his shirt.

"No, man, let Marvin drive us. Like how is a nice afternoon, we can just relax."

"Where you going?" Shad asked.

"Somewhere you don't need to know," Janet answered. She picked up her bag and jumped off the stool.

"I can't be gone long," Danny said, standing slowly. "I have stuff to do."

She slid her hand through his arm. "Pshaw, man, we not going long." They left the bar, Danny walking fast and Janet, reaching only to his shoulder, trying to keep up, two steps to his one, in her red stilettos.

Shad watched them disappear around the corner. On the radio behind him, the words of one of Sly and Robbie's classics started pouring through the bar, a song that kept repeating the chorus, *Murder she wrote.*

CHAPTER TWENTY-FOUR

A s soon as Eric opened his eyes he remembered it was his parents' wedding anniversary, a day anything but warm and fuzzy all his years growing up. Old as he was now, he still groaned when it came around. The very date was scarred by the annual rage of his mother because his father was absent again, marked by the exchanged grimace with his brother, David, when the quarreling started in the kitchen that night. When he was nine, the family had moved to the suburbs, and Eric had hoped it would lead to a middle-class truce between his parents. But apart from the slightly larger house and a new school, the only change to the family had been an address closer to the printer where his father worked the old Heidelberg press, and closer to his father's favorite pub.

"There was a bar in our neighborhood with your name," Eric had said to Danny Caines soon after he met him. "The Danny Boy, a little place in Shaker Heights." Caines had smiled absently while he punched numbers into a calculator.

The anniversary didn't go well from the outset. After a breakfast of cereal with milk starting to sour, Eric discovered that the Jeep's key was missing. To make matters worse, it was a Saturday and Shad wouldn't be coming in until later and couldn't help him with the search. There was only one key to the Jeep and, since only he and his bartender drove the vehicle, sharing the key was seldom a problem. When not in use, it hung on a nail outside Eric's apartment door.

After searching his apartment and the kitchen without results, Eric looked at the rusting Jeep sitting in the parking lot. Nothing came to mind about the location of the key. He'd never thought of himself as forgetful, but here it was, a reminder he could do without, that his memory was going. The platinum-white hair, the wrinkling of facial skin (looking more sinister every year under his bathroom light), were evidence of advancing age that he tried to ignore, but to have events disappear from his memory, that he found reprehensible.

"Just shoot me when I start forgetting stuff," he'd said on more than one occasion to Arnie across from his desk long, long ago.

He returned to the kitchen and poured himself another cup of coffee. If he calmed down, he decided, the key's location would come back. Sitting at his usual table, sipping his coffee, feeling the morning breeze springing up, watching it ruffle the leaves of the almond tree on the island, all that came to him was a feeling of apprehension about what was ahead.

"Morning!" Danny walked in from behind, startling him.

"Morning," Eric answered. He wiped a few drops of coffee from his leg and licked his finger. "Coffee?"

"I'm good." The investor pulled out the chair beside

Eric and sat down. He seemed quiet, thoughtful even, a change that had been coming on since his first exuberant days in Largo.

"Had a good Friday night?"

"An interesting night, you could say."

Eric shot a glance at his companion, hoping he would lighten things up with a joke, but the man was looking at his fingernails now, his face stern.

"You ready?" Danny said suddenly.

"We have to use your car, though."

"No problem," the younger man said, standing, pushing the chair in, anxious to be gone. Eric jumped to his feet and they walked to Miss Mac's driveway, where the rental car was parked.

The morning's agenda was to drive to nearby locations researching the competition, the other small hotels on the northeastern shore. The first stop was a hotel in Port Maria. Danny pulled up on the side of the road and they sat in the car and eyeballed the Spanish-style mansion with its sagging shingle roof and overgrown garden.

"The guests have to cross the main road to get to the beach," Eric pointed out.

"And the beach is full of seaweed."

"The owners, nice people, have been struggling for years."

"Why?"

Eric slung his arm out the window. "Probably poor marketing, I don't know. Never seems to have a lot of guests, from what I can see."

"That's our problem right there."

"My place was pretty full."

"Yeah, but you didn't make any money."

"If there'd been a few more rooms, like the new place—"

Danny shook his head, still staring at the stucco building. "I don't know. It'll take a lot of promotion, much more than we budgeted."

"You're right," Eric said, and sighed, excuses exhausted. It was make-or-break time for Danny and the project, he knew. He, too, had almost reached the point of throwing up his hands and saying it wasn't worth it—the budgeting, the applications, the upcoming Parish Council committees—with no profit guaranteed. Owning and operating a new hotel was going to be a bitch. Even running the bar had become a balancing act he'd tried to block out, and he was tired, plain tired of it all. He'd lain in bed the night before and figured that, as deep in the hole as his overdraft was, if he sold the bar, he could pay off the debt and start again, living out his life on his Social Security check in Miss Mac's boardinghouse.

They drove into Port Antonio, Eric directing Danny to a hotel on top of a knoll. Four two-story buildings surrounded a grassy central area, a parking lot to one side. The men got out and stood looking down at the circular harbor below, where three sailboats lay at anchor.

"Great view, eh?" Eric said.

"Amazing," Danny agreed, pivoting on his heel to look at the activity behind them. Two tennis courts and a swimming pool were abuzz with visitors with varying degrees of sunburn, lying, talking, swinging rackets.

"Somebody's making money here," Danny commented. "What's different about this place?"

"It's a little bigger than the last one, twenty-five units,

all town house–style. The owners sold off half the units while they were building, sold them as condominiums. The corporation collects monthly fees, manages the condos, and rents them out when the owners aren't in them. Then they rent the rest in a hotel operation."

"I like that," Danny said, rubbing his chin with his hand. "It'll give us cash flow at the beginning, makes a whole lot of sense." He liked it a lot, and all the way down the hill and winding back along the coast road, he talked of selling some of the units in the new hotel prior to construction.

"My mother and her girlfriends would love that. I know about five people right off who would buy. I could keep one and my mom could come down and relax. She needs to stop working so hard, anyway. She would love it here, it would remind her of St. Croix, and I could get Cameron to sell off the rest, what you think?"

While Danny was driving in half reverie, Eric started thinking about his own parents and how they'd never visited Jamaica after he moved down. Granted, they'd been older than Danny's mother, but they'd never come, never wanted to come. On further thought, he hadn't extended a genuine invitation for them to come down. It was too late, of course, with them in the ground all these years. His reverie continued aloud when he called Simone later.

"I'm feeling guilty," he said. "But all I can remember about my folks is the bickering, and I didn't want it in my space. I didn't want them bringing it to the hotel. They always seemed so angry, you know."

"I hear you," she said, sighing. "I always thought it was my mother's bitterness that drove my father to drink."

"I went back for the funerals, but—"

"Stop beating yourself up about it."

"Easier said than done."

"They're dead now and it's over." She had on her wise-woman smile, he could hear it. "Maybe in your next life you can fix it."

"Shit! Don't tell me I'd have to come back with them two." He groaned and she chuckled.

"You didn't turn out so bad. Anyway, change of subject. Have things improved down there?"

"Danny was close to pulling out of the deal, I could tell, but today I took him to see a place that's making money, and he got really excited. I think he's back in the saddle."

As he slipped off his shorts to get into bed that night, Eric thought about how quickly some things could change—like people's minds, and worries about senility (with the finding of the car key under a notebook)—and how other things stayed the same, like bad memories from childhood.

"Happy anniversary, yer Irish bastards," he murmured into the pillow, certain they were still fighting, wherever they were.

CHAPTER TWENTY-FIVE

D rink?" Roper asked, his hand resting on a crystal decanter, the silver tag around its neck declaring it whiskey.

"Thanks." Danny nodded from the antique chaise lounge he'd perched on. His skin blended into the chaise's mahogany arm, Sarah noticed. He was looking especially handsome tonight, with a pale yellow shirt and matching handkerchief in the pocket. She was glad she'd covered the roots of her hair with a dye she'd found in Port Antonio, and she was glad she'd been bold enough to ask Sonja if she could invite him over.

"Sure," Sonja had said right away. "Do you think he'd like lamb?"

Her hope was that her hosts would like Danny enough to make him a regular guest at the house and she wouldn't have to sneak him downstairs anymore.

Over dinner later, Sonja and Roper got into a discussion about a scandalous memoir that a musician had written about his family, and Ford and the couple argued about whether artists should cross over between genres or stick to their own. Their voices got louder while Danny struggled to cut his lamb chop with his fork.

"Maybe if you use your knife," Sarah said under her breath.

His eyes sought Sarah's. "No American style, huh?" He switched his fork to his left hand to pick up the knife and sawed away at the lamb.

The ease with which the residents of the house had eaten and chatted on previous evenings had evaporated tonight and an awkward formality had replaced it. Roper was argumentative, Ford distant, and Sonja off balance. After the debate died down, they ate dessert with the hum of the overhead fan keeping them company, but the tension seemed to lessen when they moved to the deck for brandy.

"How many businesses do you have now?" Sonja asked Danny.

"It depends what you mean," Danny answered. "I have a few malls and—"

"And you started with—" Roper said, handing him a brandy snifter.

"Beauty salons."

"Interesting," Roper said. He sat down and threw one arm over the back of his chair. "You must have been pretty young when you started."

"My mother was a beautician and I ran errands for her, then managed the place."

"You didn't go to college?"

"No time and no money," Danny said with a sad smile. "Had to hit the ground running."

Sonja raised her glass. "Let's have a toast to hard work and the hotel. Heaven knows we need it."

"Money all round!" Roper added, sounding a little tipsy

193

already, and they all raised their glasses and toasted the new venture.

"You come from St. Croix, I understand," Sonja said.

"Yes, I come from a town called Frederiksted."

"How big is the island, anyway?" Ford asked.

"Twenty, thirty miles, I forget," Danny answered.

Roper frowned. "That's tiny."

"You were quite young when you left," Sonja commented.

"Yes, but I went back a couple times with my mom in the summer. We stayed with my grandmother, but she lived in the projects, you know, so it was kind of . . ." He was using his hands, pushing them together like crowded furniture. "That's all I remember, how small everything seemed when I went back."

There'd been no tension, none at all, yesterday afternoon when Sarah and Danny had lain intertwined in her room, the beds pushed together and the sheets tangled under them. She'd been relishing the security of his thick arms around her, when Danny rubbed her cheek with his thumb.

"Why you holding back?" he'd asked.

"What d'you mean?"

"I can tell you want to have sex, but it's like you're holding your breath, and you keep your eyes shut tight the whole time."

"Doesn't everyone?"

"Not the way you do it, like you want to get it over with."

"I'm fine, I'm fine."

"You not enjoying it, though."

She'd sighed, hating to sound like a woman lamenting.

"It's always been that way, something I've learned to live with."

"What's going through your head when you have sex? Talk to me."

"I want to have sex, like you said. I do, I swear it." She'd pushed back her hair and looked up at him. "Believe me, there's nothing I want more. But when we start, it's like the brakes go on. I get this—a kind of panic attack, and my heart starts racing. I can't explain it." She stroked his arm. "Let's not concentrate on me. I want you to enjoy it. I want you to go for it and not wait for me."

"Is that how it was with your last boyfriend? You told him to *go for it*?"

"John? He got used to it. I haven't had many boyfriends, by the way. My roommate thinks I'm a bit weird."

"I'm not going to get used to it, trust me."

"I understand, really, I do. We don't—"

"I have an idea." He'd pulled back to look at her, his eyes now serious and dark. "Let's stop having sex for a while. Let's just spend time with each other, get to know each other better. Maybe we rushed things too much. From now on, we just going to take it nice and easy."

"You are the sweetest man." She'd given him a kiss, holding his bald head between both hands, and she'd felt him getting hard against her leg, but they'd dozed off together for a half hour before he left.

More relaxed by the brandy, Danny took control of the conversation, talking about boutique hotels and condominium hotels. Roper answered his questions, saying that he'd visited all of them and giving his opinions of each. When that topic was exhausted, Sonja asked about his family.

"My father was from Grenada and my mother from St. Croix," Danny said, shrugging. "They never married. My father went to New York before I was born and my mother came to the States as a maid and brought me up there." He dabbed at his scalp with the yellow handkerchief.

"Your father—" Roper started.

"My father was a character, I'm telling you. He was a sailor, worked on ships going up and down from New York to the Caribbean. He couldn't settle down, not in one place, and not with one woman, not my father!" His parents' indiscretions appeared to amuse him, if anything.

Soon after, he thanked his hosts, and Sarah walked him to the door. "You want to take a swim tomorrow after painting, maybe go to this place I heard of, Boston Beach?" he asked.

"Sounds good."

When she got back to the deck, her housemates were on their second brandies. Judging from their silence, she knew that they'd been talking about Danny or her or both.

"Friendly chappie," Roper said after a minute, the words thick with scotch and wine and brandy.

"A good business head," Ford said.

"I'm glad you approve," Sarah said, and took a sip.

"Just what Eric needs," Sonja added. "A man who looks at the bottom line."

"I'm sure he looks at the bottom line," Roper said, wriggling his eyebrows and chuckling.

"Stop talking about the guy behind his back," Sonja protested.

"I'm not talking about him behind his back, not Sarah's back, anyway," Roper declared. "He's a good businessman, but I have to be honest. I—"

"It's none of your business, Roper," Sonja said sternly. "Leave it alone."

"I'm just trying to explain to Sarah, my love, that Danny is not—you know—from her background." He turned to Sarah, fatherly all of a sudden. "I hope you don't plan to have anything long-term with the man, Sarah. He's a nice enough fellow, but a bit too rough around the edges for anything serious. No college education. Mother was a maid, parents not married, father a womanizer. Unstable background, wouldn't you say?"

"Roper—" Sarah started, her throat going dry.

Ford sat up. "I don't think—"

Roper kept going, reasoning it out. "I mean, the apple doesn't fall far from the tree, you know. When we met him, he was dating one woman. Now he's seeing you. He's probably like his father, not ever going to be happy with one woman, I wouldn't think. And he didn't even blink when he talked about his father, did you notice? That's not a good sign to me." Sarah stopped breathing. Unable to speak, she looked at the man she'd started respecting, thought of his multiple paintings of nude women and knew that his talk about fidelity was as much about himself as about Danny.

"You've had too much to drink, Roper," Sonja admonished him. "It's Sarah's friend you're talking about!"

"I'm just stating the facts, sweetheart," Roper answered, one hand waving by way of explanation. "They have very little in common. Sarah is a cultured young woman, her father a physician. She's had a good education, exposure to people in the arts. She'd have to start from scratch and teach him how to hold a knife and fork, how to match his verbs to his subjects, all—all kinds of things." He stopped and scratched his beard. "Not somebody she could take home to mother, is he?"

"I'd rather not—" Sarah started, wanting a civilized end to it, the words *don't make a fuss* colliding with her anger.

Roper ignored her. "I mean, England is the kind of place—"

"You're too damn snobbish, that's your problem, Roper," Sonja interjected. "You forget you're a black man yourself, and we didn't come from a *cultured* British background, neither one of us. We came from slaves, unless you've forgotten. You sound like those brown people who look down their noses at—"

"This has nothing to do with color, Sones, it's about class." Roper shrugged. "The man has no class, pure and simple."

"I think we should change the subject," Ford said, clearing his throat.

Roper ignored him. "I know I sound old-fashioned, Sones, but let's talk the truth here. Danny would be totally out of place with Sarah's lot in England, and I'm sure she'd feel out of place with his friends in—in the Bronx or wherever he's from."

"Roper," Sarah said as calmly as she could, hearing her voice shaking, "I appreciate your opinions, but I'm old enough—"

"You know what I mean, Sarah. Can you see him browsing art galleries or bookstores or a museum? His life and yours are going to be miles apart. I'm just suggesting that you make it a holiday affair, that's what I'm trying to say."

"And maybe you should make it none of your business," his girlfriend responded.

Sarah stood up, knocking over the small table beside the lounge chair and sending her glass flying. She stared at the shattered glass at her feet.

"I'm sorry, but I've had quite enough," she blurted out before fleeing the deck.

CHAPTER TWENTY-SIX

T he diaper bag heavy on his right arm, Joshua heavy on his left, Shad bent down carefully and picked up a stone, feeling the damp spreading under his armpits already. He straightened and pushed his sunglasses farther up his nose with his shoulder.

"Miss Maisie!" he called, banging the stone on the dented number sign on the gate. Shifting Joshua in his miniature blue jeans and sneakers to a more comfortable position, he banged again.

"Who calling?" Maisie emerged onto the porch in a housedress, shielding her eyes from the morning sun.

"Shad, ma'am."

"What happen, son?"

"I have a problem, Miss Maisie. Beth gone to work and she tell me to take the baby to Miss Livingston next door. But Miss Livingston say she get a message from her daughter and she have to meet her in Manchioneal, and she can't take Joshua today."

The old lady contemplated Shad, the squinty eyes in her dark moon face sympathetic as always. "You want me to take him for the day, is that you saying?"

"Yes, ma'am, if you can help us."

"I cleaning the house right now, and with the arthritis it take me a little time, but I can pick him up around eleven."

"I have to go to work, though."

"Carry him to the bar and I come for him."

Back on the main road, Shad headed to work. Two empty taxis roared past, racing one another through the village. Shad yelled after them to slow down, but they were gone in their clouds of dust before he could finish.

"Pshaw, man. They have no respect for decent people walking on the road, nuh?"

Two children passed him in their school uniforms. "Hurry, hurry, teacher going to vex with you," he said irritably, and the children started running.

A little farther ahead under a bush, a mother hen and her three chicks were clucking around in the sun-speckled dirt. "You see that?" he said to Joshua. "That is how it supposed to be. The mother chicken stay with the baby chickens until they can take care of themselves."

In answer, Joshua reached for his father's sunglasses, trying to pull them off, and Shad drew back. "Whoa, star, don't touch the shades."

Behind them, a car came to a stop. "Need a ride?" the driver called.

"Yeah, man," Shad replied, and Danny leaned over to open the car door. After climbing in, Shad sat the baby on his lap and pulled the seat belt around them. The new smell of the Toyota blanketed him, the best smell a man could surround himself with, in Shad's opinion. Cameron, the real estate guy, had rented a Mitsubishi, but it smelled the same, the newness of both reminding of a better world.

"Going straight to work?" Danny inquired, accelerating back onto the road.

"Yes, and I have to carry Josh with me this morning. His mother gone to work and the lady who take care of him can't do it this morning." Shad gazed at the familiar houses passing his window and gave a snort. "I tell his mother this was going to happen, but she don't want to listen."

"That's how it goes with kids, I guess."

"You have any children?"

"Never had time for it. I was talking to Sarah about that yesterday. I love how on Sundays you see all these cute kids going to church here, all the little girls in their frilly dresses and the little boys in their shirts and shorts. Reminds me of when I was a boy. You see stuff like that and you wonder if you did the right thing, not having kids."

"It's not too late."

"Maybe not."

"Tell me something," Shad said, ruffling Joshua's thick hair, and the baby looked up at him. "What happen with Janet that afternoon, when the two of you go off in Marvin's taxi?"

Danny said nothing while he parked in Miss Mac's driveway and turned off the ignition. He lowered his sunglasses with one finger, opening his eyes wide. "That's one crazy bitch, man."

Shad released the seat belt and handed the baby his keys to buy time. "What happen?"

His companion threw his head back onto the headrest. "So we get in Marvin's taxi and go off to Oracabessa, and we come to this place, the Hibiscus Inn. You heard of it?" Shad nodded.

"We go into the place," Danny continued, "and Marvin leaves before we can tell him when to come get us, but I figure we can get a taxi back. Janet is hungry, so we have dinner—great view, too." Danny jerked his head up and looked at Shad. "I kept thinking we could use the cliff here for something like that, make it a restaurant with a lookout point, you know.

"Anyway," he said, settling his head back again. "We get finished with dinner, and I'm ready to come home but Janet wants to go next door. There's a little bar there, she says." The storyteller was almost locked in a trance now, reliving the scene. "We go into the place, a dark kind of joint, and there are only a few people there. We dance a little. Two hours later we're still there, the place is getting crowded, and I'm getting nervous. I'd promised my mother to call her at ten and I'm not carrying no cell phone no more since they don't work in Largo, you know. I go to the restroom and I come back and I'm drinking my drink, and it's tasting kind of oily. And I tell Janet the drink is tasting nasty, but she just laughs and says I must be drunk."

Joshua stood up on his father's lap while Danny continued the saga. "She says we can go back next door to Hibiscus, because she's booked a room there—like she's planned the whole damn thing—and she starts to get all romantic, kissing up on me and shit, and I tell her I'm going home. I walk out and stop the first taxi I see. Then Janet comes running out and jumps into the taxi with me, all vexed and going on about how I don't love her no more.

"The taxi is coming back now and it's weaving all over the place, like the driver is drunk, but at least we're heading in the right direction. Then Janet takes a little bottle out of her purse and she sprinkles some of this oil on my hand and she starts to rub it, saying she's giving me a massage. But the oil smells funny, like the drink in the bar, and I tell her I know what she's up to, that it's some kind of black magic she's trying on me, all this oily shit. I know it, because we have it in the Virgin Islands. She starts going on, and the taxi man stops the car in the middle of nowhere and tells us to get out, because he doesn't like no quarrelling in his car. Then Janet opens the door and gets out. I tell her to stop the craziness, just to get back in the car. She starts crying and the taxi man tells me to get out, too, but he's a little guy so I stay right where I am and I tell him not to leave her.

"The whole thing is like out of a movie, man. Janet won't get back in the car. She's saying the only way she's getting back in the taxi is if I promise her I'm not going to break up with her. This time the taxi is driving alongside her while she's walking, walking in them high heels, and the taxi man is cursing all kind of bad words now and saying he's going to drive off and leave her. And it's crazy shit going on, crying and cursing and yelling. So I tell her I'll keep going out with her if she just get back in the car, and she stops crying and asks me to promise, and I promise, and she gets in the car and we come back to Largo."

The beating of Joshua's little fingers on the dashboard filled the Toyota, and Shad gathered the boy's hands, quieting them. "You seen her again?"

Danny shrugged. "I promised her, you know. It's not like she's a bad person—"

"Puss eat your supper then." Shad climbed out of the car and hoisted the baby onto his shoulder. The cat had eaten Danny's supper—and Danny.

CHAPTER TWENTY-SEVEN

Eric examined his new conch-shell path and wandered into the parking lot. His call to Simone had gone to her voice mail and his imagination was running wild, seeing her with someone, a man, no doubt. He looked at the Jeep, his steed of seventeen years, and kicked a nearly bald tire. It would be a waste of gas to drive aimlessly along the coast, but he sure as hell didn't feel like sitting on his verandah, missing her. He'd tried playing around on the laptop, writing her a letter inviting her to the groundbreaking if it happened, but his fingers had gotten confused on the keys and made too many mistakes. Still without an Internet connection, he couldn't send it to her, anyway, so he'd shut off the computer.

"I'm going next door," he called to Shad, who was sweeping out the restaurant.

"Mister Keller?" Miss Mac said when she opened the door. She was in her old housecoat although it was only five o'clock, her head tied with a scarf over bumpy rollers. "You paying me a visit?"

"Is Danny here?"

"No, he gone out."

"I'm paying you a visit, then."

Sun-spotted hands trembling a little, the woman opened a cupboard and took out two cups. "Something on your mind, I know."

Eric threw himself into a chair at the kitchen table. "Just a bit restless."

"Thinking about the hotel—or a woman?" A wrinkly smile played around her lips.

"Let's stick to the hotel. We're taking Horace out tomorrow to see the island, Danny and me."

"Horace told me." She always liked to talk about her son, *in whom she was well pleased,* she liked to say.

Her former boarder rapped his fingers on the tabletop. "I hope he's serious about the deal."

Miss Mac filled a kettle with water and placed it on the stove. "He says he has big plans for the campsite. He sounding serious to me."

"I hope—" Eric started but snipped the thought. Miss Mac might have been his confidante in the past, but she didn't need to know the ups and downs of bringing the hotel deal together with her own son.

"Something bothering you?" she asked.

Eric crossed his legs under the table. "The whole thing of applying for permits and waiting for the Parish Council to schedule meetings and give approvals, it's taking forever."

Miss Mac lifted the whistling kettle off the stove and poured hot water into the cups. After inserting teabags, she placed the cups on the table and sat down. She looked at Eric steadily, her glasses sliding down her nose and catching on one of her moles.

"Patience is a virtue," she said. "Everything in Jamaica

THE SEA GRAPE TREE

takes time, you know that. All these years I waiting on somebody to come along and buy my property, and look how Danny want to buy it now. Pshaw, man, don't worry, everything going to turn out good. You going to have your hotel and I going to sell my house and land, even if Danny don't buy it." She blew on her tea and cackled. "Then I moving into Horace's house before he put me in a nursing home."

Walking back to the bar after his visit, Eric sucked his teeth, a tepid but satisfying version of the gesture. His options were disappearing, one by one. He couldn't keep the bar open the way it was losing money, and now his plan B was out. There'd be no moving into a room at Miss Mac's. She'd be leaving soon, one way or the other—and the boardinghouse would be gone.

A bus passed, filled to the doors with schoolchildren on a rare outing, their faces lit up. A few waved at Eric through the open windows and he waved back. When the dust cleared, he saw a woman walking toward him along the main road, a tall, thin woman with a straw hat, the English artist, Sarah. He waited until she looked up, smiled, and made a sipping gesture, suggesting she should have a drink in the bar.

"Thank you," she called when she was within hearing distance. "I could do with a bit of water."

A few gulps of ginger beer later, the woman leaned back in her chair at Eric's table. She removed her hat, and bright red hair sprang up in its place, startling him for a second.

"You like walking, do you?" the bar owner asked, rubbing his knees. He felt odd being alone with her, the high cheekbones and plump lips unnerving him.

"Yes, but I try to avoid the beach. The sun turns me into a lobster, so I'm stuck with the dust on the road, I suppose."

"How d'you like Largo?"

"The scenery is amazing, isn't it? And the people are nice and warm. But what I find a bit—what surprises me, I guess, is the—the—"

"The poverty?"

"Well, that. But I was more thinking of the people's attitudes, you know. There's a way of thinking about life that I wasn't expecting."

"Like what?"

Sarah pressed her lips together. "Hmmm, let's see if I can describe it." She took another sip and sighed, and he could see that she'd needed this, needed to unburden herself. "I was expecting a certain level of racism, perhaps, black against white, because Jamaica had been a colony. I mean, what would stop them from hating the Brits after all they've been through with slavery and everything? I know I would. But I haven't found that, I've found a real tolerance for white people. But what I've experienced—and I was thinking about this walking along—is a superiority—the way some local people put other people down."

Eric put his feet up on the chair beside him. "You mean the class lines, don't you? You're surprised that black people can discriminate against their own." When she nodded, he lowered his voice and looked around at the few customers. "You know, as one expat to another—I just want to call a spade a spade, no pun intended—one of the hardest things to get used to is the fact that black people can be just as prejudiced as white people. In America we divide people up according to race. You're white, you're black, you're Asian, and so on. That's what we're comfortable with. Most tourists come out here expecting one of two things. Either the same thing that they're used to back home, the same old race prejudices, or the idealistic kind of Bob Marley version of life—peace and love, you know."

He looked at his scaly toes and twiddled them. "But what we have here, the reality, is that class is more important than race in this country. With Jamaicans, if you're from a family that has been educated for generations, whatever the color, where they speak Standard English rather than patois, where they've gone to the best schools and colleges—then you're upper class, or upper-middle at the lowest. It doesn't matter if you don't make a go of your life, as long as you're from an educated family, you're always considered up here." He raised his hand, then dropped it. "The bad news is that if you were born down here, you pretty much always stay down here."

"Can't people work their way up?"

"A few people from the lower classes either have a successful business or get a profession, but that doesn't make them upper class. It takes a few generations for that family to move into the upper classes. That's just the way it is."

"Rather like England, isn't it? Our accent, our origins, our education determine what other people think of us. Until recently, if you were in the trades, in business, you were looked down on. Even today, although things are shifting a bit, if you speak with a rural accent, even if you make a lot of money, you're thought of as rather crass, really."

"A holdover, I suppose."

"Where does race come in here then, or does it?"

"Oh, it comes in." Eric nodded firmly. "Don't worry

about that. You tend to find the lighter-skinned people—
the *brownings,* they call them—higher up the food chain. It's
been that way for a long time. But things have been changing. There are now educated people, high-class people, who
are very dark skinned and in positions of power. It's education and social background that count, ultimately.

Race isn't as important. When it comes to marriage,
a lot of those high-class people, black and brown, marry
white people, so intermarriage isn't a big thing. In fact, for
some people it's rather prestigious to marry a white person,
regardless of their class. There used to be discrimination
against white people during the seventies and eighties, so
I hear, anyway, but that wave has died down and the old
class prejudices have come back. You'll even find black and
brown upper-class people talking against each other sometimes." He flapped his hand. "It's all mixed up, kind of
crazy."

"How do you know all of this?"

"I get to hear all sides."

"What status do *you* have, if you don't mind me asking?"

Eric snorted. "White foreigners automatically fit into
upper-middle or upper class, a throwback from colonial
days, I guess—even more so when you're a big fish in a
little pond."

"I'm not quite sure where I'd fit in," the woman said,
shaking her flaming head. "Not that it matters."

CHAPTER TWENTY-EIGHT

The lone car was taking forever to pass. Later, she would recall it down to the smallest detail, was able to see, hear, and smell everything, to stretch time out and contract it like a rubber band, especially the approach of the car.

Rubbing one sandal against what felt like a mosquito bite on the other leg, Sarah waited to cross the road to Roper's driveway. It wasn't even noon, her watch was saying, but she'd finished painting for the day and packed up, among her accoutrements one of the thirty-six-by-twenty-four-inch sheets. The paper had seemed monstrous when she'd taped it to the board on her easel, but her new determination to get out of Roper's house as quickly as possible had fired her up to make a start on the large painting.

The morning had been heavily overcast, the coconut leaves making an empty, rattling sound in the wind gusts. Unlike itself, the ocean's aquamarines and turquoises had turned a solid mass of gray. Its life force seemed diminished without sunlight. The color of the sea was that of a dying human, she'd reflected while she painted it, ashen like her father in the hospital.

No one had passed on the beach today. No child had

come, finger in mouth, to stare at her or her painting, and what little enthusiasm she'd started with was now gone. She'd awakened that morning determined to get done with her host's challenge. No more dillydallying, she'd told herself. Her naive fascination with Jamaica was gone, helped in part by Roper's behavior and Eric's explanations. It was time to finish the painting and go home to the familiar. But other than a watercolor of a lusterless gray sea and sky four inches wide and six inches long in the middle of the sheet, the paper she'd brought was still largely blank. With a charcoal cloud darkening the air by the second, she'd packed up and trudged to the side of the road.

"Get on with it," Sarah muttered to the approaching vehicle. The car slowed to a crawl, the occupants looking straight at her. She thought about crossing in front of it, but decided against it. She'd already seen drivers racing side by side down the narrow two-lane road, once seen an Ocho Rios taxi drive onto the sidewalk to overtake a car. It was an illogical country this place, a madhouse, and she would wait.

Danny hadn't come today. He hadn't come yesterday either. He'd explained when he dropped her off after their trip to Boston Beach that he had several appointments coming up. The excuses weren't a surprise; she'd been waiting for them.

Things would probably come to a halt, she'd thought, after she admitted to not enjoying sex. Despite his gallant suggestion that they should continue seeing each other but be celibate, despite the dinner on Monday night and their day together on Tuesday, she knew that her sexual phobia, whatever it was, had put a damper on things. He was a virile man, Danny, a man who would want lusty sex with a willing partner, and she didn't blame him. Of course, he wouldn't tell her to her face what the cause of his absence was, because, even if he wasn't schooled in the proper use of cutlery, he was a gentleman, unlike Roper.

If it had only been Danny's pulling away, that would have been one thing, but it was the news he broke while they were paddling around at Boston Beach that had made her flounder, quite literally. He'd started talking about the small hotels he'd visited recently, saying there was one that he'd seen last weekend that he really liked, a hotel on a cliff.

"Did you go with Eric?" she'd asked.

"No, I was with Janet," he'd announced with his usual honesty, sounding nonchalant. She'd let go of his shoulder and for a few seconds couldn't touch the sand below. She'd had to paddle hard to stay afloat in the tossing waves, one wave covering her head and panicking her, while he plunged underwater, preventing further questions.

She still couldn't think of an appropriate comment when he waded ashore behind her, but it was obvious why he'd returned to Janet. While they were toweling off, their backs to each other, he started to say something and stopped, changing it to tell her he had *stuff to do* over the next few days and would be busy.

"You're a free agent," she'd answered.

Last night, sitting alone on her porch in the moonlight, she'd decided, firmly this time, that she was going to stay away from Danny Caines. Not only did her host disapprove of him, which made it difficult to bring him to the house again, but he was quite openly having a relationship with two women at one time, one of them being her, the other woman not to be messed with. It was too much like a telly drama. These kinds of things never happened to her, at least not until now. Her only comfort was that Danny had been honest with her, even if it was to confess his infidelity. Penny would have called him a rotten cheater. Roper would have called him lower class.

Her mind was made up. Despite her email to Penny the week before—the first in weeks—telling her she'd met *an interesting man,* despite her tentative foray into sex and the excitement she felt whenever she saw Danny, it was over. *Fini,* as her mother would have said. The only solution was to paint the bloody painting and get out.

She'd wanted desperately to tell someone, Sonja perhaps, about Janet's tirade in the bathroom. Her decision had been to keep quiet about the incident, but in doing so she'd felt more alone than she'd ever felt, which was saying something, because aloneness had lived with her all her life. Since the bathroom incident, her sense of injustice had grown. Janet, Roper, and now Danny had merged into one alien behemoth and she was trapped, the damn painting blocking her exit.

Since her argument with Roper she'd stayed largely to herself, saying little or nothing at dinner and excusing herself before dessert on the grounds of having gained weight. Sonja was keeping a low profile, spending most of the day in her office, and Ford was rehearsing endlessly, the sounds of his trumpet filling the house, alternating between scales and wails.

The white car drew up alongside and stopped. Two men were inside.

"Yow," the young man in the passenger seat greeted her, his arm raised. He looked to be in his early twenties and he had unusually square lips framed by an even squarer jaw. His hair was cut close to his head and shaped in neat points at the corners. Certain they were asking for directions, Sarah was about to tell them she was a stranger here herself when the man opened the car door and stepped out.

"May I help you?" she asked.

"Your name is Sarah?"

"Yes."

"Then you can help me, yes," the man said, in no hurry. On the other side, the driver got out of the car, both car doors left open, the engine running. Sarah's heart began to pound in her chest and she stepped back.

"You coming with us," the driver said. He was a bigger man, in his thirties, perhaps, his arm muscles swelling the white T-shirt. He wore a thin gold chain around his neck and several gold rings on one hand.

Sarah clutched her easel box between them. "No, thanks, I'm going home." She looked quickly up and down the road but saw nothing, no cars, no people. A feeling of déjà vu sent a shiver down her spine.

"We just giving you a ride," the square-jawed man said, and reached for her arm.

"I don't need a ride," she said, snatching her arm away, standing her ground, taller than the first man, the same height as the second. The younger man grabbed her wrist. She'd been here before, seen a man's hand grabbing her wrist before, felt his fingers chafing her skin.

"We not asking you, we telling you," the driver said in a growly voice, talking as if he was in charge. His eyebrows overhung his eyes, making them almost invisible. "You coming with us."

She looked at the square-jawed man fiercely and tried to pull her wrist free, tried not to look afraid. "Let me go!"

The driver pulled the box and bag out of her hands. The stool he threw down. "Get in the fucking car." He pronounced it *focking,* the brutishness of it never forgotten.

"No!" she said, pulling away, tugging at her arm, feeling the man's grip tighten. She wanted to say they had no right to do this, no right whatsoever, but her voice abandoned her. The younger man dragged her to the back of the car and yanked the door open just as the first raindrops came splattering down.

"Get in," the driver ordered. "Don't make me use the gun."

He walked up close beside her, one hand raised to slap her. "Get in the *raas claat* car."

Square Jaw shoved her into the backseat and her head was forced into a black hood as the smell of sweet, damp earth rose up and filled her nostrils.

CHAPTER TWENTY-NINE

Opening the drawer all the way and lifting his briefs, Shad complained to invisible listeners. "Pshaw, man, the thing just disappear." He patted the bottom of the drawer.

Two minutes later he found what he was looking for—the little plastic bag with his grandmother's grave dirt. Better than any obeah man's oil, his good luck charm went with him everywhere. He tucked the bag deep into his trouser pocket, walked through the living room, and was closing the front door when he heard footsteps coming up the steps.

"Evening, Dadda," Rickia called in a tired voice. She was carrying her books, and the skirt of her school uniform had dirt on it.

"You okay?" Shad said, and reached out to his daughter's arm and its fresh bruise.

"Matthew pushed me down."

"That ignorant boy, he probably just like you. That's what boys do when they like a girl. Tell him if he trouble you again, he have to face me, you hear? What happen to Joella?"

"She gone next door to pick up Joshua."

"Okay, homework time now. No TV, you hear me?"

"Yes, Dadda. Walk good."

Fingering the bag of red soil from the Holy Sepulchre Baptist cemetery, Shad started along the main road to his evening shift. He definitely needed Granny's stubborn faith today, needed to remind himself of her prophesy that he'd be a man of means one day, because that day was looking further and further away, what with Janet upsetting the only man who wanted to put money into Largo. When he'd told Beth the story, she'd shaken her head over the shirt she was ironing. It was pure blackmail, she'd declared, and no good could come out of it.

Changing course, Shad turned down the lane where Janet lived.

"Hold the dog!" he called at the gate. He could see Janet having a beast prowling the yard.

"Who that?" a voice answered from inside the house.

"Me, Shad."

"Shadrack Myers, what you want?" Janet appeared barefooted on the verandah in a half-sewn dress, the seams turned inside out. Chalk marks at the top of the dress hinted at a plunging neckline to come. Without makeup, her face looked shiny and tired, forty-year-old bags under her eyes.

He climbed the stairs and sat down. "I want to talk to you."

Janet put her hands on her hips, the corners of her mouth turned up. "This the first time you ever come to my house since I come here from Port Maria. It must be something serious."

"I want to talk to you about something that concern everybody in Largo, especially you."

Janet crossed her arms. "What you talking about? I don't have no time to waste today."

"I don't even think you know what stupidness you doing."

"Look here, boy, I older than you. Don't tell me what I can do." She spun around to go inside, but turned to face him again. "What you come to tell me, anyway?"

"Sit down."

"The dress have pins."

"Sit down."

After making a face at him, Janet went inside and returned wearing shorts. "I don't even want to hear it, all this *stupidness* you think I doing."

Shad looked at her in silence until she sat down with a pursed mouth and crossed her legs.

"I hear you make Danny promise—" he started.

"Is none of your business."

"You know where this could end up?"

"With me going to America."

"You realize you could kill the whole town with all this scheming to get a green card, and all the obeah you putting on Danny?"

"Is *you* talking stupidness now."

"If he ever find out you put oil-of-whatever on him, you don't think he going to get vex and leave Largo? You know what that mean? He is the *onliest* man who ever interested in building up the town. Nobody else going to want to come down here, to this little hole at the end of the island. And if you get him vex and he gone back to America, you think we getting any hotel?"

The woman stood up and put her hands on her hips. "Just get out my yard, you hear me."

"You just being selfish if you keep running the man down."

"Leave my yard."

"I leaving," Shad said, getting to his feet. "But know this, if the hotel business fall down because of you, the whole town going to be after you. Everybody hoping to get little work and little money from the new hotel, and they going to know that is *you* kill they dreams. You not going to be able to sew nobody's clothes, because everybody going to say is you put obeah on the hotel."

Janet pulled in her bottom lip. "You just jealous. You think I don't know you want to go to America, too?"

"If it go well, I happy for you," Shad called behind him as he jogged down the steps. "But don't come back to my bar if everything mash up. You not welcome no more. No more freeness—like how you never pay your bill—and no place else for you to meet American men in Largo. Remember that!"

He was striding down the main road, still hot from his meeting, when he saw a man sitting on the beach in red trunks, his naked back to the road. Arms resting on his crossed legs, he was perfectly still, staring out to sea like a fisherman's widow.

It was almost sunset and Shad was pouring a drink for Minion when Danny walked into the bar still in the red swimming trunks. He looked angry, sorry, sad, down on his luck, all rolled into one.

"I know you don't want a white rum," Shad commented, waving the rum bottle.

"I came to ask if you could take me to the airport on Monday. I know it's your day off."

Shad rubbed his head. "You leaving?"

"Yeah, time to get back."

"I have to ask the boss for the car, but I sure is okay."

"We need to leave about nine o'clock. Sorry it's so early."

"I never knew you was leaving, though, kind of sudden like."

Danny was all business. "I need to drop the car off in Port Antonio first, so you can follow behind and then drive me to Montego Bay, okay?"

"No problem, man." Shad finished pouring the rum for Minion. He slid it along the counter before turning to Danny. "Drink on the house?"

"I'm kind of sandy and wet—"

"These bar stools made for water, don't worry." The bartender opened the fridge and pulled out a beer. "On the house."

Popping the bottle open, Shad tilted his head at Danny. "Look like a bad day, man."

"Life," Danny said, looking down at his fingers wrapped around the red-and-white label.

"Life rough, yes."

The big man took a swig and licked his lips. "Maybe Jamaica does that to people."

From the end of the counter a call went up from Eli for another rum. Shad filled the order and returned to lean across the counter. "You know what happen, star? Problems follow people to Jamaica, and the country throws them back in their face. You can't run away from yourself, even on an island."

"I don't know where you get your wisdom from, boy, but you make sense."

"How things going with Janet?"

"Same shit, different day. I always seem to attract these kind of women." Shad raised his eyebrows and spread his hands. "That's the shit I brought with me, you mean?" The bartender shrugged, leaving the man with his own words.

Danny wiped his forehead. "I tell you, Janet is like a fucking vine. I can't get rid of her."

"You play with puppy, you catch its fleas."

"The lesson I just learned," Danny said to the beer in his hand. "I should have known better. Forty-five damn years and I don't know to leave the crazy ones alone."

Shad walked to the wall next to the kitchen and snapped on the lights. Stark shadows suddenly appeared, his signal to tune the radio to a song that would make the starkness more tolerable, tonight a song about red-red wine.

"How is the artist lady?" he ventured when he turned to Danny. "You not seeing her no more?"

The man's eyes were dark under the lightbulb, his nose spreading a broad shadow over the lower half of his face. "She left."

"Left? When?"

"This morning. Just packed up and cleared out, didn't tell a soul." Danny dabbed at his scalp with a napkin. "Maybe it's a good thing, I don't know."

Shad frowned and felt for the stool behind him. "What you telling me, she leave Largo and nobody know?"

"She told the maid she was going painting this morning and that's the last anyone has seen of her."

"Who told you?"

"I went by the place where she always paints. It was around lunchtime, around one, when she usually takes a break, but she wasn't there. I figured she was up at the house, so I drove up there. The housekeeper told me Sarah had gone. She said she didn't say a word to anyone, just left when no one was looking."

"But she went to paint, you say. She leave then?"

"Apparently, she went out painting like normal, but at some point in the morning she came back and packed up."

"That sound strange," Shad mused, looking across the darkening bay toward the house on the far end. "She go painting and then come back and pack up, don't sound right. And she didn't say good-bye to nobody?"

"Not even a note."

Offshore, the island was just a silhouette with the red strands of clouds behind it. It was that slippery time between day and night when nothing looked real. "She don't seem like a woman who would do that, just disappear sudden like that. I thought she was a woman with *broughtupsy,* you know, good breeding."

Danny drained his bottle. "Jamaica does funny things to people, man."

"And you don't know *why* she leave? Must be a reason."

It took the man a while to answer. "I have an idea, a couple of ideas, really. She might have left because she felt kind of trapped. Roper paid her plane fare one-way from England. He said he'd pay the other half of the trip when she painted even one large picture. She usually paints these little things," he added, making a square with his thick fingers. "Beautiful things, but always small, but she never painted a big picture the whole time she was here. It was like she couldn't do it. She might have got frustrated and just gave up."

"You want another beer? You have to pay for it this time, though."

Danny nodded. "She said she had a plan, though. She was going to paint bigger and bigger until she got up to a real big painting. Maybe she couldn't do it."

"No apology, no explanation." Shad shook his head and grunted. There was something unnatural about it, a suddenness that didn't suit the woman's personality. "You said you had a couple ideas. You thinking she know you don't like white women?"

"No, I'd gone past that and we were getting along real good. I was doing like you said, just seeing her for who she was inside, a real sweet woman. I was even starting to feel that maybe I'd missed the boat in the past by focusing on the whole color thing with women." A shrug, a boyish gesture on him. "No, I think it was something else."

Shad placed a Red Stripe in front of Danny and waited. There was always another reason, every customer had one.

The American took his time, sipped his beer, took a breath. "I told her I'd gone out with Janet again. She never said nothing when I told her, she didn't even seem upset. But now I'm thinking she was angry and that's why she left."

"That sound more like it," Shad exclaimed. "I knew it! No woman going to leave because of a painting. Women act from their heart, not the head. She was feeling—"

"How much I owe you?"

"Two dollars. You going to call her in England?"

Slapping a couple US dollars on the counter, Danny stood up. "She never gave me her number. See you Monday."

CHAPTER THIRTY

Everything seemed to be coming apart, Eric reflected as he looked at the loafers he'd worn to work many moons back, New York written all over them. The upper leather of both shoes was moldy from sitting in his damp closet, and the soles were separating from the rest of the shoes—a metaphor for his life.

"Mistah Keller," Ras Walker said, tossing his salt-and-pepper dreadlocks back as he bent over the shoes, "I think you have to throw them shoes out. You can't wear them again."

"But I've hardly worn them."

The shoemaker rubbed his polish-blackened finger around the edges of the shoes. "No, man, these shoes finished. Like how you going to be a manager again, with a new hotel and everything, you need nice shoes. You can't be walking around in old shoes or rubber sandals no more. Take my advice, throw them shoes out and buy some new leather ones in Ocho Rios."

Eric took the shoes from the man and stuffed them back in the brown paper bag while Ras Walker bared his large teeth in a smile, two teeth missing unashamedly from the top row. He leaned on the inverted metal boot in front of him. "I glad you come anyway, suh. I meaning to ask you if I could have a shoe-shine stand in the new hotel lobby. Not a big one, you know." He looked off into the distance, his mental image of the stand painted already. "A pretty red, yellow, and green one, with a sign saying *Reggae Boots*. What you think?"

Eric grunted. "I don't know if tourists need that, Ras. They wear sandals the whole time they're on the island."

"But when they go dancing at night, they want to look nice, right, or if they having a wedding or something? And I was thinking I could have a little sandal section if they want to buy sandals."

"You thinking about that from now?"

"I thinking about my nephew Saul. He almost finish school and he going to need a work. He could manage it for me. His mother say she don't want him hanging around in Port Antonio. She afraid he going to get into trouble."

"Let's talk about it when the hotel is further along, Ras. It's going to be a year or two before it's finished."

"So long?"

"Yes, ma-an," Eric said in his pseudopatois. "We still have plenty paperwork left to do, then we start construction. It's going to take a while."

The Rastafarian stroked the metal boot and looked up at the bar owner, his smile fading. "I was speaking to Mistah Delgado the other day. He said it going to take about nine months to build, as long as we don't have no strikes or nothing. I was talking to him about doing little extra work myself during the building time. My father show me how to do little carpentry, you know. Like how times sort of tight, and not much shoemaker work happening now, I was thinking I could make a little money myself."

Eric neatly folded the top of the brown paper bag. "Let's talk about it down the road, okay?"

It was the answer he'd given to at least a dozen Largoites in the last few weeks. There'd been requests for construction jobs, housekeeping jobs, gardening and maintenance jobs. Even Solomon had approached him the week before, wielding a knife and a yellow onion, to ask if he was going to be the chef in the new hotel.

He would be first chef in line for his old job, his employer had informed him. "But you're going to need help," Eric had added. "Twenty rooms means forty meals three times a day, plus staff meals. You think you can handle that?"

"Pshaw, man, that just child play," Solomon had answered, waving the knife. "When I was chef at Three Seasons Hotel in Mo Bay, is three sous chef and four hundred meals a day I have." Ever since the conversation, Solomon had been as cheerful as a dour man could get. He had been coming to work on time, drinking less at the bar in the evenings, and taking fewer days off for his indigestion.

Nothing like a little hope, Eric thought as he drove away from the shoe repair hut. Everyone in Largo was speaking of the future hotel in glowing terms. The idea, floating only mirage-like on their horizon at first, seemed to have drifted into the villagers' consciousness and now become as solid as reality. It had become intertwined with their personal dreams. The place had even been given a name: The New Largo Bay Inn, they were all calling it. Every time Eric heard it, it felt like one more thorn in his side, reminding him that it was all or nothing at this point.

That evening, his son drove the point home again. "What

do you mean the investor . . . waffling?" Joseph asked. He was speaking on a cell phone that kept going in and out.

"He was all gung ho when he first came, really excited. But things haven't been working out." Eric sat down heavily in the kitchen chair. "He's going back to the States."

"What's wrong . . . the financials hold up?" Eric pictured his tall son frowning, the brown curl falling into his eye.

"Your report has held up, no problem."

"Something must have turned him off," Joseph commented dryly.

"It's more expensive than he thought," his father replied, defending himself during three fade-outs, explaining the setbacks, the time it was taking to get approvals from the Parish Council, the added costs. "And then Horace is holding out about installing the infrastructure on the island, so that's kind of up in the air." He sighed and looked out the window. There was a choppy sea today, afternoon glare bouncing off the waves.

"I guess if it's going to work out, it'll work out," Joseph sighed—a different Joseph. His son had never been a fatalist, not that he knew, anyway, but the words could have come right out of someone else's mouth.

"How's Raheem?" Eric asked, trying to sound casual.

"I think he has a job coming up in Bombay."

Eric pictured his son's elegant friend modeling designer clothes in India, a photographer trying to capture the moment, the crowd and the cows getting in the way. "His parents—I know they're Trinidadian-Indian, right?—they must be excited—the mother country and all."

"I'm sure they are." Joseph paused and his voice rose an octave. "Hey, guess what? I got my first client."

It was another pivotal moment for father and son, who'd seen each other rarely since Joseph had turned nine, when Eric's wife had divorced him and moved to Virginia. Joseph's recent trip to Largo to write the business proposal—at his father's urging—had created a shift from their former polite exchanges and, when the thirty-one-year-old delivered a fine report, he had won his father's respect. Eric took a dish from a cupboard while Joseph told of a client hiring him to analyze her agency and write large grant proposals. He recounted the meeting, almost verbatim, and how he'd shown the executive director the proposal he'd written for the new hotel.

"She was impressed, I could tell. I have to thank you for that." Eric spooned rice and peas onto the plate, grateful that his son had something to thank him for at last.

"You did a great job."

"They just called me . . . got the job," Joseph continued, his voice light with happiness.

"Terrific! When do you start?"

"April first."

A sea breeze gusted through the window and Eric pushed his hair out of his face with his bent arm. "You're sure you want to start then, April Fools' Day?" he said, chuckling.

"Dad, you . . . crap like that." Joseph went back to talking about the hotel. "No, seriously, dude, it's got to work," he urged, no longer fatalistic, the boy whose diaper he'd changed in the middle of Central Park, now giving him orders. "You need to get Caines back in that good mood. You don't have anything else to fall back on—"

A click. Eric found himself holding a dead phone and a plate of cold rice and peas. He'd wanted to mention the laptop.

CHAPTER THIRTY-ONE

Sunlight had made its way through the leaves of the tree outside the window and fell in small triangles on the snow-white tiles. An unseen dog made whimpering noises while it scratched its fur. A tap dripped in the bathroom. In the distance a car horn; a few minutes later the sound of a bigger vehicle not far from where she was, the rattling engine fading away.

Sarah lay on her side curled up, her heart still pounding in her throat, her arms wrapped around her legs. It would be about two in the afternoon, maybe three. Yesterday she'd started marking off the days with a pencil and there were two one-inch marks on the wall near the floor beside the bed.

She was hungry but her stomach was tight, her mouth sour. A tray sat on the table beside her. Food had been brought for her again, this time a soup with thick bread, and again she hadn't eaten. When she'd drunk from the tap, the water had tasted metallic, but she'd given in, too thirsty and tired to care.

The room she'd inspected and paced for the last two days was a white bunker, the only furniture being a double bed, a side table, and a plastic chair. A locked wooden door led to the corridor and an open one to the bathroom. On one wall, louver windows, three feet above the floor and six feet long, broke the monotony of the room. Vertical burglar bars covered the windows at four-inch intervals (she'd measured them with her fingers) and were intersected by heart-shaped designs, both ensuring her safety and preventing escape.

It was not a new house. She'd known it from the beginning, the stale smells of food and musty furniture reaching her under the hood when the driver had pulled up to the house—Square Jaw beside her still clutching her wrist. She'd heard the driver getting out of the car and opening a gate. He'd driven about a hundred yards before stopping again. Dragging her out of the car, they'd pulled her up some steps and into a room. Someone pulled the hood off, her head jerking back with the tug, the fabric scratching her cheeks. She was standing in a large room with armchairs arranged along bare walls. Visible through the louver windows was the ocean; the house was on a hill.

A thin, worn man with graying hair had been standing in the room smoking a cigarette and staring at her. He wore a white shirt with long sleeves rolled up to his elbows, and his eyes had ashen circles around them. When he spoke, his voice surprised her.

"Anybody see you?" he'd said, his voice high-pitched and nasal, almost as thin as his body.

"You think I stupid or what?" the driver had answered. They'd hustled her down a corridor with several closed doors. They opened one door and pushed her inside.

"What—what are you going to do to me?" she'd managed to say when they released her.

"Rest yourself," Square Jaw had said. She'd retreated

231

to a corner as they latched the door on the outside. A few minutes later they'd returned with her large suitcase, which they'd thrown down in a corner of the room. She'd stared at it numbly, realizing it must have been in the trunk. The easel box and her painting bags they'd stacked on the folding chair, plopping the large sheets of paper on top. The computer was missing.

Who her captors were and what they wanted she had no clue. They wouldn't answer her questions and she could hardly understand a word they said, even when they spoke as if she were deaf or stupid.

Shortly after Square Jaw and the driver had left her that first day, a woman in a gingham dress had entered the room with a pillow and a pink flowered sheet. Sarah had been standing in a corner of the room hugging her arms, and she'd been startled to see the woman enter as if she were making up a hotel room. While she was tucking in the first corner of the sheet, the woman had said something without looking up and Sarah had stared at her.

"Likkle cocoa-tea?" the woman had repeated, louder, and Sarah had shaken her head, not wanting anything anyone would offer her here.

For a long time after, there'd been no other visitors. She'd finally shuffled to the bed—her hands shaking—where she eventually lay down on her side in the fetal position. The first rational thought she'd had was that someone had entered her room at Roper's uninvited, had pulled her underwear and painting clothes out of the drawers, taken her dresses off their hangers, and packed them up. Everything had been planned in advance, and the men had been waiting for her to leave her painting spot. Her mind kept circling back to Janet and she'd gone through a series of protests, in case the woman appeared and accused her of carousing with Danny.

"I teach him art, that's all," she was going to say. "I haven't even seen him for days."

After it got dark, she didn't switch on the light, but lay in the same position, willing someone, anyone, to come and rescue her. When the door was unlocked and reopened, she'd pretended to sleep until the door closed again.

She hadn't slept that first night, her whole body rigid, waiting for whatever, sure something would happen. It didn't seem right that someone could disappear and be locked up without the police being called. She lay in wait for a siren. Surely, surely, she'd soothed herself, Sonja or Ford would report her missing and the police would come. But there was only the dripping of the bathroom tap. At least once an hour she'd raised her head, listening for cars real or imagined, hearing footsteps coming down the corridor. A door had opened and closed. Someone speaking loudly had passed, the syllables harsh and disjointed.

Just before dawn, a rooster had crowed loudly somewhere. She'd felt her way to the bathroom and turned on the light. While she relieved herself, she looked around the stark, windowless room, even whiter than the bedroom. It had no shower curtain or mirror and only a bar of soap and one thin towel.

She must have fallen asleep after, because she'd awakened to find the old woman bending over her, the round cheeks and stubby mustache making her look like a walrus. She was wearing a striped dress this morning and her breath smelled of coffee.

"Likkle breakfast," she said, a drop of saliva falling on Sarah's arm.

"Where am I?" Sarah had ventured, but the Walrus had only shrugged and left the room.

The day had passed uneventfully, the prisoner waiting for something to happen, wondering why her abductors hadn't come back, refusing to eat again, drinking from the dripping bathroom tap. By afternoon, she couldn't stand her own grime and decided to take a shower, even if the water splattered on the floor. She'd found clean clothes among the mix of things thrust into her suitcase and showered with as little water as possible, looking over her shoulder through the open door, thinking of the movie *Psycho,* which she'd watched with a cousin, and drying off with the pink towel on the rack.

After dressing, she'd taken her first look out the window. To her left was a tree that rose higher than the louvers. About twelve feet in front of her was an expressionless blue wall, separated from the house by dry dirt interspersed with weeds. As tall as a man and running parallel to the house, the solid concrete wall held a sparkling and terrifying detail. Cemented into the top of the wall was a sinister line of broken bottles, the jagged brown and green points translucent in the afternoon light, scoffing at the distant ocean visible above.

She'd turned and walked to the door, the porcelain tiles cool beneath her bare feet, and put her hand on the knob. It turned easily, but a latch prevented it from opening. Peeping between the door frame and the door, she'd seen a shadowy obstruction above the knob, a thick bolt, it looked like. No one appeared to be around, no sound of movement or footsteps.

Imagining who else was in the other rooms along the corridor (residents, captives, other women?), the artist had passed the rest of the afternoon sitting on the bed, first cross-legged, then with her back to the headboard and legs straight, and then on the edge of the bed. She'd drunk water from the noisy tap, made her first scratch on the wall to mark the days. At one point she heard distant noises from what she assumed was the kitchen, the clanking of a pot on a stove, the rattle of china. When the tray was brought in, the woman had removed the last untouched meal and gone away down the corridor, sucking her teeth.

That second night she'd slept fitfully, aware finally of light creeping into the room and the rooster crowing again, over and over. Breakfast had been early that morning. Walrus had been wearing a pale yellow dress with long sleeves and a large hat.

"You haffe eat," she'd declared. She deposited the tray, removing the uneaten meal, and left. What looked like salt fish, ackee, and breadfruit, recalled from breakfast at Roper's house, sat on a white plate, the concoction swimming in oil, forcing Sarah to put the tray in a corner. Shortly after, the still of the house was broken by a church choir singing a cappella, the church perhaps a few hundred yards away. One woman's voice rose above the rest, pleading with God to aid her somehow. Sarah had paced for a while when all was quiet again, then lain down and slept. When she awoke, there was a fresh tray on the bedside table. She was still lying in the fetal position when the latch was slammed open.

"You have money on you?" It was the driver, asking the question even before he got into the room. He stopped just inside the door and left it open. The corridor behind him was empty. Sarah sat up on her elbow, her heart jumping to her throat. Driver leaned on one leg. He had a scar that ran from the front of his ear down to his throat, unnoticed before.

"You deaf or what? I said, mon-*ey*."

She tried to swallow. "I don't—a hundred, maybe, a hundred and fifty American dollars."

"I going to need it to buy food for you. The boss don't pay us yet."

Sarah stood up, steadying herself on the bed. "In my wallet, but I don't think—"

The driver opened his mouth—about to curse again, she could tell—and she ran for her handbag and handed it over.

"You—you can't keep me locked up," she blurted out as he rifled through her wallet. "It's against the law."

The man's wide mouth slackened and one side pulled up in amusement. "Is foolishness you talking. You don't see where you are? *You lock up,* you can't get out." He waved toward the window. "You see any police coming for you? *Blood claat,*" he said, after he'd withdrawn the money, "only eighty dollars."

"Why am I here?" she pleaded. "You can't just kidnap me like this."

"You think anybody care?"

Tears bubbled up inside. She sank with them to the floor, determined not to cry. "I haven't done anything wrong, believe me. Somebody has made a mistake. Please let me go, please, please. I haven't done anything, I swear to you."

"Get up!" the man barked.

Walking on her knees, Sarah approached the man holding out her hand. "I'll do anything you want, anything," she pleaded. "Just let me go, I beg you."

"Anything?" he asked, and threw the bag on the bed.

"Anything, whatever you want."

"Cook my food, wash my drawers?" He snickered, enjoying his own wit.

"Anything, but please, please let me go."

"I love it, Englishwoman on the floor begging me." A sudden frown brought his eyebrows low over his eyes. "You ever see my trial? Nothing I can't stand more than a begging woman." He slapped her outstretched hand away.

"I promise you, I won't tell them anything. I won't tell them what you look like or what the house is like. I'll pretend that I don't remember."

They stared at each other, not moving, she not daring to breathe, outside the window only the sound of a scratching dog.

CHAPTER THIRTY-TWO

J ust a couple hours to Montego Bay now," Shad said, shifting down and glancing at his passenger. Danny was staring out the window, his big hand on the side mirror. He was somewhere else, Shad could tell—back in New York, perhaps—not seeing the inverted canoes and rocky beach passing the vehicle. "Your mother going to be glad to see you, man."

"Yeah."

"You really want to go home, though?" It was worth pushing the American a little before depositing him at the airport.

Danny looked straight ahead. "Back to reality, you know."

"But Jamaica sweet, man. Every tourist who come here say they don't want to go home. You going to see for yourself when we open the hotel. Two drinks at the bar and they start planning how they going to move down here. And when they leave, they always say they coming back."

"I don't even know if I'm coming back, man."

Shad opened his eyes wide, wanting the man to see, if not feel, his disappointment. "What you saying, that you not going to build the hotel again?"

The man shrugged. "Maybe, maybe not."

"But you like Largo, though?"

"What's not to like?"

"So is what?"

Shaking his head, Danny sighed and hit the mirror. "Things just seem so—kind of crazy. I don't like to do business when things don't go smoothly, and nothing has gone right with this hotel. Horace has been like a mule from the get-go. Then the government red tape is never ending. The cost of everything seem to go up every time we discuss any changes. And even if we get through all of that, Lambert was telling me that strikes during construction happen sometimes. That's more money. I'm superstitious. If things don't happen like that," he said, sweeping a flat hand above the dashboard, "then they're going to be sticky all the way."

"But that's how it always happen in Jamaica, star. If you want to succeed here, you have to hang on until everything go like that." He imitated Danny's sweeping hand.

"I don't know, man. I'm not feeling it."

"I think you hurt because your painting teacher gone, too."

His passenger turned away, gave his distraction to Port Maria's parish church, the stone walls holding two hundred years of secrets. "I—yeah, I don't know. It was kind of weird, how she just left and didn't say nothing."

Shad shook his head. "She was so polite, she don't seem like a person who would just disappear." He shifted to a lower gear. "If you like her, you should call her when you get to America."

"Like I told you, I don't have—"

"Can't you just look her up on the computer? I hear you

can look up everybody on the computer, so my daughter says."

"I guess I could."

"Yeah, man, every woman like a man to go after her—if she like him. And I think she like you. She used to follow you with her eyes, and when you talking she would nod her head, like everything you say was important to her."

Danny tucked his chin in. "You think so?"

"I'm telling you, the woman like you." Ahead of them, a donkey cart full of breadfruit slowed them down. After two cars rushed by, Shad overtook the cart, waving to the old man sitting up front with a switch.

"You see that man?" Shad tilted his head back at the cart as he sped up. "He always riding up and down this road. He don't have no Jeep to take his breadfruit to town, but all these years he using that cart and that donkey. And sometimes the donkey get sick, and sometimes the cart wheel come off, but all these years he making his little money and feeding his family. And now his youngest son getting ready to go to school in Kingston to be an accountant, so he tell me in the market. That is how everything in life go. You don't think so? Slow and steady. You do what you have to do to keep going, work through the hard times."

The small man's voice rose a notch. "You understand what I saying, Danny? You can't just give up. Whether it a love thing or a business thing, success don't come quick, it take time and effort. Then you get little *experience* under your belt and you gone clear, that what I tell my children. Sometimes you don't succeed right away, but you have to keep trying, man."

It felt odd giving this strapping man advice, a man older

than him who owned malls in New York, but Danny's eyes were swiveling between the passing scenery and the speaker as if he was listening. Shad kept coming back to the subject for the rest of the journey. This was his last shot, he knew, his last opportunity to let Danny know he held the village's dreams in his hands. Better that he do his preaching, like he used to do in Kingston Pen after he'd gotten so riddled with guilt that he couldn't help it—preaching to the other young men who couldn't wait to get back on the streets—than do nothing and regret it for years to come. The worst that could happen was that Danny wouldn't come back and then it wouldn't matter if he agreed or not.

Turning into the road to the airport, Shad glanced at Danny. "Think about it, star, just hoping that the hotel coming is keeping a whole lot of people alive."

"I'll think about it, bro, but don't hold your breath."

Shad screeched to a halt at the check-in, off-loaded Danny's suitcase, fist-bumped and hugged him, praying for his return.

"He going to think about it," he assured Miss Mac later.

"That's good," she said, examining a book he'd picked up for her in Port Antonio. "I have to sell this house, man. I getting tired of fixing this and fixing that."

"What you need to fix now?" Shad pulled out a chair and sat down.

Miss Mac pointed upward. "The roof leaking in the bathroom and I always have to put a bucket in there. A guest shouldn't have to use a toilet next to a bucket, you know? It not civilized."

"Good thing Danny didn't come in rainy season." Shad laughed.

"But rainy season coming next month, and I need a new roof. Is plenty money to do it, but I don't have it. I trying to hold out until I can sell the place."

Shad promised to come back with his friend Frank to take a look.

"You always take care of me, eh?" The old lady nodded. She cut into the coconut cake on the counter and placed a slice in front of her visitor. "I hope all the reading and signing not in vain and that the hotel going to get built, because if it don't, I going to have to move to Horace's house and leave this house empty. Next thing, some squatter going to come and live in it. They did that with the Franklins' house in Manchioneal and squatters burn down the house. My father would roll over in his grave if that happen to my house."

"You know what I thinking, Miss Mac?" Shad mumbled through cake. "I thinking that if Danny don't want to invest in a hotel here, there must be other people with money who interested. We have a beautiful beach, nice scenery, good people. What you think?"

Miss Mac sat down with her own slice of cake. "Maybe Danny was not the person. You could be right."

"Why you say so?"

"I don't know." The old lady sighed. "I not supposed to talk my guests' business."

"Whatever you thinking, you should speak it now, before it too late. Beth always say it not good for a woman to keep something on her chest. I don't know what would happen if she keep it on her chest, because every woman I know speak they mind."

Miss Mac munched on her cake. "I didn't like the kind

of people Danny was dealing with, you know? He bring that *facety* woman here, Janet, and she act like she better than me. I mean to say, she come in my house and ask me if I don't have anything to drink. You ever hear anything like that? I tell her if she want to buy a drink she can go next door to the bar. Then she look at me with her eye kind of funny, and since that day she walk straight past me in my own house and don't even say a good evening. She walking into *my* house, making noise in *my* bed in Danny's room, acting like she own the house. You ever hear such a thing?" The home owner dabbed at her mouth with a napkin in disbelief.

Shad scraped the last crumb of grated coconut off the plate and licked the fork. There was nothing to be said about Janet. Everybody knew she was a woman with no shame at all.

Meredith MacKenzie looked up to the ceiling. "And then there was those two men who came to see him couple weeks back. Remember, the big man with the cross and his brother? They didn't talk much and they say they prefer to wait outside on the verandah for Danny. What business they have with him? I don't know, even though I want to sell the property, maybe is a good thing he gone, yes."

CHAPTER THIRTY-THREE

Eric plodded up the steep driveway, his breath getting short, perspiration breaking out on his upper lip. There'd been a time eight years ago when he'd fought winds of 180 miles an hour to climb this hill, with no thought about whether he would make it or not. But he felt like he'd aged thirty years in the last decade. Running up mountains was for men like Joseph and Danny now, men who didn't have paunches and didn't smoke pipes.

"You look like you need a lemonade," Jennifer called from the verandah as he approached. She was holding a frosty glass in her hand, the white shorts a perfect contrast to her tan.

"And you look like a nurse to the dying," Eric answered, climbing the steps. He'd always liked Jennifer and he'd always been envious of Lambert for having a shapely, young wife from Florida who'd taken to upper-class life in Jamaica like she'd been born to it.

She pulled a rocking chair forward. "You better cool down a few minutes, boy. I don't want you having a heart attack on my porch."

Eric threw himself into the chair. "God, every time I climb this hill it gets steeper."

"I've been telling you, if you'd go to the gym in Port Antonio . . ."

Eric took a slurp of lemonade. "And I've been telling you, it'll be a cold day in hell before I do." They smiled at each other, two refugees from the north.

Jennifer's blond hair blew across her face in the light breeze and she shook it back into place. There was a confident elegance to the simplest thing she did, a clear understanding of what was right at a particular moment in time. She lowered to a chair beside him, her thigh muscles getting taut.

"Roast beef sandwiches and salad—that good enough for you?"

"Of course." Eric glanced over his shoulder toward the living room, needing to look away. "Where's Lambert?"

"He'll be home soon. He called from the site to say you were coming and I was to have lunch ready for you. Miss Bertha's getting it ready."

"I heard your mother wasn't doing so well. Sorry about that."

"She's stabilized now, so I thought I'd come back for a couple weeks," Jennifer said, her voice softening. "Keep the home fires burning, you know?"

"Good idea, although I'd make sure that Lambert—"

"Uncle Eric!" A small boy barreled out of the house and threw himself at Eric's knees.

"Little Wayne, my man!" Eric hugged the child's head and shoulders. "You're getting so tall, we're going to have to ship you off to school soon."

"School, school!" The boy looked up at him, nodding hard, his face shining.

Jennifer reached over and rubbed her son's wavy black hair. "He keeps asking if he can go to boarding school with Casey. Isn't that right, son? You want to go to school with your big sister?" She straightened Wayne's shirt. "You're going to school in Port Antonio this fall, sweetie. Remember the one we visited, the school with all the kids?"

Lambert's Range Rover roared up the driveway, a trail of brown smoke in its rear. After parking in front of the steps, the contractor climbed out.

"When are you going to stop polluting the place?" Eric yelled, fanning the air.

"When you find me something cheaper than diesel fuel," Lambert replied. He mounted the steps and kissed his wife's upturned mouth. Little Wayne raised his arms and his father scooped him up and held him above his head so the child could touch the sloping ceiling.

"A few more of those lifts and you'll be flying up to the States for a rotator cuff operation, boy." Eric chuckled. "Don't you know that old men shouldn't be—"

"The only old man around here is you, my man," Lambert said, swinging his son to the ground.

"Okay, you two, time for lunch." Jennifer stood up and led the way inside. "And you, Mr. Wayne, are going to have lunch with Miss Bertha in the kitchen. Daddy and Mommy are going to eat with Uncle Eric in the dining room."

Throughout lunch, the conversation stayed local. Jennifer mentioned the unannounced departure of Roper's guest, the Englishwoman. She seemed upset about something, Sonja had said. Lambert talked about the impact of the new government on the village, only the main road paved before the elections.

This felt like home to Eric: the easy chatter with people who cared about him, the well-decorated rooms with their soft chairs and tasteful paintings, the leisurely lunch served on good china. It was almost as if his daily existence among bare walls and cheap furniture was a temporary one, and this was his reality. While Lambert was talking about the plans for a new open-air market in the square, Eric realized that he could never have made it in the years since the hurricane without these two people, even if that help brought with it Jennifer's ongoing curiosity about his personal life.

"How's Joseph?" she inquired after they'd sat down in the living room for coffee. She lifted the silver coffeepot, biting her lip with the weight of it.

"Just got a big consulting contract, he tells me." His son was back on track, he wanted to say, and he was in touch with him now, like any good parent.

"And Simone?" she ventured, her eyes fixed on the coffeepot in her hand. "Is she coming back soon?"

Vintage Jennifer, Eric thought, watching the woman's elaborate Indian-style earrings splicing through the strands of her hair as she passed a cup to her husband. There were times, usually late at night when he sat alone on his verandah, when he thought of Lambert's winter-spring marriage and wondered if he could do the same. But a man had to think ten times before he launched into the Big M, he'd often mused, because commitment came with a price. A woman in a man's life was both a blessing and a curse. A man focused on the blessings first, realizing too late that there were unpleasant little habits that came with the package, like nosiness and unpredictability.

Eric had decided years ago that he'd never understand women, largely because they were totally irrational. The decision had come after his ex-wife, Joseph's mother, had announced one night, just when he arrived home from work, that she was leaving him. She'd said it in a matter-of-fact way, stated that she, a devout Catholic, had no interest in holding it together because of the pope, and it had struck him like a bolt of lightning as he stood in the hall, still holding his briefcase, that Claire, all women, in fact, were unfathomable. He'd refused to try to understand them ever since. Enjoy them, yes, understand them, never. And just yesterday, in one of his rare moments of giving Shad advice, when the bartender had told him that Roper's guest, the English artist, had suddenly disappeared, he'd advised him not to get involved.

"I think she left of her own free will, man. Something was bothering her. She found Jamaica hard to—she had a lot going on in that head of hers. Artists are like that, anyway, deep thinking, but you can never tell with women. They give us only these little glimpses into their minds and, to tell you the truth, it looks like twisted, tortured stuff to me. They agonize endlessly over things that men would just forget about. The woman left, just accept it."

Jennifer was no different from other women—a prettier package, maybe, but just as nosy and scheming, asking about Simone, no doubt wanting to know if they still had a relationship.

"She might come for the groundbreaking," Eric replied. Lambert raised one bushy eyebrow at his friend, signaling that he wanted to talk more about the hotel, and Eric launched in with updates about the quantity surveyors' reports, relieved to move from the quicksand of his love life to the solid ground of facts.

After Miss Bertha had waddled away with the coffee tray, Jennifer disappeared inside. It was only then that Eric confided his fears to Lambert.

"The whole thing is looking shaky," he ended. "Nobody but Shad seems enthusiastic at this point."

"What about Horace?"

"We took him over to the island, Danny and I. He asked a lot of questions but he didn't say much. I think it's gotten too complicated for him with the solar panels and cisterns."

Lambert patted the sofa's cushion next to him, its tulips cringing under his burly hand. "These things are always touch and go at the beginning. That's normal."

"I don't think we have a prayer now that Danny's taken off."

"The important thing," Lambert said, stroking his mustache down one side and then the other, "is whether you've lost interest. Do you really want this thing to happen?"

Eric sighed and ran his hands through his hair. "There was a time when I just wasn't interested, but the bar is losing money like water through a sieve." He leaned forward and put his cup on the coffee table. "I don't want to close down, because people need it, you know. It's the only place in town where they can have their wedding receptions and parties, you know, Lam. It's kind of the community center or something. I don't care for the place that much myself, but it's part of Largo now." He'd disappointed the villagers once before, reminded every day by the ruins of the inn that had thrown dozens out of work when it closed—and he wasn't going to do it again. "And

I couldn't do that to Shad and Solomon—they have families, you know."

"I thought you were going to live on your Social Security at Miss Mac's," Lambert said with a curling lip.

"Who am I fooling, Lam? The woman is older than me. One way or the other, she's going to sell up and leave town; then where would I live? At least I have my apartment now, even if the bank could close us down any day."

"What's your option then, if Danny loses interest?"

The bar owner leaned back. "If he doesn't want to go through with it, maybe we can find another investor." It was Shad's idea, a shot in the dark.

Lambert frowned. He seemed to be digesting the idea, telling from the way he was staring at the view through the open front doors. "Where are you going to find him?"

"Or her," Eric said, and shrugged.

CHAPTER THIRTY-FOUR

Listening to the Walrus slide the top bolt closed after bringing in the breakfast tray, Sarah held her breath for a second, waiting until the second slid shut. The assault of locking noises outside her door had sorted themselves out after the first few days, and she knew there were two bolts outside. She always waited now to hear if both bolts had been slid shut when someone left. It sounded as if sometimes the bottom bolt was closed with one foot or hand simultaneously with the latching of the top bolt, making it sound like a single noise, but sometimes they were closed separately, and sometimes the bottom bolt wasn't closed at all.

Her visitors never knocked. She seemed to be a job that had been thrust upon them. Respecting her privacy would have been one task too many. Conversation was limited and brusque, which suited her since she could barely understand what they were saying. Walrus had been her most consistent visitor in the four days she'd been held captive. She'd push the door open with one shoulder, always with a frown and a puffy upper lip, the red plastic tray clasped tightly between her arthritic hands.

The thin man had appeared once with another man,

251

who'd fixed the leaky bathroom faucet. With all of his front teeth missing, the plumber had chatted to his companion as if he were conducting a major repair while he replaced a washer, and he'd smiled at her when they were leaving.

"You can't keep me here," she'd said, holding her voice steady, before the men got to the door. "The British High Commission will come looking for me."

The plumber had looked uncertainly at the thin man, who'd pushed him out and slammed the door behind them, sliding both bolts noisily on the other side.

On Sunday night she'd heard a discussion coming from the living room. She'd tiptoed to the door and put her ear against the tiny gap between door and frame. The low, guttural voice of one man, the driver, it sounded like, was followed by the older man's higher, clearer words.

"—can't *do* that here," the thin man was whining.

"The boss say so," the driver had grunted.

"Remember she *English,* and next thing Scotland Yard come down, and all of us end up swinging from a rope. Is not everything the boss tell you to do you have to do. Remember, she don't even pay us yet."

The driver said something inaudible and the skinny man said something about a passport. He seesawed up and down, louder now. "Like how she don't see nothing coming here, she not going to know how to find us if we leave her near the airport."

"Don't give me no *bumba claat*—" the other shouted.

The conversation got more heated, impossible to translate. The men seemed to be coming to blows and she pushed her ear harder against the gap, straining to hear more about the recurring *she* of the conversation. The debate ended as quickly as it had flared up with the slamming of the front door. Afterward, she'd sat in the middle of the bed for over an hour, waiting, her arms wrapped around her legs, heart thumping, listening intently to the muffled noises outside.

After a night of dark dreams with no details she could remember, she'd started eating on Monday. Even though her pulse still ran high day and night, even though her ears pricked up at the slightest sound, making her jump in the middle of the night, she'd decided to *live,* a decision not made lightly. Since she was being allowed another day of life, she reasoned, and since they were feeding her as if she was expected to survive, she needed to live as normally as possible. Not only would it demonstrate maturity, but it would also keep her sane. Cleanliness and sanity were bedfellows, her mother's aunt used to say. Sarah had started by sorting the clothes in her suitcase into three piles—dirty, clean, half-clean—and started washing the dirtiest items with the cake of bath soap and hanging them over the shower rail.

Her mother had come to mind while she washed her underwear, her mother who insisted on taking packets of detergent on trips. Bent over the bathroom sink, she chastised herself for not writing her mother and Penny more often. They would have missed her postcards and emails and made inquiries, sent somebody to find her. It had never occurred to her before that she needed them, that she needed anybody. She'd often thought she could live entirely alone as long as she could paint, had even flirted with the idea of living on the outskirts of London in a less expensive flat, a place where she'd know no one. But now the absence of the two people closest to her was even more palpable than her hunger, joining the hollowness inside. She wanted to put an arm around her mother's thinning shoulders, needed to laugh at Penny's startling comments. But there was nothing she could do now but wait—and take care of herself as best she could.

Eating was a necessity, she'd decided, if she was to be strong enough to escape or fight or run. That afternoon she'd started nibbling at the tray's contents and discovered that Walrus's food was tolerable.

"You try the food," the woman had commented, her frown almost disappearing when she saw that the prisoner had eaten.

"It was good, thank you," Sarah had replied with a small smile. "A little less oil next time, please?" Walrus had pulled her whiskered chin into the folds of her neck, but the breakfast the following morning was less greasy.

"What's your name?" Sarah asked the woman when she came back to get the breakfast tray. "My name is Sarah."

Walrus reached down to pick up the tray. She had whiskers growing out of her ears, too.

"My name Clementine," she said in a voice so low that her listener had to crane her head forward. Sarah thought later of the Jamaican mother who'd loved her baby enough to name her after a small northern flower, and she pondered the fact that her captors might be from the lower classes, as described by Eric, but that there was a kindness to Clementine that Roper lacked. And she was genuine, like Danny. Her mind sharpened by captivity, Sarah decided that kindness and authenticity trumped race and class for her now, would always trump it going forward. She'd tell her mother if she got a chance.

After Clementine left, Sarah walked to the plastic chair in the corner, still piled high with her easel in its traveling box and the bag with her paints and brushes. She'd thought about it the evening before and concluded that, if her jailors were ever to release her, they would have to see her as a person in control of her life, not as a quivering victim. She'd made two decisions. The first was that she wasn't going to beg anyone ever again to release her, no matter what happened. As the driver had said, there was nothing more disgusting than a begging woman, and she was already ashamed that she'd groveled at his feet.

The second decision was that she was going to start painting again. Worrying about her fate, puzzling over why she'd been kidnapped and when she was going to be rescued, would lead to nothing but anxiety. After testing the burglar bars and ruling them out, she'd decided that her best course of action if she was going to escape was to let her captors get to know her. She would humanize herself to them, get them to like her, and perhaps negotiate a release that way.

She set up the easel and the chair beside the window, resting her supplies on top of her other bags. In case she had to provide evidence of her imprisonment, to a police force that couldn't care less about a missing woman, apparently, she began on one of her large sheets—only slightly creased, thank goodness—with a four-by-four sketch of her bed. She paid particular attention to the cheap, varnished headboard with oceanlike swirls carved along the top. On the same sheet she drew the open door to the bathroom, the curtainless shower a dark cave within.

The third sketch she made from the bed. It was of the

three vertical windows and their parallel wooden louvers, which she'd started closing at night, unsure of who might look inside while she slept. She added the bars last, paying special attention to the hearts in the decorative overlay. The wall in the background and its glittering crown of glass she couldn't bring herself to draw.

When she came out of the bathroom later, Clementine was leaning over the bed, looking at the drawings.

"You is a ahtist."

"What's that?"

"A ahtist, a say, you is a *artist*."

"Yes."

"It nice," the woman said, and turned away quickly with the breakfast tray, like she knew she was overstepping her bounds. After Clementine left, Sarah pulled her chair up to the window, angling it to the left so she could sketch the tree.

It was a sea grape tree, Danny had told her, its presence bringing back a day with him on the beach. He'd loved the fruit and said that he and his sister used to eat the salty-sweet fruit that hung, grapelike, in the summer. But it was the flat, open leaves that had fascinated her from the beginning. They were almost perfectly circular, each with a red vein dissecting it, and she'd thought that it made the tree look more animal than vegetable, with warm blood running through its most intimate parts, and she'd wanted to paint one of its leaves ever since.

She reached through the burglar bars, her hand escaping for the first time, assisted by her elbow on a louver. Her fingertips touched the leaf closest to the window. She traced the vein down its center with her index finger and circled the firm outer edge. It was a survivor, this sea grape tree with its strong leaves and smooth cream bark. No one touched or climbed it. No one looked at it. But it had stayed alive all these years, found nourishment in the soil, lived one day at a time, the way trees did, and survived behind a wall of jagged glass.

After wetting some toilet paper, Sarah wiped the dust off the three leaves nearest her, touching each one as if it were a baby's arm. The leaves turned a brighter green as she wiped, the veins more alive, and she thought of their connection, of her own red hair and the leaves' red veins. Later, while she drew a leaf on her sketch pad, she thought again of Danny, wondering where he was and why he hadn't come to find her. A thought startled her and made her stare at the wall. Danny could be involved with her imprisonment. He might have wanted her out of the way, for some reason she didn't know. Maybe he'd told her something he shouldn't have. But no, that didn't feel right. She couldn't believe he was capable of harming her—being unfaithful, yes, but not having her seized and locked up.

More likely, it was a kidnapping for money. If that were the case, her captors could be anyone, a group of fishermen fallen on hard times, perhaps. The teenagers who'd stopped her on the beach, desperate for money. Maybe they'd cooked up the scheme with some friends. Oh, God, she thought, holding her breath, someone might be asking Danny or her mother for money while she was sitting in here. Phone calls might have been made and a ransom demanded. She leaned back in her chair and closed her eyes. To someone somewhere, she was either a threat or a reward. Anything was possible, anyone could be involved.

CHAPTER THIRTY-FIVE

There are those people in the world,'" Shad read slowly, keeping his voice low, two fingers underlining the words on the page, "'who have a natural curiosity.'" He shifted on his bar stool and nodded. "'If you give them a set of facts, they tend to see a pattern. These are the people who make the best private investi—*investigators*.'" He looked up, amazed that the author knew him almost as well as he knew himself, knew that he could spot a pattern in a set of facts. At a table in front of him, two tourist couples sat eating a lunch of curry goat, needing nothing but each other's company for the moment.

The book the bartender was reading had been sent to him years ago by a guest named Gerry who'd bent his ear for the seven nights he'd stayed at the old hotel. On the last night, the man had told Shad after several rum and Cokes that his full name was Leroy Fitzpatrick Gerard, and that he'd never wanted to be a doctor; that had been his father's idea. He'd wanted to drive a train.

"Wasn't there something you wanted to be when you were a kid?" Gerry had asked Shad.

"A private detective," the inn's bartender had replied without hesitation, "because when I was little I used to listen to a radio show after my granny went to sleep. It was a detective show and it was about some place in England, and the detective used to solve problems that nobody else could solve. I always like that."

After he got back to Kansas, Gerry had sent Shad the book, and he'd stowed it away in his bedside table after struggling with the first couple pages. But Miss Mac's reading classes were paying off, and Shad had returned to *The Secret World of the Private Investigator,* excited that he could finally slip into that world.

"Hello there!" One of the tourist men had his arm raised, signaling another round of drinks, and Shad put the book aside. Two rum punches, a club soda, and a banana daiquiri served, the bartender reopened the worn orange covers of his book. Just as he found the page he'd dog-eared, the phone started ringing on the counter behind him.

"Largo Bay Restaurant and Bar," he answered snappily.

A subdued voice answered. "Shad, it's Danny." It almost didn't sound like Danny, it was so serious.

"How it going, man? Everything good when you get back?"

"Yeah, no problems."

"You want the boss?"

"No, man. It's you I'm calling."

Shad closed the book. "How I can help you?"

"Remember you said I should call Sarah when I got back?"

"Yeah, I—"

"I took your advice. I googled her name—"

"Google?"

"I looked it up on the Internet, like you was saying, and

found the name of the gallery where she sells her paintings. I called them and told them I was a friend from Jamaica and I was looking for her. They took my number and her roommate called me back last night. She said she hasn't heard from Sarah, man."

"She don't go back to England?"

"The roommate says she could have gone to her mother's house, but she don't hear from her yet."

"She not at her apartment and her friend don't know where she is?"

"What you think, man?" the American urged.

Shad leaned over the phone. There must be a pattern here he could find. "I going to check it out."

"Call me back and let me know what's going on."

"I don't have the pass code to make a long-distance call, and the boss don't give nobody. You call me back tomorrow, same time. I have something for you tomorrow."

The hour dragged on until Shad's lunch break, time he passed by reading a chapter on interviewing witnesses, a chapter that called for listing all the questions the detective was going to ask, and, while he toted the departed guests' dishes back to the kitchen, he made his mental list. As soon as his break came and Eric relieved him, Shad walked down the road, had a quick sandwich at home, and went on to Roper's house. Carthena let him into the kitchen.

"Funny how the Englishwoman just leave without a trace," he commented to the housekeeper. The warbling sounds of a trumpet were coming from deep inside the house.

"Funny, yes."

"I bring you some thyme and scallion. Beth grow plenty this year."

She took the brown paper bag from his hands and set it on a counter.

"What time she leave that morning, the morning when she left for good?"

"She go painting early in the morning, and when I go to clean up her room later, everything gone. She must have come back and pack up." The young woman picked up a bowl with coconut meat and started grating it.

"What time that was, when you went in her room?"

"Around twelve o'clock." The woman stopped grating the coconut, the beads in her hair chattering when she looked up at him. "Why you want to know?"

"I just thinking that—"

"You say you come to give me little thyme and scallion from your garden. How come you asking me all them questions?"

"Is only—"

"Thank you for the seasoning, then. I busy, and I telling you I don't see the woman. I in the kitchen and I don't see nothing. She don't say nothing to me and I don't know nothing." She turned back to her grating, muttering about *people who fast in other people's business.*

A knock on the back door swung their heads around. A man and two women, one holding a tiny baby, were visible through the glass panes. Carthena started toward the door, Shad behind her.

"The musician man still here?" he said quickly before she opened the door. "The one who play the trumpet?"

"Yes."

"Call him for me. I want to tell him something, like how he going to play in the bar."

Carthena opened the door and the visitors walked into the kitchen. They were strangers to Largo, a tall woman with hard, judgmental eyes that she narrowed at Shad, followed by a young couple, the girl holding a child. The baby looked like a newborn, a blue bonnet perched sideways on its head. Nodding to Shad's greeting, the man sat down on the kitchen stool as if he expected to take the best seat in the house. His hair was shaved close to the skull and his jeans hung below his T-shirt almost to his knees. He was one of those youths that you saw in the Pen, the same flat expression whether you gave them a job or the end of a knife. Beside him, her belly still swollen, the girl stood swinging the child from side to side with a wordless baby-mother smile as Shad slipped out the door.

When Ford appeared in the backyard, Shad waved him farther away until they stood between the clotheslines, the musician's chin well above the white sheets flapping against the trumpet in his hand.

"I just want to ask you," the bartender started, "if you hear anything from the Englishwoman? She call or visit or anything?"

"Sarah? We haven't heard a word."

"You don't find that strange, like how she spend all that time here? You would think she would call to say she arrive safe, you don't think?"

"She wasn't exactly happy when she left."

"You mean about Danny—?"

"No, I mean about Roper."

Shad frowned. "What you mean?"

Ford looked down at his instrument. "I don't know if I should be telling you this, man."

"I just asking so we could invite her to the bar when you play, like how she really want to hear you."

"Everything's changed since then." Ford grimaced. "Sarah and Roper had a—a disagreement before she left. I thought he was talking shit, to tell you the truth, but I figured he'd had too much to drink, so I didn't say anything. I've known him a long time and I'm staying in his house, you know. I didn't want to—"

"And she act different after the disagreement?"

"She was real hurt, I could tell."

"So you weren't surprised when she left."

"I was and I wasn't. I think she expected me to defend her, but I didn't. I still feel bad about it, but I have enough of my own stuff going on. . . ."

Shad looked over the clothesline at the ocean, seaweed floating on top of the foamy waves, the sign of a storm at sea. "And you think she just get on a plane and go home."

"That's what we all think."

"She musta had an open ticket, when you can leave anytime. That was the kind of airplane ticket that Simone, the woman on the island, had."

Ford shook his head. "She only had a one-way ticket to Jamaica that Roper had bought for her. Someone must have sent her the money or bought the ticket for her, because she didn't have any money while she was here. So she told me, anyway."

"No money?"

"She used to joke about being penniless." About to leave, Ford turned back. "I don't think she was good with money. She was broke, but she bought a new dress, you know what I mean?"

Late that night, after he'd shifted the gawky kitten off the bed, Shad slid in beside a silent Beth, her back to him. Her hips made a dark mound in the light through the curtain. It had been a busy evening, with a birthday party for a young man who'd gotten drunk and vomited on the floor of the bar.

When Shad's head touched the pillow, it was met with the crisp rustle of paper. "What that?" he said. His hand brought out a small rectangular slip.

Beth rolled over. "My first check," she said sleepily, but he could tell she was smiling.

He put the check on the side table and reached for her gratefully, thinking of the Englishwoman who'd been penniless.

CHAPTER THIRTY-SIX

Grimacing, Eric put the receiver back in the cradle to cool down. He couldn't think of anything he couldn't stand more than a telephone hot with someone else's conversation. Behind him, Shad was counting the liquor bottles under the sink, doing the monthly inventory.

"We going to need another case of red wine, boss."

"Make it a half case this time."

Eric picked up his ginger ale and walked away, still irked by the phone call Shad had just ended. The bartender had jumped up from doing inventory when the phone rang. His greeting had been followed by a hunched back over the receiver, ten minutes of mumbled sentences, and the frenzied waving of one hand. After he hung up, Shad had bent to look at the bottles right away.

"Who was it?" Eric had asked.

"Danny. He want me to do him a favor."

With no intention of asking what the favor was, and a burning curiosity about what his possible future partners would want to talk about that didn't include him (coming quickly to the phrase *two against one*), Eric had poured himself a ginger ale. If they wanted to have their secrets, that was their business. He'd have to trust Shad, who'd always had his back, had to trust that he was keeping Danny en-gaged and the hotel venture in mind.

There'd been little on Eric's mind but Simone for the last few days. Snapshots of their time together had kept popping into his head. Earlier that morning, after doing a few side bends on his verandah, he'd remembered exercising when she was on the island, and how embarrassed he'd been to think she might be watching him in his old box-ers with his paunch flopping around. In mid-bend, he'd straightened and swept a lock of white hair away from his face. By the time he got to the third and last squat, perspi-ration trickling down the groove of his spine, he decided that he couldn't avoid the truth anymore. He wanted to see her and hold her and make love to her, even if she had to pay her own ticket down.

He leaned on a post facing Simone's island, the name the Parish Council woman had rejected.

"It can't be *Simone's Island*," she'd protested, disdain in her wide eyes. "It have to be Simone Island. It don't belong to her; it belong to *you*. And we can't have no apostrophe, the computer don't like it."

The island sparkled in the midmorning sunshine, a light wind twirling the flat leaves of the almond tree. It was going to rain later, the weatherman had said, the beginning of the springtime rainy season.

"Have the buckets ready?" Eric called to Shad.

"The new roof not leaking too bad, boss," the muffled answer came from under the counter.

It had taken Eric five years or more to get used to the Caribbean seasons, to the dry seasons and the wet, but now he couldn't imagine anything resembling four seasons. That very morning, while taking the cold shower he endured since he'd cut off the hot water, he'd created another of his little ditties to remind himself why he stayed in this god-forsaken place. Strumming his imaginary guitar with the bar of soap, he'd rumbled the verse.

> *Give me a cloud of rain* (his voice trembling like
>   Elvis's),
> *A little sun,*
> *My old flip-flops,*
> *And I'm ready for fun.*

He'd sung to Simone once. She'd invited him to sit down on her writing bench because she was lonely, and she'd asked him to sing one of the songs he used to sing when he played lead guitar. When he finished, she'd told him he was good, and he'd known she was being kind.

Today he was going to tell her casually that he'd finally gotten Horace to come to an agreement about the infra-structure on the island. Actually, he and Lambert had gone together to see the lawyer and Lambert had talked him into it. Horace had admitted that he'd liked what he'd seen on the island the week before. He and his partner were still in-terested in the campsite. Sensing victory, Lambert had got-ten him to agree that it would be best for them to install the steps, walkways, cistern, and solar panels themselves, and build them just the way they'd like them. He'd taken out his calculator and showed him how cost effective it would be to take out a building loan and deduct it from the rent for at least five years, enough for a good head start on the project.

"Shad is definitely going to be a partner," an embold-
ened Eric had added. "And the share split stays the same."

"Please yourself," Horace had said, then he'd sucked on
a back tooth and gone back to talking about the campsite.

The phone had cooled down when he punched in the
numbers later. "Do you have a minute?" he asked Simone.

"I'm in a meeting," she said, sounding confident and
businesslike, like she was trying to impress someone nearby.
"Can I call you later?"

Walking the phone to its holder on the counter, Eric
did his version of sucking his teeth, causing his bartender
to mimic him.

"Boss," Shad said after he'd finished laughing, "I was
thinking, why we don't connect the laptop to the Internet,
like what Rickia was saying? It going to cost us a little
extra, but we would be saving money because you wouldn't
have to make so many long-distance calls. Joella say you can
telephone people on the Internet."

"You could have something there," Eric replied, a lack-
luster answer.

"We can't move forward unless we put one foot first,
right, like how Joshua learning to walk."

"And like how you're learning to read better, you mean,
and want to learn the computer yourself."

"Exactly, and what we don't know, we can ask the children. They always know these things. Rickia say she sending emails to some girl in Australia now who live on a sheep
farm. You ever hear anything like that—a child in Jamaica
talking to another child in Australia, on a sheep farm?"

Shad raised his shoulders up as he talked and dropped
them suddenly. "If we don't keep up, the next generation

going to pass us out, even control up the hotel business and the tourists. We have to keep up with them, keep learning, right?"

Eric sighed. "No peace for the weary."

"Plenty time for peace when you dead, boss."

CHAPTER THIRTY-SEVEN

Y ou think it look like me?" The young man straightened his head to look more like the sketch he was
holding.

"I think so," Sarah said, walking toward him with her
paintbrush.

Square Jaw raised his eyes. "I really look so serious?"

"That's how you look."

"I can have it?"

"Let me see it first."

He handed her the drawing and she looked at it, pursing
her lips, as if she was trying to make up her mind. "I don't
know. You'd have to tell me your name first."

"Why?"

"Drawings and paintings have to have a name, and I
can't just make up a name and pretend you're somebody
else. Clementine's has her name."

The man frowned and ran his hand over his head. He'd
been lured into the room by news that Sarah had drawn his
portrait. The maid had clasped her hands against her gingham chest when she first saw it that morning. Clementine
had already been given her own portrait the day before, to
thank her, Sarah had said, for the top sheet she'd added to

the fitted sheet. The Walrus had tried hard not to smile when she saw the drawing, but she'd puffed up her top lip more than usual and announced she was going to take the drawing home to show her grandchildren.

The two portraits, both a bold six inches square, had been drawn with care, each on its own large sheet, the edges cleanly marked with a ruler, the spacious white margins emphasizing the drawings' charcoal lines and shadows. Her subjects looked handsome and proud, almost heroic. Clementine with a curve of the lips, her kidnapper looking straight at the viewer. Sarah had worked on them from memory, late into the last two nights, finding the end results just as good as those of the Bayswater sidewalk artists. While she was bent over the drawing of Square Jaw, she'd thought that maybe she should substitute her restaurant work for tourist portraits, once she got out.

She'd laid the drawing of Square Jaw on the bed to await the maid's breakfast arrival.

"It look like him, for true," the woman had said. "You even get the way his hair shave close to his head," she'd added, sweeping her finger across her forehead. "I going to tell him."

Square Jaw had arrived an hour later. He was wearing light blue running shoes with a navy blue swoosh on the sides, probably new by the way he was walking, with his feet sticking out like Charlie Chaplin, and he'd asked in a few gruff words to see the drawing she'd made of him.

He hadn't visited the room in the last three days, his voice absent from the voices rising and falling in the living room, and she'd found herself almost relieved to hear him outside the day before. She had the impression that he respected her more than the driver did, that he saw her as more than a job. He'd entered the room once to search through her bags. When she stood behind him, asking why she was still being held here, he'd told her to sit down and said something about asking too many questions.

"What are you looking for?" she'd demanded, when he'd finished tossing her clothes out of the bag.

"You have any scissors or knife?"

"Of course not. You can't take them on an airplane."

He'd stood up and brushed off his knees. "We don't want you trying to—"

"I don't deserve this, you know," she'd called after him while he left the room mumbling to himself, irritated with somebody.

She'd returned to her work with a vengeance after that, keeping at bay the anxiety that lived with her day and night. Nothing would come from giving in to fear, she knew. Her only salvation would be to clear her mind of clutter and find out as much as she could from the people around her. *Better the evil that you know.* Her mother's words had come back to her after she'd made her seventh scratch at the foot of the wall. Evil or not, the square-jawed fellow was someone she wanted to know better.

The young man looked up from the drawing. "Me can have it?" he asked her in broad patois, waving the drawing in his hand.

"You still haven't given me your name."

He scratched the back of one hand. "Batsman," he mumbled.

"Batsman, then." She dug around in a bag and found a pen. "Played cricket, did you?"

The man shook his head, wiping his laugh away with his hand. "No, Batsman, like Batsman and Robin, the guys in the movie."

After writing the name at the foot of the page, she handed it back to him. "Has anyone ever drawn your picture before?"

"No, but ah have plenty camera pictures."

His description of his older brother's photography tumbled out, something about his brother having a camera and taking family photographs. She grabbed on to the few words she could understand, stringing them together to create a chain of visuals of a family and a celebration when someone visited from overseas.

What had at first seemed impossible, that she could understand the harsh language around her, had turned into a challenge to learn what her captors were saying, to learn patois. As soon as she heard voices outside, she'd stand at the door and press her ear to the gap, separating out the words she understood from the ones she never would. The cadence had been a struggle at first, with the forceful upward swings and quick descents, the staccato intervals and abrupt endings. She'd practiced saying a few phrases to get the hang of it, thinking of her uncle, a linguistics professor at the University of Kent, who would have learned it by now.

After Batsman had gone, Sarah settled in front of her easel and her work of the last couple days. With her watercolor pad now completely filled, each page slightly warped, and her sketch pad unable to take paint, she'd started in on the one large sheet left of the five she'd originally brought from London. Today she was painting another sea grape leaf. It had started to age, one brown edge curling in death, a nice contrast to the two other paintings of healthy green leaves on the page.

She leaned her head to one side and squinted. Three rectangles were scattered around the page already, each four by six inches, two horizontal and one vertical, each a different leaf, one with a lizard sitting on its stem. If she continued like this, filling the page with squares, inserting boxes between the boxes, she'd fill up the entire sheet—to create one large painting. She allowed herself a tiny smile to think that she'd be able to fulfill Roper's challenge in the most ironic of ways. It would be a jigsaw of miniature boxes.

While she continued painting, she thought about her dream the night before. It had awakened her, her chest constricted, and she hadn't been able to get back to sleep. She'd lain afterward with listening eyes wide, thinking of the dream in all its detail. She'd been back in Maidstone and she was young, an adolescent changing out of her choir robe. Penny Clutterbuck was there and had giggled something about Peter inviting her to the cinema.

"But he's too fat," she'd whispered, so the others behind wouldn't hear.

Penny and the nameless others had disappeared and she was suddenly alone under a streetlight on the Old Edgecombe Road. Traffic was sparse, a Sunday evening, she knew. It was dark already, cold, and she hadn't brought gloves. She'd known somehow that the day had been overcast, making the colors on the leaves look dull all day until they faded into autumn darkness. She'd turned up her collar and dug her hands into her coat pockets. It was a coat she'd actually worn and loved at that age, a dark blue cloth one with padded shoulders, but under the streetlight it seemed bleached yellow and her shadow had circled her like a black ball.

Her mother was to fetch her after church, but she was late. She'd looked up the road. A bicyclist and one car passed. The church grounds were dark behind her and she didn't know where else to go. A man and a woman walked by holding hands, the woman pregnant in a bright red coat. They were talking as they passed.

"She did no such thing!" the woman said to the man, then looked at Sarah questioningly. They'd turned the corner beside the church and disappeared, leaving the young girl alone and Sarah wide awake.

CHAPTER THIRTY-EIGHT

T he stool lay on its side behind a patch of weeds. Shad leaned in to examine it, making sure to stay well away because Beth wouldn't tolerate him snagging the new khaki pants she'd bought him. It was a simple wooden stool with a round seat, the kind you'd find in a kitchen, or that an artist would sit on. Already late for work, he walked quickly toward the beach. Just before the end of the path, he stopped and made a full turn.

Earlier that afternoon, Sonja had pointed to the path Sarah used every morning to go to her painting spot, and he'd descended the driveway to inspect it. He was now standing in a clearing large enough for someone to set down a stool, yet have privacy behind a couple of coconut trees. Peanut shells were scattered among the fallen palm leaves. Shad crossed his arms and stared at the spot where Sarah must have painted. She was disciplined, Sonja had said, and she'd painted up to the day she'd left. He rested his cheek on the fist of one hand and looked at the waves, pounding and dragging, a few yards away.

Shad's excuse for coming to Roper's house on a Saturday—when Carthena wouldn't be around—was to ask for Ford. He knew he wasn't at home, since he'd seen him heading out of town with Roper. The bartender had told Sonja he wanted to recommend some backup musicians to the trumpeter. She'd invited him inside when he'd appeared at the door, something a little unusual for a lady of her standing, but Sonja was different from the other browning women, her hair worn natural like she was proud of her kinky hair.

The writer had told him that Roper and Ford had gone to Ocho Rios, and the bartender had thanked her and started toward the door, turning back just as his hand reached for the brass knob.

"I sorry to hear that the artist lady gone," he'd said sadly. "I wanted to see her paintings."

Sonja's eyes had become unfocused. "I'm sorry, too."

"People always have a reason for running away like that, you know, and I been wondering what make her do it."

The woman had struggled with what she should say, he could see, her hand to her throat. She'd walked out to the deck in her long dress and leaned over the rail, as if she were expecting Sarah to appear on the steep driveway below.

"She used to walk down to that path every morning carrying all her art stuff. She insisted on doing it herself, never wanted any help. Every day she'd do that, except on weekends, just like she was going to work. She was really serious about her art."

The bartender had nodded. "Strange, eh? She don't say nothing, just slip away like that."

"Women do strange things when they're upset."

"She was upset? I hate to know she leave Largo upset."

Sonja had cupped her left breast with her hand, like she was carrying something heavy on her chest. Shad had leaned on the rail and looked toward the village's rusty rooftops peeking out between the coconut trees.

"What happen to her?" he asked Sonja, because he knew she was an honest woman.

She had leaned on the rail and sighed, blowing the air hard out her nostrils. "One evening, a few days before she left, my—boyfriend, partner, whatever—sometimes I don't know what to call him—he said something to her. He didn't approve of her dating Danny and he let her know."

She couldn't look him straight in the eye, a person who always looked straight at everybody. It was the class thing, Shad knew, the same kind of foolishness that had kept Jamaican people apart from before Granny's time, that had made Horace want to deprive him of success, the wall that he and his children would have to climb all their lives. Maybe Danny Caines had dropped an *h* and his grammar had failed him, or he'd told them that his parents were poor. One way or another, the American had slipped up, enough for Roper to classify him as lower class.

"We hardly saw her after that—she stayed out of our way, gobbled her dinner without saying much. I think she was really uncomfortable here." The writer had turned toward the front door, ready to have him leave, but Shad had stroked his chin.

"She was having a good time, you don't think?"

"I thought so, but something happened—even before the argument with Roper. She started getting kind of anxious a couple weeks before."

"After the night you all come to the bar, the night you ordered the jerk chicken?"

"Could have been, I don't remember exactly when. She

never stopped painting, though. Right up to the day she disappeared, she went off painting in the morning."

"She come back to get her things?"

"I didn't see her if she did. We left in the morning to go into town. Roper had a doctor's appointment and I wanted to go shopping, and Ford tagged along because he wanted to see Kingston. When we came back that night, she was . . . She must have planned to pack up and leave after we were gone."

"So she must have had a taxi come and get her with all her things."

"Carthena said she never heard anything."

"She had a ticket to go back, then."

Sonja shook her head. "Not that I know of."

"She didn't go into town to buy a ticket?"

"Maybe with Danny, but not with us," she'd said, leading him to the front door.

After examining the trampled coconut fronds at Sarah's painting site, Shad walked back to the main road. High above the road, Roper's deck was empty and there was no sound coming from the house. Wiping his damp palms on his pants, the bartender crossed the road and walked up the driveway slowly, glancing up at the deck and the windows to check for onlookers. His excuse, in case he was seen, would be that he forgot to leave the names and numbers of the musicians for Ford.

Avoiding the steps leading up to the front door, he slipped behind the grove of bamboo that he'd seen from the deck. It was the kind of wall that thoughtful hosts planted to provide privacy for visitors—and for a guest room. On the other side of the bamboo was a stone patio with some chairs. Shad peered through the sliding glass doors. Inside, two twin beds faced the terrace, both neatly made up with colorful spreads. It was empty—no luggage, no clothes—a room standing ready for the next guest.

It only took a sharp penknife to work the lock and Shad slid the door open, remembering other doors he'd opened exactly like that, a long time ago. He slid the door shut behind him. The sandy soles of his sneakers crunched on the tiles and he tiptoed slowly toward the chest of drawers. A quiet examination of its six drawers yielded nothing but a few American coins and a hairpin. The drawers of a small desk and bedside table were similarly empty.

After turning on his heel in the middle of the room, Shad asked himself what Ellis J. Oakland, author and detective, would have done next, then he carried the desk chair to the closet and set it down without a sound.

CHAPTER THIRTY-NINE

Eric picked up the banana from the kitchen bowl and marched it into the bar with a disgusted mouth.

"Do you see that?" he asked Shad, who was pouring a white rum for the evening's first customer. Eric pointed to the dime-shaped hole in the side of the banana. "We have a rat, and he's eaten my Chinese banana."

"The bar is open, boss, anything can come in. You forget we in the Caribbean, plenty roaches and spiders and mosquitoes. You don't think we going to have rats?"

"But we have an exterminator, that pest control guy with the green truck."

"You stop paying him, remember?"

"Rats everywhere," Tri called gleefully from the end of the bar. "They going to be here after we gone, Mistah Eric. Rats going to be king."

"Somebody should have covered up the bananas or something." Eric threw the fruit into the garbage and washed his hands. "I'm going to set a rat trap tonight and catch the son of a bitch."

"You better set ten traps for the whole family," Tri suggested.

"And, boss," Shad murmured, "if you going into Port

Antonio to buy the trap, don't forget to pay the phone bill. They cut off the phone this morning."

"One damn bill after another."

"So life go, boss."

"Where's Solomon? He's late."

"Maisie say he get a cut on the bottom of his foot, so he must be walking slow."

"Good thing we don't have any customers yet."

"Tri is—"

"You know what I mean."

"Boss," Shad said. "I want to ask you a little something." He walked partway to the kitchen, spinning the towel in his hand. Eric followed him, in no mood to explain why he couldn't give him a raise or why his parents had been unhappy.

The small man turned and stretched the towel between his hands. "Can a foreign person—a real foreigner, not a Jamaican living abroad—can they leave Jamaica without a passport?"

"I don't think so. Once upon a time an American could get in on his driver's license, but not anymore. Everybody has to have a passport."

"What about an English person?"

"Same thing." Eric tucked his hair behind his ears. "Why do you ask?" Shad's reasons for asking questions were always as good as the questions.

"Remember I tell you that the English artist gone, just disappear one day? Well, she leave her passport."

"You're kidding! How you know that?"

"Somebody tell me."

"You tell the person that if her passport's here, she's

282

probably still in the country, unless she left with a fake passport."

"She don't look like the kind of lady who would make a fake passport, though."

"If she has a real passport, she wouldn't need one."

"You're right, you're right," Shad said, starting back to the bar, snapping the towel as he walked.

"And tell the customer who's coming in that we're not ready to serve dinner yet," Eric called, "unless they want corn beef sandwiches."

CHAPTER FORTY

The dream was as clear to her in the light of day as when she'd awakened earlier in pitch darkness gasping for air. It was a continuation of the dream the night before. In this last dream she'd been an adolescent again, thirteen, she'd known somehow, the numbers *one* and *three* clear in her mind. She was wearing the same blue coat, still standing outside the dark church waiting for her mother. A taxi had approached and slowed in front of her, the profiled driver looking out from the murky interior, motioning with his finger, asking if she needed him. She'd shaken her head and he'd driven off.

Then she'd swung around in a circle on tiptoe, her arms extended, practicing a ballet step, and as she turned she'd blown her breath out through her mouth to see if it steamed up around her, but it hadn't. Her new patent leather shoes made a grinding sound on the sidewalk and she turned again because she liked the sound.

Four boys were walking past the closed offices and shops and coming toward her, their voices forced, almost vicious. They'd been drinking, she could tell. One taunted another while the others laughed. They'd started glancing toward her as they approached, and she pulled her coat closer around her. When they passed in front of the church sign, they grew quiet, listening to one boy talking. They were all around the same age, eighteen, maybe nineteen. At the steps leading up to the church, they'd gathered in a circle, but she couldn't hear what they were saying. She wanted to run away but she didn't want to attract attention, and they could outrun her, anyway. They were blocking the gate to the churchyard, the only opening in the black iron fence. A car turned the corner, followed by another. They drove past to the end of the road and were gone.

The boys started walking toward her with energized, self-conscious steps. Although she couldn't make out their eyes, she knew they were looking at her, coming straight for her. She stood still, frozen to the spot. One boy said something and the others laughed. They wore leather jackets and greasy hairstyles. The tallest one was in the front, their leader, the only one with brown skin and wavy black hair that he'd tried to plaster flat.

"'Allo?" he said, and stopped in front of her, his beer breath hitting her in the face. He was a few inches taller than her and had a pimple on his nose large enough to have a shadow. The others circled her.

"What's your name, then?" he said, the trace of an accent in the way the words came out. "Something like Jane, innit?" He tilted his head back, tickled by his own wit. The streetlight showed a broken tooth in front. His followers echoed him with their own cocky laughs. She could hear her heart beating in her ears, and she hoped they couldn't hear. Beside them, the road was silent, dotted on both sides by empty streetlights.

"Sarah Louise," she'd answered, trying to control the

shake in her voice. They laughed again. Their intensity pawed at the air around her and she knew she was their prey.

A thump to her pelvis made her hunch forward and look down. The leader, a silver chain still swinging from the belt of his pants, had hit her in her privates with his fist, startling her even though it was muffled by the heavy blue coat. The boy straightened his black-leathered arm to do it again and she took a step back. There were spots of dried cement on his jeans like he was a brickie, a bricklayer's apprentice. He grabbed her arm and she felt the pressure of his fingers through the woolen sleeve. She tried to pull away.

"Where you going, Sarah Louise?" he taunted her. "Just having a little fun, right, boys?" She glanced back at the church gate, measuring the distance.

"Where you going?" the others repeated, touching her, jostling her.

Sarah had awakened with a jerk and lay in the dark, panting. She wondered where it had come from, this dream so real she could still feel the mental version of the thump. Was it a prediction, a warning? After stumbling to the window, she'd watched the sky turning pale yellow, then pale pink, with a smattering of clouds above the ocean. She'd hung on to the bars and breathed deeply, the air faintly salty from this distance.

By breakfast, she'd sketched an addition to the growing watercolor painting on the large sheet. It was a view of the ocean sliver above the wall—and the jagged glass. She'd had to draw it leaning against the bars, the drawing board braced with one hand and the free hand sketching. The awkwardness of the position made it difficult to think of the dream and the insult to her privates.

Clementine didn't approve. "You can't make a picture standing up like that," she said with a scowl. Another Sunday and the Walrus was in a starched purple dress and a matching hat with a wide brim. Another Sunday and ten scratches on the wall. After Clementine left, all was quiet. Then the church choir started up again, the soloist screeching at the top of her voice while Sarah painted bronze glitter along the edges of the broken glass.

She was sure that the distasteful dream had been inspired, if one could call it that, by the driver, who'd grabbed her chin and tousled her hair the night before, touched her as if he owned her. It had started when he knocked on her door, the first person to do so, the visit coming in the middle of a celebration in the living room. She'd heard people collecting in the early afternoon, until there were about six men's voices getting gradually louder, as if they were drinking. They'd talked about her. One man had asked about *de woman* and Batsman had answered that she was *cool*.

"She don't give no trouble," he'd said.

There was talk of a birthday, and she'd stood listening, both hands pressed to the door, smelling its cheap varnish, anxious about the change in the number of voices and the volume, surprised that these people celebrated birthdays like ordinary people, rituals with a prisoner in a nearby room. Music had suddenly erupted, a dancehall song that drowned out the voices and vibrated through the tiles into her bare feet.

The knock had come shortly after. "Who is it?" she'd answered, jumping away from the door.

"Man-Up." The driver, using his name for the first time. There was nothing she could do but tell the knocker to come in, every visit bringing hope and terror. After sliding the bolts, the driver had pushed into the room along with the throbbing music.

"You good?" he'd said after he spotted her beside the bathroom door. He was wearing baggy jeans and a black T-shirt, black sneakers. Taller than Clementine and Batsman, he crowded the room, the rough tones of the dancehall singer a fitting backdrop.

"I come to tell you something," he'd announced, slamming the door closed. He swaggered like he'd been drinking and was in a good mood. He walked to her easel and stood looking at the painting, an unfinished box showing a budding leaf projecting from the tip of a branch. "I hear you is a ahtist. Batsman show me the picture."

Sarah had pulled down the hem of her shorts, glad she'd worn a bra. "I paint—yes."

He'd lifted the board off the easel and walked toward her, examining the painting. "You paint good, yes, man." His uplifted eyebrows almost vanished into the hairline above his narrow forehead. "Your day almost come, you know." He'd glanced at her over the board. His face was expressionless except for the tiny muscles making his eyes squint.

She'd run her tongue over her lips. "What—what do you mean?"

"You going to get out soon, one way or another, dead or alive," he'd said with a snorting laugh. He'd thrown the board onto the bed. "First, you have to paint me, though."

To Sarah's slow nod, he'd continued, "I want a nice painting for my sitting room. No pencil drawing, you hear me? I want you to paint it with color. I come back later."

He'd departed the room with a smirk and appeared again after dinner, after the other men had left. "You ready?" he'd demanded, and she'd moved to the easel and chair she'd set up near the bed. The bare bulb didn't give enough light, but she'd said nothing, knowing every detail of his face already.

"We need another chair," she said.

"You didn't need nothing for Batsman."

"He didn't pose for me."

After he'd settled on the red velvet chair he brought in, Man-Up straightened his shoulders and turned toward the window.

"That good?" he'd asked, glancing quickly at her and back into the dark outside.

"Yes, but—" she said, gesturing to her own neck, and he'd straightened his black shirt under the thin gold chain. Black wasn't a good color for him, she thought. It didn't offer enough contrast with his ebony skin, skin almost as dark as that of the bartender who smiled a lot.

They'd spent an hour in silence except for the few times when she'd asked him to turn more to her or center his chain. She was glad he'd asked her to paint him. She wanted him to see that she wasn't the begging woman at his feet, but instead a sensible woman who could take the pressure, not make a fuss. Once he got up and left the room without explanation, returning after a few minutes.

"Tell me—Man-Up," she'd started when he sat down again, as if she was asking for his opinion on the weather, "why am I here?"

"I don't come to answer no questions."

She'd caught his eye, looking from her to the window

and back again. "I just thought I should ask. You're holding me here, not—"

"Don't ask me *nothing*," he'd said, his voice callous now. "I didn't come here for no fucking interview, you hear me? Just paint the *raas claat* picture." He seemed to slip seamlessly from good mood to bad.

After the drawing was completed and she'd begun to paint, Man-Up had started moving his feet around restlessly between the chair's legs.

"You can go now, if you'd like," she'd said. "You don't need to be here for the whole thing."

He'd stood up and stretched, pulling the T-shirt taut against his stomach with its small spare tire. He'd walked over to look at the portrait. "Nice, nice."

She'd kept her eyes on the painting until he reached for her, cupping her chin hard in his hand.

"You a sweet woman." The smell of beer had oozed out of his pores. "Anybody ever tell you that you sweet?" She'd tried not to shrink from his touch, stared instead at his teeth and the small spaces in between.

"And I like your red hair," he'd added, rubbing his hand roughly over her head. "Watch me, I coming back to take you up on your offer." Then he'd pushed her head hard to one side before stalking out and bolting the door behind him.

CHAPTER FORTY-ONE

n the two-room police station in Port Antonio, Shad slid lower in the rickety chair, waiting for Sergeant Neville Myers to get off the phone.

"Go to the police," Danny had said on the phone the day before. "Tell them what you told me." Shad's first instinct had been to select a few choice words to describe the Port Antonio police force that never had time for little Largo, but he'd held his tongue and followed the suggestion, even if it meant taking his day off to do it.

"Yes, ma'am." His police cousin nodded patiently into the receiver, raising smug eyebrows with each sentence. "It sounding suspicious, you right. But we can't come and arrest your helper. We don't have no proof that she stole the ring." Neville swung his captain's chair toward the dusty window, adjusting the blue uniform shirt over his belly. Stumpy like all the Myers men, he made up for it with girth and authority.

The men didn't like each other. One was the representative of the Constabulary Force (on whose side Neville had invariably fought when they were boys playing in the bamboo), and the other a former renegade and convict, something that had hung in the air between them for the last seventeen years.

At a smaller desk behind their superior, no computer in sight, two young constables were reading the contents of a file folder, one standing and leaning over the other. The seated youth glanced up at his colleague with a grin, amused by what they were reading. They weren't making more than two hundred US a month, Shad knew, but the red stripes down their pants seams gave them the right to know people's private lives. Maybe carrying a gun made it worthwhile.

"Yes, sir," Neville said, having disposed of his caller. He spoke wearily, his younger cousin still an embarrassment. "How can I help you?" He creaked back in the old captain's chair and swung it around, showing all three stripes on his right sleeve.

"How is Aunt Jasmine?" Shad smiled.

"She good, getting old," Neville said. "So what bring you here?"

"An English lady, she used to come into the bar—"

"What happen to Beth?"

"Nothing like that. This woman is a artist, she disappear from Largo."

"What you mean she disappear?"

"She was staying with another artist man in Largo, a man called Roper. You ever hear of him?" His cousin stared back blankly. "Anyway, she was staying there and she just disappear one morning. Her clothes gone, everything gone—well, almost everything—but she never come back and she don't contact nobody since then."

Neville pulled a pad toward him. "What were the circumstances of her departure?"

"One day they come back to the house and she gone."

"No forced entry?"

"No."

"No witnesses?"

"No."

Neville pushed the pad aside. "Pshaw, man. The woman just leave on her own."

"She don't have no money."

"How you know that?" Chubby cheeks getting chubbier, Neville shook his head, a man of the world. "She could have money and nobody know. White people don't talk their business like black people, especially money business."

"She don't just move somewhere else. She don't know nobody."

"The woman get on a plane and leave, you hear me?"

"Without a passport?"

Neville frowned. "How you know?"

"Somebody tell me," Shad said, swallowing hard. "She leave it in the room on top of a closet." He could still see the small, blue book hiding at the back of the shelf.

"She still on the island then," the sergeant said, rubbing his chin. "She have any *enemies?*"

"No, she don't have no enemies." Janet intruding into the bathroom didn't give her an enemy, nor the argument with Roper, not enough to make Neville sound more like a judge. "She not that kind of person, she quiet like. She just go about her business and paint every day."

Neville harrumphed. "I think I know what happen. Them artist people like to smoke weed when they come down here. They free up themselves and do all kind of things."

"You can't come to Largo and investigate?"

"Investigate what, some artist woman who smoke weed?"

"She not smoking weed, man. She don't even smoke cigarette."

"Trust me, boy, the woman gone off to some Rasta man's yard to smoke weed. I have a case last year of a woman who never go back to New Jersey, and her parents come down and want us to investigate. And when we check, the woman was living with a Rasta in St. Ann. Them cases easy to solve. We don't have no time to waste on that kind of business. Is serious business we doing here, catching criminal and thing. We put our lives on the line every day." Neville's eyes started to bulge, like when they were playing police and he'd caught Shad in his grip, yelling, *I catch you now, I catch you now.*

He poked the desk with a fat finger. "You know is *sixty* police dead in Jamaica since 2002? This job is not a joke, not no cops and robbers we playing. Is *criminals* we have out there, mistah! You think we want to run around checking on some woman who don't come into the bar anymore?"

"She disappear, nobody know where she gone."

"Then how come the people she was staying with don't come in? How come her father don't call us? How come the British diplomat people don't tell us to look for her?"

Shad rose to his feet. "I just saying that things looking suspicious—"

"You know what the word mean, though? All you doing is looking at detective show on television and you trying to play detective, saying things looking *suspicious*. Just leave the investigating to us, you hear me, boy!"

Feeling like a ten-year-old who'd just wrested himself out of a bully's hands, Shad galloped down the stone steps of the police station, reminding himself to tell Beth not to invite Neville to the wedding. It was one thing to have his idiot cousin suggest that he had a thing going on with the woman, but it was another to talk down to him in front of two green corporals. They were probably laughing at him right now.

The Jeep didn't cooperate either. It started bucking near Boston Beach, hiccupping like it was going to shut off at any minute. A mechanic in the gas station told him he had water in the gas tank, and it took another hour to drain the tank and two thousand Jamaican dollars from his wallet. By the time he got back to Largo, he was in no mood to deal with anyone, much less the seamstress waiting for him in the parking lot, her eyes bright with news.

"You hear from Danny?" Janet greeted him as soon as he stepped out of the Jeep. She was wearing shorts and gold sandals, their last meeting on her porch apparently forgotten.

"The phone not working since Saturday. They coming to fix it today."

She patted the shiny, brown curls cascading to her shoulders. "He coming back."

Shad slammed the car door. "What you telling me?"

"Danny coming on Wednesday, day after tomorrow."

"Why?"

"He taking me to the American embassy in Kingston to get a visitor's visa."

"I thought you was looking for a green card."

"Pshaw, man, that take too long. I call them to find out. You have to get marry first and wait five years. Who have that kind of time?" To Shad's upraised eyebrows, she smiled, sweet moon eyes all innocence. "If I get a visa I can pay him a little visit in New York, give him some loving-up. Every man need a woman to keep him warm, like how it cold up there. You know what I mean?"

Shad's forehead deepened into a frown. "Is your idea, this visit you going to make?"

"Of course is my idea," Janet said, tossing her new locks. "You ever hear a man have an idea that a woman don't put in his head?"

"Don't get me vex, you hear?" Shad started toward the bar, keys in hand.

"Don't forget," she said, sandals clattering on the gravel behind him, "he want you to come for him at the airport. Wednesday at three o'clock, he say." Shad kept walking, and she touched his arm.

"You hear me, Shad?" The bartender shook off her hand, raising one impatient finger with the keys, and the clattering stopped.

CHAPTER FORTY-TWO

Eric threw the rest of his sandwich into the garbage can, guilty of having broken his own rule of not eating behind the bar. There was usually no one around to notice on Mondays, when he worked alone at the counter, few customers to impress.

In the parking lot, Shad was being detained by the dressmaker woman, who was stroking her wig as she talked. She'd come into the bar earlier asking for the bartender and Eric had told her he'd be back soon and she could wait there. Instead, she'd chosen to stand in the parking lot, slapping her thick, shiny legs for mosquitoes every now and again, and Eric had imagined Danny Caines riding the woman, and he'd thought that it must have been a pleasant ride because she was a round little thing with no bony hips to contend with. The thought had been followed by a trip to the kitchen, where he'd slathered mayonnaise onto a slice of hard dough bread, topped it with onion and two slices of ham, and started devouring it behind the bar.

"Boss," Shad greeted him, a hard look on his face as he strode across the dusty concrete floor. "Business good?"

"Same as usual." Eric dried his hands on the kitchen towel and perched on Shad's stool.

"You remember to sweep today, though?"

"The wind is doing it for me."

"I returning the keys," Shad said, placing them on the counter and putting his hands in his pockets. "But I going to need the Jeep on Wednesday. Danny Caines is coming back. I have to meet him at the airport."

"Caines is coming back? Well, Janey Mac!" Eric beamed, delighted with his rhyme and his mother's favorite expression. "That must mean he's serious about the hotel, don't you think?"

Shad turned away, wiping his scalp. "I don't know—"

Eric slid off the bartender's stool. "You told him that we're free and clear to start construction, right? The permits are signed and we came to an agreement with Horace. You told him that, right?"

"I tell him long time." The bartender was hovering, not rushing away like he always did on his day off. He was shuffling from one leg to the other, putting his hands in his pockets and taking them out.

"So, what's up, bud?" Eric said, still glowing with delight.

"I want to borrow the Jeep again. I want to go into Port Maria, since it's my day off—"

"I'll come with you. I'll even drive."

"You working the bar."

Eric spread his arms to the emptiness. "What work?"

With the liquor stored under the sink, the refrigerator and kitchen locked, the men were on their way in half an hour. It was the perfect afternoon to get out from under, low clouds scudding across the edges of a blue sky, sunshine everywhere.

"Not much traffic, eh?" Eric commented, changing down to fourth. "Why we going to Port Maria?"

Shad rubbed his hands on his jeans. "I think the artist lady, Sarah, still on the island, and I want to start looking for her."

"It was her passport you were inquiring about, wasn't it?"

"Same thing."

"I had a feeling, I just had a feeling." Eric leaned toward the passenger seat, ready to wink if Shad had been looking at him. "Who found the passport?"

"Boss, some things you don't need to know."

Guided by his companion, Eric drove toward the upper end of Port Maria and away from the ocean. The first lane they turned into was narrow and crowded with small cement houses, dusty yards separated by chicken-wire fences.

"Stop here," Shad said, pointing to a house with high windows.

"Who lives here?"

"A man called Boxer. I know him long time—from Pen days. He know everything going on in Port Maria."

"You know you're being melodramatic. She's probably somewhere—"

Before he could finish, Shad was knocking at the wire gate. A solid-looking man wearing boxer shorts came onto the tiny verandah. He greeted Shad and gestured for him to come inside. Beside the driver's side of the Jeep, a small boy in a stained T-shirt stared up at Eric, two fingers hanging on to the wire fence between them and two fingers in his mouth.

"You seen any Englishwomen hanging around?" Eric asked the child, who turned and ran into the house.

Five minutes later, Shad jumped into the vehicle. "Up the road," he declared. He slammed the door twice until it caught. "Drive to the end and turn left."

Eric slipped the gear into first. "Where we going?"

"We looking for a big yellow house up the hill."

"Whose house?" Eric asked, turning left around a small bar with an umbrella table and three chairs out front.

"Janet's brother live there. They call him Lizard."

Eric chuckled. "Sounds like a drug don or something."

"Boxer tell me he in the business."

"What kind of business?"

"Is three of them in town, Boxer say, three dons in Port Maria." Shad slung his arm out of the window, his face expressionless. "Lizard is one of them."

"Jesus Christ!" Eric exclaimed, hitting the steering wheel. The Jeep chugged to a stop. "Janet's brother is a *don*? How'd you make the connection?"

"I know she from Port Maria and, since Boxer know everybody around here, I thought we should start with him. He know her family, yes, just like I thought."

"Does Danny know this?" Eric opened his eyes wider. "Oh, God, maybe he's—do you think Danny's—tell me it's not so, because I'm not going into business with a drug dealer!"

"We don't know anything yet, boss." Shad was as cool as he'd ever been, wouldn't even look at him.

"What do you think we're going to do, knock on some don's door and ask about a missing woman who may not even be missing?"

"They can't do us nothing, we just inquiring." Shad nodded. A smile played along his lips as he turned away.

"And, besides, you safe. You disappear and embassy people coming around asking plenty questions." A remark that did little to curb Eric's jitters.

The mustard-colored mausoleum was visible from the main road. It stood alone at the end of a long uphill road, dominating the banana trees on either side of the road leading up to it. The cantilevered verandahs on the upper floor made it look like a dusty bomb above the wall surrounding it.

Eric stopped the car a hundred yards in front of the elaborate wrought-iron gate. "This is crazy—you know that, right? We shouldn't even be here."

"We just looking, boss, just looking."

"I'm not driving any closer, I'm telling you right now. Just because we can't see anybody, doesn't mean they're not watching us. I bet they have a camera on us." He gestured with his chin, not daring to point. "And if you hadn't noticed, there's an eight-foot wall around the place. They're going to have dogs."

Shad shook his head and grinned, the gap between his teeth none too comforting this time. "Boss, you never going to make a private investigator."

"You damn straight."

"You saying, you not coming inside with me?"

"Shit, I wouldn't go inside with my own mother." Eric pulled his head back. "You know what those people do for a living? They don't only export and import drugs, you know. They wouldn't think twice about killing you if you asked too many questions. Hell, they don't even have to have a reason to shoot."

"Don't worry, I seen enough," Shad said, patting the air. He settled back in his seat. "I just wanted to check it out."

CHAPTER FORTY-THREE

A craving for Danny had come on that morning after she'd forced herself awake from yet another in the series of terrifying dreams. In this one, the strong fingers of brickies had been holding her, dragging her up the stairs in front of a Gothic church, probing under her blue coat, all the while calling her name.

Think yer too good for us, don't yer, Sarah Louise?

Think we're dirty jobbies, don't yer?

We're going to fuck yer brains out, Sarah Louise, and I bet yer a bloody virgin.

She'd awakened, heart pounding, and the rest had appeared like the gradual lifting of fog from warm earth. Memories, fresh in their rawness, blocked for two decades, had emerged. She remembered first the smell of greasy hair and beer, felt the press of the metal fence against her spine, saw the leering brown face inches from hers.

She remembered the shock of his rough hands and fingers making her breath catch and freezing her tongue, and how they'd cursed her, all of them, throwing out her name, laughing as she struggled in dumb silence. And then it came suddenly, the memory of one of them, the one who had thumped her, trying to have sex with her against the fence, holding up her coat, pulling down her pants, and pushing into her pubic area with his limp penis, and how the others had laughed at him. And she remembered him cursing her again and shoving her to the ground and the damp coldness of the earth under her fingers after they'd left. And she remembered standing up and pulling up her panties. She'd brushed herself off, watching the boys walking down the road, two of them still guffawing, and she'd felt bruised, her privates throbbing and huge. Then her mother's car had come from the other direction even before the boys had turned the corner. She'd run to the car and jumped in, looking straight ahead.

"You're late," she'd said, still shaking, wanting her mother to know.

"I'm sorry, darling. I forgot, to tell the truth, but when Aunt Phyllis asked about you I suddenly remembered. Terrible of me, I know."

She'd hugged herself, lips shut tight.

"You're all right, are you, Sarah Louise?" her mother had inquired when they rounded the corner, the boys nowhere in sight. "You're looking a little—"

"I'm fine, Mum, I'm fine," she'd said, knowing that her cheeks were red and the car was dark. Her mother had started talking about Aunt Phyllis's latest boyfriend and how he'd popped in while they were having tea. Nothing more had been said, nothing, nothing to anyone, although she'd asked her parents never to call her Sarah Louise ever again and they hadn't. She'd stopped taking ballet and buried herself in the quiet of art classes.

When she was fully awake and the dream-reality of probing fingers and her mother's indifference had been pushed aside, she'd lain quiet for a few minutes, hugging her ribs, staring at the white ceiling with its stupid spackling, and it came to her that this position, this familiar hugging of herself, she'd been doing for a long, long time. And it all started to make sense. The dreams were her history, rejected and blocked. She could now understand the hollowness inside, the walls thickening each year, keeping everyone out, keeping them away from her soft insides, an awareness followed by a yearning for the one person who'd refused to be kept at a distance.

"Danny," she'd whispered. "Come for me, please, please, please." It wasn't about sex, every sexual impulse having died since Batsman held on to her beside the road. It was instead a yearning to be found, to matter to someone.

Half an hour later she was sitting on the floor, her upper body extended over her straight legs, stretching her body, trying to escape the mental jumble. She'd felt a compulsion to stretch and made a couple forward bends. The memories uncaged by the last dream had left her in turmoil and called for pacifying. Outside her window, the unseen dog started scratching, whining with pleasure as he scratched. She was about to stand up and attempt a headstand, when the memories started forming themselves into an organized procession. Pausing with her hands on her knees, she allowed the images to fully materialize, allowed the feelings to emerge along with them.

After the assault, she remembered, she'd only felt shame, embarrassment that these crude young men with their accents and rough hands had found her attractive, had touched her. She'd smothered the memory into obliteration, blaming herself. Thirteen years old, and she'd never mentioned the incident to any living being, not even to Penny.

Her silence had been meant as a punishment to her mother for being late. It was deeper even. It was anger with her mother for being self-centered, a woman who had to have the floor, whose turn it always was to make a fuss.

She stared at the blue sky outside the bars. Yet again, she had Man-Up to thank for bringing back the worst of the memories. He'd come into her bedroom the evening before, talking as he entered.

"Where you passport?" he'd demanded, no mention of the painting.

Her mouth was full of toothpaste and she'd stood with the brush in one hand, pulling her nightgown close with the other. "I don't know."

"What you mean?"

She'd spat out the toothpaste into the bathroom sink. "I'm telling you. I don't have it. Whoever packed the bags didn't put it in."

Man-Up had walked to her suitcase and looked down at it. "Where it is then?"

"I have no idea."

"Don't lie to me."

"It was with all my stuff, and it's not here."

He hadn't taken her word for it, knelt down and plowed through her clothes, threw some papers and a map of Jamaica on the floor, went through her pads and papers one by one. He looked up at her, still on one knee, his face suddenly like a spurned lover's.

"Look how we treating you good and you lying to me. You hiding the passport."

"I'm not."

Sauntering over to her, his eyebrows hanging like thunderclouds over his eyes, Man-Up balled up his fists. "Give me the passport!" he shouted, and slapped her, shocking her, snapping her head back. "This is your *one* chance to get out! You better take it."

She held her cheek. "I—I told you—I don't have it."

He'd held on to her upper arms and shaken her, his calluses scratching her skin. "Like you don't understand. If you want to leave Jamaica alive, you have to tell me where the *blood claat* passport is and you have to do it now."

"It wa—was—on a sh—shelf—in Roper's house," she'd stammered as he shook her again.

"What shelf?"

"In the closet—in my room."

Man-Up had stalked out, slamming the bolts back into place behind him. He was *vexed,* Danny would have said, proven by the loud discussion in the living room afterward—three men's voices shouting, interrupting, contradicting. She'd made out bits and pieces, an argument about the passport, and she'd sat on the floor beside the door, crying with dry eyes, holding on to her ribs.

"Two shots and everything over," Man-Up had declared, his vicious voice stabbing through the gap, uncaring if she was listening.

"—the woman named Holloway, the one in Aruba?" the thin man had responded.

"No, man," Batsman interjected, his voice lower than the other two. "The woman don't do nutten."

When the argument had died down and there was silence again, she'd crawled to the bed and lain under the sheet, whimpering, praying, eventually drifting off to the dream and the memories, the imprint of sandpaper hands still on her arms and swollen face.

CHAPTER FORTY-FOUR

S had stopped the Jeep on the weed-packed road leading up to the house, well away from the gate. "This is it."

"Janet's brother lives here?" Danny slid both hands over his head, his fingers interlocked. His hands came to rest behind his head. "That's a big fucking house, man."

"So the dons like they houses big-big. I wanted you to see for yourself."

The American sighed and shook his head. "She never mentioned it. She don't seem like the kind of person—"

"I tell you, nothing in Jamaica seem like what it is, star."

"You think the brother is involved?"

"It seem like too much coincidence that Janet hate Sarah, Janet's brother is a don, then Sarah disappear. I see-ing a *pattern* here, you get me? You never can tell, maybe he kidnap her for money."

"Or she just took off on her own, moved into a hotel or something."

"She didn't have no money, plus she left her passport."

"Okay, if it's a kidnapping, maybe it's somebody else."

"Is only a couple of people. Carthena, the maid who work for Mistah Roper. She don't seem to like Sarah either."

"But why would she want to harm her?"

"Jealousy, maybe."

"I don't get it—"

"And Mistah Roper could be another suspect"—the delicious word Elliot used on *Law & Order: SVU*—"or his girlfriend."

"Because she didn't do the painting? I don't think so."

"We don't know that, star. People have all kind of motive."

"Anybody else?"

"You."

"Me, a *suspect*?" Danny yelled. An artery on his forehead bulged. "You can get that out of your head right now, man. Why would I come back to find her?"

Shad shrugged and gave a half smile. "You could be pretending. Who knows? But to tell the truth, I believe you, because I know if you had any problem you can jump on a plane and leave. You don't have to hurt nobody."

"I'm glad you remember that." Moving his shoulders around a little, Danny got back to business. "Who else?"

"Somebody in England might want her out of the way."

"From what she says, she has a pretty quiet life in England."

"You call her roommate again?"

"Yes, she said Sarah's still not home and her mother hasn't seen her either. I told her about the passport, and she said she wouldn't be surprised if Sarah had gone off somewhere on the island. She kept saying *I'm sure she's having a great adventure*." Danny's attempt at a British accent, complete with wagging head, tempted Shad to laugh. "She said if I come down and still can't find her, to get back in touch, so they could notify the police."

"Then is not a kidnapping for money. They would have heard from the kidnappers by this."

"Why are we here then?"

Shad shrugged. "We have to start somewhere. Janet have a motive and her brother have the means. And another thing," Shad said, stroking the sides of his chin, "I don't like how Janet suddenly change her tune from getting a green card to a visitor's visa. She always talking about getting married and getting a green card, and now she suddenly happy with a visitor's visa. Like she would do anything to get to America and don't care about the getting-married part. I don't understand that—Beth would never switch up like that. Something not right there—I don't trust her."

"But I'm just not seeing Janet—"

"You right, you not seeing her," Shad said, and lifted a warning index finger. "Like how you tell her you coming back to get her the visitor's visa."

Danny shook his head hard. "Is that what she told you? No way. I told her I was coming back to check on the hotel. She said something about a visa, but I didn't want to get into that on the phone. I'd been trying to call you and Eric, but all I kept getting was a busy signal, so I asked her to tell you I was coming. But I came down to find Sarah, you know that, I swear to you."

"Wake up, star, Miss Janet have big plans for you."

"She's in for a bigger surprise then."

Shad stared at the yellow fortress ahead, creaking the gearshift into reverse. "Two things we know: Janet still planning to trap you, and the artist lady still on the island."

On the drive from Port Maria to Largo, it was agreed that they should take action. "We need to ask Lambert to come with us," Shad said. "He have a gun. And if Lambert come, the boss have to come, is a package deal."

"Shit, we going to guns now?"

"I going to bring mine, too."

"*You* have a gun?"

"Short life, long story."

Danny brought out a handkerchief and wiped his forehead. "I guess I'm still getting to know my partners."

"You right, even after you tie the knot, still plenty to find out."

As soon as they drove up the driveway, Miss Mac emerged onto her verandah. "Nice to see you again, Mistah Caines," she said while the men mounted the stairs. Danny greeted her warmly and went into the house with his suit bag, and she looked at Shad behind him and made a funny mouth.

After they deposited the luggage, the men went in search of Eric next door. He was kneeling on the grass outside the bar fixing a water faucet, his white hair hanging like a curtain over the wrench.

"Boss, we have a job for you," Shad announced.

"And I have a job for you," Eric answered, wiping sweat from his forehead. He banged the faucet's rusty spigot. "Damn salt air. Everything rusts in a year." He stood up slowly, holding on to one knee, and shook hands with Danny. "Hey, man, good to see you. Sorry I haven't called since you left, but the phone's been dead. It's back now, though. I got that hooked up this morning."

"Did you tell them about the Internet?" Shad asked him.

"Next month, they said. They'll put us on the list."

"That's great," Danny put in. "You'll be online and we can email—"

"Right," Eric said. "But it's always better doing business in person, you know."

"It's good to be back, I can't lie," Danny said, wiping his hand on his jeans. "Largo feels almost like home now."

"Glad to hear that." Eric nodded. He swung the wrench toward Shad. "So what's this job you're talking about?"

CHAPTER FORTY-FIVE

After laying two of her scarves on the side table, Sarah wrapped the thin pink towel around her hand, holding it tight in her fist. She took up her position beside the door, the first minute ticked off by the thumping behind her ribs. Five minutes, feeling like twenty, went by. At the end of ten minutes, her chest had gone numb and her feet were starting to sweat in their tennis shoes, feet that had gone bare for thirteen scratches on the wall.

She'd hatched the plan that morning. As she'd stood in the shower, trying to wash off the sensation of scratchy hands on her face and arms, probing fingers in her privates, the reality of her rape had poured slow rage into her. It seemed to clear her head somehow, forcing her to sit on her bed afterward assessing her situation.

Her gut told her that the men in the living room had come to some conclusion about her fate, were probably planning it already. The idea of putting her on a plane had been scotched, she guessed, her passport not located. Another plan for her disposal had to be made and, according to Man-Up, they'd be coming for her soon.

They wouldn't expect her to do anything. Her docility, her painting of leaves, the amiable sketching of her captors had lulled them into an assumption that she was a passive person. Her most frequent visitors had started chatting to her when they entered. Clementine had stopped closing the door when she brought in her meal and Batsman had told her that his portrait was now in a frame. The maid had confided that she'd been named for the song her mother loved, and not a flower. She'd even warbled a few lines from the song.

Unwrapping the towel, flexing her hand, Sarah began to have second thoughts about her plan. Maybe it was safer to wait. If she tried to escape, a million things could go wrong. She started toward the bed, then turned back and took up her position again.

The familiar steps started shuffling down the corridor. She caught her breath. The shuffling drew closer. One bolt was drawn back, then the lower bolt, this time with a groan (she pictured the middle-aged woman stooping low, knees gaping, one hand gripping the tray). The door opened and Sarah ducked behind it. On her way to the bed, Clementine glanced at the closed bathroom door, from behind which came the sound of the shower.

"Your breakfast come," she called.

Sarah pushed the bedroom door until it was almost closed. She tiptoed toward Clementine as the maid set the tray down and straightened. In a flash, she drew the towel tight across the woman's mouth. Clementine clawed weakly at the towel as Sarah pushed her facedown on the bed. After knotting the cloth behind the woman's head, Sarah snatched up the ends of the top sheet and tied them around her legs.

"You're just going to have to lie here for a bit, old lady," she said as she turned her captive over. With one of the scarves, she secured the maid's shaking hands, hands that had fed her.

"I'm not going to hurt you." She stood in front of Clementine, hands akimbo, the way the maid had often stood over her. "I just want a chance to live, really. Wouldn't you?" The woman lay still, a puzzled, almost hurt, look in her eyes, while the artist tied her sheet-wrapped feet with the second scarf.

Sarah took a last look at her captive, a pink mummy lying diagonally across the bed, before creeping to the door. She waited, listening. Only a few bird calls outside her window. She entered the corridor, pulling the door almost closed behind her, and tiptoed in the direction Clementine came from every day. Four closed doors lined the corridor, two on each side, and she glanced at them as she crept past.

A kitchen, dark and gloomy, lay straight ahead. When she got to the doorway, she paused and took a breath. It was an old-fashioned, L-shaped kitchen, and she could just make out a gas stove and laminated counter along one wall, a sink and refrigerator along another. Straight ahead was a door, probably to the exterior, and she started toward it.

A creak in the corner made her freeze. The older man was sitting at a table; a thin line of smoke streamed upward from an ashtray beside him. His startled eyes looked ominous above his coffee mug.

"Where the *fuck* you going?" he screeched, slamming the cup down.

"I'm getting some tea for Clementine," Sarah said. "She's not feeling well."

He jumped up. "Get back to your room, you trying to run away. You think I fool."

"I'm not running away," Sarah said, backing into the corridor. "I'll get Clementine."

She turned and ran down the corridor, past the door to her room, and to the living room, the man pounding on the tiles behind her.

"Come back here!" he screamed.

The living room was empty. She darted to the front door and turned the handle. It was locked. The man grabbed her arm and swung her around, his nails digging into her.

"No woman, I don't care where they come from," he snarled, "is going to escape from me."

She wrenched her arm loose and ran to the louver windows, barred like hers. He grabbed her from behind.

"I tell them to send you away long time," he whined, his off-key voice in her ear as he dragged her back down the passageway. "They didn't want to listen to me. Like somebody need to teach you a lesson."

When they got to her room, he kicked the door open. Clementine was lying across the bed in her pink cocoon, red eyes bulging above the towel.

CHAPTER FORTY-SIX

T his isn't a good idea," Lambert declared, throwing his sunglasses onto the Rover's dashboard. "We're too exposed." Early-morning sun was painting the eastern side of the house golden, the rest of the towering building in deep shadow.

"I don't know why we had to come out so early, anyway," Eric put in.

"Dons don't get up early," Shad said, "and Lambert have to go to work."

"We're sitting ducks here," Danny said. "Anybody can look out the window and see us."

Shad leaned over Lambert's shoulder. "Just ease the car forward, like you don't mean no harm."

In the front passenger seat, Eric rolled down his window. "I say we reverse and reconnoiter, like—"

"No, boss," Shad said. "We can't come all this way and not find out nothing." It had taken too much time, valuable time, to get the four men and two guns together.

"It's too late, anyway," Lambert muttered, his eyes on the rearview mirror. All eyes turned in time to see an emerald-green BMW pulling up behind them, the windows tinted jet-black. It came to a halt in reptilian silence close to their rear bumper.

"Keep the engine running," Shad instructed. He took the Glock out of his pocket and placed it on the seat, glancing at Danny. As soon as he opened the car door, the driver's door of the BMW opened. An athletic-looking fellow unfolded from the car, navigator sunglasses hiding his eyes. He wore basketball shorts and a neon orange jacket, on his feet matching orange sneakers, one of the imports, with a logo on the side and the strings removed. Even with the expensive clothes, he looked disgusted and fearful, another candidate for the Pen.

The man sauntered toward Shad, jamming his hands into the jacket pockets. "Like you lost or something." His voice was surprisingly smooth and deep like a radio announcer's.

"We not lost."

"What you want?"

"We want to see Lizard."

The man turned his head a few inches toward the car and shrugged. "What you want with him? He tired."

"We looking for somebody."

"Who you looking for?"

"That between him and me."

Shifting from one sneaker to the other, ready to teach somebody a lesson, the man took his left hand out of his pocket. "Don't move."

He walked backward around the front of the BMW, facing the Rover until he got to the passenger side. The window rolled down with an elegant humming noise and he bent and said something. A few seconds later, he beckoned to Shad.

"He say to come."

Shad approached slowly, his heart in his throat, thinking

of the gun he'd left on the seat next to a startled Danny. If he didn't have his back, maybe Lambert would.

"Stop there!" the driver ordered.

Shad halted in front of the vehicle's gleaming emblem, the circle of blue and white looking like a dartboard. He stared at the man's bright sneakers while the man patted him down, front and back, up and down, fingers not yet as invasive as a prison guard's. When he bent down to pat Shad's crotch, a gun handle stuck out of his jacket pocket. Satisfied, he gave a languid wave toward the passenger side. "He in there."

The window was still down. Lizard was sitting with his mouth pouted at Shad, annoyed already. He was smaller than the photographs in the newspaper made him look, the rounded features and big eyes stamping him as Janet's family. Wearing a heavy cloth coat, he looked like he'd come back from a trip.

"Excuse me—" Shad started, bending toward the window. The driver stood close beside him, his hands again in his pockets.

"What you want?" Lizard said. "What you sneaking around my house for?"

"We looking for an Englishwoman, she name Sarah, a tall woman with red hair."

"And why you come to me?" The man's surprise looked genuine, his eyebrows arching and relaxing.

"We can't find her nowhere. We was wondering if you see her or hear anything, like how you run things, you know."

"I never hear of her."

"We just checking, you know. We asking everybody around the area."

"Nothing here to check, so just go on about your business."

Shad nodded and started back to the Rover, Orange Jacket still close. When they got to the front of the Beemer, they peeled off to their separate vehicles.

"Pull to the side so he can pass," Shad said after he climbed in. Danny handed him the gun and Lambert pulled the Rover over. The blackened windows of the BMW glided past, slowly enough for its passengers to take a good look at them, and the wrought-iron gates opened silently to admit them. Lambert reversed to the end of the road where he could turn around.

"What did he say?" Danny asked.

"He say he don't know any woman named Sarah."

"End of mission," Eric said.

"Not yet," Shad replied.

"We have to make them think we're leaving," Lambert said. He revved the car engine and turned the corner.

"But we not going to leave," the bartender said sharply.

Lambert slowed down. "What now?"

"Damn, Shad," the boss moaned.

"There's a banana walk just before we turn onto this road." Shad nodded. "Turn up there." Lambert found the narrow dirt road, lined on each side by banks of fifteen-foot banana trees, and turned in.

"We can't see anything from here, man," Danny said. "This stuff is too thick."

"At least it's hiding us," Eric said.

"Get up close to the house," Shad urged, "as close as you can get."

The car bumped along the farm road until the large house rose to their left, its verandah balusters high above the trees.

"Stop here," Shad said. "I going to get closer." After Lambert stopped, the bartender climbed out.

"I'm coming with you," Danny said.

Their footsteps silenced by the floor of dead leaves, the two men slid between the tree trunks, pushing aside the ripening fruit in their blue plastic bags. The wall was taller than it looked from the road.

"We can't see nothing, man," Danny said. "We can't even see over the wall."

"Help me up."

Stepping onto Danny's bent leg, Shad grabbed the top of the wall and pulled up. The house ran eighty feet or longer, parallel to the wall, Lizard's green chariot now parked on its circular driveway. Underneath the overhanging balcony was a construction job in progress, an addition to the house. Unpainted concrete-block walls stood behind piles of sand and gravel. Bags of cement were stacked inside an unfinished doorway.

"What you seeing?" Danny hissed.

"Not much," Shad whispered back. About to step down from Danny's knee, he clutched onto the wall. "Wait, I hear something." There was a stirring at the front of the house, a door opening and closing. "Somebody leaving."

"Can you see who it is?"

A woman in a red skirt appeared on the circular driveway, her back to them. She walked around the green car and toward the gate. The bold stride of the woman was familiar, something about the way she swung her hips and kicked out her feet when she walked.

Shad snorted softly. "It look like—no, it can't be—but it could be—"

"Who is it, man?"

"You never guess."

CHAPTER FORTY-SEVEN

Eric chewed the inside of his cheek as Shad and Danny climbed into the Rover's backseat. He'd had enough of Shad's rescue missions. One day they'd be arrested—or killed, dammit—and for what? There was no hope of Danny investing in a hotel, anyway, not after this crap, and now this caper looking for a missing tourist who had nothing to do with the hotel.

Beside him, Lambert turned to the men in the back. "What happened? Why did you run back to the road? I didn't know if we were supposed to follow you."

"We have to go to Annotto Bay," Shad said.

"We saw Carthena," Danny said, closing the car door quietly behind him. "She knows where Sarah is, man. She says she's in another house."

Eric swung around. "You're kidding! I thought we were on a wild-goose chase."

"She didn't want to talk at first," Danny said. "She said all she was doing was visiting her mother."

"You should have seen her face when we jumped out in front of her," Shad said, snickering.

"And you got her to talk—just like that?" Lambert asked.

"She was vexed when we hold on to her," Shad replied. "She say we shouldn't frighten a person like that. I ask her what she was doing in the house, and she say her mother sick and she come to see her. I ask her why her mother living in Lizard house, and she say none of my business. I tell her to talk if she know what good for her, and that I want to know where the Englishwoman is. But she so *facety,* little and fresh, she just suck her teeth at me. She say she don't know anything about the Englishwoman. *I tell you she leave and gone back to England,* she say. But then she say she glad she gone, that she never like her, and how she want to take every man she see, even the trumpeter man Ford. And, right then, I know she know something, just the way she happy that Sarah gone."

"I took a photograph on my cell phone while Shad was holding her," Danny said, "and I told her I was going to show it to the police and put it on the Internet, and I was going to say that she and her mother was family to Lizard, a known drug dealer. That seemed to get to her."

"I think it was the gun on her neck." Shad chuckled. "I never meet a woman yet who not afraid of a gun. Is a good thing she don't know I don't have no bullets. When I tell her to run down the road toward town, she start flying down the hill, you see."

After they'd gotten back to the main road and were heading west, Eric broke the silence. "So, why are we going to Annotto Bay? You might as well tell us."

"Carthena tell us Sarah in a house in Annotto Bay."

"Oh, God," groaned Eric, his only comfort knowing that Danny wasn't in the drug business, or didn't seem to be.

It was seventeen long miles to Annotto Bay and, one eye

on Lambert's speedometer, Eric counted them off, ignoring the lush fields of bananas flying past his window. He'd never liked the parish of St. Mary, too competitive with Largo's parish of Portland, everybody fighting for skimpy tourist dollars far away from Montego Bay.

In Annotto Bay, Lambert drew up outside a redbrick Baptist church. "Where to now?"

"She said the house is on a hill, a house with a blue wall," Shad said. "That was all she would say."

"Sounds like another don," Lambert said. "Or somebody in the business."

"How do you know?" Danny asked.

"They like the hills because it make a good lookout," Shad said.

Lambert frowned. "We're looking for a blue wall. That's all you know? There must be a hundred blue walls in this town."

Danny leaned over his shoulder. "Why don't you get a good vantage point? Maybe a place where we can look up at the hills so we can spot a blue wall."

"Good idea." Lambert nodded and pointed the car toward the waterfront.

CHAPTER FORTY-EIGHT

The bedroom door banged open and Man-Up stood in the doorway, hands on his hips, feet apart.

"Slim Jim tell me you tie up Clementine and you trying to run away," he shouted. "You must be a *ee-diot*."

Sarah folded her arms around her knees and looked outside. It was midmorning, no sunlight falling inside the window yet, and nothing to lose.

"I speaking to you!" he demanded.

She stood up and smoothed the top sheet that had bound Clementine, who'd called her *ungrateful* and refused to look at her as Sarah had untied the sheet and scarves.

"What do you expect? You have me locked up, won't tell me why I'm here, won't tell me who's behind this."

"I asking you a question, why you running away?"

Her answer was to walk to the window. She could see the dog for the first time. It was lying near the wall, a large black-and-white dog with fur that needed to be brushed, an old dog on a chain who'd kept her company.

"What come over you?" the driver insisted behind her. "You not acting like yourself. Now you causing trouble."

"We can try, can't we?" she answered carefully, holding the rage at bay.

He walked around the bed toward her and reached for her arm. "Come here."

She yanked it out of his reach. "Don't you bloody touch me!"

He laughed. "Remember, you were down on your knees begging me?"

"The offer has expired."

"I touch you if I feel like," he said, and snatched at her, the scar popping out of his sneering cheek. She dodged him and ran to the open door. He raced behind her, caught her by her elbow.

"You not going nowhere, not until I finish with you, then all this foolishness stopping today."

"What are you going to do?"

"You find out soon enough." He dragged her to the bed. "First, you and I going to get friendly."

"Fuck you!" Sarah said, and spat at him, the spittle falling short. "You're going to have to kill me first."

He screwed up his lips and spat. "Is the first time I ever spit on a white woman," he said, grinning, boasting.

She wiped the spit from her cheek. "If you think you're going to—"

"I don't think, I know." He reached for her head and she ducked. "You think is game I playing?" He grabbed her by the hair and yanked her down to the mattress.

A piercing ringing at his waist, sounding like an old-fashioned phone, made him loosen his grip and look down.

Sarah pulled her head away. "Answer your phone!"

"More important things to do," he said, and lunged for her breast.

"Somebody!" she screamed, turning her head to the open door, kicking at him. *"Help me!"*

"Nobody coming, man, they know you deserve it. After what you done?" He threw himself down on the bed beside her, the old-fashioned ring still pealing. "Who you think Clementine is? Just some stupid old woman you can disrespect? You don't mess with her, tie her up and thing, and don't get what coming to you."

"Batsman!" she shouted.

An annoyed voice from the door. "She making too much noise," the whiner said.

"Shut the *raas claat* door!" Man-Up roared.

"Help me!" Sarah called, reaching one hand toward the thin man, but the door slammed shut.

Man-Up put his hand over her mouth. It smelled of raw meat.

She yanked her head free. "Stop it! *Stop!*"

"Like you need little persuasion." He held on to her arm with one hand, pulled a gun out of his pants pocket with the other, and put it on the mattress beside him. "Now we can have a good time, right?"

She gulped and glared at him. "You big bully. Just because you have a gun—"

"You going to thank me after, man." His hand darted out and grabbed her blouse, ripped it open. "I going to give you something no white man ever give you."

326

A full minute went by before the door opened. A thin, tired-looking man stood in the doorway.

"What you want?" he said, glancing behind him.

"Lizard send us," Shad said, one hand in his pocket, two fingers touching the bag with Granny's grave dirt, the other three wrapped around the gun. He hoped his sunglasses hid his racing heart. Beside him, Danny stood with arms folded across his chest, keeping his mouth shut as directed.

The man at the door pursed his lips. "Why Lizard send you? How come I never see you before?"

Inside the living room, a youth sat on a red chair staring at them.

Shad cleared his throat. "He say you might need *reinforcements.*"

"What that mean?"

"You need some help, so we—"

A piercing scream came from deep inside the house, and the man swung toward it.

"Sarah!" Danny yelled, and pushed past Shad through the door.

The skinny man grabbed Danny's arm. "Where you going?"

"Get out of my way!" Danny said, striking the man in the face. The two fell to the floor, the American twice the size of the other. Shad pulled the gun out of his pocket.

"Let him go!" he shouted, pointing the gun at the skinny man. His hand was shaking and he held on to it with his other hand.

The man in the red chair jumped up, drawing a silver gun. "Get out!"

Danny rolled on top of his opponent, pinning his arms. "Man-Up!" the man screamed, looking toward the corridor.

A burly man rushed out of the hallway, zipping up his pants with one hand, a thick, black gun in the other. "What the *raas claat*—"

He stopped in the middle of the room and pointed the gun at Shad. "Drop it!"

"Police outside," Shad yelled. "All around the house."

"Batsman, take his gun," Man-Up ordered, straightening his shirt. "Check the door."

Batsman yanked the Glock out of Shad's hand and glanced around the yard before closing the door. "Nobody outside," he said. He stuck Shad's gun in his pants pocket and pointed his own at the bartender.

"Why the damn dog didn't bark?" Man-Up growled.

"He too old," Batsman said. "I tell you that long time."

"What you want?" the big man demanded, looking from Danny to Shad. "Who send you?"

"We want the Englishwoman," Shad said. "Let her go and we won't go to the police."

"Sarah!" Danny shouted as his opponent struggled up.

"Shut up!" Man-Up said, brandishing the gun. "I should just kill the two of you one time."

"I tell you, no killing in my house," the thin man said, standing and brushing off his pants. "All them DNA tests—"

"You hear what the man say," Danny said as he got up. "Just let Sarah go and there'll be no killing."

Man-Up threw himself into an armchair. He smiled a slow, easy smile. "Oh, is *you*—the black Yankee man. I hear about you. You own all kind of beauty shop and thing, man, making plenty money." He said the last sentence with an American twang.

Danny frowned and shook his head. "All we want is Sarah."

The thick man laughed. "Is two of us have guns on you, star. Don't get excited. You watch your manners and you can have little piece of the business."

"I don't want no part of your business, whatever it is."

Man-Up dropped the smile. "Is *you* don't understand, Yankee. You might as well get comfy, because she not going nowhere and you not going nowhere."

"Danny!" All heads turned to Sarah, standing at the entrance to the corridor holding her torn blouse together. She was sweaty, her face almost as red as a poinciana flower, almost as red as her wild, frizzy hair.

Danny threw a fist toward Man-Up. "What you do to her, man?"

"Get back to your room!" Man-Up shouted at her.

"No bloody way!" Sarah shouted back, a new fire in her eyes.

"Let her go," Shad urged.

"What you going to do with us?" Danny said at the same time.

"You can't kill us," Shad said. "Is three of us, and if you kill one you have to kill all three, then they going to hunt you down. We tell them where we coming."

Man-Up sucked his teeth, an ugly scar rising with his cheek. "I don't believe you one damn. You don't tell no-body." He sighed. "You put me in a terrible position. We going to have to take you to a cane field and shoot you. All they going to find is three dead bodies. They never going to know who leave you there." He nodded to the thin man. "Tie them up."

"With what?" the man complained. "I don't have no rope."

"Pshaw, man, you want me think for you now? Just go in the back and find something." The man headed to the corridor. As he passed her, Sarah gave him a dirty look, and slipped farther into the room.

"Stop!" Man-Up barked at her, sitting up in his chair.

"Bollocks! Don't tell me what I can do!" she retorted. Batsman looked from Sarah to Man-Up, nibbling his lip.

The skinny man returned with a plastic clothesline, and Man-Up told him to tie Danny and Shad together by the wrists, haranguing him as he did so.

"Don't even have twine or nothing to tie up a person. You just as stupid as your dog. The boss tell you what to do, but you don't want to do it, arguing with me whole time. All you can talk about is putting her on a plane. Then we can't find her passport and now you can't find your friend in Montego Bay to make a new one." The man didn't respond, just finished his task and pushed Shad and Danny onto two of the red chairs, Shad's left wrist bound to Danny's right.

"And now you see what it come to?" Man-Up continued. "If you listen to me—"

"I telling you," Shad interrupted, "the—"

"Shut your *raas claat* mouth," Man-Up threw at him.
"Nobody know you come here. We can do what we want
with you."

The front door banged open. Man-Up jumped out of
the chair and the older man jerked around. Lambert was
standing in the doorway, his gun planted in the elaborately
braided hairdo of the woman he was clutching. She was
thin and wiry, not an ounce of fat on her, a woman with a
powerful voice, the kind of woman you didn't mess with if
you could help it.

"Lemme go!" she snarled as she struggled, the angry,
protruding eyes above the straight nose reminding Shad of
someone, somewhere.

"A volunteer hostage," Lambert said. He wasn't smiling,
but his voice had a proud lift to it.

"What the *blood claat*—?" Man-Up shouted, and raised
his gun.

"Why you don't answer the fucking phone when I call
you?" the wriggling woman yelled, three gold teeth parad-
ing along one side of her mouth. "I was calling to tell you
them was coming."

"I was busy."

"Just when I need you, you *busy*?" the woman shrieked,
the tight skirt sliding up her thighs.

"Who are you?" Sarah flung at her, advancing one step
closer.

"Is the boss, Lizard woman," Man-Up said. "Gecko she
name."

"I know you," Sarah shouted. "I saw you with Carthena in the bar—"

"And you was with her in the kitchen—" Shad added.

"Why'd you have me kidnapped?" Sarah demanded. "I never did anything!"

"What dis? What going on here?" Another angry woman's voice—Janet's. She was standing behind Lambert, trying to peep over his shoulder.

"Get him, Jan!" Gecko called. "Grab him balls!"

"You grab my balls, you never forget it," Lambert snarled, turning his head toward Janet. He spread his elbows to fill the doorway.

"Get out my way," Janet yelled at Lambert, a midget on tiptoe plucking at his clothes, kicking at his ankles.

"You not going nowhere," the contractor grunted.

"You bitch!" Danny shouted at Janet. "Look what you started!"

"What you mean what I start?" Janet yelled, one eye visible around Lambert's right arm. "Is *you* promise me a green card. Then you change you tune—"

"You promise her a green card?" Shad snorted, staring hard at Danny. "You told me—"

"That was before Sarah," Danny answered, his jaw working.

"See what I mean?" Gecko spat on the tiles and glowered at Sarah. "You come along and turn the man's head. We couldn't let you mess up everything. And you would be *dead* if these idiots had listen to me. But no, because you is a woman, they feel sorry for you. I should have get women to work for me. They would have shoot you and dump the body long time."

"I'm telling you, drop your guns!" Lambert shouted, jerking his head toward Man-Up.

Gecko yanked one hand free of Lambert's grip and pointed at Danny with a long blue fingernail. "And you is a idiot, running after a white woman. You could have been *rich*. All you had to do was give Janet a visitor's visa, not even a green card. We make it easy for you. She would have just come up to visit you and disappear—don't even have to take her shopping or nothing—and if you want to, you could have help her run things in America and use your businesses them as a cover. Easy, easy, everything in place already. Man-Up going to handle things down here, collections and shipments. We plan it long time."

"You never said nothing about no *drug* business," Danny called to Janet. "You talking trash, talking how you love me the whole time."

"Love you?" Janet yelled, tugging at Lambert's arm. "You ever hear the song say, *What love got to do with it?* This about business, star." She frowned at Sarah. "And you have to mess up everything. You teaching him to paint, taking him to dinner with big people, and he stop calling me, don't want no more sexing up. All we had to do was get you out of the way to make the obeah work good."

"I knew it—obeah!" Danny exclaimed. "Jesus—"

"Let me tell you something, Mistah Savior," Gecko said, pointing the vicious finger at Danny again. "You not going to mess up our plans, you hear me? I going to make sure Janet get her visa even if I have to pay plenty money for it. We still having our business in America, and I going to be in charge." She spat on the tiles. "So *all* of you have to dead because I don't take no prisoners. Just shoot him, Man-Up!"

The skinny man put his hand up. "I tell you, I don't want no killing in my house."

"You too damn coward," Gecko retorted. "If I woulda know you was so coward—just shoot him, Man-Up!"

"Shoot if you think you bad," Lambert roared, twisting the gun deeper between the woman's braids.

"Don't shoot," Batsman called, glancing from his prisoners to Gecko. "You could dead, Franchette, or he could miss and kill Janet."

"Leave him, Bertie," Lambert's prisoner yelled.

"The boss say I must shoot," Man-Up answered, cocking the gun. He took aim, the pink tip of his tongue sliding out of his mouth. Suddenly, a screeching wail sliced through the room.

"What that?" Gecko screamed. The bloodcurdling alarm rotated its shrill invasion, only a few feet away, it sounded like.

Man-Up covered one ear. "What the *blood claat*—"

Everything happened quick-quick after that, Shad told Beth later, just like you were taking one-one photographs. Sarah darted behind Man-Up and kicked him hard behind one knee, sending him crumpling to the floor. Her arms had shot up high like a football player who'd scored a goal, showing a flash of white breast, before she ran behind Lambert. She snatched off Janet's wig and delivered a blow to her jaw that sent the seamstress flying out the door. At that, Shad and Danny leaped up together, their wrists still bound. Danny kicked Batsman in the groin and Shad kicked him on his arm, knocking the gun out of his hand and sending the youth to the floor. And just as the skinny man reached for the gun, Danny grabbed him with his free hand and Shad picked up the gun with *his* free hand. And it wasn't over yet, because Man-Up rolled over and fired toward the four men in their tight huddle, and Franchette and the thin man screamed at the same time, the sounds of gun and pain exploding over the siren.

Blood sprouted from the man's shirtsleeve, and he held his arm. "*Bumba,* you shoot me!" he yelled at nobody and everybody.

Shad jammed the gun against Batsman's scalp, the scalp that had been almost clean shaven in Roper's kitchen when he'd appeared with the two women and the baby.

"Man-Up, take your pick," Shad shouted. "You can shoot again and kill either Lizard's woman or his little brother, maybe both. And you know Lizard coming for you then, and it going to be a long, slow death. Which one you want to dead first, girlfriend or brother?"

CHAPTER FIFTY

Securing her easel with one hand, Sarah swooped a line of acrylic up the large page Roper had given her. She held her breath with the boldness, the bigness of it. After several more stripes, she dabbed her brush in the dark green paint on the palette and started feathering in the narrow leaves springing from the stalks. Her subject was the bamboo grove encircling her patio. Once unsightly to her, she now welcomed the privacy it afforded from passing cars and the curiosity of strangers and journalists who wanted to see *the Englishwoman who was kidnapped*.

She missed her sea grape tree. She thought of it often, saw its flat, red-veined leaves outside her cell window, wondered who would look at it now. Who would learn what it taught about perseverance and survival, about living behind a wall of jagged glass? Maybe a dog, she decided, a dog grateful for its shade.

The fluttering in her chest hadn't stopped yet, although she could feel it starting to slow with her painting. Her hand holding the brush was only shaking a little. It felt good to paint again, her way, she knew now, to soothe the anxiety that had plagued her for two decades. Since her release the day before, there'd been no rest. Even the bedside lamp that stayed on all night hadn't helped her to sleep. When she did doze toward morning, she'd dreamed of being buried alive in a coffin lined with a pink sheet, and she'd awakened suddenly and moaned into her pillow.

There was no escaping the reminders. Every minute of her ordeal was replayed either in her head or in her reluctant words. Earlier that morning, Sonja had come to tell her that a Sergeant Neville Myers was there to see her. The man was waiting for her with a young corporal who'd lugged all her baggage into the living room. Squeezed into his uniform and squeaky shoes, the sergeant had spent an hour asking her questions, the corporal taking notes, and she'd tried to be patient. She'd shown him her sketches of the room where she'd been held captive, but he didn't seem interested. He seemed to have other things in mind.

"And you say you didn't know these men before they took you in the car?" he'd asked her twice.

"I'm totally sure," she'd snapped the second time.

When the sergeant got to his feet, Sarah had jumped up. "Why didn't you come looking for me? In England—"

"No one reported you missing," Myers had said, and shrugged, as arrogant as any London copper. As soon as they left, she'd returned to her room and set up to paint as far from the ringing phone as possible. There was nothing she could do about the swirling thoughts but try to paint them away.

"Visitors?" a hesitant voice said behind her. It was Danny at the open door to her bedroom. He was barefooted, his face and arms sweaty.

"Of course."

He walked across the patio's flagstones and kissed her upturned cheek. "If you want to paint—"

337

"No, it's fine, honestly," she said, swirling her paint-brush in the jar of water. "Did you walk down?"

"Ran on the beach, needed it." He sank into a lounge chair and pulled up his shorts.

"Hey, you're working on the whole page!" he exclaimed softly. She nodded, unable to say that she'd lived every minute in her cell with terror and rage and longing, enough to fill many large sheets now that she was free.

"Sonja tells me the phone is ringing off the hook," he said. He was trying to sound cheerful, she could tell. "Every newspaper and TV station in the Caribbean and England want to talk to you."

She shrugged. "I'm not taking any calls, although I had to talk to a man from the British High Commission, from Intelligence or something."

"You're a celebrity now. You thought about that? It'll probably make your paintings more valuable, particularly if you paint a Jamaican series, like you been saying."

"That's what Penny said."

"You spoke to her?"

"And my mother, last night." She dipped the brush in a blob of lime-yellow and stroked on a few highlights. "They want me to come home right away."

"Are you leaving?"

"Roper said I could leave or stay as long as I wanted, but I'll probably go next week. He's got his painting, the one I—the one of sea grape leaves. The police brought it with my things."

"Aren't you going to keep it?"

"Oh, God, no." She shuddered. "I don't need any reminders, and it was part of the deal. I think what he really

likes is the painting of Man-Up on the back, even though
it's unfinished. He calls it a *two-fer*."

"How are you feeling, by the way?"

She pushed at her hair with one hand, the hair she'd
decided to keep red. "Not quite the old self yet, but I'll get
there."

Danny stroked his scalp as he looked down. "Listen, I
have to—I want to—I'm sorry I got you mixed up in this."

"It's I who should be thanking you. I mean, you bloody
well rescued me."

"But if it hadn't been for me and my—my—the whole
Janet thing, you wouldn't have gone through this. I didn't
have a *clue* what she was up to, honest, but I still feel re-
sponsible."

She squeezed more acrylic onto the palette. "Apology
accepted, I suppose."

"You may not believe me," he said, leaning forward
over clasped hands, his smoky eyes with their yellow circles
pleading. "I was really *really* worried about you. That's why
I came back. I had a hundred things doing in the States,
but I couldn't—like I couldn't concentrate. I kept thinking
about you, wondering why you left—just like that—and
where you went to." He reached out to touch her arm and
she drew away, the gesture making him pause.

"I thought—I knew you were mad at me," he said at
last.

"I was."

"When the housekeeper told me you'd left, I was
stunned."

She lay down her brush. "Stunned? How do you think
it felt being kidnapped for no reason, not knowing what

you'd done wrong? And I still can't believe that someone can disappear and nobody look for her. Thank God, Shad kept looking. If it hadn't been for him—I called him last night to thank him."

"I was in touch with him—but if I'd thought—"

Heat rose from the base of her spine, steaming into her chest, until she had to stand up to give it space. "Thought what, Danny? That somebody could snatch me right under everybody's eyes and nobody notice? That you and everybody else could go on with your lives as if nothing had happened? Nobody even reported me missing, did you know that?" She tried to hold her voice down, tried and failed.

"I told Shad—he went to the police—"

"I've been *locked up* in a room, men with *guns* to my head, my life threatened almost every day."

She put her hands on her hips and gave herself permission to speak as loudly as she had to. "I *waited* and *waited* for somebody, anybody, for Christ's sake, to come and get me. All I could think was that nobody cared if I lived or died. I thought you'd all *forgotten* about me. Then I started to imagine all kinds of things, that you'd had me kidnapped—"

"Me?"

"I thought you wanted me out of the way, or those two men you were with when I first met you, maybe, had kidnapped me for—I don't know—money or something."

Danny shook his head. "Alphonsus is an Anglican minister, and his brother has a grocery store. Why would you—?"

"*Dammit,* Danny!" she shouted. "What do you expect? My mind was all over the place. I was in *prison,* for God's sake. You have no idea what I've been through. I was terrified the whole time. All I had were my thoughts, my suspicions to keep me company. I even thought Roper had me kidnapped because he didn't want to buy my ticket home."

"Oh, God, I'm so glad we found you."

"I could have *died* and no one—"

"If I'd had any idea—but I swear to you, I thought you'd just—*left,* you know, because you were angry with me. You had every reason to leave. I'd told you I'd broken off with Janet—then I got back with her. I couldn't blame you for being angry. I called Penny—"

"Much good it did me."

"—and she said you hadn't come back, and that's when I started to get worried. Then Shad found your passport." He pulled the dark blue booklet out of his shorts pocket and handed it to her. "He ask me to give it back to you, by the way—and we knew you were still here. That's why I came back to Largo. I'm just glad we got to you in time."

She answered by staring at the bamboo, unmoving, and he walked to the edge of the patio and turned around, his forehead knotted.

"Sarah, I want you to tell me the truth." The great arms were helpless at his sides. "Were you raped?"

Sonja had asked the same question. The writer's perky voice had lowered when she placed a bowl of soup in front of Sarah the night before. She'd put one hand on her trembling back and leaned over her shoulder.

"Did anyone—you know—*hurt* you, Sarah?" she'd asked. "Maybe we should report it." No one, not her mother, not her father, had ever asked her that before.

The question had come after Roper had apologized for—*everything,* he said before rushing out of the kitchen. Sonja had sunk into the chair beside her, miserable, explaining that they hadn't called the police because they were sure she was furious with them, especially with Roper (*he can be so damn controlling,* the writer had said with tears rolling down her cheeks). They were too embarrassed to try to call her in London, she said. They'd thought she'd call when she was ready. A kidnapping was the last thing on their minds. Everything had been cleaned out of her room, after all, and she'd had reason enough to leave. She'd begged Sarah's forgiveness and Sarah had said she forgave her, although she hadn't, part of her still behind the blue wall.

Danny leaned over in front of her, the dove-gray eyes not allowing her to escape the question again. "Talk to me, Sarah. Did he rape you?"

It was her turn to walk away until the bamboo stopped her. She reached out and grabbed two slender stems. The leaves felt stickier and sharper than she'd expected, not rounded and comforting like sea grape leaves.

"No, he didn't," she said without turning her head. "He tried, but I wouldn't let him—I got this enormous—wave of strength, and I—I couldn't let him do it." The rage was subsiding, allowing her to breathe even though her voice was shaking. "Got a bit dodgy before you lot came in, but I was fighting and kicking like hell. I told myself that if there was ever a time to die, it was now. If there was ever something I would die for, it was—to protect myself. Nobody would get away with it ever again, not this time. *No* man would—"

"What do you mean *not this time?*"

She shook her head wordlessly, the anesthesia of twenty years putting the words to sleep. Danny came up behind her and slipped his arms around her waist. He kissed her long neck gently, like he was blessing her.

"Take all day, all week, all month if you have to, years if you need to, but we're going to talk about it."

She turned and buried her face in his still-damp T-shirt, smelling his odor, seeing herself as an egg nestling into his earth. It was her series of paintings come alive, never to be painted but to be lived. And inside of her, she felt a cracking and opening, and sensed the hollowness filling up with a river of tears, heard the sobs of a hysterical teenager, and knew it was finally her turn to make a fuss.

CHAPTER FIFTY-ONE

The music was sweet, flowing right into Shad's and Beth's swaying bodies. She was wearing the orange dress he loved, the one with the neckline he had to snuggle in close to enjoy. All around them, the dance floor—the restaurant reborn—was packed with dancers, even Horace MacKenzie with his date, a buxom woman nobody knew. They were all moving to Ford's trumpet as he wound through "My Mother's Eyes," one of the classics he'd said when he introduced it. Around the bar the fairy lights blinked on and off, almost in time to the music.

"Your cousin Junior playing nice on the guitar," Beth murmured as she rocked in his arms.

"I promised to run the bar for his next dance party."

"We should have more dancing here, man."

Shad looked down at the tops of her breasts glowing orange inside the dress. He drew her closer, glad she was his woman, glad he wouldn't have to kill Horace or even curse him out. "The boss can't afford no live music. We lucky tonight."

"We lucky you alive, you mean."

"Pshaw, man, I not going nowhere."

"I should fling away that detective book. It only causing you to get into all this *cass-cass* confusion. Every few months is another excitement, somebody trying to shoot you or something." She pulled back and looked at him hard. "You know what would happen to me and the children if you dead?"

"Not a thing, now you making big money at the library."

"I *serious*!"

"Just keep going to church and praying for me. You always say prayers is powerful."

She nestled close and sucked her teeth right in his ear. "Powerful enough to make you get married, you mean."

She looked at him again, chin down, her no-joke look. "If July come and go and we not married, is trouble, you hear me, Shadrack Myers?"

At the back of the restaurant, the end of the song was approaching with a long final note from Ford's trumpet. When he finished, the dancers on the floor clapped and hooted.

"Beautiful!" Danny called. Beside him in her aqua dress, Sarah continued clapping after everyone stopped.

"Thanks, folks," Ford said into the mike, nodding in Sarah's direction. "We're going to take a little break now and we'll be back in ten."

Shad walked behind the bar to check on Tiger, one of the wayward village men he'd set straight who now did bartending for big parties. Solomon was slouched on Shad's stool grinning from ear to ear, like he was serving himself as much as he was serving the customers. At the end of the counter, Maisie was selling beef patties and plantain tarts, the cash in a jumble in front of her.

"You need help, Miss Maisie?" Beth called, and the woman beckoned her over.

The bar counter was filling up with thirsty dancers and Tiger raced to fill orders. Rising reluctantly from his stool, Solomon took an order for three beers from a group of young women still swaying to the music. Shad placed the Red Stripes on the counter and Tiger collected the cash.

Making their way through the crowd, Danny and Sarah joined Eric, Lambert, and Jennifer, who were sipping wine at one end of the bar.

"Drinks on the house for the handsome couple," Eric called to Shad, and the bartender shook his head. The boss must be getting soft in his old age, giving away free drinks and playing the odds with Danny, calling him handsome. He was attractive, maybe, tall like the Englishwoman, but they looked odd together. Sarah was pale like a baby chick, and Danny dark and sturdy like a tree. Janet had looked better with him. She was evil itself, but they'd looked more like a couple. It just went to show, two people could look good together and still be poison.

"Look like we making money tonight, eh, Solomon?" Shad commented to the man at his elbow. "We don't have a crowd like this in a long time. I think we making enough money to get us through another few months, what you think? Like how we don't have to pay Ford nothing. He even paying the musicians himself, say is to give thanks that Sarah come home safe."

"But it don't seem right without Janet," Solomon sighed. "She would have like the party. I don't know what make her mix up in all that drug business with Lizard girlfriend."

"Queen of diamonds, that what she call herself, right?"

Beth reminded them. "She forget to tell you the diamonds she was talking about coming from cocaine and ganja."

Maisie handed a customer a bag of patties and brushed crumbs off her hands. "She make her bed, she have to lie in it," she declared.

"She making her bed in Port Antonio jail tonight," Shad said, "she and all Gecko posse. And they don't even make a dollar yet." He placed two beers on a tray and walked them over to Eric's group.

"I thought you had the night off," Danny said as he took his bottle and handed Sarah hers.

"I just helping out," Shad said.

Jennifer touched Shad's arm, her bracelets tinkling. "I hear you were helping out big-time the other day, too."

"Your husband don't tell you he saved us?" Shad replied. "If he didn't come in—"

"Good thing you spotted that woman, man," Eric said to Lambert.

"How did you grab her, anyway?" Sarah asked, leaning one hand on Danny's shoulder like she wanted to stay glued to his side.

Lambert waved his wineglass. "After Danny and Shad knocked on the door, we saw Danny and that man—what was his name?"

"Slim Jim," Shad threw in. "The sergeant said he owned the house, a longtime criminal."

"Yes, so we see him and Slim Jim fall to the floor fighting," Lambert continued, "and we know we have to do something. I drive along the side of the wall around the house and we get out, but we can't climb over the wall because of the damn glass. So, we're creeping along beside the wall when a taxi pulls up to the front gate—and who should jump out of the taxi but the woman, Francine, whatever her name is."

"Franchette," Shad corrected him.

"We decided to split up," Eric said, nodding.

"I catch up with the woman as she's opening the gate," Lambert continued. "She sees me and starts to run toward the house, but I grab her and drag her up the driveway to the door—and she's cursing and fighting me the whole time."

"Thank God, Janet arrived after in her cousin's taxi," Danny said, chuckling. "If they'd come together, boy, you woulda had two crazy women to deal with."

"When you walk in the door with Gecko"—Shad shook his head—"I swear to you, you look like an angel—"

"With a devil on his arm!" Danny added.

"I didn't even know she was the leader of the gang," Lambert put in, looking as bewildered as Lambert could look. "All I was thinking was that she'd make a good hostage."

"You got in the way of history, boy," Eric said. "She would have been Jamaica's first woman don."

"I still have a question for you, Eric," Jennifer said. "How'd you make the car alarm go off?"

"I knew all hell would break loose once Lambert went in the house with a hostage. And then I saw Janet pull up in the other taxi, and I knew I had to do something. I had this idea that I would ram the gate with the car or something—I hadn't even thought it through or anything—but the damn car door was locked when I got back to the car. I was sure Lambert had left the key in the ignition, so I tried pushing the window down so I could pull up the door lock—and the thing went off! The loudest fucking alarm (sorry, ladies) I ever heard in my entire life, right in my ears."

"Best mistake you ever made, boy," Lambert said, shaking his head.

"What I loved," Danny added with a sharp nod, "was how Sarah kicked Man-Up's leg in. I couldn't believe it was the quiet woman I knew." He looked at his companion with mock amazement. "You saved us, you know that?"

She wagged her head at him. "I suppose I did, really. I was so—so furious with Man-Up for roughing me up, and I could have killed Gecko for kidnapping me. I swear to God, it was all or nothing for me at that point."

"It give us time to jump up and hold Batsman," Shad said with undisguised glee, and, with a whinny and a spin on his heel, Shad did what Shad did best. He reenacted the entire scene from start to finish: Danny and Slim-Jim falling to the floor, Man-Up running in zipping up his pants, he and Danny getting tied up by the skinny man, Lambert breaking in with Franchette, Janet trying to battle Lambert from behind, the alarm shocking them all, Sarah kicking Man-Up and punching the daylights out of Janet, and, at the end, there wasn't a person who wasn't roaring with laughter, Sarah with tears in her eyes.

"What I want to know," Danny said when the laughter subsided, "was how Shad knew the young guy, Batsman, was Lizard's brother."

"Easy, man," Shad said, a warm feeling inside him, knowing he knew something that the rich American didn't. "He brought his baby to show Carthena, and she is Lizard family. They all look so much alike, same short people,

349

same round face, it hard to miss the likeness. Then Batsman and Franchette call each other by home names, not street names—only family do that."

"That's right, she called him Bertie," Lambert recalled.

"He was either brother to Franchette or Lizard, but he stumpy like Lizard, so I took the chance."

"And Clementine, the helper who took care of me, was his mother," Sarah put in.

"Mother to Janet, Carthena, and Bertie," Jennifer said, counting them off on her fingers.

"And don't forget Lizard," her husband reminded her. "Mother to the don himself."

"A real family affair," Danny said.

Eric waved his glass around the group. "Does anyone know anything about this Franchette?"

"She come from Bog Walk, near Kingston," Shad said. "My cousin tell me that she living with Lizard five years now. You can't live with a man like that and not get into the business. What make her different was that she was planning her own operation. Lizard is working England now, but they can't touch him yet—so Neville say. She was going to start the American branch, like how she don't have no record."

"Lizard must be some kind of a liberated man, to let the girlfriend head part of the operation," Jennifer said, winking at her husband like it was a private joke.

"I bet police hoping they can get to Lizard through Gecko," Shad said, "make her talk."

"The whole thing was—I don't know—kind of flimsy," Eric commented. "I mean, kidnapping Sarah in order to get a visa—how crazy is that?"

"That's how most small businesses start," Danny whipped back, "with one crazy idea."

"It was actually quite brilliant when you think about it." Surprised eyes turned to Sarah, who had a new shimmer of importance about her. "I was the only fly in the ointment. They already had Danny lined up—" She glanced at her dance partner, who looked away guiltily.

"And they'd set up an infrastructure ready to swing into action as soon as Janet got up to the States—" Jennifer added.

"—with Lizard's experience behind them," Lambert said, finishing his wife's sentence. "Not to mention millions hanging in the balance if they'd succeeded."

"I guess all they needed was one small detail—the visa," admitted Eric.

"A little obeah and Sarah out of the way," Danny said, "they thought it would be all tied up." He stroked his companion's hand as he said it.

Roper and Sonja joined the group, glasses already in hand. "Sorry we're late," Sonja said. "A policeman came to ask all kinds of questions about Carthena."

"They're going to charge her, right?" Sarah asked.

"Apparently not," Roper said, dropping his eyes. "We've fired her, of course, but—"

"But she was an *accomplice,* for God's sake," Sarah interrupted him. "She *must* have packed my bags and handed them over."

"She denies it," Sonja said, "and there's no way to prove it, since there were no witnesses. Plus, she's cooperating with the police. There seems to be some bad blood between Janet and herself that goes way back. Plus, Carthena is furious with Franchette for getting their mother—what's her name?"

"Clementine," Sarah said.

"Right, for getting her involved and causing her blood pressure to go up, but she's even angrier with Janet for bringing their little brother into the whole thing, and he just got out of the Pen. She's singing like a bird, told them that Janet and Franchette had been planning the business for a couple years now. No love lost between them, apparently."

Shad frowned. "If Carthena was angry with Franchette, why'd she call to warn her?"

"She didn't," Roper said. "According to what she told the police, she called her mother to tell her what had happened and the mother told Franchette, and she must have called Janet."

"And to think," Shad said, the man who usually knew everything in Largo, "that nobody in Largo knew that Janet and Carthena was sisters, that they were even related."

"Or that the woman in the bar with Carthena was a don—or a don in waiting," Sarah added.

"A wicked family, Lord!" said Beth, who'd just joined the circle holding two beers. She handed Shad a bottle.

"Janet never talked about her family—a brother who's a don and another brother who just got out of prison," Danny protested, looking around at his companions, each engrossed in his or her drink. Shad fingered the edge of his starched collar. He knew they were all thinking the same thing: that the man from New York had been running after *pum-pum,* trading green-card promises for a piece of ass.

From outside the circle came Ford's low drawl. "You guys like the set?"

"Brilliant," Lambert said.

"I love the last song," Beth said, slinging her arm through her man's. She gave Shad her one-up smile. "Maybe Ford can play it at our wedding reception in July, right, sweetness?"

"A wedding!" Jennifer said.

"Oh, God." Shad rolled his eyes up to the thatch as *ooh*s and *congrats* came from the women in the group and the men grinned.

"Sure, I'll play." Ford nodded. "Just find me a place to stay—"

"No problem," Sonja said. "You're staying with us."

"Not too late to change your mind," Eric said to Shad, eyebrows high.

Shad rubbed his neck. "Too late, boss, but when I walking down the aisle in July, all of you have to bar the doors to make sure I don't run."

"I'll be happy to do that," Danny said. He looked at Sarah. "Like to come back for a wedding? We might need you to kick Shad behind the knees."

She put her chin on his shoulder, her nose almost touching his. "As long as—"

"I won't leave your side, I promise," Danny said, looking contrite. Sarah gazed back at him through squinty eyes, eyes that weren't sure they could trust him again.

"You have to come, everybody wants to see Shad tie the knot," Roper insisted. "And of course"—nodding to Danny—"you can both stay with us."

"Thank you," Sarah said, her prim, clear syllables making a point.

Danny took a swallow of beer. "We might as well make

it an even bigger celebration. Miss Mac says she's definitely selling us the land, and by July we should be ready to go." He turned to Shad and Eric. "What do you think, guys, a groundbreaking ceremony after the wedding?"

Eric's eyes were as wide as saucers when he turned to Shad. When he opened his mouth, nothing came out.

"Don't you want to think about it," Shad pressed Danny, "after all this kidnapping and thing?" It was a risk, he knew, asking the man to reconsider, but if they were going into something big like a hotel, Danny needed to declare it publicly—with as much commitment and as many witnesses as a wedding.

"He's right, my friend," Lambert put in. "Jamaica isn't an easy place. You've seen that for yourself."

"I thought about it, and at first I thought I should just cut my losses, you know, but what came to me was that one bad apple don't make the whole basket bad. Like how the Mafia comes from Italy, but people still going to Italy, millions every year. My mother said she could hardly see the fountains in Rome for all the tourists."

Danny waved his hand westward, toward Port Maria and Annotto Bay. "If we let Janet and the Geckos frighten us away from Jamaica, then they running things. I'm not going to let them win. I love this island. I want to get into the tourist industry and this may be my one chance to do it. Besides," he added, "I couldn't disappoint the folks here, not after they've been so nice to me, giving me a welcome party and everything."

"Here, here!" Eric hollered, making the patrons at the bar turn to see what the old white man was up to now.

Shad leaned over to Eric. "You inviting a certain lady to come for the groundbreaking, boss?"

"Absolutely," Eric muttered, his mouth twitching.

"Onward to the groundbreaking!" Lambert shouted, like he was going into battle.

"To the New Largo Bay Inn—and to us," Danny said.

"The New Largo Bay Inn," the group echoed, raising their drinks.

"Amen," Solomon called from his stool.

Shad clinked bottles with Beth. "Cool runnings," he whispered, because tonight there'd be no dark water, no sharks circling Largo. Tonight he'd be stroking the baby hairs on his woman's shea-butter neck. Tonight he'd be filled with the warm fullness of knowing there'd be money coming in for a hotel and a campsite and glass-bottom boats, money for books and a computer and a mattress that didn't sag, and one day—maybe not right away, but eventually—money enough for a small-small diamond.

ACKNOWLEDGMENTS

By the third book in a series, one is tempted to lessen the expressions of gratitude, but the truth is that I am constantly aided by others in the completion of each novel. In this case, my thanks first goes to the village of Long Bay in Jamaica, which I visited while writing this book and which continues to serve as the rough inspiration for the setting of the series.

I also want to thank the following people for their support during the completion of this novel under particularly difficult circumstances: Sonja Willis, Lauren Baccus, Sarah Jones, Heather Royes, Gabriela Royes, Larry and Maria Earl, Deborah Huntley, Louise Santana, Ruth Cooke Gibbs, Baji Daniels, Beatriz and Ricardo Hayes, Stephanie McIver, Ursula Folkes, Mable and Jimmy Densler, Barbara Blair, the president and staff of the University of the Virgin Islands and others too numerous to mention.

And, as always, my editor, Malaika Adero, continues to offer her sage and gentle advice, which always serves to improve the content and for which I'm deeply grateful.